A SELLSWORD'S COMPASSION

Book One

of

The Seven Virtues

by

Jacob Peppers

D1731464

**A Sellsword's Compassion
Book one of the Seven Virtues**

Visit the author website:
www.JacobPeppersAuthor.com

To my mom for teaching me that there are other worlds out there

To my dad for giving me the courage to find them

To my brothers for showing me the way

And to my wife for going there with me

To stay up to date on new release info as well as upcoming promotions on Jacob's latest projects, visit his website at www.JacobPeppersAuthor.com.

CHAPTER ONE

THE SHACK DIDN'T LOOK like the type of place anyone in their right mind would live. In fact, it looked more like the kind of place a man might go to, say, get tortured and die and, if the screams coming from inside were any indication—screams loud enough to be heard even over the roaring wind and thundering rain—that was exactly what was happening. The house's walls were rotten and crooked, like an old beggar's teeth, and the door sat askew in its frame as if the carpenter who had built it had been either drunk or blind. In truth, it seemed more like a thieves' hideout than a home, and in this way it resembled any other house in the Downs, the largest and poorest district of Avarest.

There was nothing to distinguish the house from the buildings that surrounded it. Nothing, of course, except the two men standing on either side of the rickety door, frowning into the night, their muscled arms folded across thick, barreled chests. And the screams, of course. A man would be hard pressed not to notice those. Not that anyone would be coming to investigate—it was the Downs, after all, and rarely did a night pass without such screams. There were a few guiding principles which the denizens of Avarest's poorest district lived by: rich men were made for robbing, ale was made for drinking, and, most of all, it was better to be deaf than dead. All rules Aaron made a point of living by himself, or *had,* at least, until the damned woman had shown up, flashing her gold and her smile.

He sighed heavily and pulled his cloak tight against him in a useless effort to ward off the driving rain. *She'd damn sure better be good for it,* he thought. She'd promised him triple his usual rate and that was the *only* reason why he was here. Anything less than that and he would be warming his hands in front of the fire at the *Juggling Bear* instead of standing in the middle of one of the worst storms Avarest had seen in a year and getting ready to get his fool ass killed.

The man screamed again, this one louder and shriller than those before, and Aaron winced. He was no stranger to death or pain but that kind of screaming wasn't something a man could get used to. It was the desperate, wailing cry of a man who'd lost any hope of living and only wanted the pain to stop. It was *also* a sign that the triple he'd been promised was growing less and less likely by the second. Right. No time to scout the area, no time to devise a plan, or take any of the other precautions his father had taught him so long ago. Triple, she'd said, but only if he got the unlucky bastard out alive. Cursing himself for a fool, he checked the cloth bundle strapped across his back to make sure it was secure, pulled the hood of his shabby brown cloak over his head and stepped into the street.

The two men were professionals, good at their work; they spotted him the instant he moved out of the shadows. He stumbled toward them with the meandering, purposeless walk of a drunk, whistling out of tune as he did. Had he appeared armed or at all threatening, the men would have no doubt charged him, cut him down in the street, and worried about why he'd been there later. It was true that corpses didn't answer a lot of questions, but one thing that his life as a sellsword had taught Aaron was that they didn't argue much either.

As it was, the Downs was full of drunks and beggars, men who'd given up on life or had life give up on them and had decided the only recourse was to drown their sorrow beneath the bitter taste of ale and wine. The sight was common enough, innocuous enough, that he managed to make it within three strides of the guards before one of them brought his hand to the hilt of his sword challengingly. "Stop there!" Three strides. A reasonable distance, maybe, but if a man was good, if he was quick, it was close enough. He changed his mind about the two soldiers. Maybe they weren't so good after all.

In one smooth motion, he tore the cloth from the bundle at his back and slung it at the guard who'd spoken. The man grunted in surprise as the coarse wet blanket wrapped around his face. Aaron pulled his sword free of the sheathe at his back and lunged forward, plunging the cold steel through the heart of the other man before he had a chance to draw his own blade.

He kicked the man in the gut and ripped his sword free, spinning to the side and narrowly avoiding a thrust that had been aimed at his back. When he turned to look, he was surprised to find that the guard was still tangled in the horse blanket and had been stabbing blind. Not stopping to question his luck, Aaron stepped forward and shoved his sword into the mass of tangled cloth and flailing arms. The man screamed and a flood of crimson mingled with the rain as Aaron pulled the blade out and rammed it in again. The unfortunate guard stumbled, choked out a rattling wheeze, and crumpled to the rain-soaked cobbles. Aaron shook his head as he stared at the man's still form, the blanket serving as a burial shroud as blood began to pool beneath it. Iladen really was a fickle god, and there was never any telling how his dice would land.

He reached for the door and caught himself. Two men on the outside. That left two, maybe three on the inside. Two, maybe three men who'd made a career out of killing and even over the claps of thunder and the beating rain, they had to have heard the screams. Unless they were a band of deaf hitmen, and somehow he doubted that even Iladen's favor—if he'd had it—would make him *that* lucky. Going in the front entrance, the *only* entrance, was an errand he'd have been happy to avoid. A fool's errand.

He hesitated, staring at the door, his sword held at his side, the wind pushing at his back as if urging him forward. *A man would have to hate himself an awful lot,* he thought as he studied the light spilling beneath the door. *I could leave,* he thought, his hand hovering above the door handle, *I could just leave.* After all, it didn't matter how much money the woman paid him if he wasn't alive to spend it. If he turned around now, he could get away clean, without any worries about the men in the house being able to track him down. He knew that, but he also knew that he wouldn't. He knew he was going in, had known it since before he'd stepped into the street. The screams had made sure of that.

Shaking his head at his own foolishness, he sheathed his sword and drew two shorter blades from where they hung at his hips. Each blade was about a foot long and despite the nicks of hard use on their surface, each bore an edge sharp enough to shave with. They were short, brutal weapons made for close, brutal combat. He'd always preferred the sword, but he preferred breathing more, and it would be too easy for a longer blade to get caught on something once he was inside. A small, tight space, meant close in work, and the shorter blades would be better for that. If, like their comrades, the men inside carried only swords, it would give him an edge. He'd have preferred an army, but he'd take what he could get.

Before he could question the foolishness of his decision, he backed up, took two running steps, and slammed his shoulder into the door. The rotten wood burst apart in a shower of damp splinters, and he hit the ground in a roll. He came to his feet in an instant and swept his eyes around the inside of the shack. A bare-chested man hung loosely from where he'd been tied to a wooden support in the center of the room. Blonde hair, lank with sweat, hung in the stranger's drooping, haggard face but did little to cover the bloody ruin where one of his eyes had been. The prisoner's chest and arms were covered in jagged, dripping cuts, and a short, stocky, bearded man stood beside him, a bloody knife in his hand.

Movement flashed in the corner of his vision, and Aaron barely managed to duck a sword that would have taken his fool head off his fool shoulders. Growling, he whipped around, drove both blades into his attacker's gut, and barreled forward, slamming him into the wall. The swordsman's screams turned into shrieks of agony as Aaron jerked the blades upward, and the man's sword clattered to the ground.

Footsteps behind him, and he tore one of the blades free before turning and throwing it at the approaching man. The blade sank into his chest, arresting his charge, and he crumpled to the ground with a groan. Aaron started forward, managing only a step before arms wrapped around his chest from behind like bands of iron. *Bastard's quiet,* he had time to think before his head was rammed into the wall.

His vision erupted in a burst of white light at the impact, and he growled in pain and anger as he struggled vainly against the man's grip. The soldier pulled him back by his hair and started toward the wall again, but Aaron managed to get his legs up in front of him. His feet struck the wall, and he pushed off with all the force he could, grunting with the effort, and he and the man holding him tumbled backward.

They landed hard, and the man's grip loosened. Aaron spat out a mouthful of coppery-tasting blood and was crawling to his feet when a booted foot struck him in the side and knocked him onto his back. He groaned, and blinked, trying to clear the fog from his eyes. His vision was just coming back when thick, hairy fingers wrapped themselves around his throat. He grasped the man's wrists and snarled as he struggled to keep from being throttled.

The soldier was surprisingly strong and, despite Aaron's desperate efforts, he was able to do little more than keep enough pressure off to draw a few choking breaths.

"No ... you don't ... bastard," he said. He let go of one of the man's wrists, pawing drunkenly at his boot, his vision fading to a thin tunnel of light as the man applied more pressure. He felt a surge of relief as his fingers touched the handle of the blade secreted in his boot, followed directly by a moment of panic as the knife caught on the leather. He grunted, his struggles weakening, and suddenly the blade came free, and he shoved it into his attacker's side.

The bearded man's eyes bulged, and he grunted in surprise as the blade slid home. His grip weakened, but only for a moment. Then he growled, a sound more like that of an animal than a man, and began to shake Aaron by the throat, slamming his head against the floor. Fighting against the darkness overcoming his vision, Aaron pushed the blade in a second time, then a third, until he could feel the man's hot, sticky blood coating his hand and arm. When he was sure that he couldn't take anymore, that his head would burst from the pressure, the man's grip suddenly slackened. The bearded soldier wavered for a second, then his eyes rolled back in his head, and he collapsed on top of Aaron, dead.

Aaron lay there for several moments gasping and hacking through a throat that felt as if it was on fire, oblivious of the dead man lying on top of him or the warm blood covering his shirt. Then, when he felt that he could get some air—though each breath made his throat feel like it was laced in razor wire—Aaron heaved the corpse off of him and struggled to his feet. He shuffled to where his knives lay, wiped them on the tunic of one of the corpses, and slid them back in the sheathes at his waist with shaky hands. He took a moment to fight off a fresh wave of dizziness, then stumbled toward the figure tied to the pole. "Don't you be dead, you bastard," he said, rubbing at his throat, "don't you dare be dead."

"Not ... yet." Came the stranger's reply, so quiet that Aaron almost didn't hear him. The man raised his head groggily, and Aaron winced in sympathy. He had high cheekbones, and—apart from the marks of his recent torture—a smooth, unblemished face. Once, his would have been a face women would have giggled and whispered about but those days were behind him now. As it was, the ragged, puckered hole where his eye had been and the blood that matted his face and hair made him look more like a corpse than any of the dead men littering the room.

"Good," Aaron said, struggling to keep back his rising gorge as he forced himself to look the man in his remaining eye, "that's good."

One side of the stranger's mouth turned up in a grizzly smile, and Aaron wondered how the man could talk let alone smile considering the wreck the men had made of his body. Aside from the damage to his face, the skin of his chest and back had been flayed off in places, and he bled freely from several deep puncture wounds. "T-twenty years," the man whispered, his head lolling, "twenty years of war and blood and fighting and more coming." He coughed and a fresh wave of crimson wound its way from his mouth. "I-I just wanted it to end. I just wanted to protect them—to stop it."

The man didn't look any older than Aaron's own twenty seven years, and somehow the sellsword seriously doubted he was involved in war at the age of seven, but considering the state he was in, it was no surprise he wasn't making sense. Still, the man's words awakened an old anger in him, and Aaron grunted and spat, "There isn't any stopping it. The strong take what they want and the weak suffer. It's the way it has always been—the way it always will be."

The man wheezed a breathy laugh, "My brother ... would agree with you." He raised his head shakily with what looked to Aaron to be a monumental effort and met his gaze with a piercing, blue eye. "You're angry."

Aaron frowned. The man's words sounded almost conversational, "I'm angry because I don't like fools, now come on. We gotta get you down from there. I know some people that can--"

The man shook his head slowly, "It's too late. I'm dying. Even *she* can't stop it—not this time. It seems that ... Belgarin ... has finally gotten his wish." He smiled a sad smile and the hole in his face puckered in a way that made the sellsword's stomach clench, "I'd thought he'd changed. When he asked to see me, to discuss an end to the war, I'd thought perhaps," He burst into a fit of hacking, wrenching coughs that made his entire body shake. "I thought t-that he'd become a good man."

Against his will, Aaron thought of his father, a general in Prince Eladen's army who'd only ever wanted to end the war, to make a better life for his family and his city. He thought too, of the way he'd found him and his mother, their throats slit, lying in a pool of their own blood. "There's no such thing as a good man," he said, "not anymore and people don't change."

The man's face twisted in the same ghastly smile, "Y-you'd be surprised," he whispered, then his head fell forward, and he let out a single rattling breath and was still.

"Oh no you don't, you bastard," Aaron said. He rushed forward and jerked the man's head up, "Don't you die on me. She told me triple damnit! Triple!" The stranger's icy blue eye stared back, cold and glassy in death. "*Shit.*" He let the dead man's head fall back with a sigh. Something red flashed in the corner of his vision, and he jerked his blades free, but when he turned nothing was there. He frowned, glancing around the room, but there was no one there but him. Him and the dead. *Spending too much time around corpses. No wonder I'm losing it.* He slid his blades back, looked around the room for any tell-tale sign of the thing he'd seen then grunted and headed back out into the night.

As he walked, the man's words replayed in his mind, forcing up memories of his parents' death, memories he'd spent a lifetime trying to forget, and he grew angrier with each step. Soon, he found himself searching the shadowed alleyways, hoping that some unfortunate footpad or thief would try to rob him. None did, though, and eventually his thoughts turned to the woman. She had some explaining to do. Usually, he didn't mind not knowing much about a job—at least that way you rarely had to worry about your employer trying to dust you later for knowing too much —but this wouldn't stand. It had taken him a minute, what with the missing eye and the wounds, but he'd finally recognized the man. It'd be hard not to since he'd seen him on more statues than he could count, not to mention on a picture that had hung in his father's study so many years ago. The corpse, the one that he *wouldn't* get paid triple for, had once been Prince Eladen, son of the late King Marcus, and one of the leaders of the rebel armies. What had the woman got him involved in? He considered the possibilities as he made his way farther into the city and decided that triple hadn't been enough. Not nearly.

CHAPTER TWO

AARON APPROACHED THE SMALL HOUSE where he was to meet his employer and knocked. The space between his shoulder blades itched, and he swallowed past his burning throat, glancing behind him at the street. No one was there and, yet, he could *feel* eyes watching him, had felt them since he'd left the torture shack. Had one of the assassins still been alive? Was he maybe, even now, staring out at Aaron from one of those dark alleyways?

Don't be a damned fool, he scolded himself, *you've been around enough death to know it when you see it. Those boys won't be following anyone anytime soon, except maybe the Keeper through the fields of eternity.* He was shaken up, that was all, and who could blame him? It wasn't every day that a man stumbled in on the assassination of a prince. But *could* the man have really been Prince Eladen? And, if so, how? The prince was the second oldest of the nine siblings, and, according to all accounts, was at least fifty, but the man he'd seen hadn't looked a day over thirty summers.

Still, there was no mistaking that face—ruined or not. He'd heard enough about the prince to know him on sight. His father, after all, had held great respect for

Eladen. When Belgarin, the oldest son of the late King Marcus, had two of his siblings assassinated and war broke out between the remaining Royal Seven, Aaron's father had quickly joined the prince's army in hopes of helping him bring a real, lasting peace to the people of Telrear.

Aaron frowned and spat. What the man had brought was death. Not just to himself, but to Aaron's parents who had believed in him. Because of that royal bastard, he'd spent the last years of his childhood in that cruel excuse of an orphanage. As far as Aaron was concerned, the man had got off cheap. He turned back to the door and knocked hard enough to make the weak wood shake in its frame. Still no answer. "To the Fields with this," he growled. He took a step back and kicked the door. It flew inward and slammed against the inner wall with a *crack.* Aaron took one last look behind him, saw nothing, and stalked inside.

At one time, the building must have been used for storage by some merchant. The walls were lined with shelves, and there was a small trapdoor to a cellar in the back of the single room. He thought he could detect the faint smell of vegetables or fruit, but there was none in evidence, nor had he seen any when he was summoned here the night before and offered the job—not that he'd been paying much attention with the woman talking about paying him three times his normal rate.

In fact, he realized now that he'd acted a fool. He should have known that something was up—no one started off offering that kind of gold for no reason. Instead, he'd set out with a will, questioning, bribing, or threatening all of his contacts until he finally discovered someone who'd heard a rumor about a man being taken prisoner in the Downs by a group of hired men. Not that it'd taken long. Information, like almost everything else, could be bought in Avarest's poor district as long as you had the gold to spend. The only problem had been that his source hadn't known the exact location, and Aaron had spent precious time finding the house where the prisoner had been taken. For the prince, it had proved to be too much time.

Not only had he been too late to earn triple his usual fee, but he'd also nearly gotten himself killed in the process and for what? To save the very man who was responsible for his parents' death? Never before had he been so reckless, and though he'd like to blame it all on thoughts of the gold, the truth was that the woman had a nice rack and a pretty smile, and he hadn't been thinking much at all by the time he went out in search of the prisoner.

Still, it wasn't the way he'd acted like a fool for the money, or even how he'd let the woman's smile work on him that bothered him the most. It was the fact that he hadn't been *careful,* and sellswords who weren't careful lasted about as long as a pig on feast day. *You can never know enough about your enemy,* his father had told him once, and he'd always followed that advice. Always, that was, until the woman had shown up wielding her damned smile the way a swordmaster might wield a blade.

He glanced around the room and wasn't surprised to find the place empty. In the center stood the same old, beat-up table the woman had set in, flanked by two guards, when he'd first met her. In the center of it sat a small bag, and a note. He lifted the bag in his hand, hefting its weight. "That's damn sure not triple," he muttered sourly as he slid the money into his tunic; that done, he unfolded the note and scanned it, growing angrier with each word.

I have been made aware that you were unable to complete your task. Contained within the bag is your normal rate, reward for your valiant effort. I would not let your failure trouble you. They were long odds at best. I will call on you again.

He noticed that the paper was wrinkled in a few spots, as if the woman had been crying as she wrote it. He turned it over, expecting something more, but that was it. She'd given no name in the note, just as she hadn't when he'd met her. *Failed?* He thought angrily, balling the paper up in a fist. What had the crazy woman expected? Of *course* he'd failed. The Downs was a big place, home to thousands of people, a maze of back alleys and sidestreets. The fact that he'd even been able to *find* one particularly unlucky bastard in a city full of them had been a miracle, but that wasn't enough, was it? No, she expected Aaron to find him, take on five hired killers, and then breathe life back into the man like Nalesh, the father of the gods, himself.

But he wasn't a god, and it would have taken nothing short of that to have saved the prince's life. And what was that last bit about calling on him again? The woman had some gall that was sure. She'd never told him there were going to be five men, let alone that the man he was being sent to save was none other than Prince Eladen himself. If he'd have known either, or if she hadn't been quite so good-looking, he would have told her to go screw herself and called it a day.

He sighed as he wondered, yet again, just what he'd got mixed up in. From his experience, good looking women had a way of doing that to a man, but this was too much. Angry husbands and death threats were one thing—dead princes and professional hit squads were quite another. He didn't care if the woman came offering him a palace and enough gold to swim in, there wasn't a chance he was going to work for her again. He stuffed the wadded-up note in his pocket and walked out.

In the street, he pulled his hood tight against the freezing rain and started out for *The Juggling Bear,* his mood growing worse with each step. The streets appeared empty, but although he appeared to be the only person foolish enough to venture out into the driving rain, he scanned the dark alleys and shadowed corners of the shops and booths he passed out of habit. He didn't see anyone, but his hands never strayed far from the blades at his side. In the Downs, what you saw was rarely what you got and careless people had a way of becoming penniless at the best and corpses at the worst. Not that he felt too far from either just then.

By the time he reached the inn, his throat was swollen and each painful, forced breath made him curse the day he'd accepted the woman's job. He pulled his cloak tightly around him, covering his bloody tunic, and pushed his way past the two bouncers flanking the door without so much as a glance. Once inside, he ignored the steady drum of conversation and laughter coming from the crowded tables and stalked to the bar. "Flinn," He croaked, tipping his head.

The innkeeper nodded his balding head from behind the counter and focused his attention back on the mug he was cleaning, either unaware or unconcerned with the blood on the sellsword's tunic or the rasp in his voice. To hear him tell it, Flinn had once been a soldier in the army back before King Marcus died and threw the kingdom into chaos. As his last act, Marcus had split the kingdom into seven portions, ignoring his eldest son Belgarin's claim to the throne. Instead, he'd wanted his children to lead Telrear together, stating in his will that he believed that no single man or woman should rule over the entire kingdom. Aaron supposed that he'd get his wish one way or the other.

After all, it had been twenty years since Marcus's death, eighteen of which had been filled with wars and battles while each royal heir or heiress squandered thousands of men's lives because they'd decided that a man just couldn't make due with ruling only a seventh portion of a kingdom. Eighteen years of bloody ambushes and assassinations as each sibling tried to eliminate the others, and they showed no signs of slowing. *Yeah,* Aaron thought bitterly, *the old king will get his wish. Before much longer, there won't be much of a nation left to rule.*

And what could a man do about it? Nothing but become another corpse in a sea of them and what was the point of that? "A mug of the strongest shit you got,

Flinn." He said, rubbing a hand over his aching throat, "It's been a long night."

The innkeeper grunted in acknowledgment and turned to get the bottle. Aaron believed that the old man *had* been a soldier—he didn't care enough not to—but the man's fighting days were done, that was certain. His was a muscled frame gone to fat. His chest was still broad, his arms thick, but a massive gut hung over his trousers, wobbling back and forth sickeningly as he poured the drink, and he was always winded as if he'd just finished an all-day march. Of course, if neither of these things were evidence enough that his soldiering days were long behind him, then the wooden pole that served for his right leg damn sure was.

Aaron shook his head. The man had fought and bled on another man's orders, no doubt believing that he would be rewarded with honor and glory for his dedication to the cause and this was what he had to show for it, a shabby, beaten-down inn in a place where a man would gut you as soon as look at you—sooner really—and a wooden leg. Aaron didn't know about the glory of serving a just cause—he wasn't convinced there were any, and if there were they were destined to fail, but he did know one thing, Flinn wasn't going to win any races anytime soon. It was a stupid, pointless way to become a cripple. Still, he liked the innkeeper well enough—as far as he liked anyone. The man talked little and knew how to mind his business.

He took a long pull from the mug, wincing as the ale burned its way down his ruined throat. "Damn, Flinn." He coughed, "This tastes like horse piss."

The burly innkeeper smiled, running a hand through his gray beard, "Yeah, but the best horse piss money can buy."

Aaron grunted and took another swallow. It wouldn't make the pain go away or push back the memory of the prince's screams, but another drink or two *would* make him care less and that was about as good as a man could expect. He was raising his mug again when someone bumped into him from behind nearly making him spill his ale. His knife was halfway out of its sheathe at his side before he spun and saw a man smiling at him, his face red from drink.

Examining the stranger through narrowed eyes, taking in his young, acne-covered face, Aaron decided that he wasn't a man at all, but a kid that couldn't have been a day over eighteen summers. "'Scuse me," the kid said in a drunken slur, "Didn't mean to bump ya." He glanced back at a table where two women and a man— apparently friends of his—were watching, laughing and whispering to each other as if someone had just told a joke. He turned to the sellsword with a lopsided, drunken grin, "Say, friend, how about you buy me a drink?"

The kid let out a squeak of surprise as Aaron grabbed him by the collar of his shirt and jerked him close. "I'm not your fucking friend, kid. How about instead of buying you a drink I give you some advice. Take your ass back over there to your woman and your friends before your night ends up getting a whole lot worse."

"*Easy,* man," the youth said, trying—and failing—to pull away from Aaron's grip. After a moment, Aaron let him go. "Just take it easy," the kid said, making a show of straightening his shirt, "I was just foolin' with ya."

"I am taking it easy," Aaron growled. "You don't want to see me when I'm not. Now get out of my face."

The kid looked to Flinn for help, but when the bartender only shrugged, his expression blank, the youth swallowed hard, "S-sorry," he mumbled before turning and hurrying back to his friends.

Aaron sighed and met Flinn's gaze, "Kids these days."

The fat man barked a laugh as he picked up a mug and began cleaning it with a linen towel, "Pity the old generation. 'Course, we were all young once."

"Not that young," Aaron said, downing the rest of his ale. Flinn poured him another without waiting to be asked and walked away as someone else shouted for a refill. Aaron took his time with the second drink, trying to get his thoughts in order, trying to decide what to do next. He wanted to talk to the woman, to figure out just what she'd gotten him into, but he didn't know how to reach her, and he had better things to do with his time than comb the city in search of a woman whose name he didn't even know. Namely, drink.

A sudden thought struck him and his arms broke out in gooseflesh. What if someone had seen him leave the place? What if they'd gone in and seen the prince's body, had recognized him? "Damn her," he muttered under his breath. The citizens of the Downs were great at ignoring or forgetting anything that might prove to be inconvenient for them, but they were also opportunists.

The dead men were probably being stripped down for valuables even now. *And why by all the gods didn't I think of that?*

Now that he considered it, he realized without a doubt that someone *had* seen him leave; the woman had said as much in her note. How else would she have known that he hadn't got Eladen out alive? "Another?" Aaron looked up at the waiting barman and was surprised to find that his mug was empty.

He considered for a moment then shook his head reluctantly. Suddenly, getting drunk didn't seem like a very wise decision. "What are you trying to kill me?" he said. "No thanks. Just put the two on my tab."

"Sure."

Aaron nodded at the man, "Alright then." He rose and made his way up the stairs to his room where he was surprised to find a hot bath waiting. He locked the door and, with a grunt of satisfaction, began to undress. He'd only been staying at the *Bear* for less than a week—as a sellsword he was never short of enemies, and he made it a point not to stay in one inn for too long—but he thought he could really grow to like Flinn. The man might be a cobbler's worst nightmare, but he was a fine innkeeper.

He sighed contentedly as he settled into the hot water, and it wasn't long before his thoughts drifted back to the prince. What *had* the man been doing in Avarest's poor district? In some ways, the Downs was a fine place. A man didn't have to go far to find cheap boarding, cheap liquor, and—best of all—cheap women. Of course, he didn't have to go far to get robbed or murdered either and most of the women were only worth the money with the lights off.

Aaron didn't doubt that the prince, like all men—or women for that matter—had certain lusts that were most easily sated in the near lawless streets of the Downs, but he was also just as sure that one of the perks of royalty was being able to order out for that kind of thing. So, then, what had brought him to the Downs and how was the woman connected? Even more troubling, how did a fifty something year old man—for if he really was Prince Eladen that would be his age—manage to appear like a man of no more than thirty summers? He doubted that even royal dandies had access to *that* kind of powder and face paint.

The questions ran through his head, unanswered, until the bathwater grew tepid and his fingers were wrinkled. Aaron had always believed—since his parents' death and his time spent at the orphanage at least—that it was best to keep to yourself, to mind your own business and let everyone else mind theirs. After all, no one could stick a knife in your back if you didn't let them get close. He avoided authority and causes like they were death itself, and the last thing he needed was to get mixed up in a prince's assassination. If his parents' murder had taught him anything, it was that when a man got involved with princes and politics he tended to end up dead.

Still, as much as he hated it, he *was* involved now. The woman had made sure of that. It was all well and good to avoid others, to keep yourself distant, but it was just plain bat-shit stupid to ignore everything going on around you until you felt the prick of the blade and nothing after. He decided that no matter how tempting it was to try to forget everything that had happened and go about his own business, he couldn't. Instead, he would find the woman, and she would tell him just what he was involved in, or—pretty or not—he'd make sure she regretted ever hiring him.

That settled, he rose from the chilly water, dressed in a pair of clean trousers, and laid his knives on the night stand before climbing into bed. It wasn't until his head rested on the cheaply-made linen pillow that he realized how exhausted he was and despite the jagged pain that tore at his throat with each breath, he was soon fast asleep.

CHAPTER THREE

AARON AWOKE WITH A START, jerking up in bed. "Who's there?" He asked, blinking the sleep out of his eyes as he stared around the darkness of his room. There was no answer. He stilled his thoughts and listened for the tell-tale noises that would indicate an intruder, but the only sound was the rapid beating of his own heart. He sighed and shook his head. He didn't remember what he'd been dreaming or what wakened him, but he'd been sure there was someone in the room with him. *Just your nerves,* he told himself, annoyed. *The woman's got you jumping at shadows. Next thing you know you'll be hiding under the covers with a candle, scared that some bogeyman is going to get you.* He yawned heavily and glanced out the window of the room. It was still dark, and judging by the gritty feeling of his eyelids, he hadn't been asleep for more than a few hours. The large, rickety window let in enough moonlight for him to see that no one shared the room with him. Why, then, did he have the unshakable feeling that he was being watched?

"Because you are." A voice spoke from beside him.

"What the fuck!" Aaron fumbled for his knives, miraculously managing to grab the handle of one without slicing his fool hand open and whirled to the sound of the voice only to find nothing there. He frowned, blinking his eyes, "I must be losing my mind."

A girlish giggle, behind him. He turned and lashed out with the knife reflexively. It struck the headboard of the bed and was knocked from his grip, falling to the floor. He hissed a curse, jumped out of the bed, and scanned the room, poised in a fighter's crouch. He was just becoming convinced that he really *was* going crazy when a small orb of glowing magenta, no bigger than his hand, winked into being and hung in the air in front of him. He lashed out with his fists, calling on speed and reflexes honed from years of training, but the orb danced around his strikes with ease.

What kind of magic is this? He struck again, and the orb of light retreated to the other side of the room. He grabbed the bed and, grunting with the effort, upended it and heaved it at the ball of light. The mattress and the box springs slammed against the wall with a crash. He waited for several seconds, sucking in deep heavy breaths then grinned, satisfied. "Got you that time, bastard." He shuffled to where his blade lay and was reaching for it when the ball of light winked into being in front of his face. He stumbled backward, nearly tripping on his own feet, and swung at it again. This time the orb did not move, but instead of striking something solid, his fist passed through the glowing light as if it was no more tangible than air. The only evidence that he'd touched it at all was a tingling sensation that lingered in his hand.

"Enough!" He shouted, backing up a step, his fists still raised, "if you've come to kill me stop wasting my time and do it!"

I haven't come to kill you. The voice didn't speak out loud this time. Instead, the words came from inside his head as if some being shared the space of his mind with him. It was a woman's voice, and he frowned at the laughter he could hear in it.

"If you didn't come to kill me then why are you here?" He demanded, "What in the name of the gods *are* you?"

"I am here because you are here," the orb answered, and he was relieved, at least, that it spoke out loud once more, "and if you like, you may call me Co. My last companion did."

"What are you *talking* about?" He realized that he was shouting but didn't care.

"You are my master—my new companion. It is only right that I should be here."

He watched the orb floating in front of him disbelievingly for several seconds. Finally, he barked a harsh laugh and rubbed at his eyes, "I've got to be dreaming. Damn Flinn, what did he put in that drink?" He shook his head, "I'm going to have to have a talk with that innkeeper he—"

"*Wait.*" The words were shouted, aloud and in his head at the same time, and he grunted, grabbing his temples.

"Not so loud, damnit."

The orb flickered for a moment then its color darkened to a deep, foreboding crimson. When it spoke into his mind again, the humor was gone from its voice, *They are here. They've come for you. You must run.*

Aaron squinted his eyes, confused. "I swear this is the strangest dream I've ever had."

"This is no dream, Aaron Envelar," the orb said, its voice tense with emotion. "They have come for you, and if you do not leave this place now, they will have you."

He frowned at that and took a cautious step back. "Wait a minute. How do you know my name?"

The orb flickered and wavered from side to side, clearly agitated, *There's no time. You must go* now.

Aaron laughed, "Go where? Listen, I'm not in the habit of listening to dreams, and even if I wa—" His voice cut off as a woman's scream echoed from downstairs. Dream or not, she sounded terrified. "What in the name of Talen was that?" He slung his sword across his back and hefted his knives, reassured by their weight in his hands. No sooner had he done so, then a blood-curling shriek—far worse than the first—split the silence and sent goose bumps up his back. Slowly, painfully aware of the wooden floorboards creaking beneath his feet, he crept toward the door and eased it open with the blade of his knife.

A roar of anger from downstairs, and Aaron recognized the voice as Flinn, the barkeep. He eased out of his room, went to the head of the stairs and peered into the common room of the inn. What he noticed the first was the corpses, half a dozen lying scattered across the plank floor like broken dolls. Five men stood in the center of the room, their swords drawn. Two more had pressed the innkeeper against the counter, and Aaron saw that his mouth was bloody.

A thin man walked out from behind the others with an unmistakable air of authority. He frowned at the innkeeper, his hands behind his back as if he were out for a stroll in some lord's garden. "We know you know where he is, old man," he said in a nasally, bored voice, "there is no reason for you to make this anymore unpleasant than it already is. The man's crimes have nothing to do with any of you here, and His Highness Belgarin rewards well those who serve him."

Belgarin, the High Prince, Aaron thought, his heart hammering in his chest. *Gods, I'm fucked.* The thin man started to say something else, but his words were drowned out as the innkeeper roared, broke free of the hands holding him, and slammed his fist into one of the men's face. The man's head snapped back, blood and teeth flying, and he crumpled to the ground as if he'd been clubbed. Flinn bellowed another roar and charged the thin man, but one of the others stepped forward and rammed his sword into the innkeeper's chest, and the blade exploded from the innkeeper's back in a spray of blood. Time seemed to freeze for a moment as the innkeeper's wide eyes took in the bloody steel protruding from his chest.

Then the man ripped the blade free with a sickening squelch. Flinn grunted, tottering. He took one shuffling step toward forward then collapsed in a heap. "You bastards!" It wasn't until the soldiers turned and looked up the staircase that Aaron realized he'd shouted the words out loud.

"*That's him,*" the thin man screeched, "get him!"

Idiot, Aaron cursed himself as the men started toward the staircase, his mind working rapidly. Eight men inside. That meant probably three, maybe four waiting outside in case he got away. "Damn that woman," he growled. He ran back to his room, slamming the door closed behind him. Footsteps sounded on the stairs as he grabbed the flipped over bed and heaved it in front of the door.

His gaze darted across the room frantically in search of a means of escape. He took in the small table, the turned over bed and, finally, the window. *Probably a man outside, watching it.* The men had obviously known he was here or at least that he *had* been here, and they'd been willing to kill in cold blood to find him; they wouldn't have taken any chances.

The footsteps outside his room grew louder and with a curse he rushed to the window and threw it open. He could only hope that the darkness would obscure him from anyone watching from below. He was barely halfway out the opening when something struck the wall beside him. He snapped his gaze to the side and saw a crossbow bolt quivering in the wall, close enough to touch. He ducked his head back in, scanning the shadowed streets below him but couldn't make out anyone in the darkness.

Behind him, there was crash as something struck the door. He risked a glance back and saw that a large crack running up the wood. "Shit." He risked another peek out the window and saw the outline of the edge of the roof only a few feet above him. He stretched his hand out, but it was a good two-hand lengths out of his reach.

Growling with frustration, he braced his feet on the windowsill and took a deep breath. Another few seconds and the men would be in the room. His only option was to jump and to pray to Iladen, God of Luck, that the clay tiles of the roof didn't slip out of his hands. That was, of course, assuming that he managed to reach them without falling and bashing his head on the street below.

There was another crash, louder than the first, and the door flew off its hinges in a shower of splinters. "The window, fools!" The thin man shouted.

Aaron saw something out of the corner of his eye and turned. The orb was floating in the air beside him. *You can make it,* the young girl's voice spoke in his mind, *but you must go now.*

Another crossbow bolt zipped by him, striking the wall only inches from his face, and he winced. "Must be nice to float around all day," he growled. And then he jumped. For a moment, he was sure he wouldn't make it, sure that he would fall and splatter on the ground like some rotten fruit, and he let out a breath of relief when he felt the clay tiles beneath his hands. He started to pull himself up, but the roof was slick from the recent rain, and his fingers began to slip. One of his hands lost purchase as the tile he'd been holding slid away, missing him by inches and smashing on the streets below.

Desperately, he lunged at the empty space where the tile had been and was able to get a firm hold. He glanced at the scattered pieces of tile in the street and swallowed hard. *Thunk.* His eyes widened as another bolt struck the wall nearby. Gods, but the son of a bitch was a good shot.

If not for the darkness, he was sure he'd have been hit already.

Not willing to trust to his luck for another shot, he heaved himself up, oblivious of the tile scraping and cutting his arms and chest as he drew himself up over the lip of the roof. He was almost over when something flew out of the darkness and stuck into his leg. Pain, hot and fierce washed over him, and he let out a choking gasp, nearly losing his hold. He turned to the street and could just make out the crossbowman's shadowy form near the opening of an alleyway. The man was bent over his crossbow, cranking it back and preparing another shot.

Aaron bared his teeth and jerked himself over the side of the roof. He rolled away from the edge and lay on his back, gasping against the pain. He looked down and saw a crossbow bolt sticking into the meat of his right thigh, blood staining the leg of his trousers crimson. "Son of a bitch shot me," he hissed, tearing a strip from his shirt and hastily wrapping it around his leg to stem the flow of blood.

They are trying to kill you, the girlish voice spoke, *you must flee.*

Aaron glanced over at the orb floating next to him and frowned past the pain. "Really?" He growled, "What gave it away? As for fleeing, I'd love to, you see, but the thing is I have a gods-cursed *arrow* in my gods-cursed *leg.*" Gritting his teeth, he took hold of the shaft of the bolt and broke it off, hissing in agony.

"It is the pain," the orb spoke out loud, "it is too much for you."

"Rather good at stating the damned obvious, aren't you, Moe?"

"It's Co," the orb said testily, "and I can make the pain lessen."

"Yeah? How about you go kill all those bastards while you're at it." A head peaked over the edge of the roof and Aaron lashed out with his good leg. The soldier screamed in pain and surprise and was still screaming as he flew out into the empty air, disappearing from Aaron's view. He struck the street below with a crash and the screams came to an abrupt halt. Seconds later, an arrow struck the corner of the roof, and Aaron rolled away as splinters of tile and wood scattered around him.

He struggled to his feet and hobbled toward the other end of the roof in a low crouch. The treacherous footing of the rain-drenched tiles was compounded by the agony that lanced up his right leg anytime he put any pressure on it, and he only just managed to keep himself from falling as he trudged stubbornly along the rooftop. With each step, the pain grew worse, and less than halfway to the other end it forced him to a panting stop.

As soon as he was still, the orb floated to his leg, and began to drift around it in lazy spirals, touching it from time to time and making the flesh around the wound tingle. Aaron opened his mouth to tell it to stop, but before he had a chance the orb flickered brightly, floated toward his leg, and disappeared. "What the—" he stopped speaking as a dull numbness spread over his wound, easing the pain. It still hurt, but it was a small ache when compared to what it had been before, and easy enough to ignore.

Now go, the voice spoke inside his head, and he was sure that he could detect a hint of strain in it, *while there is time.*

He was just about to ask the orb what it had done when another head peaked over the edge of the roof. He reached down, pulled one of the clay tiles up, and threw it, but the man had already ducked back down. He surveyed the area around him and, seeing no other options, started across the slippery tiles in a limping, shuffling run. "I don't know what you did," he muttered, "but we're talking about this later, Joe."

It's Co, the voice said, but he paid it little attention, focused instead on the rapidly approaching roof's edge and the five foot gap between it and the next building. Under normal circumstances, the jump would have given him little difficulty, but the water-soaked tiles made the footing treacherous even without taking into account his wounded leg.

He glanced back and saw that one of the men had made it on the roof, and that there was another coming up behind him. No time to stop, no time to think. He sped up, almost slipped, recovered his footing, and leapt.

He fought the urge to close his eyes as he soared through the air, sure that he was going to plummet to his death like a bird with a broken wing. Instead, he went farther, faster, than he'd intended, and he hit the roof in an awkward roll, grunting as the wind was knocked out of him on the hard tiles. Gasping, he rose and forced himself into a stumbling walk across the rooftop. When he made it to the edge, he turned and looked back. In the pale moonlight, he could just make out the forms of four of the soldiers as they came to a skidding halt at the end of the roof. One of the men didn't manage to stop in time and nearly stumbled over the edge before one of his companions grabbed him and pulled him back.

He smiled smugly at their curses for a moment—then he remembered the crossbowman. The man would probably be circling around. It would take him longer on the ground than on the rooftops but not much. Aaron guessed he only had a minute or two tops before the man was able to work his way through the alleyways. He walked to the edge of the roof, careful of his footing, and looked down. The roof of the building didn't overhang as much as the inn had—thank Iladen for that.

He crouched low and lowered himself over the edge carefully, terribly conscious of the hard pavement of the street below. Unlike the inn, the building had enough windows that he was able to work his way down, using the sills as hand and foot holds. He took extra care to be quiet; the last thing he needed was some wench screaming her head off because she saw him in her window and thought he'd come to steal what little virtue she had left. After what he estimated could have been no more than a minute and a half, his feet came down on the pavement, and he breathed a shuddery sigh of relief.

Still, there was no time to rest. He glanced down one side of the shadowed street and then the other. "What do you think, Blinkie, which way's he coming from?" The orb didn't respond. "Fine then," he said as he headed for the shadowed entrance of a nearby tailor's shop, "be that way."

He tucked himself into the doorway, satisfied that he was hidden in the darkness and as he waited, he focused on getting his breathing under control. A hiding place didn't do much good if you were breathing like a blacksmith's bellows.

It wasn't long until the bowman appeared out of one of the nearby alleyways. The man scanned the rooftops warily, his crossbow held at the ready as he made his way down the street drawing closer and closer to where the sellsword was hidden. Aaron resisted the urge to draw one of his blades. The night was quiet, and the slightest sound could give him away. He waited until the man was only a few paces away from him then lunged out and grasped a fistful of the soldier's hair. Before the man could cry out, Aaron jerked his head back and brought a fist down on his throat.

Something in the man's throat gave under the blow, and he let out a hacking, gurgling sound, struggling against the sellsword's grip, but Aaron held on grimly, hitting him in the throat again and again until the other man's struggles weakened then he let him fall to the ground in a heap. "Surprise."

Watching the man labor in vain to get a breath past his ruined throat, Aaron felt an unexpected stab of pity. The man was dying, that was certain. He was dying because Aaron had killed him. Not just dying either, but suffering. *So what?* He thought, angry at the unexpected shame he felt as he watched the man squirm and paw at his throat helplessly, *the bastard tried to kill me.* It was true—he had the wound to prove it—but the nagging, unfamiliar feeling of guilt didn't go away.

Suddenly, an image of a young boy came to him, a boy—not him as a child, but not so different either—waiting at home for his father. The boy was waiting for his father, excited to tell him about his day without any idea that his father wasn't coming home, that he was busy laying in some deserted street, breathing his last breaths as those in the nearby houses of the Downs listened but did not hear, watched but did not care.

Before he knew it, he'd dropped to one knee, all thoughts of the other soldiers forgotten. In that moment, his only thoughts were for the dying man staring at him with wide, panicked eyes as he sucked desperately, his hands clawing at his throat. Already, the bowman's face was beginning to turn a sick shade of blue. "I'm sorry," Aaron said, meaning it and not knowing why. He drew one of his blades and slowly, gently, slid it through the side of the man's leather jerkin and into his heart. The man let out a final rattling gasp and was still.

The sellsword withdrew the blade and slid it back into the sheathe at his side. He leaned over and closed the man's eyes with an almost reverent gesture. Shouts rose from down the street and he looked up to see four of the soldiers and the thin, sharp-faced leader approaching in the moonlight. He blinked, confused, like a man waking from a vivid dream, shaking his head to clear it of the strange, alien thoughts. *What in the name of all the gods is wrong with me?* While he'd been wasting his time with the dead man, the one who'd tried to *kill* him, the soldiers had caught up to him. He swallowed hard, furious at the unexplainable lump in his throat.

Studying the approaching men, he rose to his feet and drew his sword. One wounded man against five trained soldiers. Those weren't long odds; they weren't odds at all. He considered running but immediately dismissed the idea. With his hurt leg, it wouldn't take them anytime to run him down, and then he'd be even more exhausted than he already was. Besides, he'd be damned if he gave the bastards the satisfaction of chasing him down in the streets like some rabid dog.

The soldiers drew their swords and fanned out as they approached. Aaron frowned, his gaze turning left then right as he tried to keep all of them in view. "Well, come on then," he shouted, "who dies first?" The soldiers stopped and stared at him, and a confused moment passed before he realized they weren't staring at him after all but *behind* him.

He snatched a quick look over his shoulder and at first saw nothing. Then, as he watched, two forms seemed to materialize out of the shadows. The two figures were dressed all in black, even their faces wrapped around with black cloth so that only their eyes and the dusky skin around them could be seen. "Akalians," he breathed, his words a hoarse croak. He'd never actually seen one, but he'd heard enough stories about the master assassins to know them for what they were. It was said that the Akalians dedicated their lives to Akane, God of Shadows and closest sibling to Salen, the God of Death, and that they endured a hard, merciless life of training in order to become the most skilled killers in the world. It was also said that they performed dark rituals where they mutilated and tortured themselves in worship of their dark god until they became something more—or less—than human.

Aaron had always thought the stories exaggerations if not outright lies, but seeing them here, floating across the pavement like two phantoms of shadow and menace, he believed. Little was known about the cult of Akane but it was rumored that they came from the desert land of Elanar. Of course, the rumors had never been proven. No surprise, that, considering that most men who saw Akalians up close—as he now did—didn't live long enough to confirm any theories. "This day just keeps getting better and better," he said.

It was said that with an army of Akalians, a leader could conquer the entire world, but the soldiers of Akane were exceedingly rare and their services were said to be expensive enough to beggar a king. They were figures out of story and legend, murderers of kings and queens, creatures to be laughed away in the day and watched for in the dark of night, beings feared only a little less than the gods themselves. The appearance of two of them in a shithole like the Downs was beyond belief, and if not for the stiffness in his leg, and the too-real knot of fear in his stomach, Aaron would have thought he was dreaming.

Long, thin blades appeared in the hands of the figures as if by magic, and the two Akalians held them at a low angle to the ground as they approached with fluid, smooth strides so graceful that he could barely tell they were moving at all. Aaron swallowed hard and backed up toward the side of the street, his eyes darting between the Akalians and the group of professional hit men, the handle of his sword now slick with sweat.

The leader of the soldiers whistled sharply and more men spilled into the streets from the nearby alleys until there were at least twenty of them.

The Akalians drew even with him in the street and he tensed in expectation, but they didn't so much as spare him a glance, and he watched in shock as they glided past, toward the group of nervous, pale-faced soldiers.

"This has nothing to do with you. This man is hunted by his Highness Belgarin himself, and any who aid in his capture will be rewarded handsomely." The nasally voiced leader shouted at the Akalians, and despite the armed men gathered around him, Aaron was sure he heard a quaver in the man's voice. The black-garbed figures did not respond, but continued forward with the inevitability of a thunderstorm. "Fine, damnit," the thin man yelled, turning to the men with him, "kill them and then kill the sellsword. He knows too much."

I don't know a damned thing, Aaron wanted to say, but he decided to be quiet. He didn't want to remind the Akalians of his presence, in case, by the grace of Iladen, they'd somehow forgotten he was there. He backed up again until he fetched up against the wall of a building.

"Excuse me, master," came a man's cultured voice at his side.

Aaron cursed and spun, raising his sword. He stopped cold as he took in the short, chubby man before him. The stranger wore a simple brown robe similar to a priest, and his hands were clasped behind him. He bowed deeply to the sellsword revealing a head of thinning gray hair. "I hope I'm not intruding."

Aaron just stared. "Who the fuck are you," he whispered harshly, "and what do you want?"

The chubby man bobbed his head in deference, his double chins jiggling, "You may call me Gryle, sir." He said in a formal voice, "It is a pleasure to make your acquaintance. Forgive me for being so forward, but I wonder if you could be persuaded to accompany me to a more ... discreet location."

Aaron glanced meaningfully at the two figures, swathed in black, and the score of soldiers before turning back to the man. "Nah," he said, "how about we ask all of these fine gentlemen for tea instead?"

The man seemed to consider for a moment then he shook his head, "I do not think that would be wise, Mr. Envelar. I was under the distinct impression that they wanted to kill you."

Aaron eyed the man for a moment, at a loss for words. Then, "How do you—no never mind that. Let's go."

The chubby man looked surprised. "Aren't you curious as to where?"

"Anywhere's better than here," he growled, "now *move!*"

Gryle glanced up at the two groups, as if he'd only just realized they were there. "Ah," he said, nodding, "I take your point, sir. This way."

Aaron followed the man down a nearby alley. As they were turning on another sidestreet the night stillness was shattered by the sound of screaming. Apparently, the Akalians had begun their bloody work. He didn't think they had a chance against so many soldiers—no matter what the stories said—but he was just as glad that he wasn't among them. Salen's bell would ring loudly this night as the Keeper of the Dead called to his new servants, leading them across the fields of eternity.

CHAPTER FOUR

"WHERE IN THE NAME OF THE GODS are you taking me?" Aaron asked, scowling at the fat man's back. If his escort heard, he gave no sign as he trod along the broken cobbles of the street, marching purposefully past whore houses and shady bars with the air of a servant showing a visiting dignitary to his master's study. *I should have taken my chances with the Akalians,* Aaron thought, but he sighed and followed after the man. He'd been in Avarest, and specifically the Downs, for several years, and he'd thought that he had a handle on the maze-like huddles of shanties and shacks, the labyrinthine, haphazardly constructed streets and alleyways. He'd been wrong.

He was utterly and hopelessly lost. For a man who, as a matter of course, had plenty of enemies who would be happy to catch him off guard, it wasn't a good feeling. What's more, the pain in his leg was beginning to grow worse. "It is not far now, sir." Gryle answered as if he'd read the sellsword's mind.

Just when Aaron had decided that he wasn't going to take another step without some answers, the stranger stopped at a small, indistinct home and rapped on the door once, paused, and rapped twice more. The door swung open, and a thickly muscled, familiar form moved aside to let them in. "Why am I not surprised," Aaron muttered as he followed Gryle into the house.

Inside, a single, flickering candle gave off enough light for him to recognize the figure standing by the opposite wall. Her features were smooth and soft and held a beauty unlike anything a man would ever expect to find anywhere, let alone in the Downs, the asshole of Avarest. A long mane of dark brown hair framed her face, and he thought he detected a hint of amusement on her blue eyes. "You." He lurched toward her, but a fresh wave of pain, by far the worst yet, tore through him. His knee buckled and the next thing he knew he was lying on the floor.

I'm sorry, Aaron, the voice spoke inside his head in an exhausted tone, I can hold it back no longer. You are safe, now. From his place on the floor, Aaron glanced at the woman seated at the table, at the chubby, pink-faced man who now stood behind her, as if waiting to fill her cup, then turned his head to look at the two thickly muscled men who watched him silently. He barked a harsh, tired laugh through teeth gritted against the pain. Oh yeah, safe as a baby in its mother's arms, he thought, and then darkness reached up and took him.

CHAPTER FIVE

HE AWOKE WITH A GASP, his body bathed in a cold sweat. He was surprised to find that he was in an unfamiliar bed, and he shook his head furiously in an effort to clear the visions that still lingered there. He'd dreamed of the bowman, lying in the street, choking and gagging on his own wasted throat. His stomach turned threateningly at the memory. *What is happening to me?*

It wasn't as if the man was the first he'd killed. A sellsword didn't survive long without wetting his blade from time to time, but never before had it left him feeling so ... guilty. After his parents' death and his time at the orphanage—where he was administered beatings almost daily—he'd learned that a man must have tough skin to survive in a world where everyone was out to take what was yours.

"*You feel.*" The familiar voice spoke as the glowing, magenta orb floated into his field of vision.

He jerked up in bed, "*You,*" he growled, "this is your fault. What are you doing here, and just what in the name of the Keeper's Bell have you done to me?"

"It is Kevlane's Bond."

He frowned in thought. "Kevlane? What in the name of the gods are you—wait a minute. Do you mean *Boyce*

Kevlane?" He barked a laugh, 'you'll have to do better than that, firefly. I'm no child to be told a bed time story. Everyone knows the wizard never existed."

"The same way that they know that talking balls of light don't?" The voice asked. Aaron frowned at the hint of amusement in its tone but didn't respond. "You're wrong," the orb said after a moment. "Do you remember the story?"

Aaron scowled, "Of course I remember it."

The orb drifted closer, "Tell me."

"No thanks. I have better things to do than recite a children's tale I haven't heard since I stopped pissing the bed."

"Fine," the orb voice answered, annoyed, "I will tell you then. Thousands of years ago—three thousand, seven hundred and sixty three, to be exact—during the Age of Kings, dozens of Warlords fought and warred in an effort to become the ultimate ruler of Telrear. They were selfish, cruel men who cared only about power, and the land and its people fought, bled, and died to feed their ambition. Crops were burned, families starved, and it seemed that there would be no end to it until one rose who wished only to bring peace to the land, to end the killing—"

"Hah," Aaron said. "Seems fools existed even then."

"The man," the orb went on, as if he hadn't spoken, "was Aaron Caltriss, and it is from him that you get your name."

Aaron recoiled as if slapped, "How could you possibly know that?" When he was young, he'd made the mistake of telling some of the kids in his home city of

Yalet about his namesake, and he'd spent the better part of his childhood being teased because of it. No matter how many fights he was in, no matter how many bloody noses he gave or received, it had not stopped. The teasing had even followed him to the orphanage somehow, but of course it hadn't been the kids that had taunted him then but the headmaster himself. After one of the regular beatings, when his back was bloody from the headmaster's switch and tears of anger and pain stung his eyes, the old man would lean down with a humorless smile on his face. *You're no Caltriss, boy,* he'd say, *and life's no fairy tale.*

Aaron could hear the bastard's voice even now, harsh and raw from his poorly hidden addiction to his Tamarang pipe, could see his hunched form holding the bloody switch, smiling as he scratched the puss-filled sores long use of the drug produced. Still, the beatings hadn't been the reason Aaron had killed the man in the end. The truth was, the headmaster had been right; life was brutal, cruel, and there were no happy endings. Hard lessons but important ones. Some people didn't learn them until they were much older, until one of their children died from the wasting sickness or the nobles raised the taxes so high that they could barely feed their families. As for Aaron, he'd learned them at the end of the old man's switch, and in a way, he knew, he should be thankful for that.

No, it wasn't the beatings that had made him kill Headmaster Cyrille. If he was being honest with himself, it wasn't even the old man's sick use of the young girls under his care—though the cold, dead looks in their eyes had certainly paid for his death a thousand times. Aaron had been young then, too young to understand the depravities the children were forced to endure. A good reason to kill a man, but it had not been his. He had not killed Cyrille for all of the children; he'd killed him for one of them. *Owen.* The name came to his mind unwillingly, and he fought it down with a will. Some memories were better forgotten.

"I know it because you know it," the orb said simply, pulling him away from his dark thoughts. "Caltriss fought the armies of the barbarian kings in several pitched battles, but despite the fact that his army was much smaller and ill-equipped, he always managed to win."

"He led his army across the width and breadth of Telrear, engaging the vicious legions of the barbarian kings in quick, fluid skirmishes instead of the large-scale conflicts they were accustomed to and disappearing with his smaller force before the mighty armies of the kings could corner and destroy him. It wasn't long before the name of Aaron Caltriss began to spread and soon people were searching him out in order to join his army, or to join the city of Palindra, the city it was said he'd created in the deep tracts of the Olindash forest in the west of Telrear."

"You see, people didn't join Caltriss just because he won victories—all of the barbarian kings won great battles against the others the Time of Blood. No, people flocked to Caltriss because of who he was, because of what he believed in. In those days, as in most, when a city was sacked or conquered, widespread looting, rape, and killing were common. The armies of all of the kings took their toll from any city they occupied—all except for Aaron's. He left the people in peace. Instead of setting his men to theft and murder, he set them to rebuilding homes and businesses, to helping those who needed it, to fixing the damage that the war had caused, and the people loved him for it."

The orb paused then, and for a moment, Aaron thought it would not continue. When it finally did, its voice was soft, almost wistful, "Caltriss was more than a man. He was hope in a hopeless world, rest to the weary, peace to men and women whose entire lives were stained with blood. The citizens of those ancient cities came to him in search of something better until his numbers swelled to rival even those of the greatest barbarian kings. It seemed, then, as if it was only a matter of time before he united the entire continent."

"Fearful of his gathering numbers, the barbarian kings united their armies against him. Caltriss tried to fight, but despite his growing numbers, the combined might of the kings was too much, and soon his armies were forced back to the city of Palindra, surrounded by hordes of bloodthirsty men."

Aaron shook himself. Listening to the orb, he'd felt himself being drawn into the story despite himself. "You talk as if you were there," he said with a laugh.

The orb's light grew pale and weak, almost sad. *As if a lightning bug can be sad,* he thought. When the orb didn't answer, he sighed, "Why are you wasting my time telling me all of this anyway? Everyone knows the story. Boyce Kevlane, Aaron's most powerful wizard betrayed him. He killed Caltriss and the barbarians took the city. They call it Kevlane's Folly because he thought that betraying Caltriss would grant him favor with the barbarian kings, but they threw him from the castle parapets as soon as they entered the city."

You know nothing! The voice hissed, and Aaron winced at the words seemed to burn in his mind. "Kevlane never would have betrayed Aaron." It continued out loud, "they were friends since childhood, closer than brothers. No, in their darkest hour, when the barbarians crouched outside the city, hungry for blood, Caltriss called for Kevlane and his seven greatest apprentices. Kevlane and the others had spent years working on a spell that would bind into a normal man those virtues that they believed made the perfect warrior and commander: Strength, speed, intelligence, charisma, perception, adaptability, and compassion."

"Caltriss told them that there was no more time, that their spell would have to be tried now. Kevlane protested that it wasn't ready, that the sorcery hadn't been perfected, and that it would almost certainly kill any man who it was used on. But Caltriss, seeing his people losing hope, would not relent. He demanded that the wizard and his apprentices perform the ritual on him, for he said that he would not ask anything of anyone else that he would not do himself."

"At first, Kevlane denied him, but as the gates shook from the barbarian horde and siege engines lobbed fire into the streets and homes of his people, Caltriss demanded it of the wizard first as his king, then as his fellow man, and finally, as his friend. In the end, with tears sliding down his cheeks, the High Wizard relented and ordered the beginning of the ritual." The orb paused before continuing, "No, Aaron. Kevlane's folly—as Caltriss's—was not betrayal, but hope, not hate, but love."

"The mages threw their all into the ritual, desperate that it succeed. Each apprentice was to focus on the summoning and shaping of one of the seven virtues, while Kevlane himself was to handle the nearly impossible task of weaving those virtues into Caltriss. Perhaps, the magic proved too much even for a mage of Kevlane's power, or perhaps the gods feared that such a spell would bring men close to their own power and decided to intervene. Whatever the reason, the magic failed and, instead of being instilled with the Seven Virtues, Caltriss was killed. Wracked with grief, blaming himself for his friend's death, Kevlane charged headlong over the castle parapets where he fell to his death. No more than an hour passed before the barbarians burst into the city and put its citizens to the sword, including the seven apprentices who lay in the floor of the throne room, too exhausted to defend themselves."

"It wasn't until later, after all those involved were dead and Palindra overthrown, that the spell achieved some small measure of success. You see, though Caltriss died, the virtues *had* been created. As the corpses of the seven apprentices were burned along with the rest of the city's dead, those virtues formed, somehow taking with them some of the human aspects of their creators. The virtues were young then, new to the land of the living, scared and confused. They fled, and in fleeing, scattered themselves across the land of Telrear."

Aaron's eyes widened, "So then, you ..."

The orb's light intensified until it grew so bright that he was forced to shield his eyes, "I am one of the Seven Virtues, created from Kevlane and Caltriss's desperate hope for peace, born in the fire and smoke of a mass grave, and infused with some small part of my creator." The light drifted closer to Aaron, floating only inches away from his face, "I am Compassion. You may call me Co."

He barked a laugh. The story didn't follow anything he'd ever been told about Caltriss and Kevlane. Caltriss was always talked of like a hero, sure, but the wizard was pretty much the world's most famous traitor—excluding, perhaps, Belgarin who, unwilling to share the rule of Telrear, had turned on his brothers and sisters, assassinating two before anyone knew something was amiss. Of course, Belgarin was still alive and breathing, and few were the people who were brave or stupid enough to label him traitor in a stranger's hearing. The prince wasn't exactly known for his tolerance.

The fabled city of Palindra, the most powerful wizard of the Age of Kings being misunderstood for all these years, a bunch of sentient virtues created by magic? Aaron grunted. A crock of shit is what it was. Fairy tales cooked up to help children sleep at night.The problem, of course, was that one of the damned things was floating in front of his face even now. A thought struck him, and he narrowed his eyes at the orb. "You said you're compassion?"

The orb bobbed up and down, as if nodding. "So are you the reason why I almost blubbered like a cursed baby when I killed that archer?"

"Yes," the orb answered, "It is Kevlane's bond at work."

Aaron started at a knock on the door, "Well, you better make it *stop* working," he whispered harshly, "The last thing a sellsword needs is to start crying every time he has to ghost somebody."

The knocking on the door grew more insistent. "I'm coming, damnit!"

The orb floated closer, "I will hide within you, it is best that no one knows we are bonded."

"No thanks, firefly" He said, waving a dismissive hand at the bobbing light, "not interested."

The orb drew closer still, and though the words were spoken in his mind, he felt as if they were whispered in his ear, *Not many know of me and the others—for most, we are nothing but a children's tale—but there are those who do. There are those who hunt us, who seek to bring us all together, as Kevlane tried to do so long ago. Such men pay fortunes to assassins and trackers, and they would not hesitate to kill you if they found out that you were bonded.*

Aaron frowned, "I've already got enough people trying to kill me thanks to that damned woman." He considered for a moment then sighed irritably, "Fine, but don't go screwing around in there again. You understand me? It's my head. You're just visiting."

Without replying, the orb flew into him, disappearing into his chest, and he grunted as the all-too familiar tingling sensation ran through his body. The door opened a moment later and the two men from the night before walked in and took up positions on either side of the door. They folded their arms across their massive chests displaying identical tattoos--a sword with a rose wrapped around it—and watched him, their faces expressionless.

Aaron frowned. He'd seen such men before. Men such as these, with their blank expressions and stances that were relaxed, yet at the same time prepared to do any violence asked of them, prided themselves on following orders, on adhering to what they considered their 'duty' no matter who it hurt. When Aaron was young, his father had been a general in Prince Eladen's army, and Aaron'd had occasion to meet many like this. As far as he was concerned, any man who valued a cause over his own life or the lives of others was barely a man at all. "Well, howdy, boys." *Bastards are wide as a damn house,* he thought. "It's good to see your mistress feeds you well. You must be a couple of good dogs."

The man Aaron had met the night before walked in with a cough, "It is, perhaps, unwise to taunt them, sir," he said in an apologetic tone, "Eagan and Deagan are two of Telrear's fiercest warriors."

Aaron turned to the man, Gryle, raising his eyebrows. The man met his gaze and, suddenly, the craziness of the last day was too much and he broke into a fit of uncontrollable laughter. Gryle frowned, "I do not see that there is cause for laughter. The two are brothers, they—" The fat man's tone was all offended dignity.

Aaron laughed harder, "I don't doubt that. Two big, dumb, and ugly bastards like these? Keeper's lantern, they'd *have* to be related."

The expressions of the two men remained as still as stone, their eyes showing no hint of anger or any emotion at all, for that matter. The chubby man sighed and opened his mouth to speak, but a soft, amused voice came from the doorway. "Do not let him bother you, Gryle. He insists on acting more foolish than he is."

Aaron turned and watched her stride into the room. She wore tight fitting leather trousers that accentuated her curves, and his laughter cut off as he swallowed hard. Her soft leather boots were of a make much too nice for anyone who spent much time walking the refuse-filled streets of the Downs, as was the white silk shirt she wore—not that he didn't appreciate the way it clung to her. She pushed a strand of long brown hair out of one eye and smiled at him. *Some folks cut with a blade,* Aaron cautioned himself, *and some do their cutting with a smile. Either way, the result is almost always the same; a dead man or one that wishes he was, and in this case, that man is me.*

"Still," she said, as if she didn't notice his eyes on her, "there are things that we must talk about."

"Damn right there are." He said, forcing his eyes up to her face "for one, how about we talk about the fact that I damn near got killed because of you, or about how you sent me on a rescue mission and somehow forgot to mention that the target was none other than Prince Eladen himself. I don't give a damn how easy you are on the eyes, lady, you're one mean bitch."

Gryle gasped in shock, but Aaron paid him no mind as he and the woman studied each over for several moments. "I'm flattered," she said finally, her smile widening, "that you think I'm easy on the eyes."

He grunted, "Don't get it twisted. Because of you, I got shot in the leg, was chased across rooftops like some kind of damned animal, and watched a man who I was beginning to like get killed. I've a mind to get up right now and bend you over my knee."

The chubby man stepped forward, "You wouldn't *dare.* Who are you to speak to Mistress—"

"Enough, Gryle," the woman snapped. She turned back to the sellsword, a frown on her face. "I am sorry for the innkeeper. I did not mean for him to become involved. In fact, I didn't think that you'd been seen at all." She considered for a moment, "Still, I find it surprising that a man who sells his blade to the highest bidder should much care about a man he knew for less than a week."

"Wait a minute," he said, "how in the name of Salen's Fields, do you know I knew him for less than a week?"

The woman's smile returned, "Of course, we have been watching you, Sir Envelar. I do not take the hiring of men I don't know lightly. Still, you haven't answered me about the innkeeper."

"I'm no sir." He threw the covers aside and noticed for the first time that his leg had been wrapped with a clean bandage. He also noticed that, aside from the bandage, he was completely naked. *Damn. No help for it.* His father had always told him to strike while he had the momentum and, by Talen, he had it. "Now listen, lady. I don't give a rat's ass about the innkeeper or your questions." He struggled up onto wobbly, unsteady legs, "Now you're going to tell me what I want to know, or this is going to get ugly."

"You really shouldn't—" The woman began.

"I'll do what I will," he barked, gesturing at the two fighters, "you might be able to boss those two fools around, but not me." He took a step forward and grunted as his weight came down on his wounded leg. It buckled, and he had time to spit a curse before it gave beneath him, and he fell at the woman's feet for the second time in as many days.

Someone whistled. He looked up, scowling, and saw that the woman was covering her mouth with one delicate hand, as if to keep herself from laughing. He sighed. *This is going to be a long damn day.*

Truer words, never spoken, the voice said in his mind, and he was sure he didn't imagine the laughter lurking under its surface.

CHAPTER SIX

EAGAN OR DEAGAN, HE WASN'T SURE which and didn't much care, helped him to his feet. Aaron dressed and then the brother guided him to a small room with a table. Eagen—or was it Deagan?—eased him down into a chair surprisingly gently, and stepped away, folding his arms once more, his face still expressionless. *An obedient dog waiting for orders,* Aaron thought. The woman sat down across from him, a look of concern on her face. "The scars on your back--"

"Are none of your damn business," he growled. "Now why am I here, and what do you want with me? Haven't you fucked my life up enough already?"

"I'm sorry for the trouble I've caused you," She said, leaning forward and placing a hand on his, and despite his anger Aaron found himself thinking about how soft her skin was, like rolled silk, "You must believe that I didn't want any of this to happen. I just ..." she paused and a deep sadness came into her eyes that surprised Aaron, "I picked you," she said, looking away from him, "because everyone says you're the best. I knew that saving El— *Prince* Eladen was a long shot but with your reputation ..."

He frowned suspiciously. "What reputation? Who told you I was the best?"

The woman looked surprised, "Most everyone. I had my men ask around in the Downs, and everyone pointed us to you. They didn't know where you were, of course, but they told us to seek out a man named Envelar. They said that you were a skilled swordsman, and that once you'd taken a contract you always saw it through."

He leaned forward, his elbows on the table, "What else did *they* say?"

The woman hesitated. When Aaron continued to stare at her expectantly, she continued, an obvious note of reluctance in her voice, "They said that you wouldn't ask too many questions as long as the money was good."

Aaron laughed, "That sounds closer to the truth. Best be honest with me from now on, princess. We peasants kind of have a thing about that."

Gryle let out a gasp of surprise, and the woman leaned back in her chair, her eyes wide. Even the two guards raised an eyebrow in surprise. "H-how could you know?" She asked.

He grunted. "These people, did they also tell you I was a fool? A man would have to be blind not to see it." He gestured at the short, chubby man, "This one here follows you around like a puppy, and his speech is much too cultured for us lowly commoners. Still, I think it strange that you would be so bold as to bring your chamberlain along."

He leaned back in his chair with a smile, satisfied at the frightened, uncertain look in her eyes. "Not many people can afford the price of two Akalians either," he continued, "but I suppose one of the royal blood could." He nodded his head at the brothers, "As for those two, if those tattoos aren't the mark of a personal guard, I don't know what is. But what really gave you away is the fact that you hired me at all. After all, you clearly have men who could have done the job. Why, then, pay me? The answer is that you didn't want anyone to know that you were involved with your brother's attempted rescue." He frowned, "Better to let some sellsword take the heat than bring any anger down on that pretty head of yours."

"I wonder, princess, what do you think your brother, Belgarin, and the others will do when they learn you're trying to swap sides? Come to think of it, why *have* you swapped sides? From everything I've heard, you've followed him since the beginning, so what's changed?"

For a moment, the princess didn't speak. Her sky blue eyes got a faraway look, as if staring at something only she could see. "Nothing's changed. My brother Belgarin is a bloodthirsty fool, intent on ruling all of Telrear or destroying it."

Aaron stared at the woman for a second then glanced at the chamberlain, noting the man's worried look, and a realization struck him. "You haven't just changed sides, have you?" He asked, sure even as he said it, that he was right. "You've been working for Eladen all along. So when you heard news of his capture, you were forced to abandon the charade and attempt a rescue, is that it?" He barked a laugh, "Lady, if your brother didn't want to kill you before, he damn sure does now, or he *will* once he finds out you were the one who hired me."

"Y-you would betray the Princess?" the chamberlain said, wringing his pudgy hands.

"Relax, Gryle," The woman said, her eyes never leaving Aaron's. "Please, call me Adina."

He raised an eyebrow at the flustered chamberlain, smiling at the man's obvious discomfort, before meeting the woman's gaze. "Fine, Adina. Tell me this, why would you leave your palace in Edrafell? Surely, you would have been safer there, behind your guards and your army."

Adina scowled, a look of bitter hate flashing in her eyes, "I have no army. They are Belgarin's men now, bought and paid for, as are most of my household staff and my personal bodyguards." She gestured around the room, indicating the two men and Gryle. "What you see here, is what's left of my *army.*"

Aaron's eyes widened at that, and he stared at her for several seconds before breaking into another fit of laughter.

"I'm glad that my misfortune amuses you," she said, frowning.

He wiped at his eyes, "A princess without a palace, a commander without an army. Looks like you chose the wrong side, lady. Oh, and forgive me if I don't have a lot of sympathy just now. After all, you *are* the same princess who very nearly got me killed because she didn't want to get her royal hands dirty."

She opened her mouth to speak, an angry remark clearly on her lips, but stopped herself at the last moment. Then she took a deep breath and tried again, "I have already apologized for that."

He snorted, "Apologies don't mean shit to the dead, lady. Now why don't you tell me why you brought me here, so I can tell you to go to the Fields and get on with my day?"

The chamberlain gasped, and one of the brothers started forward, but the princess forestalled them with a raised hand, "With Eladen slain, Belgarin will try to consolidate his holdings in the north, as he did with my brother Geoffrey's lands in the east, and my sister Ophasia's in the south after he had them assassinated. If he succeeds, he will not only control nearly half of Telrear, but also nearly half of our country's armed men."

The sellsword gave a mocking look of surprise, "Oh? Surely you must be mistaken. Certainly, Eladen's nobles and soldiers would not so quickly betray him. After all," he said with a wink, "what is more important to any man than peace?"

"You mock me," she observed, her expression troubled, "but does your cynicism reach so far that you believe all of Ophasia and Geoffrey's armies and nobles took the assassination of their leaders in stride and pledged their loyalty to Belgarin without hesitation?" She shook her head slowly, 'If so, then let me assure you that you are wrong. There were many, commanders and soldiers both, who would not bow to Belgarin's rule. That was, until the highest ranking officers were made examples of. They and their families were declared traitors to the crown, escorted to the city square by the very men they'd fought beside for years and executed publicly for all to see."

A hard look came in her eyes, and when she spoke her voice was little more than a snarl, "Women and children were dragged from their homes, kicking and screaming and burned alive. No, Eladen's armies are loyal to him and to his cause, but with Eladen dead and no one to lead them, their loyalty will lie with their families. As for the nobles, it is my belief that Claudius, Eladen's second in command and now ruler of his capital city of Baresh and all its surrounding lands, works for Belgarin. In fact, I believe that he was instrumental in my brother's capture."

Aaron shrugged. "You still haven't told me what any of this has to do with me. I'm just a common sellsword, lady, not some tourney knight in gilded armor."

"I want to hire you." She said. "Claudius has ever been a coward and a fool, but the man beneath Claudius, Ervine Deckard, is a good man. If something was to happen to that simpering craven Claudius, Deckard would gain control of the north's army, and he would not stand idly by as Belgarin marched in and put the city to the sword."

Aaron shook his head. "You must be out of your mind, lady. What do you think this is one of your nurse's stories? At least with the last job it was a short walk to nearly get myself killed. Now you want me to journey halfway across Telrear, somehow sneak into a *castle* and assassinate the land's new ruler; this all in opposition to the most powerful man in the nation, a man who—by your own admission—enjoys making examples of people? Impossible. And even if I *did* manage it, the people wouldn't thank me. I'd get the executioner's axe if

I was lucky, but more likely, they'd make me suffer before I traveled the Keeper's Fields."

"You will have help."

He laughed harshly, "What kind of help? Are you able to call Talen, God of soldiers on command? Or, even better, Iladen? Because for a job like this, a man couldn't have enough luck."

Her cold blue eyes did not waver from his gaze. "You know that I cannot. You will be well compensated."

He sighed, "Let me guess, fifty virgins? An honorable place among the minor gods, maybe? Am I to rub shoulders with Hectar, the god of Blacksmithing? Sit for a drink with Oberon, God of ale and inns?" He shook his head, "I don't think so."

"Damn you," Adina snapped, her composure breaking, "Don't you care about anything but yourself?"

My parents. Owen. But they're all dead. Aaron forced the thoughts down with a will, smiling to cover his anger, "Not really. I'm not much for causes, princess. They have a way of getting good men killed." He shrugged, "Well, men anyway."

She took a deep breath and made a visible effort to calm herself. "What happened to you? What made you hate people so much? What made you lose your belief?"

His expression turned hard, and she looked away from his cold gaze. "Life. That's what happened. Not that I expect a *princess* to know anything about it. Kind of hard to learn about loss when you've got people like these fools waiting on you hand and foot. When you were a child, sitting in your castle, and spending your time mocking the dirty peasants or fretting over whether to wear the blue silk or the white, us *common* people were busy *dying* for you and your family's *causes."*

Adina recoiled as if slapped, a look of genuine hurt on her face. *You wound her to no end,* Co said in his mind.

Life wounds, he thought back harshly, *best that she starts learning it.*

"I cannot help my birth," The princess said finally, her voice little more than a whisper, "but don't you understand that you could save hundreds? Thousands?"

"Yeah, or die for nothing and feed the maggots in a land I've never been to. The Downs aren't much, princess, but they're my home—as much of one as I have, anyway. Now let's stop wasting each other's time. I have enough to worry about now that I'm being hunted by the gods know how many assassins, and I'm sure there are things you need to be doing for your little rebellion." He rose from the table slowly, careful not to put too much of his weight on his wounded leg. The wound didn't hurt much, only itched, but he wasn't prepared to risk falling on his face again. It wouldn't have fit well with the kind of exit he planned on making. "There's nothing you can offer me that is worth my life. Good day, Adina."

He was halfway to the door when she spoke, "Fifteen thousand gold coins."

He stopped and let out a deep sigh. "You just don't learn do you?" He asked, not bothering to turn around. "A dead man has no use for coins."

He started for the door again. "Fifty thousand." She said.

Gryle gasped, "Princess, you can't."

"The treasury will matter little if Belgarin takes control of Baresh, Gryle." The princess said in a tired voice. She said something else, too, but by that time Aaron wasn't listening. *Fifty thousand gold.* With that kind of money, he could live like a king for years.

I wish that we could help her, Co spoke in his mind, *but you're right; it would be suicide.*

You think it unwise?

Of course.

He nodded and turned back to Adina. "That settles it then. You give me traveling money and pay for expenses. When the job's done, fifty thousand marks and not a penny less."

For a moment, she looked as if she was about to smile, but instead she only nodded, "You have my word."

He shrugged, "I don't care for your word, but your gold will do." *How do you like that, firefly?* He thought smugly, *looks like we're going on a little trip. Maybe next time you'll think twice before making me blubber over a man I've never met.*

A wave of feminine laughter washed over him, and he frowned, confused. *Wait a minute ... you said you didn't want to ...* "Damn."

The princess and the chamberlain jumped in surprise at his shout, and the two guards went for their swords. "W-what is it?" She asked.

"Nothing," Aaron said, "it's nothing." He jerked a thumb at the two guards, "Now, tell Butch and Woofers there to heel. We've got things to discuss."

CHAPTER SEVEN

"I SAID NO, DAMNIT." Aaron sat back in his chair, sighing. They'd been at it for hours now, and he was growing impatient. "You're not coming. I'm going to have a hard enough time avoiding getting killed by one army or another without carting around a princess and her handmaid," he said, gesturing to Gryle, "Might as well kill us both now and save us the walk."

"He's quite right, princess," The chamberlain agreed, choosing to gloss over the handmaid comment, "it is much too dangerous on the road. Belgarin's spies and thugs are everywhere. It would be better to find a nice, quiet place to—"

"No, Gryle." Adina said, "I will not stand idly by while Belgarin throws all of Telrear into chaos." She turned to Aaron, "You need me."

He laughed, "I hate to tell you, princess, but I need you like I need the plague. What do you think we're just going to ride off and make everything right? I'm no story book hero, and this is no fairy tale. This is life, and in life there are no happy endings."

The princess said something, but Aaron wasn't listening. He felt something, at the back of his awareness like a thing seen from the corner of a man's eye.

Something wasn't—*there are men approaching,* Co said, her voice worried, *you must go.*

"—really would be better if—" Gryle was saying.

"Shut up," Aaron said, "listen." The chamberlain looked hurt, as if he was a child being sent to bed early, but he lapsed into silence. Aaron cocked his head, listening for any betraying sound but could hear nothing except the rapid beating of his own heart. Despite this, the feeling of foreboding didn't subside. *How many?*

Too many, the Virtue answered, and he could hear the fear in her voice.

Good enough for me. "They know we're here." He said, abruptly rising to his feet. "We have to move." The two brothers—who'd been standing like statues throughout the course of the discussion—jumped into action, vanishing into the bedroom and appearing in the doorway moments later, each wielding a curved, wicked looking sword. Eagan or Deagan—Aaron couldn't tell which—tossed him his knives, still in their sheathes, and his sword. He strapped the sword on his back, hiding it under his cloak, and secured the knives at his waist.

Where are they?

See for yourself.

Aaron gasped as strange sensations rolled over him in silent, invisible waves of force. One moment he felt as if a thousand pins were piercing him, the next, he felt as if he was being buoyed up by something, held aloft in a raging sea of torment. Then that feeling, too, was gone, and he was overcome with a sense of something slick and greasy, that left him feeling dirty in its wake.

He dropped to one knee, closing his eyes and holding his head between shaking hands. *It's too much.* He thought, *it's too loud. Make it stop.* He let out a pained groan. He could hear the others speaking to him, but he couldn't make out their words past storm in his thoughts.

Focus, Co hissed, *you have to focus. Do not try to take it all in at once. You are too close.*

A hand touched his shoulder, and he jerked away, snarling in sudden rage and bloodthirst. *Kill. I have to kill them. Belgarin will be pleased.* The thoughts, not his own, crowded in his mind insistently, pushing against his consciousness, making his head feel as if it was going to explode. Then, as abruptly as the fury had come, it was gone. What replaced it was still anger, but of a different kind. He was angry at his brother, Belgarin, at what he'd become, at the atrocities that he'd subjected the people of Telrear to. It was a cold, powerful anger, but tempered with hope, with a belief Aaron hadn't possessed since he'd found his parents murdered—the belief that, somehow, things would work out. It was a strange, unfamiliar feeling, but another instant passed and it too was gone, replaced by fear. Fear that he would fail his Mistress, that he wouldn't be able to help her to make the right decisions, that, in the end, he was useless, and that he would fail in his promise to his King.

More thoughts crowded into his mind, too many to count, a raging sea of fear and anger and hate, and he felt himself being pulled apart by the force of it. *Aaron!* A voice screamed in his head, and suddenly the voices, the thoughts, grew silent. *Concentrate. You must not let yourself be swept away. Look closely.*

He stared into the churning tempest inside his mind, and as he watched, the wants and desires began to coalesce into vague shapes. After a moment, he could make out the outline of the room he was in, could distinguish the forms of the others as roiling masses of various colors, each color, he knew instinctively, representing an emotion in a way that his mind could make sense of. Turning, he looked at the wall, looked past it, and into the street. Outside of the small house's door, a group of men gathered in the street, their forms blazing angry reds with coiling chains of a sickly green he took for selfishness and ambition snaking their way through each.

He shook his head, expelling the vision with no idea as to how he did it. His sight snapped back to his body with a sickening, disorienting lurch that left him dizzy. He barely managed to fight back the urge to vomit, and when he came to his feet he saw that Adina and the chamberlain were staring at him with wide eyes. Even one of the brothers watched him with an eyebrow raised. "There are twelve of them," he gasped, out of breath, "Too damned many." He turned to the princess, "Tell me you've got another way out of here."

The woman met his gaze, and he could see the question there. He said nothing and finally she shook her head "That is the only door."

"Well," he said grimly, "that's that then. Sure you can't call up a couple of Akalians? The bastards would be awful handy right about now."

"No. Those men came to me. They told me that you were being hunted, and I sent Gryle to bring you back. I've no idea why they got involved."

The window.

Aaron smacked himself in the forehead, *Thanks, firefly.* "Come on." He rushed into the room where he'd slept, not bothering to see if the others were following, and eyed the window. It would be a tight fit for the brothers, but that's what the bastards got for being so damned big. The chamberlain let out a squeak of fear as someone knocked on the door loudly. "Go," Aaron said, grabbing Adina and pushing her toward the window, "We've got to go before the bastards get smart and circle around."

The princess hurried to the window and climbed out, dropping to the ground on the other side. "You next." The sellsword said, motioning to the chamberlain.

The man nearly slipped on his own feet in his haste. He made it through the opening up to his gut and then grunted with effort as his bulk got stuck in the frame. Aaron used his boot to help the man along, and the chamberlain squealed in surprise, grunting as he hit the paving stones of the street.

A second series of knocks banged against the door, louder and more insistent than the first. He turned back to the two men. "Come on, guys. You're next."

The two brothers shook their heads, and he saw that they hadn't sheathed the large, strangely curved swords. "You go." One of them said.

He stared first at one and then the other, taking in the grim set of their jaws, and the determined look in their eyes. "You mean to stay," he said, incredulous.

The two nodded. "We will hold them as long as we can." The one who hadn't spoken before said, "You must protect the princess."

I don't give a damn about the princess, Aaron thought. "Don't be fools. We have to go, now."

There was a resounding crash in the room beyond. Another hit like that, maybe two, and they'd be in for sure. "You're out of your damn *minds,*" Aaron shouted, "you're talking about suicide."

The two brothers smiled small, knowing smiles. "Keep her safe." Something smashed against the door, and Aaron heard the wood crack. The two brothers met each other's gaze, nodded, and walked out, closing the door behind them.

"Damned *idiots.*" Aaron started for the door then stopped, looking back at the window. There could be others out there, creeping up on the princess and the fat man even now. The two of them wouldn't stand a chance. Of course, neither would the brothers, not against that many. As soon as the door came down, the fools would probably be peppered with arrows.

They chose their fate, Co said, her voice low and sad, *it is a noble end. You must look to the princess.*

"A pointless end," Aaron grunted, fighting back an unfamiliar tide of emotion that threatened to overwhelm him, "but you're right about the last." He started toward the window, "After all, if she dies, who's going to pay me?" Another crack, louder than the first two, split the silence. *That'll be the door coming down.* He broke into a run and did not look back as he dove through the window and into the waiting daylight.

CHAPTER EIGHT

AARON SCANNED THE NEARLY EMPTY STREET with a frown, his hands on his blades. On an average day, the streets would be packed with people. Merchants would set up stalls and hawk wares ranging from the cheap to the extravagant—the latter of which had often once belonged to some unlucky noble or rich merchant from the finer parts of the city. Avarest's poor would shuffle home from a long day of work that rarely left them enough coin to feed their families, their gazes downcast and empty. Interspersed between these unfortunate souls, one could always pick out nobles, lords and ladies out for a day of slumming, searching to fill some perverse hunger that could only be sated in the dark by-ways of the Downs, and though they no doubt thought their disguises made them blend in with everyone else, they could easily be spotted by their manner and the inbred arrogance that clothed their kind far more thoroughly than any robe or tunic ever could.

Drifting through and around the nobles and the poor alike, one could always find those who made their livelihood from the suffering or desperation of others: Pickpockets, muggers, sneakthieves, sellers of "magical" medallions and trinkets, whores, all of them watching and waiting for the opportunity to make use of their own personal brand of thievery. From time to time, priests would travel through the Downs, condemning the citizens for their lawlessness and threatening them with the names of their gods if they did not repent—such as these were often found in some back alley the next day, their clothes and possessions gone, their throats slit by some kind citizen who decided to send them to their gods early. To Aaron's mind, the fools got what they deserved. After all, who wanted to hear about repentance while their children starved?

The nobles often gave speeches about the blatant, appalling crimes that took place in the Downs but it was rare that anything ever came of it. Aaron believed that in part, this was due to the fact that the ruling council of Avarest generally concluded that it wasn't worth the vast expenditure of money and manpower it would take to tame the city's poor district, but mostly, he suspected, it was because the nobles, for all their talk, enjoyed indulging in the darker pleasures the Downs offered too much to risk losing them.

Still, from time to time, the city guard would march into the poor district in force, scattering the poor and the criminal alike as if they were mice fleeing from a brush fire. After such cleansings, the crimes would stop. At least, for a while. Then a day would pass, or a week, and slowly, inevitably they would begin again. The nobles enjoyed hearing themselves talk about the Downs as an evil, godless district, but as far as Aaron was concerned, everyone was out to screw you if they could get something out of the deal. At least the people of the Downs were honest about it.

Still, crime-filled or not, Avarest's poor district held the vast majority of its population, and in the middle of a cool autumn day like this one, the streets should have been packed with people spending money and stealing it in nearly equal measure. Instead, the lane was nearly deserted. A short distance away, an old woman haggled angrily with a stall keeper. The argument was heated, but seemed half-hearted to Aaron, a feeling that only increased as he watched them scan the street constantly with nervous, shifting gazes. Farther on, a beggar dressed in ratty clothes shook a can against the paved street. *Clink, clink, clink.*

"What now?" Adina's voice came from beside him, but he didn't turn. He watched the beggar, saw that the dirty old man was sparing too many glances in their direction. *They know.* Aaron wasn't surprised. Word traveled fast in the Downs, word of rich nobles out for a night on the town, word of recent scores and newly "found" merchandise, or the town guard making one of their rare visits, but most of all, word of hits. Of course, the last person to know was always the one with the price on his head.

A scream of pain came from inside the house, jerking Aaron back to the present. He turned to the princess and her chamberlain, taking in their pale, scared faces. "Come on. There's someone we need to talk to."

He set off at a fast walk without looking back to see if the other two were following. He was angry, *pissed,* in fact. The two brothers had thrown their lives away for nothing, for the hope of a peace that would never be. He'd hated his time at the orphanage, had suffered there, but he'd also learned. The only peace men were capable of was that of the grave. Only when the masses of humanity had gone room temperature and maggots feasted on their corpses, would the world know an end to war.

He hated the brothers for their choice. Surprisingly, he also pitied them, and it was that pity that made him the maddest of all. Who were they to him? Just two men working for a woman who seemed to be trying her level best to get him killed. Life was cheap—he'd known that for a long time—yet the thought of their deaths sickened him just the same.

He strode through the back alleys of the Downs in a quiet rage, ignoring the shouts of the occasional beggar that smelled of piss and worse, booting them roughly aside when they wouldn't get out of his way. Eventually, he came to a decrepit building that was larger than many of the others on the street. Other than its size, the building looked like nothing special, which was, of course, the way the owner, a heavy set redhead named May, wanted it.

The chipped paint on the walls, the hanging sign that read *Traveler's Rest,* even the two bums sitting nearby covered in rags and filth, all created the illusion that the building was little more than a run-down inn in need of repair—certainly not the place anyone in their right mind would want to stay given a choice. However, like many things in the Downs, the building was more than it appeared. Without slowing, he stalked inside. Once through the door, he was confronted with an elderly lady sitting behind a rickety, dust-covered counter.

"Surry," the woman said, shaking her head and speaking with a slur. "I'm all full up. You want yeselves a room, ye'll be needin' to try again on the 'morrow."

Aaron flicked a coin at her without slowing and walked toward the door beside the counter. The old woman moved with a nimbleness surprising for her years and snatched the gold coin out of the air. "I wonder, mother, may I smoke?" He asked.

He didn't have to look to know that the elderly woman's wrinkled, leathery face had broken out into a knowing smile. "Yes, you *may*." She answered, in a cultured voice, all traces of her thick accent gone. "And your friends?"

Aaron frowned and tossed two more coins into the woman's eager, waiting hands and motioned to the others. "The accent's getting better, by the way."

The woman beamed at him, "Room service will be right out." She reached under her desk and pressed something, and the door in front of Aaron opened.

A man scowled at them over folded arms, ludicrously big biceps pressing against the fabric of his tight-fitting shirt. "Silent," the man grunted, acknowledging him with a slight nod, "May wants to see you."

Aaron nodded and pushed his way past the bigger man, "If there's time."

The bouncer frowned but said nothing. Aaron had, after all, a bit of a reputation in the Downs, enough, at least, to ensure that people stayed out of his way when they could.

"H-how can this be?" The princess asked beside him, but he didn't answer. Most everyone had the same thought when they first stepped inside May's club. The door they'd entered gave the impression—from the outside—that it would lead into a rundown hallway in as much filthy disrepair as the entrance itself. Even knowing what waited on the other side, Aaron still always found himself surprised by the dramatic change. The club was a sprawling room so big that one could barely see to the other end of it and so richly furnished that it looked as if it belonged in some nobleman's manor.

The tiled floors were covered in rugs of various designs and make, the tables and booths expertly-fashioned. The room was bathed in warm, golden light given off by what Aaron thought must have been at least a hundred of the contraptions he'd heard called Sun Globes hanging from the ceiling. Each circular orb was worth a small fortune, and it was said that they never stopped giving off light. Of course, only a fool would think that—after all, nothing lasted forever. Still, he could appreciate how expensive they must have been, and he'd heard of more than one incident when a particularly brave—or foolish—thief had attempted to steal one despite the fact that the ceilings were at least thirty feet high and that May, the club's owner, was known for the quality of guards she kept on her payroll.

All around the room, the tables were packed with people who talked, laughed, flirted or argued as they each enjoyed their own brand of relaxation. Many smoked on pipes or cigars, so that the air was filled with a constantly shifting curtain of gray haze. On a large, raised platform in the center of the room, a woman in a skimpy dress and top sang a bawdy song about a sailor who was caught by a mermaid and "forced" to perform certain favors for her before she'd set him free. The singer's voice was off key, but she looked good enough in her red dress and high boots that no one seemed to notice, and even the women in the audience clapped and cheered her on.

Aaron had to push his way through a crowd of people as he headed for the bar. Finally, he made it to the counter and nodded to the bartender. She had emerald green eyes and the type of body that men usually only saw in their dreams. Though she looked to be no older than twenty or twenty one years, Aaron knew her to be, in fact, in her early forties, and the blue silk dress she wore revealed even more than the singer's. He suspected that the guards earned their keep just convincing the male clientele to keep their hands to themselves.

The woman noticed him and smiled revealing a set of perfect, pearly white teeth. "Well, my, my, if it isn't the Silent Blade himself!"

Aaron grunted, "Celes."

"The Silent Blade?" Gryle asked curiously, pushing his way beside Aaron, "does it refer to your stealth in combat?"

The bartender let out a girlish laugh and ran a hand through her long, blonde hair. "I don't know much about fighting, hon, but our friend here does everything silent."

She winked at the chubby man, "and I do mean *everything.*"

Aaron sighed as Gryle's face turned a deep, embarrassed red. The chamberlain tried to reply, but his words came out as stuttered, incomprehensible sounds, and Celes laughed throatily. "You're cute." Aaron hadn't thought it possible, but the man's face managed to go an even deeper, angrier crimson.

"Still," the bartender said as she draped her arm around Aaron, "I'm a one man woman, and I'm already taken, aren't I, sugar?"

He swallowed, hard, conscious of the firm softness of her pressing against him, "You know I'm not good enough for you, Celes."

She grinned and spun in a circle with the grace of a dancer before leaning forward and kissing him on the lips. "Maybe not, sugar," she said as she leaned back, "but you'll do until the good gets here."

Aaron laughed despite himself.

"Is there a *reason* why we're here?" Adina asked, scowling.

"Uh-oh," Celes said, grinning mischievously as she glanced between the two of them, "Now don't tell me you've been cheating on me, Silent. Why, I think my heart would break from the strain of it."

He smiled. "Of course not. You know me better than that, Celes. She's just my employer."

"Right," Adina snarled, "and as such, I think it's about time we got down to business, don't you?"

He glanced over at her face, saw the anger flashing in her bright blue eyes, and his smile died. "You're right."

When he turned back, the barmaid's eyebrow was raised in silent question, but he ignored it. "Celes, I've run into a bit of a snag, and I need some information. Is Lucius in?"

The blonde frowned, "I don't know why you waste your time with that bastard, Silent. He's a world-class weasel if there ever was one."

Aaron grunted in acknowledgment, "Easier for him to keep his nose to the ground then." The truth was, Lucius *was* a weasel, the kind of guy that made you want to wash your hands just by talking to him. He was also a world class liar who would sell out his own mother if he thought he could make a profit off the deal. Still, there was no denying that the man knew of almost everything that went on in the Downs.

Celes sighed and pursed her lips in a pout. "Well, if you would rather spend time with that gutter trash than me that's *your* affair. You'll find him at his usual table." She gestured disgustedly to the far end of the room, "Oh, and Silent," she said as Aaron started to turn.

"Yes?"

"Are you alright?" She asked, her expression one of concern, "You seem ... different."

"I'm fine, Celes. Thanks for asking." He pushed his way through the crowd, thinking of the brothers again, and of Flinn, all men who had died, in some way, because of him. *That's bullshit,* He thought angrily, *Stop screwing around in my head, firefly.*

That wasn't me, Co answered, *but you must not think that way. It wasn't your fault. You didn't kill those men.*

"I *know* it wasn't my fault," he muttered angrily, "and who cares if it was? Who were they to me?"

"Did you say something?" The princess asked beside him, and Aaron shook his head, glad of the noise made by people too drunk to know or care that they were making asses of themselves and others who were doing their level best to get that way as quickly as possible. He would really have to watch that. The last thing he needed was for somebody to figure out that he had the orb; he had plenty of people wanting him dead already. Many more and they'd have to form a line and make appointments.

He weaved through the crowd of people, pipe smoke parting around him like a curtain of graveyard fog, and he finally spotted the table he'd been searching for. "Stay here," he said to the princess and the chamberlain, "this will only take a minute." Adina eyed him for a moment but finally nodded, and he turned and walked up to the semi-circle booth. "Hello, Lucius."

The small man sat in between two scantily clad women, smiling. Their breasts were pressed provocatively against his shoulders as they leaned in and whispered something into his ear. The women were young—eighteen or nineteen at most—and their eyes held only a small portion of the apathetic disillusionment that could always be found in the gazes of hired women, as if they still retained some of their innocence. *Innocence,* Aaron thought, *a rare thing in the Downs. Rare and expensive.* He wondered idly how Lucius, a small-time crook, could afford such company. It wasn't by his looks—that was certain.

Celes hadn't been far wrong when she'd called the man a weasel. His nose was long and pointed, giving his face a stretched look, and his smile revealed a set of crooked, pointy teeth. As he turned to Aaron, he ran a hand through long black hair lank with sweat and grease. "Well, if it isn't my dear friend, Silent. How do you fare in these remarkable times?"

Aaron frowned. Lucius was a notorious coward, and the fact that he didn't seem the least put off by the sellsword's arrival didn't bode well. "I think you know. Send the hirelings away, Lucius."

The greasy man gasped in mock surprise, "You must be kidding. These are my two cousins, only recently arrived from the cold north. Why, what kind of man would I be if I were to fail in my duties to warm then with good cheer and better company?"

Aaron growled, out of patience. While he was wasting his time with this asshole, those men were no doubt combing the streets in search of him and the others, and it was only a matter of time before they came here. The women squealed in surprise as he reached across the table and jerked the greasy man out of their arms. Glasses of wine toppled, staining the table a crimson red, and Lucius squeaked, rat-like, as Aaron dragged him across the table. "Let's try this again," he snarled, leaning down to look the suddenly pale man in the eyes, "Someone tried to dust me today, Lucius. Quite a few someones, actually, and I'm betting you know something about it."

"Let him go." Aaron turned and saw two men scowling at him, their hands fisted at their sides. Tattoos ran up and down their massive arms in dark spirals. Their heads were shaved bald, and their noses and ears looked like little more than malformed balls of clay on their face—the marks of any long-time street tough. All in all, they had a fearsome, brutal appearance, one that wouldn't win them any beauty contests, but did add a certain amount of credibility to their experience in their chosen profession. He glanced back and saw that a small crowd had begun to gather around the princess and chamberlain, most likely in the hopes of seeing a fight. He frowned. The last thing he needed was to attract attention, but there was no help for it. He turned to the man who'd spoken, "Let him go?"

"That's right," the bruiser said, cracking his knuckles, "before we make you."

Aaron slung the little man back across the table in disgust and turned to face the two men fully. "You don't mean to tell me you work for this little bastard?"

The man shrugged, "It's a job, and the pay is good. Besides, one asshole's not so much different than another."

Aaron sighed, "Well, I guess that's true, but listen. There are some questions that I really, *really* need to ask your employer, alright? So, if you'll give me just a minute, I promise to leave him mostly alive when I'm done with him."

The man shook his head. "Not gonna happen. Best leave while your legs can still carry you, little man."

Aaron grinned, "Little man, huh?" Not something he was called often. He was six foot, three inches, and a hundred and ninety pounds, but considering the fact that both of the men were about twice his size, he guessed it made sense for them to think so. Still, it wasn't something that a man enjoyed hearing. He felt the familiar, cold anger that had driven him his entire life beginning to assert itself.

There is no reason to fight these men, Co said into his mind, *after all, so what if the man does know something? What use could it be? You already know that men hunt you and the princess. What possible knowledge could this man possess that would make it worth it?*

Aaron nodded slowly. It was a good point, as far as it went. Of course, that would mean letting the slimy bastard get the better of him. "You see, Silent," Lucius said smugly, unaware of Aaron's battling thoughts, as he leaned back and took a calm sip from the only wine glass still standing, "I won't be your whipping boy anymore. I've got *friends* now. You'll have to find someone else to push around." Aaron met the man's gaze, and Lucius looked away, his smile twitching nervously.

Aaron forced himself to take a deep, calming breath. *You're right*, he thought at the virtue. *What would we benefit from forcing a fight here?*

Exactly, came the Virtue's satisfied response.

Aaron popped his neck and turned back to the two hired men. "So, there's really no way I can talk you two guys out of it?"

The men shook their heads in unison, "Not going to happen," said the talkative one.

Aaron shrugged, "Well, you can't fault a man for asking."

"Of course not," the man said with a sympathetic nod.

Aaron glanced back at the fidgeting Lucius once more, then over at the princess and chamberlain who were both shaking their heads. He sighed heavily, "Well, alright then. I'll go. Maybe another time—when the money runs out."

The bruiser nodded, watching him warily, "When the money runs out."

Aaron stepped past the two men and noticed that the gathering crowd was still relatively small. Apparently, the possibility of a fight wasn't enough to lure many of the club's patrons away from watching the singer's performance. *There's no reason to fight here,* he told himself for the second time. *No reason at all except pride, and pride never fed a starving man as dad used to say. Best to let it lie, best to just--*"There's just one problem," he said, stopping.

"Oh?" The big man said, turning, "what's that?"

"The truth is, I've always been a pretty prideful man, and I've never needed a fucking reason." The men were bigger than Aarion, stronger, but they were slower too. By the time they realized what he was doing, he was already inside their reach, kneeing the silent one between the legs as hard as he could. The man let out a broken cry and crumpled to the ground, gripping his crotch in two massive hands. A woman in the crowd screamed, but Aaron barely heard.

The talkative one swung at him with a paw as big as a shovel, surprisingly fast, and the sellsword only just managed to sidestep the blow. He bumped into the table, scattering trays of food, caught his balance, and grabbed the first thing he could—a toppled wine bottle. The man rushed forward, reaching for him with arms as big as tree trunks, but Aaron lunged to the side, away from the hired man's grasping hands, and swung the bottle into the man's face with all the force he could muster.

Glass shattered and wine flew as the bruiser stumbled backward, bellowing curses and pawing at the pieces of bloody glass sticking out of his face. Before he could recover, Aaron stepped forward and kicked him in the shin, hard. The street tough howled in pain and stumbled into a spectator who'd gotten too close to the show, knocking him over as he tried to comfort his leg and bloody face at the same time. The tough was so preoccupied that he didn't look up at Aaron's approach. With a burst of movement, Aaron grabbed the man's head in both hands and slammed it down on the heavy oak table with a resounding *crash.* The man's head rebounded off the table, and he dropped to the ground like a pole-axed calf.

Aaron grunted, satisfied, and turned back to the table. Lucius whimpered quietly, pushing himself farther back against the seat cushion as if trying to disappear into its surface. Aaron noted, absently, that the two high-priced hookers had vanished. Innocent, maybe, but not stupid. "Now then," he said, "are you going to start talking or do you need some motivation?"

"I spent a small fortune on those two bastards," Lucius whined, as if overcome at the injustice in the world, "a fortune!"

Aaron walked over to the bruiser that was still conscious, writhing on the floor, and kicked him in the face, hard. The man's eyes rolled up into his head, and he slipped into unconsciousness. The sellsword turned back to Lucius with a cold smile, "You paid too much."

The small man held up his hands placating, "I-I don't know anything," he said, spit flying from his mouth in his haste, "I don't know what you want, man."

Aaron reached across the table and half-heartedly smacked him across the face with the back of his hand. "Try again, Lucius. There's not a thing in the Downs that happens without your knowing it, and a hit like the one I've got on me? That's damn sure caused some talk."

The man's mouth worked for a moment before he spoke. "Y-you're wrong, man, okay?" he said, his tone pleading, "I don't know nothing about it."

"Wrong answer," Aaron said, reaching for one of the blades at his side.

"Alright, alright," Lucius squealed, his eyes so wide they looked as if they were about to pop out of his head, "Fine. I'll tell you."

"I never doubted you would. While you're at it, why don't you tell me how a small-time, no account asshole like you gets a hold of enough money to hire two high-priced streeties and these two thugs? Oh, and Lucius? It's been a long day, and I'm in a shitty mood. You really don't want to end up on the wrong end of it."

The weasel-faced man nodded nervously, "Look, it wasn't my fault, okay, Silent? You've got to believe me. This guy, he comes by my place, wakes me up out—"

"When?"

The small man shook his head, "Last night, but this guy, he tells me that there's a price of five thousand gold on your head, tells me to spread it 'round the Downs.

Says that if I don't, he'll split me from ear to ear, send me to bed early, you know what I mean?"

Aaron grunted, surprised at the large sum. He knew most of the blades for hire in the Downs, and although he wouldn't call any of them friends, there was an unwritten code among them that they all tried to keep out of each other's way as much as their professions would allow. Of course, five thousand large was more than enough to make a man forget that kind of thing. "Go on."

"Come on, man. Silent, there's *nothing* else, okay? I had to do what the man said, you see that don't you? I mean, he would have *killed* me."

The sellsword grabbed a fistful of the man's shirt and jerked him over the table, "Don't you fucking lie to me, Lucius. What do you think I'm stupid? I'm supposed to believe you just stumbled on a pot of gold on your way to Hale's, is that it?" Hale was one of the major crime lords in the Downs and Lucius's boss. He was a disgustingly fat man who'd grown rich off of other people's suffering—not that Aaron blamed him for that. After all, everyone in the Downs, no, the *world,* did the same thing. Hale was just better at it than most.

"Of course not!" Lucius protested, "I wouldn't lie to you, Silent. Man, you gotta know that."

"What I know is that you'd lie to the gods themselves if you thought you'd get away with it. Now start talking before I lose my patience."

"It's not like that, Silent, I swear!" The small man squeaked, "Look, when I woke up and that guy was just *there.* I was scared, okay? Scared shitless. But, well ... he seemed like he really wanted you, you know? Said that you had something he wanted, but he wouldn't say what."

Aaron frowned at that, and the small man swallowed hard before continuing, "Anyway, I figured that the man wanted you bad enough that he wouldn't kill me for maybe, you know, seeing if there was something in it for me."

"I swear by Iladen and the rest, it's a miracle that someone hasn't laid you horizontal long before now," Aaron said with genuine wonder in his voice. "A man wakes you up with a knife at your throat and you try to *blackmail* him?"

"No!" Lucius protested, shaking his head vigorously, "not blackmailed. I sold a service, that's all. Not any different than those high and mighty merchants up on God's Row."

"You sold me out is what you did you, Lucius." Aaron said, his voice low and dangerous, "sold me out and nearly got me killed in the process."

"No, I didn't, you gotta believe me!" The weasel-faced man squealed. He glanced up in the sellsword's face, saw the anger there, and spoke quickly, as if Aaron was contemplating killing him. Which, of course, he was. "I took the man's money, sure. What better way to throw him off your trail? I wasn't going to *tell* him anything, Silent. But better that he keeps paying me for doing nothing than finding someone else who actually *would* put the word out, right?"

"Oh, I get it. So you were actually out to help me, is that it? All those armed men weren't hitters, huh? Just

some men out to pay us a visit, had a few blades they
wanted to sell us?"

Lucius avoided his gaze. "Well ... something went
wrong. The guy started getting really anxious, you know?
No ... not anxious. Crazy. Crazy as those Priests of Death
are." A few people in the crowd whispered at that. The
Priests of Death, also known as the Reapers—though not
to their face—were men and women who'd dedicated
their lives to Salen's dark purpose, experimenting on the
terminally sick and abducting the unwary to be used in
their twisted rituals. Of course, many believed that they
were nothing but a myth, but that didn't explain the
occasional disappearances of beggars or the discovery of
opened, empty graves in one of the city's cemeteries from
time to time. "Anyway," the weasel-faced man continued,
apparently oblivious of the stir he'd caused, "He told me
that if you weren't found or dusted in two days' time I'd
be walking Salen's Fields myself—real suspicious
bastard, he was."

Several people in the audience hissed at his use of
the god's proper name. It was widely believed that to use
the God of Death's name was to draw his attention—or
the attention of his followers—on yourself and those
around you. Aaron thought it was a crock of shit, but he
avoided saying it just the same. Only a fool sticks his
hand in a snake pit unless he's *certain* it's empty. "So you
told him." He said, frowning.

Lucius swallowed hard, "I had to, man! I didn't have
a choice, don't you see that? "

"What was his name?"

The weasel face twisted in confusion, "Who's name?"

Aaron grabbed a hold of the front of the man's wine-stained shirt and shook him, ignoring his squeals and whimpers, "*The* man. The man who put the hit out on me and the girl. What was his Keeper-cursed *name?*"

Lucius broke into a coughing fit. When he finished, snot hung from his nose, and he wiped his arm across it unconsciously. "He said his name was Aster," he said, his voice whiny, that of a man getting punished for no good reason. "Aster Kalen. Said it like it was a name a man would kill to have too."

Aaron glanced back at Adina, but she shook her head to indicate she'd never heard of him. *Damn.* He turned back to Lucius, "And where were the men supposed to meet this Aster Kalen when they killed me? Where was the pay off?"

"It was an inn, alright? An inn on dockside called the uh ... uh ... the *Blindman's Mermaid.* Yeah, that was it. Said for them to come and ask for Aster, and he'd take care of 'em."

The sellsword nodded slowly, "And—"

"*Just what in the name of all the gods is going on here?*" A deep, angry woman's shout came from somewhere in the crowd, and, in an instant, everything grew silent. The singer stopped singing, the whisperers stopped whispering. The drunks kept drinking, but they did so quietly.

Shit. Aaron took a slow, deep breath and turned to see the crowd of people scattering as if an army of city guards had just marched into the building. In the suddenly empty space walked a heavy-set woman in a crimson dress that had no doubt cost a small fortune.

Ruby rings covered her fingers, glittering in the light like motes of fire. She ran a hand through red hair that had once been brighter than her jewelry, but that now held several gray streaks. The skin around the woman's mouth and eyes held the wrinkles Aaron's mom had once called smile lines. She wasn't smiling now. Her face was drawn down in anger, and members of the crowd were bumping into each other in their haste to get as far out of her way as possible. Aaron didn't blame them. The woman had such a strong presence, such a powerful personality, that he himself was half convinced that the only reason why he didn't burst into flame from her look was that she thought it would be an inadequate punishment. Altogether, she was an intimidating woman even more intimidating, in fact, than the four men that followed behind her, cudgels in hand, threatening scowls well in place.

She stopped a few paces away from him, taking in the two men on the floor with an intelligent eye that the sellsword knew from experience missed nothing. "Silent," she said.

He tipped his head respectfully, his expression grim, "May."

"Just what in Mariana's name do you think you're doing?"

Mariana was the goddess of Vengeance and Retribution, and he wasn't particularly comforted by May's use of her name. "Talking with an old friend."

May stared past him, "Do all of your friends end conversations with you unconscious? If so, it's a wonder you have any left."

Aaron glanced back and saw Lucius lying across the table where he'd left him. *The bastard fainted.* He turned back to May with a shrug, "He never could hold his drink."

The slightest smile flickered on the woman's face for an instance, and then was gone. She turned to the men behind her, revealing a ruby earring that sparkled in the low light of the room like living fire, "Take him to the back room." She turned to the gathered crowd, "Oh? Has someone started a show of which I'm unaware? Or is it my beauty that captivates you so?"

The men and women in the crowd nodded vigorously, as if a knife were being held to their throat, and shot uncertain glances at one another. "Well, then." May said expectantly, and as if on cue, the singer broke out into song, and in moments the room was again buzzing with drunken laughter and flirting, though obviously forced.

He sighed and gestured at the princess and the chamberlain. "Might as well bring them along. They're with me."

Adina opened her mouth to launch what would have no doubt been a series of curses at Aaron but snapped it shut as one of the guards approached and grabbed her by the arm. May nodded to the guards and the club's patrons watched them as if they were men headed to the gallows as they were led through the smoke-hazed club into a small, richly-furnished and decorated back room—May's office. The door slammed shut behind them with ringing finality.

The guards sat them down in three of four chairs that faced a large, oaken desk and took up positions behind them. May walked over to the chair behind the desk and sank into its red, cushion, letting out a sigh of relief as she did. "Now then," she said, the anger and threat of vengeance that had filled her voice in the main room nowhere in evidence, "tell me, Silent, what's happened?"

Out of the corner of his eye, Aaron could see the princess and the chamberlain looking confusedly between him and May, but he paid it no attention. "Someone's put a hit out on me." He said bluntly.

May nodded, "So I've heard." No surprise there. May was one of the most powerful people in the Downs, had been for years. In a place like the Downs, information was often more valuable than gold, and May was plenty rich in both. In all the years that he'd known her, he'd never seen her taken by surprise. "Still, it's not like it's the first time, is it?" She said, smiling slightly, "A man in your profession has a way of making enemies and losing friends." She gestured to one of the guards and the man poured them each a drink of wine. She frowned at him, "Never before has a hit forced you to come into my club and make a scene, tearing up the place and scaring my customers." She waited a moment for him to answer. When he didn't, she sighed heavily, "You've put me in an awkward situation. You know that, don't you?"

She was right, of course. Letting someone come into her club and tear it up without being punished would be seen as weakness and the citizens of the Downs—specifically the crime lords—pounced at any sign of weakness quicker than wolves on a wounded deer. He nodded, "I know. I'd say I was sorry, but it wouldn't mean much. This time isn't like the others. I had some questions that needed answers, and I had reason to believe that Lucius had them."

May's face twisted in disgust, "That slime always has answers. Whether they're true or not, now that's a different story. A man would have to be pretty desperate to come to him for help."

Aaron let the silence speak for itself.

"So," May ventured after several seconds had passed, "who is it this time? An ex-employer? One of the bosses? I hear Grinner is still angry at you from that last stunt of yours, and Hale has always hated you."

Aaron shook his head. "I can handle Grinner and Hale. No, it wasn't either of them."

May shrugged, as if the two bosses, possibly the most powerful men in the Downs, were none of her concern. *And if anyone can, it's her,* Aaron thought. It was well known that May was one of the richest people in the Downs, if not *the* richest but, more importantly, she was also one of the most resourceful. The bosses had tried to move in on her before, several times in fact, but they had always lived to regret it, while May herself continued to prosper. She liked to claim that she was nothing more than a simple club owner, but Aaron had come to believe that she was possibly the most powerful person in the Downs. Powerful enough, he thought, that if she bent herself to it, she could have the entire Downs, Hale and Grinner included, bowing to her within a year, but he would never tell her that. The last man who *had* had received such a tongue lashing that Aaron would be surprised if the man could sit down even still, though the incident was years gone.

It had been one of the few times he'd ever seen May angry, and he'd resolved a long time ago never to mention it to her, though he didn't understand it. His father had once told him that every man, woman, or child sought something. For some it might be fame, for others power or money, but there was always something. Often times the people didn't know what it was themselves, but his father had claimed that you could not truly know someone, or yourself, until you learned what that something was. For May, it clearly wasn't power, and, for at least the hundredth time since he'd met her, Aaron wondered what it was.

"If it's not one of the bosses, then who?" May asked, her voice bringing his thoughts back to the present.

He considered not telling her, that it might be safer for her not to know before deciding it didn't matter. She would learn of it, one way or the other. May always did. "Belgarin."

She whistled, her eyes wide. "What did you do sleep with his daughter or something?" Despite her effort at levity, she twisted one of the rings around her finger. He'd seen her use the gesture before, when she was nervous or scared. Unlike the rest of the jewelry she wore, the ring was plain, tarnished silver without ornamentation or device. She changed her other jewelry regularly, but the ring was always there, always waiting for her to touch. He'd asked her about it once. The silence that followed had been more threatening than the calm before a thunderstorm, and he'd quickly changed the subject. He had not asked again.

"As far as I know," he said in response to her question, "he doesn't have one."

"Son then?"

He frowned, and the heavy-set woman laughed. "Fine, fine. Just a little joke between friends, but surely you must be kidding. I like you, Silent. I'm one of the few people who does, and you're probably the best at your job—I know you've charged me enough in the past that you damn sure better be—but you're nothing more than an ant to a man like Belgarin. I mean, Keeper's Lantern, Silent, the man has *thousands* at his command. Why would he even bother to waste his time worrying about you?"

Because I saw his brother die. Because I know that he killed him. Because the princess, his younger sister, decided to get me involved, and is counting on me to save the Keeper-cursed kingdom. "I can't tell you that."

It was the large woman's turn to frown and when she spoke, her voice was lightly scolding, "Aaron, listen. You've never kept anything from me before. Why start now?"

"It's different now."

"How?"

"Because if I told you everything I know, I wouldn't be the only one on Belgarin's list. I like you, May, and you're a damned fine club owner—a fine dresser too, come to that—but if you show up on Belgarin's list, he'll crush *you* like a bug. A charming, interesting bug, but a bug nonetheless."

The woman smiled, clearly flattered, and put a hand across her chest, "Ah, pierced with my own blade. Well done." She turned and frowned at Adina and Gryle, "And how are these two involved?"

"I can't tell you that."

May let out a deep, unhappy sigh, "I don't like this, Aaron. Not one bit. Secrets are dangerous."

"I don't like it either, and secrets may be dangerous, but this truth can kill." He met her gaze and held it, "I need you to trust me, May." Whether he told her or not, he knew that, if she wanted, May would be able to find out everything, and he couldn't have that. She might be powerful in the Downs, but Aaron knew that even she would stand no chance against Belgarin should the man decide she was in his way. "I need you to leave this alone."

She studied him for several tense moments with a thoughtful frown. Finally, she nodded, though reluctantly. "I trust you Aaron, but I still don't like it." She held up a hand to silence him, "Fine, fine, I won't look into it, you have my word. Now, tell me what I can do."

He nodded, satisfied. It was another oddity about May that she was one of the few people in the Downs who, when they gave their word, kept it. "I need to get to an inn called the *Blindman's Mermaid.* Have you heard of it?"

May laughed, "The Mermaid? Of course. A dump of a place—nothing like the Rest. Old ale and older women. A man could catch his death there."

He thought of the man Aster, who'd put a price on his head, the man who, if Lucius had told the truth—and he was certain he had, for this at least—was staying at the Mermaid. "That's the idea," he said, struggling to keep his anger in check. "Anyway, I need to get there."

The club owner watched him for a moment, waiting for him to continue. When he didn't, she laughed, "Aaron, I'm happy to do you a favor, and I realize that this dress makes me look intimidating, but despite the rumors, I'm no goddess, and I'm certainly not strong enough to carry you all the way to Dockside."

He grinned despite himself, "Well, it was worth a shot. What I mean to say is, do you know of a way to get there without being seen—I'm a little more popular than I'd like right now."

May scoffed, "Of course I do." She paused for a minute, eyeing him, "but are you sure? Why don't you just stay here, Aaron, you and your friends," she indicated the others with a ring-bedecked hand, a princess granting a favor to one of her people, "I can hide you in the Rest. Belgarin's troops would never find you."

He shook his head, "They would, May, you know they would, and if Belgarin learned that you were hiding me he wouldn't just be after me anymore. I have to go. It's better this way."

She frowned, "If you say."

"I do."

"Very well then," she said, and then her face twisted into a smile that made him uncomfortable, "You need to get there without being seen, you said? I think I know the perfect way. Come. I will have one of my men show you."

CHAPTER NINE

AARON SIGHED AS HE STEPPED OFF THE LADDER. Overhead, he could hear the laughter of the man May had tasked with leading them as he slid the cover back in place.

"You've got to be kidding," Adina said beside him.

He shook his head in wonderment. Despite the thick darkness that surrounded them—a darkness so complete that he couldn't see the chamberlain or the princess even though they stood right beside him—there could be no doubt as to where they were. The smell that assaulted his nostrils, rank and cloying, made sure of that. "A sewer," he grunted. "Why am I not surprised?"

"*This* is the safest way?" Gryle asked, incredulous, his voice disgusted.

Aaron shrugged in the darkness, "Possibly. Of course, there was probably another route that would have worked equally well and not had the ... *atmosphere*, of this one. I suspect this is May's way of getting back at me for the scene I caused in the *Rest*."

"Yeah, what was that back there?" Adina asked angrily, "those men could have beaten you half to death and for what? A name and a place? I'm no soldier, and I may not have a lot of experience in this sort of thing, but it seems rather stupid to head straight to the man who put a hit on you. Do you think he'll pay you before he kills us? We'd do better to get out of Avarest as quickly as possible. We *must* make it to Baresh before Belgarin does or all is lost."

"If you ask me, the princess is right, sir. Better to—"

"I didn't ask you," Aaron growled, "either of you. Besides, it wasn't much of a choice. In the Downs, if you start letting people get away with crossing you, it won't be long until you wake up dead."

Gryle coughed politely, "That doesn't really—"

"Not another word out of you." Aaron reached in the pocket of his trousers and withdrew the flint and tinder May had given him. "Hold that torch close." He struck a spark, then another, and the oil-soaked torch sprang to life with a fitful, sputtering fire.

Examining his surroundings in the orange glow of the torch, he was surprised by how large the tunnel was. The three foot walkway they were on extended in both directions as far as he could see, disappearing into the darkness. An identical walkway ran the length of the opposite side of the tunnel. Between the two, a river of waste and filth flowed past. He set his jaw and turned away from it, examining the stone at his feet instead. It, as well as the wall beside them, was coated with a green, slimy substance, the origins of which he dared not consider too closely.

Clenching his jaws, trying unsuccessfully to ignore the foul odor that was so thick he could taste it, he turned to the others. Their faces were pale and sick-looking in the torchlight, "Come on," he said, "there's no hope for it.

The sooner started the sooner done." He started off at a slow walk, careful not to lose his balance on the slippery substance that covered the walkway. It had been a shitty day so far. The last thing he needed was to take a swim in the River Brown. He almost gagged at the thought as Adina fell into step beside him. In the torchlight, he saw that her lips were pressed into a thin white line.

She's angry with you, Co said.

Oh? He thought back, *I never would have guessed.*

The orb either didn't notice his sarcasm, or chose to ignore it, *She is. She is a princess, not used to being talked to in such a way. If you can't show her respect, you would at least do well to not go out of your way to antagonize her.*

Aaron grunted, *She's been pissed since May's, and the gods alone know why. Besides, what makes you think I want advice from a glowing bug?*

I am not *a bug!* Co hissed in his mind.

He laughed, and Adina turned and glared at him before turning away. *Great, now she thinks I'm laughing at her.* He thought with a sigh, *women.* "As for your question from earlier," he said in hopes of making amends, "we're going to meet this Aster Kalen because I believe it's the safest thing to do."

Adina scoffed, "Safe? Delivering ourselves to the man who's offering a purse of gold for our heads? You've got a funny idea of safe. No, not funny. *Stupid.* What's more," she continued, her voice troubled, "I've never heard of this man, Aster Kalen, and I've made it my business to know all of my brother's top men."

"So the man has chosen to go by a different identity," Aaron said, shrugging, "that's not surprising. After all, Belgarin wouldn't want to be linked to Eladen's death."

The princess frowned, "Perhaps, but I'm not so sure. This doesn't feel like Belgarin's work to me. With Ophasia and Geoffrey, Belgarin was discreet. It was not until later that we discovered he'd been behind it. It doesn't seem like him to be so open about hiring a hit on someone."

Aaron shrugged as he continued forward. It wasn't as if he didn't have enough to worry about, what with the most powerful man in all of Telrear putting a hit on him. If this Aster Kalen really didn't work for Belgarin but was after him on his own ... no, that didn't make any sense. It *had* to be one of Belgarin's schemes. What other reason would the man have to want him dead? "Perhaps your brother has decided that discretion is no longer so important," he said, "but whatever the reason is, it doesn't matter. Your brother's man or not, Aster will soon know that the hit failed. He'll be expecting us to run to the nearest gate or ship as fast as our feet will carry us."

"Which, of course, would be *absurd,*" she said, her voice thick with sarcasm.

He gritted his teeth, struggling to keep his temper "It will do us no good to stumble into the pit of vipers ahead in an effort to avoid the garden snake behind." He paused to sidestep a crumbled section of walkway, wincing as he brushed against the stinking film on the wall, "Besides, I like knowing what I'm up against."

Good reasons both, Co said in his head.

Glad to have your approval, firefly.

Good reasons, the Virtue repeated, *but not your reason. Not all of it, anyway.*

Stop poking around in there, he thought back sharply. Still, she was right. It was true that he *did* think it smarter to surprise the man. After all, what men Aster commanded would no doubt be out searching for Aaron and the others in force, leaving few to protect the man himself. Better to surprise him, to act instead of react. His father had told him once that predictability was a commander's worst nightmare, and he believed it.

It was the right thing to do—the smart thing, and a sellsword didn't survive long in the Downs without doing the smart thing. It was a good reason, but the orb was right, it wasn't all of it. Mostly, he was just pissed off. He'd been chased halfway across the Downs, taken an arrow in the leg, and was currently slinking through a gods blasted *sewer* all because some pompous bastard had walked into the Downs—the closest thing he had to a home—and started waving money around.

"Watch out!" Adina shouted, grabbing the back of his shirt and jerking him back.

Glancing down, he saw that the walkway had split off and, wrapped up as he'd been in his own thoughts, his own anger, he'd very nearly stepped off into the river of human waste that rushed past beneath them. He swallowed hard. "Thanks."

"Don't thank me," the princess said, frowning in the torchlight, "I'm just your employer, here to make sure you do the job instead of bathing in muck, no matter how much I'd enjoy watching."

He frowned. Her jaw was set, and her eyes met his in silent challenge. *If looks could kill,* he thought uncomfortably, *Belgarin would have one less sellsword to worry about.* "Don't worry," he said, trying on what he hoped was a placating smile, "I'll finish the job. I always do. Ask May or Celes, they'll tell you."

"I'm sure," she almost snarled, glancing at the map May had given them, "the directions say this way." She set off down the left branch purposefully, following the direction of the river. He stared at her back for several confused moments as the chamberlain waddled past him. He'd only meant to reassure her, but if anything she was even angrier than she had been.

He took a deep breath, grimacing at the foul smell that rushed through his nostrils, and started out after the others.

After what felt like an eternity traveling down the slime-encrusted walkway, the orange glow of the torch revealing shadows of unrecognizable debris carried along by the river of sewage, the princess finally came to a stop. "This is supposed to be it."

Aaron nodded and tossed the low-burning torch into the river. "Stay here. I'll call for you." He started up the ladder without bothering to wait for a response from either of them. If May's sources were right—and they always were—then the ladder should lead to an empty warehouse on Dockside. Still, with each rung of the ladder, his anxiety grew. Five thousand gold was a lot of money. He'd known May for a long time, and she was one of the few people who he might actually consider a friend, but anyone who'd ever met the club owner knew that she had expensive tastes. Five thousand gold would buy a lot of dresses.

He reached the top and hesitated, his hand on the latch. *Do you trust no one?* Co asked incredulous, reading his thoughts. *If she'd wanted to betray you, why would she not do it at the Rest, while you were surrounded by her men?*

You're right, he thought, *it doesn't make sense. Still, people don't always do what makes sense, do they?*

The sound of a long-suffering sigh filled his mind, *you have to trust someone sometime.*

"Is everything alright?" Adina asked from below.

"Fine," He shouted down. He pulled on the hatch, grunting as the rusted clasp resisted. Finally, the metal cover slid aside, and he crawled up and into the room. Once in, he blinked in the light of a lantern. The place was supposed to have been empty. He drew his blades and scanned his surroundings.

Around him, shadows cast by the flame of the lantern's candle danced and shifted ominously. In the low light, he could just make out piles of debris where the roof had fallen in and no one had bothered to remove it. He could see the stars shining overhead through the holes where the tiles had been, and a thin layer of dust coated everything. Everything that was, except for the footprints that led to the small table where the lantern had been placed and then disappeared into the gloom. An abandoned warehouse then, like May had said. So why the light? He backed up to where the lantern sat on an old wooden table. Judging by how far the candle had burned down, it couldn't have been lit for much more than half an hour. So someone had been here recently. Someone that, for all he knew, could even now be lurking in the shadows, waiting for the best moment to strike.

The space between his shoulder blades itching in anticipation, he glanced at the lantern again and noticed a scrap of paper beneath it. Warily, scanning the shadows around him, he sheathed one of his blades, moved the light aside, and snatched up the note.

Silent, I hope you enjoyed your journey through the sewers. I imagine it was ... interesting. Consider us even for the trouble you caused me. I don't know what you're up against, but be careful—I'd hate to lose you. Celes is a good woman, but she plays a terrible hand of cards. I suspect you won't want to hang around in Avarest for long. Under the table is a box I've prepared for you. Inside are orders bearing my seal. Bring them to the docks, to a captain named Leomin. He is a strange sort but has proven reliable in the past. He will see you away from the city. The box also contains your payment for the next job I'll ask of you when you return. Be safe, and may Iladen's dice always roll in your favor.

P.S. The princess is as beautiful in person as I'd heard. Keep her safe. I think she fancies you.

--M

Aaron smiled and shook his head, suddenly ashamed for his distrust of the club owner. "Thank you, May," he muttered. It didn't surprise him that May had discovered the princess's identity. If anything, he'd have been surprised if she hadn't. What did surprise him, however, was how wrong she was about Adina. "Fancies me?" He barked a laugh, "maybe she'd fancy sticking a knife in me. I'd say that's about it."

The two are not mutually exclusive, Co said.

Pointedly ignoring the Virtue, Aaron reached under the table and withdrew the paper and a sack heavy with far more coins than any job he'd ever done for May before. Secreting both under his tunic, he was starting back to the hatch when Adina's head poked over the top. He frowned as he watched her climb into the room, followed by a panting, red-faced Gryle. "I thought I told you to wait until I made sure it was safe."

The princess shrugged, "Either it was or it wasn't. If it wasn't, and men were waiting on us, what would stop them from coming down the ladder after us?" She met his eyes challengingly, "I will *not* die in a sewer."

He turned to the chamberlain, "And you?"

The man straightened and raised his chin, his attempts at a confident, capable appearance undermined by the disheveled state of his clothes and his red, sweaty face. "I will not let the princess venture into danger alone."

Aaron repressed the smile that was threatening to come. The man had shown courage coming after her—more courage than most servants would—and laughing at him now would wound him to no purpose. He noticed the princess frowning toward the chamberlain and realized that she must not like the idea that she needed looking after. Aaron nodded to the panting chamberlain, "Well done."

"Thank you, sir," Gryle said, beaming with obvious pleasure.

He smiled then caught himself. *What in the name of Salen's Fields? Why do I care if the fat man feels good?* His smile soured into a frown. *Co!*

Yes? The Virtue asked innocently.

Stop screwing around in there.

The orb's voice was all offended dignity, *I'm sure I don't know what you're talking about.*

A question, firefly.

Yes?

When that arrow got me in the leg, did you feel it?

Of course, the orb answered immediately, *we are bonded. I* am *compassion, after all. Why do you—Oww!*

Aaron grinned past the pain as he looked down at the red welt growing on his arm where he'd pinched himself. *Don't test me lightning bug,* he thought, satisfied.

"Are you okay?"

He turned to see Adina staring at him strangely. "Err ... right. Let's go."

They walked through rows of dusty, empty shelves that reached nearly to the ceiling, stepping over or ducking under pieces of crumbled roof or fallen shelves where they could and having to backtrack and take another path more than once when the debris proved too large. Aaron was half convinced they were going to spend the rest of their lives navigating the deteriorating maze when finally they arrived at the door. Stepping outside, he grunted. The smell here was—in its own way—no better than that of the sewer. The unmistakable tang of rotten fish permeated the air, made somehow worse by the salty ocean breeze. Night had come while they traversed the underground passages, but Dockside was filled with sailors staggering drunkenly down the streets, laughing, talking and, more often than not, groping awkwardly at the hired women on their arms, enjoying their shore leave before they sat out on the sea once more.

The masses of people surrounding them should have made Aaron feel more secure, but they did not. Instead, he felt woefully, terribly vulnerable out in the open, and it seemed to him as if everyone glanced at him and the other two for longer than normal, possible assassins out to make some coin or just his imagination running away with him? He tried to reassure himself that the people around him were nothing but the usual Downs fair, thieves and opportunists, whores and beggars, sailors and slumming nobles all out for a good time. Many of them were criminals sure, and if not honest, at least predictable. Besides, none of them seemed to have the look of hired killers. The problem was that few hired killers did.

He had to fight the temptation to draw his sword as they wound their way through the press of bodies. Though the passersby appeared innocent enough—well, maybe not innocent, this was the Downs after all—any one of them might get it in their mind to make a quick five thousand coins. "Come on."

He pushed his way through the crowd, working his way down the lane, his hands staying close to the sheathed sword on his back, covered as it was by his cloak. After a time, he looked back to make sure that Adina and the chamberlain were still with him. Their faces were pale, their expressions taut. Apparently, they too, had grasped their vulnerability. He grunted as someone bumped into him from behind. "Excuse me, sir," a voice murmured.

He grasped the arm stealthily pawing under his tunic and squeezed, hard. "I'm sorry!" The owner of the hand squeaked. He looked down and saw a youth no older than thirteen summers staring back at him, his expression a mask of pain. The boy's face was covered in dirt, and his shirt and trousers were torn and ragged.

He looked at the sellsword with wide, desperate eyes, "I'm sorry, m-mister. I'm really sorry. My momma's sick. We don't have the money to buy her th--."

Aaron squeezed harder. "Don't tempt me, kid."

In an instant, the innocent bewilderment left the kid's face, and his eyes took on a look much too jaded for one so young. True, the pity routine had been an act, but it was obvious by the kid's emaciated frame, by the look of his haggard face, and the way he swayed slightly on his feet that he was starving. Aaron stared at the boy for a moment then shook his head, "You didn't bump hard enough, kid," he said, still gripping the boy's wrist, "better to hit a man hard enough that he's worried more about not falling on his ass than he is about his coins."

The youth opened his mouth to speak, no doubt planning to launch into a scathing comment on how he didn't need anyone's help, on how he was better on his own. Aaron knew them all—he'd made them often enough himself, but the kid must have seen something in his stare because his jaw snapped shut, and he nodded grudgingly.

The sellsword reached into his purse for a few coins, paused to make sure that it was *his* idea, not some damned glowing orb's, decided that it probably wasn't, but gave them to the kid anyway. "I don't expect you to stop stealing, boy," he said, meeting the youth's eyes, "but I do expect you to get better. Next time I don't want to know a thing until I reach for a coin and come up empty, you hear me?"

The boy paused uncertainly. After a moment, he smiled and the coins vanished into his ripped and faded tunic, "Sure thing, mister. Next time, you'll never know what hit you."

Aaron nodded, "I expect nothing less."

Adina looked at him reproachfully as the kid hurried off into the crowd, "What was all that about? You probably just helped to make that kid into a thief for the rest of his life."

Aaron turned and met her eyes, and when he spoke his voice was hard, "Maybe, but he won't go hungry anymore. It's hard to worry about morality when your stomach's cramping from lack of food, and you sleep in the streets every night. I don't expect you to understand."

She frowned, "That doesn't mean that you should make yourself part of the problem. He could do something good with his life. He could grow up to be a soldier instead of a thief who lives off of others' misery."

The sellsword barked a laugh. "If we're breathing, we're part of the problem, princess, and don't talk to me about the nobility of being a soldier. There's nothing noble about cutting men down or dying fighting for some damned fool that decided the chair he was sittin' in ought to be a throne instead."

CHAPTER TEN

ADINA WAS JUST BEGINNING TO RESPOND when Aaron turned and headed into the crowd, the stiff set of his shoulders making it obvious that he didn't want to talk about it anymore. *If we're breathing, we're part of the problem, princess.* "We don't have to be," she whispered after him with a sigh. She turned to make sure the chamberlain was next to her before heading off after the sellsword. *What happened to you, Aaron, to make you so bitter?*

Thinking of the kid brought to mind memories of her own childhood. True, it had been different than most, but it had still had its own hazards, its own lessons. She was the youngest of her father's children. When she was still playing with dolls, her other siblings were grown, her brothers fighting in tournaments, her sisters marrying to seal alliance's with some of the lands more powerful nobles. All except for Ophasia. The thought of her sister, murdered by her own brother, sent a pang of grief through her.

Eladen had always been kind to her, treating her sweetly, but it had been her sister, Ophasia, with whom she'd spent the majority of her childhood. She remembered the way her sister had looked then, raven black hair always in a tangle, a constant source of frustration for their nurse maid, Gertrude, and brown eyes so dark they were almost the color of midnight. Most of all, she remembered the mischievous glint in those dark eyes, the look that often presaged a harsh scolding from their nurse.

A sad smile of loss crept its way onto her face at the memory. Her sister had always been wild, always looking for a thrill despite the consequences. At the time, Adina had believed Ophasia to be the embodiment of everything she was not: courage, daring, and recklessness. Small wonder, then, that she had looked up to her so much.

Considering her sister's bent for doing things she'd been expressly told not to, it was no surprise when her sister had begun to take Adina on trips to the dungeon. Adina had not wanted to go, had not wanted to brave the stares of the prisoners, the leers and the shouts, the memory of which often kept her awake at night. But as strong as that desire had been, the desire to not disappoint her sister had been stronger and so, in the end, she had gone. Ophasia had enjoyed taunting the prisoners, throwing stale bread at them or calling them cowards, no matter whether they were thieves, rapists, or murderers. She shook her head wonderingly at the memory. How foolish they had been.

She'd gone, true, but she'd always been too scared to join in Ophasia's taunts. Instead, she would sit back and watch, quietly terrified, sure that somehow the men would break through their cells and get her. They never did, of course, and eventually, despite her fear, she began to notice similarities between them. There was something in their eyes, in the set of their jaws that said they didn't regret what they'd done, that they'd do it again if given the chance.

Even when they tugged on their bars, shouting for mercy, their faces twisted in wretched sadness, the look never left their eyes. It was a cold, calculating look. It was a look that said that their morality, their desire to do what was right—if they'd ever had any—had withered and died long ago, leaving in its place nothing more than a walking, talking, empty husk, devoid of all its humanity.

Sometimes, she was sure she saw a similar look in Aaron's eyes, and it was that look, more than what he said, that affected her. No, that wasn't right. It terrified her. Still, with him it was different. She believed that beneath that placid surface of apathy, lurked a pain, a betrayal, that gnawed at him unceasingly, scraping away the goodness in him even as it strove to break him.

Or perhaps he was just an ass. Some people were, after all. His sharp comments about her childhood, about her being pampered, had shown as much. They had been unfair and infuriating, never mind that they were, she had to admit, at least partly true. He was clearly a greedy, selfish man. A man who didn't possess *any* of the qualities she'd been taught to strive for and seek in others. To him, honor, faith, and nobility were nothing more than a joke to be laughed at, a trap to be avoided. He was a sellsword, a man who sold his blade to the highest bidder—no matter the job. A man who would kill someone he'd never met if the money was right with little more than a second thought—a disgusting, vile excuse of a human being.

She knew all of this, so why, then, did she find her eyes following him when he wasn't watching? Why did her mind replay his words, over and over again? Even now, she realized, she was watching him, her eyes taking in his wide, muscled shoulders, remembering how he'd looked without his clothes on. The scars that covered his back had been terrible, so terrible, in fact, that she'd nearly cried out at the sight of them, yet her eyes had been drawn to his powerful, sinewy arms and the tight, compacted muscle of his stomach and chest. She felt herself blushing at the memory and forced her gaze onto her feet, shaking her head in disgust. *What is wrong with me?*

She was so consumed in her own thoughts that she didn't realize the sellsword had stopped until she bumped into his back. She stumbled, almost fell, but his arms shot out, lightning quick, and caught her. "Are you alright?" He asked as he helped her to her feet, the anger he'd shown a few minutes before nowhere to be seen.

Her face feeling as if it was on fire, she jerked away from him, "Like you care," she hissed, "don't try to act human now."

He frowned, staring at her so intensely that she thought her heart would stop, "Don't worry," he said finally, his voice devoid of any emotion, "I won't make the same mistake again. Anyway, the inn's up ahead. Come on." He turned and headed into a nearby alleyway.

What's wrong with you, Adina? She thought, furious with herself. *He was just trying to help.* She'd been trained in diplomacy almost from birth, educated on how to deal with scheming, plotting nobles with rivalries dating back hundreds of years, yet she couldn't seem to get along with a simple sellsword. She glanced to the side and saw Gryle watching her with a knowing, almost fatherly smile. Frowning, her face hot, she followed Aaron into the shadowed alley. In the darkness, she could barely see him, but she felt his eyes on her just the same. "Listen," she said, "I didn't mean—"

"Forget it," He said, his voice gruff. "Take this," she couldn't see what he was doing, but she heard a rustle and felt paper being pressed into her hands.

"What is it?"

"A way out, courtesy of May. I'm going to go check out this Aster Kalen, see if I can't figure out just how bad off we are. If I don't make it back—"

"Of course you'll make it back," Adina interrupted, suddenly, unexplainably terrified at the thought of the sellsword's death.

He shrugged. "Maybe, maybe not. If I don't, use the papers and get out of Avarest. Wait for an hour—no more. If I'm not back by then, I'm not coming back."

"Don't say that," she said, her chest feeling tight.

"What's going to happen is going to happen, princess. Ignoring it doesn't change it."

"I know that," she snapped, her fear making her angry, "I'm not a child!"

He nodded, "Okay then. I'm off." He paused a moment before turning and starting into the street.

"Be careful, sir," Gryle said.

The sellsword turned back, his outline lit by the lights of nearby shops and buildings, "Remember, chamberlain. An hour, no more."

"Y-yes, sir."

The sellsword nodded and turned away. She watched him go, desperately wanting to forbid it, to pull her rank as princess and command that he run with them now, but she knew that he wouldn't listen. The man had made it obvious that titles meant nothing to him. There was something terrible, something wonderful about that. She opened her mouth to tell him to be careful, but no words came, and in seconds he was gone, disappearing into the crowded street as if he'd never been.

CHAPTER ELEVEN

SPOILED, UNGRATEFUL BRAT, Aaron thought furiously as he pushed his way through the teeming crowd of people, keeping his eye on the inn's sign a short distance down the street.

She is emotional, Co admonished, *her brother just died. Perhaps, you could try to be understanding.*

Out of the corner of his vision, Aaron noticed a shadow separate itself from the dark mouth of a nearby alleyway. He reached under his cloak and had one of his blades halfway out of the sheathe before he realized that the target was not him but a stumbling, drunken couple ahead of him. They were laughing and kissing, oblivious of the fact that soon their purses would be much lighter. *I understand that next time I'll let her fall on her royal ass—see how she likes that.* He thought as he moved past the unlucky couple, leaving them to their fate. *Besides, whose side are you on, anyway?*

Do you really want me to answer that?

Aaron sighed, *No, probably better that you didn't, firefly.* He approached the inn and headed for the door.

Tell me you're not going in, Co hissed in his mind.

He allowed himself a smile, "Of course. What did you expect?" He reached back, threw the hood of his faded brown cloak over his head, and walked inside.

I didn't expect that you had a death wish! There are other, more discreet ways of doing this. The orb's voice was frantic and tight with worry.

We don't have time for discreet, he thought back as he glanced around the inn. May had been right. *The Blind Mermaid* had nothing on the Rest. The air in the place was rank with the smell of vomit, piss, and other smells he didn't want to think too long on. Among the scattered, dusty tables, a few small groups of rough looking men and women drank and talked in subdued tones. None bothered turning to pay him any mind as he walked toward the bar. He had a seat, ordered a mug of ale from a bored looking barman who smelled as if he hadn't bathed in a week. As he waited for the drink, Aaron surreptitiously glanced around the room.

The conversation of the place was a dull rumble punctuated by the occasional angry shout of one of the inn's patrons, or the squeal of what appeared to be the place's only barmaid. A homely, heavy-set woman who was trying—and failing—to dodge the gropes of some of the inn's drunker customers while weaving her way between the tables with pints of ale.

He searched for anyone that seemed out of place but nothing caught his eye, which, of course, was all the more reason to be sure that one of those drunks wasn't as drunk as he made out. After all, Aster would have at least one of his men keeping watch downstairs in case someone came in to receive their reward. In a few minutes, the bartender returned with a mug and sat it carelessly on the counter, sloshing ale over the sides of the cup where it mixed with the caked dirt and grime on the bar. "That'll be two of the Old Kings," the man growled. "Nobody drinks for free."

Such a people person, Aaron thought, *it's a wonder the place isn't packed.* He raised an eyebrow as he looked at the greasy, unwashed mug before him. His first instinct was to tell the man that he was out of his damned mind, that for two gold coins he at least expected a clean glass but stopped himself. The last thing he needed to do was make a scene, so he pulled two coins out of his pocket and sat them on the counter. "Thanks."

The bartender grunted as he snatched up the money and tucked it into his apron. Aaron frowned at the beer. He could get away with coming here—after all, he'd never met this Aster Kalen before, so, at best, the man would have a description of what he looked like: a tall, brown haired man with brown eyes. Yeah, good luck with that. There were hundreds, thousands, of men fitting that description in the Downs. There was no reason for them to take any special notice of him. None, that was, as long as he didn't do anything stupid to draw suspicion; anything like, say, ordering a beer and not drinking it.

He grabbed up the mug and sniffed at it, his nose wrinkling. If anything, the ale smelled worse than the room itself, no easy feat, that. *Well, no help for it.* He held his breath and took a long pull from the mug. It took all he had not to spew the contents back out onto the counter. Instead, he winced, forced himself to swallow what was left in his mouth, and grunted. "Good stuff," he croaked to the bartender.

The man raised an eyebrow at the sellsword, frowned, and walked away. Struggling not to gag at the taste of gritty bile in his throat, Aaron turned back to the room, the mug in his hand.

What now? Co asked, a distinctly satisfied tone in her voice.

Now we wait, he thought, deciding to ignore her obvious amusement at his discomfort. *For now.*

Wait for what?

A few moments passed before he caught sight of a familiar form entering the bar. *Do you think that men will always act according to their natures, lightning bug?*

It is in their nature to do so, she answered in an arrogant, self-satisfied voice.

Just what I was thinking, he thought with a thick smugness of his own as Lucius stepped further into the room followed closely by the two bruisers from the Rest. The talkative one had a black eye and a bandage over the side of his face, but other than that, he looked no worse for the wear. *Hard to get any uglier,* Aaron thought, but he was happy to see that the silent one walked stiffly, obviously in pain.

Lucius was rubbing his hands together nervously, scanning the tavern room like a mouse sensing a housecat. Aaron turned back to the bar before the man recognized him, tracking the group's progress out of the corner of his eye. The weasel-faced informant headed to the far end of the room and sat down at a table in the corner. The two men took up positions behind him, scowling at the other people in the bar. *Bastard must be paying good,* he thought, wonderingly.

After a few minutes, a scruffy, unkempt looking man who he'd thought was passed out from drink raised his head off a table on the other side of the inn, stood, and started toward Lucius. He walked past the two bruisers as if they didn't exist and sat down at the table. Lucius began to talk immediately and although they were too far away to hear, the animated way in which he moved, waving his hands in the air exaggeratedly, spoke volumes. After a moment, the scruffy man rose and disappeared up the stairs.

Gone to get his boss, no doubt, Aaron thought. He sat back in his seat, nursed his beer, and waited. It wasn't long before a tall, rail-thin man dressed in a white silk shirt and black trousers came down the steps. The man walked with a confident swagger, as if he was three times his actual size, and a small, knowing smile played at the corner of his face. Aaron frowned. He'd seen that kind of walk before. It was the kind of walk that said the man thought he owned the place and everyone in it. It was the walk of a man who would put a hit on someone without any fear of retaliation.

Aaron gritted his teeth as he studied the man. Aster Kalen's face bore a diagonal scar that started just below his left eye and stopped at his right jaw in a hooked pattern. His head was shaved so bald that it seemed to glow in the weak lantern light. The thin man's smile widened as he took in Lucius's hired muscle, then he pulled a chair out and lounged in it lazily.

"I'll take another beer at that table over there," Aaron said to the barkeep, indicating a table within hearing range of Lucius and the others. The surly old man grunted in response, and Aaron stood and walked to the table, careful to keep his back to Lucius lest the informant recognize him. He needn't have bothered. The man was too intent on his discussion to have any idea what was going on around him. Aaron sat down, his side to the group, and watched them out of the corner of his eye.

"—told you he'd come after me." Lucius was saying, his voice sharp, "he nearly *killed* me."

"You worry too much, friend." Aster replied, and Aaron had to struggle to keep his hands from balling into fists at the coolness of the man's tone. For all the emotion he showed, he could have just as easily been discussing the weather as killing a man. "He will be in hand in good time."

"And the girl?" Lucius asked, "I thought you wanted them both."

"The ... *girl* is of no consequence to me beyond being a means by which our dear Mr. Envelar might be found." The sellsword shifted in his seat. The man had only hesitated for a moment, but it had been long enough to make Aaron sure that he wasn't the only one who knew the princess's true identity. Yes, Aster knew who she was, but instead of trying to kidnap or ransom her, he was focused on Aaron instead. *What in the name of the gods does he have against me?* True, his profession wasn't the kind that won a man any popularity contests, but he couldn't remember ever having wronged the thin man in the past.

"Make it known that whoever finds them can do what they want with the girl, but the man I want alive if possible and if not ... then just make sure that his killer comes personally to claim his reward." Aaron frowned, there was something strange, he thought, about the way the man had said that, but he didn't have time to consider as Lucius's wheedling voice continued.

"You never did tell me why he's so important to you."

"I didn't tell you why I hunt him," Aster answered lightly, "because it is none of your concern."

"I think I could help you more if I knew what was going on," Lucius said in a sullen, almost whiny tone.

"I don't pay you to think, Lucius. Leave such weighty matters to your betters." Aaron didn't need to look to know that the man was smiling. He could hear it in his voice. "You are a rat," Aster said, his tone matter of fact, " a sleazy, blight on the face of humanity, but one who—by his very nature—attracts little attention, and therefore is able to hear things others would not. You are a *listener,* Lucius, not a thinker. Leave it at that."

"Maybe I won't," the informant said, and despite the fact that he tried to sound threatening, Aaron could hear the quaver in his voice. "Maybe I'm tired of listening. Maybe it's time you did some listening."

"Oh?" Aster asked in an amused tone, "is that right?"

"That's right," Lucius said, his courage increasing in the face of the man's lack of reaction, "Maybe *you* should listen now. I've done what you've asked; I've put the hit out on that bastard Envelar. Kind of funny, really. Everyone calls him Silent. Well, he'll be *really* silent soon, won't he?" He tittered a nervous, high-pitched laugh, and Aaron calmly began to consider how much he was going to enjoy dusting the bastard. "But that's not important," Lucius continued, "What *is* important, is that you understand something."

"Yes?" Aster asked in a bored voice, "and what's that?"

"I'm a man to be respected, that's what. I'm not a dog to be ordered about, to be thrown a bone once in a while to keep him happy. If you want any more of my help, I want to be a partner. The way I see it, you wouldn't bother yourself with a no account asshole like Envelar unless there was something damned good in it," Aaron could hear the greed in the man's voice, "Whatever it is you're working on, I want in. You got it? I want a fifty-fifty split or you can find him yourself."

Aster laughed good-naturedly, "Ah, Lucius. You can't begin to imagine what I'm working on. I doubt if even that sellsword understands, but he will, soon. Oh yes, he'll understand when I rip it from his fucking *chest,*" Aaron tensed at the sudden, unexpected rage in the man's voice.

Out of the corner of his eye, he could see that Lucius was leaning away from the man in fear and surprise. For several seconds, they sat in silence. When Aster spoke again, his voice was calm once more, as if his outburst had never occurred, "No, I'm sorry to say that being partners is completely out of the question."

Lucius's mouth worked for several seconds before he finally spoke. "Well," he said, struggling to sound confident as he gestured to his two goons, "it's not your decision to make anymore." The two bruisers moved forward, and the one with the black-eye jerked Aster up by the front of his shirt as if he weighed no more than a child and turned back to his employer, raising an eyebrow in question.

The informant nodded, a cruel smile on his face. "Hurt him."

The big man grunted and pulled a thick, meaty fist back. Before he struck, Aster slapped at his face offhandedly in the same way a man might wave away a fly, and the air was split with a loud *crack* as the hired man's jaw shattered and his head jerked sideways as if struck with a mace. His body followed, and to the sellsword's astonishment the hired man actually *flew* over the table, smashing into the wall with a deafening *crunch* before crumpling to the ground in an unconscious heap. Aaron felt his own jaw drop. *That isn't possible. The man's at least three times Aster's size.* Nobody *is that strong.*

It's him! Co, who'd been quiet for the length of the proceedings, suddenly whispered in a terrified hiss. *It's Melan! You must go!*

The sellsword hesitated, unable to pull his eyes away from the spectacle before him as the other hired man, the silent one, lifted a nearby chair and swung it at the thin man. Aster stepped forward, a small, knowing smile on his face, as he swatted at the chair with one hand. It exploded in a shower of splintered wood, and the big man grunted, taking two stumbling steps backward. He lifted his hands, staring at them in wonder, and Aaron saw that they were coated in blood where the wood had bit into him when it shattered.

It's him! Don't you understand? Run. Aaron, run! Aaron was so concentrated on what he'd just seen, so focused on trying to figure out how it was possible, that, despite the urgency in the Virtue's voice, her words seemed to be coming from far, far away. He watched, stunned, as the bruiser took another nervous step backward, glancing from side to side as if for help as the thin man stalked slowly toward him, his smile still in place.

Please, the Virtue pleaded, *you have to go now.* Co's words were frantic now, coming as sharp, agonizing bursts in his mind.

He jerked himself out of his chair, surprised at the pain in his head. "Stop it," he hissed, gripping his head with both hands, "you're killing me." But if the Virtue heard, she gave no sign. Instead, her screams grew louder, each word more desperate, more painful than the last, until it felt as if Aaron's head would explode.. *Run. Run. HE HAS MELAN. I KNOW HIM. I KNOW HIM. I KN—*

"I know you!" Aaron shouted, the words ripped from him in a flurry of pain and unexplainable rage and fear.

As one, the informant, the bruiser, and Aster turned and regarded him, the first two with surprise. Aster's smile widened, and he nodded, "Ah. The sellsword. Do you see, Lucius?" He asked, turning to the terrified little man who looked on the edge of bolting, "I told you it was only a matter of time." He regarded Aaron calmly, "You have something I want, Mr. Envelar."

The room had descended into silence as Aster had fought the two men, but that silence suddenly shattered as, all around Aaron, the inn's patrons began to rise from their chairs, weapons they'd had hidden under tables or behind chairs appearing in their hands like magic. He was stunned to see that even the serving girl, who'd only just been trying to avoid a supposed drunk's pinch, was gripping a kitchen knife in a white-knuckled fist and staring at him with an almost hungry expression. Slowly, but purposefully, the group started toward him. "Shit," he muttered to himself, "this was a bad idea."

Scanning the room, he saw that some of the inn's patrons were watching with wide-eyes, trying their best to be invisible. So not all of them worked for Aster—a good thing. The bad thing was that there were plenty enough who did to finish the job, even if the man himself hadn't been some kind of ... some kind of what? Later, he would have to ask Co just who in the name of the Keeper's Lantern Melan was. That was, of course, assuming that he made it out of the inn alive, an outcome that was looking less and less likely by the second.

One of the pretend drunks rushed at him, his ugly, fat face twisted in concentration. Aaron stepped to the side, grabbed a hold of the back of the man's shirt as he charged by and used his own momentum to toss him head first into the bar. Mugs of ale tumbled and shattered on the ground at the impact, and Aaron watched as the man collapsed to the ground in a heap. He was still watching when the bartender popped out from behind the bar with a crossbow pointed at him, the same bored, surly expression on his old, weathered face.

He ducked quickly enough to keep the arrow from piercing his heart—where the man had been aiming—but not soon enough to avoid it tracing a line of hot fire across his shoulder. He cried out with pain, reached for a nearby chair and flung it at the approaching men and women who were looking to be five thousand coins richer before the night was out.

The chair crashed into the closest person, a short, thin man with thick, shaggy eyebrows and burn scars on his face. Lacking his employer's incredible strength, the man staggered backward into those behind him, slowing them down. Aaron eased his way toward the door, meeting the intent expressions of the people in the room. "So who will it be then?" He growled, his sword ringing sharply as he drew it from behind his back. "Who's gonna make them some money? Lot of folks in here for only one of you to get paid though, wouldn't you say?"

His would-be killers hesitated staring first at his sword, then at each other. *Gods I love the Downs.* It was one thing to kill a man for gold. It was quite another to risk your life for a payoff you might not ever get, and judging by their distrustful, greedy expressions, they were beginning to realize it.

One of the men up front pushed at one of the others trying to ensure that he would be first. The man who he'd pushed bumped into a woman, cried in pain, and staggered away with a dagger in his chest. "He's *mine,*" the woman snarled revealing a mouthful of rotten teeth. She was just stepping forward as a fist flew out of the crowd and smashed into her face. Blood flew from her mouth in a red fountain, and she tumbled to the ground.

A tense, still moment passed. Then, as if on cue, the entire crowd erupted into vicious, frenzied fighting as people forgot all about their quarry even as they fought and bled for the opportunity to kill him. Blood and spit flew as they tore into each other like wild animals. Over the grunts and cries of pain, Aaron could hear the man, Aster, shouting at them, telling them that they were idiots, and that they would *all* be paid as long as the sellsword was his. *Too late for that,* Aaron thought with a grin. There weren't many things you could count on in the world, but the human capacity for greed was definitely one of them.

He was still grinning when a man flew straight up out of the crowd as if shot out of a cannon, screaming and flailing his arms wildly. The man's screams abruptly stopped as he struck the ceiling overhead with such force that several of the roof beams snapped. Aaron followed the man's limp, shattered body with a stunned gaze as it fell and disappeared in the roiling crowd. *What in the name of the gods*—Before Aaron could finish the thought, another would-be murderer flew out of the crowd following the unbelievable—and certainly deadly— course of the first. It was Aster; it had to be. And he was coming closer. Aaron could follow the man's course by the mangled bodies raining from the sky, and if he was any judge, Aster wasn't in a talking mood anymore. Alright then. His father had often told him that one of the most important things a general or even soldier must know is that there was a time to fight and a time to withdraw.

He shot one more quick glance at the brawling mob, at the dusty counter that the bartender had disappeared behind then bolted for the door like Salen himself was behind him. As he barreled out into the waiting night, he ran into a man and woman who'd been about to enter, knocking both of them sprawling, barely managing to avoid impaling one of them on his still-drawn sword before he sprinted off into the street, ignoring their cries of shock and anger.

He turned a corner onto a dark alley and jerked to a panting stop as two forms peeled themselves away from the shadows of the alley walls. "I told ya, didn't I?" One of them said in a nasally, self-satisfied voice, "I told ya he'd come out. Better to wait out here then be caught up in the inn with those fools."

"Yeah, yeah, shut up about it already." The man's partner answered in a gruff voice that sounded like he spent his spare time gargling broken glass.

Aaron turned his side toward them, his sword extended in front of him. Looking closely, he saw that the men—no doubt a couple of street thugs—carried cudgels instead of blades.

"Now, don't you go and be getting' any ideas, mister." The first one who'd spoken said, "you're probably tellin' yourself that that there pricker of yours is better than these chunks of wood, am I right? Fact is, I'd have to agree with ya if not for one detail."

Aaron continued to watch them, and after several moments of silence, the first man who'd spoken gave a long-suffering sigh, as if disappointed that Aaron hadn't asked, "Said detail *bein'* that there's a crossbow trailin' ya even as we speak."

The sellsword shot a look behind him and saw that it was true. The man was little more than a shadow close to the entrance of the darkened alley, but he was there, that was certain. By the pale moonlight, Aaron could just make out the crossbow in the man's hand. *I'm really beginning to hate those damned things.*

"Now, I don't know why that scarred fucker wants ya, and I don't much care," the talker of the group said, "all I care about is the coin he's offerin'. Now you can come along quietly, and might be he'll let ya live once he's finished with ya, or you can go gettin' ideas and end up spitted on the end of one of my partner's arrows. Now I ain't much for the thought of draggin' your big ass back to the inn, so what'dya say? Be a good man and make this easy on all of us, eh?"

Aaron frowned, "You talk too much."

The man sighed again, dramatically, "Why ain't I surprised. Well, alright then." He looked past Aaron and motioned, "Bronne! Plug this bastard, would ya? I've got some coins to pocket and a whore on Skinner street that needs seein' to."

Aaron glanced quickly over his shoulder again, and both of the men rushed forward, eager to take advantage of his distraction. The silent one came first, swinging his cudgel in a brutal two-handed arc. Aaron barely managed to knock the blow aside as he stepped away from a strike by the smaller man that had been meant for his knee. They came on hard, swinging their cudgels viciously, and Aaron fought desperately, dodging the clubs when he could and batting them aside with his sword when they came too close. Against only one of them, it would have been an easy enough thing to slip his sword past the wild attacks, but with both of the men attacking at once, it was all he could do to keep from getting his head caved in, and his back itched where he knew, in moments, he would feel the steel of the bolt pierce him.

He heard a grunt from up the alley where the crossbowman had been standing, but with the men pressing him hard, he couldn't spare a second to look back. A few moments later, he heard the fatal *twang* of the crossbow release and tensed in expectation.

He was surprised, then, when the smaller of the two men, the talker, cried out in pain and staggered back, grasping at an arrow protruding from his stomach. Aaron didn't have time to marvel at this, however, because the other man was still wading in behind a flurry of wild blows, oblivious of the fact that his partner had been shot. The man was strong, no doubt, and each of the strikes would have been enough to cave in the sellsword's head had they landed, but the bruiser had no skill, and without the other man to keep him busy, Aaron was able to slip past the man's guard as the club hurtled past. The hired man's eyes were just beginning to show surprise as the sword sliced through the air and made a ragged ruin of his throat. The club dropped to the ground as he fell to his knees, groping at his throat in a hopeless effort to halt the torrent of blood sluicing out.

Aaron felt a stab of sympathy at the sight of the man choking and gasping as his life's blood poured out in a flood of crimson, but he pushed it away angrily. To Salen's Fields with compassion. These men had come to kill him, and it was nothing but their own lack of skill that had kept them from it. He stalked toward the smaller of the two. The man lay on his back in the alley, his hands fluttering nervously around the arrow in his stomach, scared to touch it, but scared not to. It wasn't until Aaron was standing over him that the man looked up. "P-please," the man wheezed, "it ... it weren't nothing personal. J-just business."

The sellsword nodded. "Just business." He brought the tip of the sword down, piercing the man's heart and watching as the light faded from his eyes. He sighed, then suddenly remembered the archer and whipped around.

Gryle stood a few feet away. The chubby man's face was pale, and his fingers had gone white where they gripped the stock of the crossbow. His mouth worked soundlessly for several seconds before he finally managed to speak. "I-I came to h-help."

Aaron walked over and the fat man let out a sigh of relief as he took the crossbow from him and tossed it into the alley. Aaron turned to inspect the third member of the group who lay unconscious on the ground, a large, blood-coated rock nearby. He shook his head in surprise and turned to Gryle. "That was one of the bravest, dumbest things I've ever seen, chamberlain. Where's the princess? Tell me she wasn't so stupid."

The chamberlain shook his head savagely and though his hands still trembled, his voice was clear as he defended his mistress, "No, sir, Mr. Silent. Her royal princess is very intelligent. She is a scholar of many of the finer subjects such as math, science, histo—"

"There'll be time for her life story later," Aaron interrupted as he grabbed the man by the arm, "come on. We're not out of it yet."

He led the man through the alleys of dockside at a run, dodging the people on the street when he could and knocking them aside when there wasn't room to go around. By the time they made it to the edge of the docks, both of them were gasping for air, and the chamberlain's chubby face was scarlet and covered in sweat. By the light of the lanterns hung along the side of the docks, Aaron scanned the names of the three ships in the harbor. "Damnit," he snarled.

In the note, May had said to look for a ship named *Clandestine,* and there was no such ship in port. "Reliable my ass," he muttered, "the bastard chickened out."

"Maybe ... not, sir," Gryle huffed beside him.

Aaron turned and regarded the wheezing chamberlain, "What are you talking about?"

Instead of speaking, Gryle pointed a trembling arm out toward the ocean. The sellsword followed it and at first, saw nothing. Then, squinting into the darkness, he could just make out the form of a ship bobbing in the ocean currents. "Damn if you're not right," he said with surprise, "Still, it doesn't matter. He's too far. We'll never make it."

"W-what do we do?" The chamberlain asked beside him, the terror clear in his voice.

Shouts sounded behind them in the distance. "They're coming," he said, as if Gryle hadn't spoken. He couldn't see them yet, but they were coming just the same, all of them intent on making a small fortune off of his head. "But you'll work for your pay, you bastards," he muttered grimly, "I'll see to it." He drew his sword and one of the blades at his side then turned to Gryle, "Run, chamberlain. Get as far away as you can. They didn't come for you, but men with killing on their mind aren't always too particular."

Gryle swallowed hard but shook his head, and Aaron was just about to give him a good hard kick to get him started when he heard footsteps from further down the dock. He jerked around, blades at the ready and was surprised to see the princess standing there. "Over here!" She yelled, her long, dark hair fluttering around her in the wind. She was waving frantically, beckoning them to a space between two of the docked ships. "Hurry! There's not any time!"

Aaron stared at her in surprise then turned back to the street. It was still empty, but judging by the approaching shouts, it wouldn't be for much longer. "She's out of her damned mind," he muttered, "They'll check the ships."

"What are you *doing?*" Adina shouted, "Come *on!*"

Aaron shrugged at the surprised chamberlain and sheathed his blades, "Let's go."

They raced down the docks to where the princess waited, the sound of shouts and curses growing louder behind them. When they reached her, Aaron glanced back and saw that the mob of people had finally emerged from the streets at the far end of the docks. Even in the weak light, he could see that many of them sported bloody noses or black eyes. Their clothes were torn from their earlier fighting and many of them held blades or bludgeons coated with the blood of those around them, but they weren't fighting now. Apparently, they'd come to the conclusion that there wasn't any reason to kill each other for free when someone was going to pay them good money to kill Aaron instead.

"What now?" Aaron asked, stopping in front of the princess.

Adina was stared at the mob with wide, fearful eyes as if hypnotized.

"Princess!" Aaron snapped, shouting to be heard over the cries of their pursuers.

She blinked and finally pulled her gaze away from the approaching mob with a visible effort.

"Here," she said, waving them forward and pointing at the water. Aaron glanced down and, for the first time, he saw that a small rowboat was tied to the dock, tottering back and forth on the rough, choppy water.

"Princess," he said grinning, "I could kiss you."

Some of the fear left her expression at that, and she smiled back nervously, "I'm glad you're okay. And call me Adina."

They met each other's eyes and neither of them spoke. After a moment, Gryle coughed, "Um, excuse me, Princess, sir Aaron, but I think … perhaps, that we should go. Those uh … *people* are definitely getting closer."

Aaron knew that the chamberlain was right, but he couldn't seem to take his eyes off of her. Her long dark hair hung around a face that was tinged with red either from excitement, fear, or both, and her blue eyes sparkled like twin sapphires in the dim light of the dock lamps. "Here," he said, "I'll help you down."

She nodded, her eyes never leaving his as she stepped toward him, into his grasp. Her body was soft, yet firm beneath his hands, and despite their danger, Aaron hesitated for a moment before he finally lowered her gently off the side of the pier. "Okay," she said, staring up at him. He let go, and she dropped into the rocking dinghy.

He watched her for another moment then reluctantly turned to a pale-faced Gryle, "You're next, hero."

The chamberlain smiled self-consciously, "I'm no hero, sir. I'm a coward."

Aaron grunted, "Could have fooled me. Now, come on. Time to go."

The chamberlain glanced down at the rowboat at least eight feet down from the dock, rocking back and forth on the rough ocean currents. "I'm not uh ... I don't think I can."

Aaron shrugged. He stepped forward and the chamberlain let out a squawk of fear as Aaron lifted him off the ground, grunting with the effort, "That's alright. I can." Before the chamberlain could reply, he stepped forward, hefting him over the edge of the dock. The fat man panicked, and Aaron cursed as one of his thrashing feet caught him in the stomach. He shot a quick glance at the water them unceremoniously dropped the man into the rocking canoe where he landed with a *plump*.

As he waited for Adina to help the chamberlain untangle himself from the bottom of the boat, Aaron spared a glance behind him, noticing with dismay that the furious mob was more than halfway down the dock, rushing forward like a stampede. As he watched, a woman in the front tripped and fell and those behind her didn't even pause as they trampled over her in their haste to get at him. *Crazy bastards,* he thought, and then he turned and jumped off the dock

The princess sat at the stern of the boat watching the approaching mob with wide, disbelieving eyes while the chamberlain whimpered incoherently as he fumbled with the oars. Aaron pushed him out of the way, took the oars, and sat down. Then he extended his legs and braced his feet against the bottom of the boat. He dropped the oars in the water and pulled, grunting as pain lanced through his wounded shoulder at the effort.

Continuing to row, he looked up and saw that the mob had reached the part of the dock where he and the others had jumped off. A few of them shouted curses and obscenities at the three, but most prowled restlessly back and forth on the dock with angry scowls, like a pack of coyotes who'd lost their dinner to an inconvenient rabbit hole. *That's fine,* Aaron thought with grim satisfaction, *you just keep sitting there watching.* He said a quick, silent prayer to Talen that none of the men had a crossbow or got the bright idea to jump in and swim after them. The craft was sitting heavy in the water with the three of them, and each grunting, sweating effort he put into the oars moved them only a short distance. A few semi-decent swimmers could easily capsize the vessel.

As if reading his thoughts, several of the men and women dove into the water and started after the boat. "Damnit," he said. He looked over his shoulder where the *Clandestine* waited. A short distance, really, but just then it felt as if it was on the other end of the world. *Too far,* he thought, *too damned far.* He pushed harder, grunting with the effort, but there were six or seven of the swimmers now, and they were quickly closing with the slow-moving craft. He stopped rowing long enough to draw one of his blades. "Gryle." The chamberlain sat in the center of the boat, his fingers and knuckles stark white where he gripped its sides. He did not turn at the sellsword's voice. "Gryle!"

Finally, the chamberlain's wide, terrified eyes turned to Aaron, "S-s-sir?"

Aaron took in the man's pale face and glossy eyes and spat a curse. He'd seen such a look before. The man had succumbed to his fear; Aaron didn't dare give him the blade now. He would just as soon fumble it and hurt one of them as he would the approaching swimmers. Instead, he met Adina's gaze and held out the knife, "If they manage to flip us, we're done." The princess swallowed hard and looked at the blade as if it was a snake getting ready to bite, but he was relieved when she clenched her jaw and took it.

Despite his desperate rowing, it was only moments later when the fastest of the swimmers caught up to them and started climbing over the side. Adina brought the blade up but hesitated and the man was nearly over when Aaron grunted, reared back, and kicked him in the face. The man cried out as his nose shattered in a burst of crimson. His hands came away from the boat, and he disappeared into the black, churning water.

Aaron pulled at the oars again, but the first man had slowed them down enough for two more of the desperate swimmers to catch up with them, and the boat canted dangerously as a snarling man and woman pulled at the other side. The princess kicked at their grasping, unprotected fingers and the two of them cried out and let go.

"Behind you!" He shouted. A man had crawled into the boat and was just trying to get his feet under him. The sellsword fought the urge to let go of the oars and throw the man off. It was hard to tell in the darkness, but at least half a dozen more people were floundering toward them in the black water, and if he took the time to take care of the man, they'd be sure to catch up. The princess turned, raised the short blade, preparing to bring it down on the man's head, and hesitated again.

"Now damnit, or we're all done!" Aaron shouted. Adina let out a shout of anger and fear and turned the blade, striking the man with the handle of the sword. The force of the impact jarred it from her grasp and it fell into the bottom of the rowboat. The man grunted and grasped his head with one of his hands; blood, almost black in the moonlight, seeped through his fingers, but still he came to his feet. He grabbed the princess by the throat, and she gasped, fighting uselessly against his grip. Aaron was just about to drop the oars when the chamberlain—who he hadn't been able to see for the princess and the sodden man—brought the blade across the man's face in an awkward cut. The man cried out, grabbing at the long slash across his face, stumbled, and fell off the boat.

Adina turned to the sellsword with wide, pleading eyes as if searching for understanding, but he didn't-- *couldn't* waste energy on words. Instead, he heaved against the oars again, and again, and they began to outdistance the mob as the swimmers grew tired from fighting against the choppy currents. *Thank Iladen for the luck of rough seas,* he thought, gasping wearily as he continued to push the dinghy farther toward the ship.

Finally, exhausted and drenched in sweat, he pulled up beside the *Clandestine.* Sailors stood at the railing of the ship peering down at them, their expressions grim, if not outright hostile. Aaron had a moment—a terrible, heart in his throat moment—when he thought the sailors would just ignore them, would let them sit stranded in the water until the swimmers (behind now but getting closer) caught up to them, and he breathed a heavy sigh of relief when a rope ladder was thrown over the side.

He turned back to the others in time to see Adina take the blade from Gryle's shaking hands. She handed it back to Aaron, a look of shame on her face. He wanted to tell her that it was okay, that there were worse things than not being able to hurt a man, but he knew that she'd hear the lie in it, so he said nothing. Instead, he nodded, turned, and grabbed at the rope ladder, steadying it. "You first."

She opened her mouth, as if about to speak, but closed it again. She met his eyes only for an instant then turned and hurried up the ladder as if thankful of a chance to escape. Aaron watched her until he judged that she was far enough up, then motioned to Gryle. "Your turn."

The cherubic features of the man twisted with worry as he looked up the side of the looming ship. "I don't think I c—"

"Listen to me, Gryle," The sellsword interrupted, "I'm exhausted, soaked through, and ready to get out of this damned toy boat. Now, if you don't get your ass up that ladder, I swear by all of the gods, major and minor both, that I'll throw you into the water and leave you for our friends."

The man's eyes widened, "Y-you wouldn't. I can't swim."

Aaron just stared at him, and the chamberlain must have seen something in his steady gaze because he grabbed hold of the ladder and started up, an almost imperceptible whimper escaping him as he hefted his weight awkwardly up each rung.

The sellsword watched him go, waited until he got to the top and was hauled up by a couple of sailors. Then, he started up himself. He didn't turn back to stare at the slums of the Downs, the closest place he'd ever come to calling home since his parents' murder. He wanted to, so he didn't. If there was one thing he'd learned in his life, it was that a man was a fool to let himself grow attached to things. After all, places had a way of changing, possessions had a way of getting stolen, and loved ones had a way of dying.

It need not be so, Co said in his mind, her voice sad.

He grunted and continued up the ladder. From time to time, he looked up to judge his progress, looked at the ladder to assure himself of handholds, but he did not, *would* not look back. "Maybe it doesn't need to be, firefly" he muttered, "but it is."

CHAPTER TWELVE

AARON DIDN'T REALIZE how exhausted he was until he was aboard the *Clandestine* and in the relative safety it afforded. His legs felt wobbly and unsteady beneath him, and his shoulder still burned from the cut he'd received earlier, but he forced himself to walk up and stand beside Adina and Gryle. Around them, sailors worked, each attending to their own separate tasks and in moments the ship was sliding through the water with a deceptive quickness. Aaron didn't know much about ships. His occupation rarely gave him occasion to visit one, and the few times when it had, he'd been forced to leave as quickly as possible. As a rule, sailors didn't enjoy finding their captain beaten to within an inch of his life. It made them ... prickly. Still, despite his lack of nautical knowledge, he was impressed by the crew's efficiency. It was as if they were all cogs in some vast machine that had merely been waiting to be turned on.

Aaron was looking down at the small dinghy they'd used when the ship went over a particularly large swell. He had to grab the railing to keep from stumbling, and his stomach lurched dangerously. He gritted his teeth and breathed slowly through his nose, forcing the feeling down. He didn't know any of these men, and the last thing he needed was to look weak in front of them. Men, like vultures, tended to take advantage of such weakness, and if there was a way to look intimidating while puking your guts out, he didn't know it. He focused on taking slow, deep breaths and, after a moment, two men walked up to them. They wore simple cotton slacks and shirts, and their skin was tanned and leathery from hours spent in the sun. They stared at the three newcomers with unveiled suspicion, and it was all Aaron could do not to reach for his blades. He'd seen such looks before—in his experience, they usually came right before the blood.

The men stood, silent, for several seconds. Aaron was just about to speak when a third man came up from behind the sailors. The two men bowed and moved quickly to the side as the newcomer stepped forward, and Aaron raised his eyebrows in surprise as Adina handed the papers May had given them over. The newcomer busied himself studying the documents, a small smile on his face. While he did, Aaron busied himself studying him.

Unlike the rest of the crew who were dressed in simple trousers and sleeveless shirts, the man wore golden satin pants, a long-sleeved, sky-blue silk shirt that was ruffled at the cuffs and collar, and boots so bright red that they almost glowed. To Aaron, he looked like one of the ridiculously-dressed actors that sometimes performed in Avarest. His dark brown fingers and neck were covered in rings and necklaces of various colors that seemed to dance in the moonlight. The effect of all of it put together was so garish that, on second thought, Aaron suspected that even the troupers—known for their eccentric clothing and costumes—would find the man's fashion sense (if sense it was) too radical for their tastes.

Even more unusual, the man's dark brown skin and the long, coal black hair that dangled past his shoulders in tied, oiled locks, marked him as a Parnen. Aaron had met members of the small, sea-fairing community of the southern reaches only once or twice in his life, and he'd found them to be a dour, unassuming people. In fact, the Parnen were known all across the reaches of Telrear as quiet, conservative folk who kept to themselves and horded their coins—and their words—like misers. It was said that the only thing a Parnen did less than spend money was talk, and they did the latter so rarely that members of the race were often thought to be mute. His father had told him, when he was young, that it was true that the Parnen were a quiet, simple people, but that when they *did* speak, a man would be wise to listen.

Aaron wondered idly what his father would have made of *this* Parnen, the man who, judging by the deferential way in which the sailors treated him, had to be Leomin, the captain of the Clandestine. The man's wildly gaudy, flashy attire would have been incredibly off-putting no matter whom it was on, but on a Parnen it was a ridiculousness that seemed to border on profane.

The man finally looked up from the papers and met the Aaron's gaze with eyes so darkly green that they were nearly black—another common characteristic of the Parnen. He smiled revealing straight, white teeth. "A chance meeting in the night, aye." He said in a lilting, almost musical voice. He glanced past Aaron at the swimmers that were quickly fading from view as the ship rushed through the water and sighed regretfully. "Ah, it seems that we have left some of your friends behind."

Aaron grunted, "Are you Leomin?" The men on either side of the Parnen tensed at his abrupt tone, and he could feel the heavy stares of several of the crew, but he didn't look away from the man's gaze.

The necklaces the man wore jingled as he gave a casual shrug, "One must be who he is. We are always trying to be something different," He glanced at the princess meaningfully, "Yet even as we change, we remain the same, do we not?"

Aaron frowned, "Just what in the name of the Keeper's Fields are you talking about?"

The man flashed that bright grin again, "Ah the Fields, yes, the legions that walk them, fleeing from life or running to death? Is it the same?" He tapped his chin with a ringed finger, a thoughtful expression on his face, "An interesting question, no? Perhaps one that even the gods themselves cannot answer."

What the fuck is he talking about? Aaron thought.

The question had been to himself, but Co answered anyway. *I cannot feel him.* She sounded worried.

What do you mean, you can't feel him?

His emotions, his hopes or fears, what makes him him. *There is nothing there.*

Aaron could hear an edge of panic in her voice. *Just relax, Co.* He thought back. The last thing he needed was for her to go crazy again. In the *Mermaid*, when the Virtue had panicked, he'd felt as if his head was going to explode. It was an experience he wasn't interested in reliving. Come to think of it, what had *that* been about? The Virtue had been calm enough when he was barely avoiding getting skewered by arrows. Who was this Melan and why was she so frightened of him? He shook off the thought. He'd ask her later, when she didn't sound like she was about to have a fit. He didn't think he could survive another. *After all,* he thought soothingly, *there must be plenty of people who you can't feel, right?*

No.

He coughed and was about to respond when Leomin spoke, "I see that you are a deep-thinker, one who would spend hours yet pondering the question, and I respect you for it." There was something about the man's deep green stare, and the small, almost wistful smile on his face that made Aaron uncomfortable. He got the impossible, yet distinct feeling that the man had been listening to his internal dialogue with the Virtue. He allowed his hands to drift slowly, casually closer to his blades. "Too many folk," the Parnen continued, apparently oblivious of Aaron's reaction, "these days worry only about the present. It is a worrisome trait. Still, if one only worries about the present, and the future will soon be the present, is one not worrying about both at the same time?" He rubbed at his chin thoughtfully, "An interesting question, isn't it?"

The sellsword blinked and tried again. "So ... you're Leomin?"

The man seemed to consider this carefully, "For now?" He smiled, "I suppose I am. Though little do I resemble the Leomin who came before, and I suspect that the Leomins of the future will be more different still. Change, after all, is the curse of time, is it not?"

Aaron rubbed at his temples where he could feel a headache forming. "For a man who talks a lot, you don't manage to *say* much, do you?"

Leomin looked surprised, "Why by the gods, no! I'd hate to think it. Now, if you are quite finished talking, I believe introductions are in order," he said, turning to the two men beside him and not noticing Aaron tense as he seriously contemplated throwing the man overboard. "This," the captain said gesturing to the stocky, salt-and-pepper bearded man to his right, "is Balen, first mate of this vessel."

Apparently, the captain's calm manner was enough to assure the first mate that the sellsword and the others were no threat, because his hostile look was gone, and he nodded politely to Aaron and Gryle. When he turned to Adina, he ran a hand over his unshaven face and grinned sheepishly, "Pleasure to meet—"

"Alright, alright, enough!" Leomin barked, and the first mate's mouth snapped shut. The Parnen turned back to them shaking his head, "Balen's a good enough sort, but he'll talk you to death if you let him. The man's words walk in circles like a mutt with the shits. Still, I love him like a brother, and much farther than I could throw him."

Balen stepped back behind the captain, and Aaron was surprised to see that he was grinning like a child who'd just been given a treat. Apparently, such a rebuke was common and a source of amusement for the grizzled first mate. Leomin indicated the other man with a flourish of his ruffled right arm. The man was thin and tall with a sharp, angular face that made him look hawkish. As in the case of the first mate, the man had traded his scowl for a smile so friendly that an observer might have thought he was a man greeting a long missed friend. "This," the captain said, "is ... it's uh ..." He gestured with his hand vaguely, "Oh, don't tell me. It ... it starts with an H does it not? Something short and strong. Is it Hugh ... no, that's not it." He tapped at his teeth for a moment then nodded, satisfied, "Ah! I've got it! Hank. Yes, that's it. Hank here is the cook, and a fine one at that."

The tall man nodded to them, "Nice to meet you. The name's—" he hesitated and glanced at the captain before continuing, "Er ... the name's Hank ... but you can call me Randolph."

The captain sighed long-sufferingly, "By the *gods* what is wrong with everyone today? You've spent too much time with Balen, Hugh. His atrocious habit of running off at the mouth like a ship springing a leak has infected you, I fear. Can't you see that our guests are *tired?* No doubt, they've spent a long night partying and drinking at one of Avarest's finest, is it not so?" He winked at Aaron.

"Not really," the princess offered in an annoyed voice, and Aaron was glad to see that the captain wasn't only grating on his nerves, "we spent the day being chased by thugs and murderers, but we *are* tired."

"You see there?" Leomin said, glaring at the cook, "what did I tell you? It must have been quite the party." He gestured vaguely in the direction from which they'd come, "I insist that you take that as a lesson. A man can do too much of partying and talking both."

The cook nodded humbly, "Of course, sir."

Leomin watched him for a moment then gave a quick, satisfied nod, "There now. Where were we?" His eyebrows furrowed in confusion for a moment, "Balen?"

The first mate glanced at Aaron and the others before turning back to the captain, "You was just sayin' how you was gonna get the good folks a place to rest, I think, sir."

"Certainly," the captain said, "and what a wonderful idea. I'm quite glad I thought of it."

Balen nodded, his expression never changing, "That's why you're the captain, sir."

"Indeed," the Parnen said, pleased, "and that is—" he cut off as he glanced at Aaron closely, squinting his eyes in the darkness as he took in the wound on Aaron's shoulder, "by the gods man are you *bleeding*? On *my* ship?"

Aaron nodded, "Yeah, sorry," he said, his voice thick with sarcasm, "I don't know where my manners are."

The captain gave a long suffering sigh, "Yes, well, apology accepted. Now come, let's get that seen to and find you all a place to retire for the night. No doubt, Balen's meandering, torturous conversation has killed what little wakefulness you may have had. We will speak more on the 'morrow."

Without waiting to see if they were following, he turned and started toward the deck, "Sir," The first mate said, "It's uh ... it's this way."

The captain turned and frowned at him, "Do you mean to imply, Balen, that I don't know my own ship?"

"Of course not, sir."

Leomin stared at him for a moment then nodded and patted him on the shoulder before turning back to the others. "Balen is a good man, but not the clever sort," he said in a whisper that was easily loud enough for the first mate and cook to hear. They grinned at each other behind the captain's back as Leomin started toward the cabin, "Come. I will show you the way."

"It's going to be a long trip," Adina whispered beside him.

Aaron sighed then looked toward the distant Avarest, thinking about the would-be murderers who were no doubt even now waiting on the docks. "Think it's too late to get them to take us back?"

CHAPTER THIRTEEN

HE WOKE WITH A START, reaching for the blades at his sides only to have his hands come back empty. He pushed himself up from the bed and growled a curse as he slammed his head into the frame of the empty bunk above him. Belatedly, he remembered that he was in the cabin Balen had led him to the night before. Sitting up carefully, rubbing his aching forehead, he tried to shake off the remnants of his dream.

He'd been back in the *Mermaid,* watching in shock as the man, Aster, flung people into the ceiling where they shattered like cheaply-made puppets without expending any apparent effort. It was just like before, only this time, he hadn't made it out. This time, he'd turned to flee and the man had been there, waiting, smiling that small, knowing smile. Aster. The man who'd put the hit on him. Aster, a man who Co seemed to think was Melan. Whoever that was. *You have something I want,* he'd said. *You have something I want.* Aaron turned the words over and over in his head, but he couldn't make any sense of them. After all, the only thing he owned of any worth were his blades and—though they were good steel—they didn't come close to approaching the five thousand coin bounty the man had offered for his head. What else could he possibly have that someone would want? What else except ... *Co? Are you there?*

Aaron jumped in surprise as the orb appeared directly in front of his face. *I am here, Aaron.* Gone was the usual playfulness of Co's tone. Instead, she sounded tired. No, that wasn't quite right. She sounded resigned.

"Co, who is Melan?"

The Virtue didn't answer.

"Look, Co, I need to know. Who is he?"

There was a long pause, and Aaron was beginning to think the Virtue wouldn't answer when she finally spoke, though he could hear reluctance in her tone. "Melan was one of Kevlane's disciples. He was tasked with gathering the essence of one of the seven Virtues, so that Kevlane could conduct it into the waiting vessel."

"And?" Aaron asked impatiently, "Why are you so scared of him? I deserve to know after what you've put me through. Consider it payment for the free rides I've been giving you."

The Virtue sighed in his mind, "Fine. After Caltriss and Kevlane's deaths, when the warriors of the barbarian kings burst into the chamber, Melan, like the others, was too exhausted to defend himself. While the others struggled to rise, struggled—and failed—to summon the power to protect themselves, Melan went mad. He cursed Caltriss and Kevlane both even as the barbarians began their bloody work. He was so consumed by his rage that he was still screaming his hate, his curses, oblivious even when they cut his throat."

"But you called Aster Melan. Why would you do that unless ..."

"Yes," Co said, "your thoughts are correct. Through Kevlane's ritual, the seven Virtues were created. When they arose from the ashes of that mass grave, when they awoke among those smoking husks of humanity, each Virtue retained some of the memories and personality of its creator.

"You were ... alive." Aaron said, stunned. "You were a person."

"What matters," the orb answered sharply, "is that Melan was tasked with gathering the virtue of strength. It was his power that you saw in the inn."

"Fucking perfect," Aaron muttered, "the man can toss people around like kindling, and I can ... what? Feel guilty? Cry a lot?" He shook his head, "Damn Iladen and his dice, both."

"It is not wise to provoke the gods," the Virtue warned.

"Oh?" He asked, as he rose from the bed and slid his blades into the sheathes at his side, "yeah, you're right. I wouldn't want to make him mad, would I? My luck would go to shit. Oh, wait. My luck already *is* shit." Well, at least he and the others were safe on the *Clandestine*. The man could be the strongest person in all of Telrear—no doubt was—but he couldn't walk on water. "He can't can he?"

"Walk on water?" The virtue asked, "Of course not."

Aaron nodded, "Good." They sat in silence for some time as Aaron digested the information. Then, "Co? What was your name?"

At first, he didn't think the Virtue was going to answer. "It was not *my* name," she said finally, "You do not understand. I am her creation, the product of a spell that was, by some strange anomaly, invested with a portion of her personality and part of her memories. A freak accident. Nothing more."

"You have her memories and her personality?"

"Yes."

"What else is there?" He asked. "It seems to me that if you think like her and remember her experiences then you may as well *be* her."

You know nothing! The Virtue hissed in his mind, and he recoiled as the orb flashed a deep, angry red before reverting back to its normal color, *I am not her. I am not human—I never was. Yes, I can remember pieces. I can remember the sun on her skin, but I can't remember how it felt. I can remember the barbarians, remember the bloody slaughter they reaped, but I can feel none of it because it was not me. It is as if there is a vital part of me missing, as if they are something I read in a book. Can you imagine what that feels like?*

"No," he muttered, "I don't guess I can. But tell me this, if you—if your *creator* knew Melan, then why were you so scared of him? After all, he's just a Virtue, right? Just a—what did you call it—a freak accident?"

You still don't understand, she answered impatiently, *The Virtue of Strength is not Melan, but it* does *possess Melan's personality.*

Aaron grunted as understanding dawned. "And Melan was insane."

Correct. Which means that if this man, Aster Kalen, is not mad already, he will be so soon. There is no stopping the transferring of traits between the virtue and its partner—it is Kevlane's bond.

Aaron thought of the way Aster had slapped Lucius's hired muscle in the face, nearly killing him, or the way he'd tossed people aside, breaking bones and wreaking havoc with no more thought than a man would give to swatting a fly. Yeah, the bastard was crazy alright. Suddenly, a thought occurred to him, and he went rigid, "Before, you told me there were people who hunt the Virtues. Aster is one of those, isn't he?"

Yes.

He sighed heavily. "Great. There's still one thing I don't understand though. "

Just one? Co asked.

"Very funny," he said, but, in truth, he was glad to see the Virtue getting some of her humor back. It was bad enough having to share your mind with someone else; the last thing he needed was for her to become neurotic. "Two, actually," he admitted, "first, what decides who one of you lightning bugs bonds with?"

We do, of course, Co said as if he'd just asked if birds could fly.

"So you ... *picked* me?"

Yes.

He shook his head in amazement, "Why in the name of the gods would you do that?"

The orb bobbed in the air and despite the fact that she had no arms or shoulders to do it with, he got the distinct impression that she was shrugging. *I thought you were funny.*

Aaron blinked slowly, "You ruined my career as a decent sellsword and made me the enemy of a psychopath that can juggle people like rocks because you thought I was *funny?*"

Do not mock. I've existed for thousands of years, and I've found one thing to be true. A good laugh is hard to come by.

"You've got to be fucking kidding me."

You shouldn't curse so much, she admonished, *and no, I'm not kidding, but why don't you talk to me about it after you've lived a few thousand years.*

"Okay, ignoring the fact that you're a pain in the ass, are you telling me that Melan *chose* Aster?"

It is not Mela—nevermind. To answer your question ... perhaps. Melan—as you insist on calling him—is, as I believe I've mentioned, quite insane. Who can guess why he would have chosen Aster Kalen if he did, in fact, choose him?

"And if he didn't?"

The Virtue paused before answering, and when she spoke her voice was tight with worry, *If he didn't, then Aster has discovered a way of doing what even Kevlane could not—forcing the Virtues to bond with a person of his choosing. In this case, him.*

Aaron frowned. Suddenly, the ship's cabin felt too small. The walls seemed to be getting closer, and the air felt thick and cloying in his throat. He got dressed, threw on his weapons, and headed out the door. On the deck, the sailors were busy about their work and few of them spared him a second glance which was just how he liked it. The choppy waters of the night before were nowhere in evidence, and the ship skimmed across the ocean as if it were born to it.

He walked to the side of the ship and looked around. Water stretched on endlessly toward every horizon. It was a disconcerting feeling. It was as if the ship and its passengers existed in a world of their own, as if the land and cities he remembered were nothing but a dream. His stomach lurched at the thought, and he closed his eyes, fighting back a wave of nausea.

"Ah, good day, sir."

He turned to see the first mate, Balen, approaching. "What's so good about it?"

The first mate smiled and shrugged, "The sun's shinin' and we're breathin.' What more could you ask for?"

The ship lurched as the sail caught more wind, and Aaron swallowed hard. "Land for a start."

Balen grinned wider, "A dirt foot, eh?"

Aaron frowned "If the gods had meant for us to be in the water they'd have given us gills."

Balen barked a laugh. "So, where are your friends?"

"I don't know."

The first mate nodded and leaned in conspiratorially, "I'd watch her close, friend. It ain't often the boys get a good lookin' gal like herself on board. I'll count us lucky if every one of the damned fools don't ask for her hand before the day's out."

Aaron squashed the sudden, unexplainable anger that welled up at the thought, "Where's your captain?"

Balen shrugged, "In his cabin, I expect. Sometimes days'll go by without the Cap comin' top deck. Other days he'll work right alongside the lads 'till they're gaspin' like fish out of water. Ain't never any tellin' what he'll do."

"They've got a word for that—crazy."

The first mate's companionable demeanor vanished in an instant. "Look, stranger," he said, his voice gruff, "you seem like an alright sort, and you're alright by the captain, so I won't take offense to words spoken out of ignorance. The Cap's ... unique, sure, and he has a way of talkin' what will turn a man's head around backwards, but I've been with 'em goin' on ten years and there ain't a man breathin' that I'd rather sail with."

Aaron considered this then spat over the ship's rails, watched as it disappeared into the rushing waters below. Suddenly queasy again, he jerked his eyes away. There wasn't any use making enemies with Balen. Despite all odds, it seemed that the man really did love his captain. Apparently, Leomin wasn't the only madman on board. "No offense meant, first mate."

The man nodded, satisfied, and his smile reappeared. He'd just opened his mouth to speak when footsteps sounded behind them and someone said, "Excuse me, sir." They both turned and saw the cook from the night before.

"Randolph, enough with the sir business," Balen said, "me and you shared enough water to skip the bullshit, visitors or no."

The hawk-faced man nodded, and though he smiled, Aaron could see the worry in his eyes, "Of course, Balen. Anyway, I thought you'd want to know that there's a ship following us. They're a few days behind, I'd say, but they're following us just the same. Kurt saw them from the crow's nest."

The first mate shot a look at Aaron who shrugged to cover up the cold ball of dread that had started to gather in his stomach, "Doesn't mean they're after us, does it?"

"Big ocean," the hawk-faced man said.

"Aye," Balen grunted, studying Aaron, "mighty big ocean. You're right there, Randolph. Well, they're a few days away. Might be they aren't nothin' to do with us," he gazed behind them thoughtfully, "Might be."

Aaron turned to the tall, thin man, "I thought your name was Hugh or Howie or something? The cook, right?"

The two men shared a look and grinned before turning back to him. Balen answered, "Captain never has been much for details. Not real good with names and the like."

Randolph nodded, "Or duties."

The first mate nodded, rubbing a hand over his unshaven face, "Right. Not much good with those either."

Aaron raised an eyebrow, "Duties?"

Balen barked a laugh, "Randolph here has been the ship's second mate for goin' on eight years."

The sharp-featured man nodded seriously, "And I can't cook for shit, but don't tell the Cap."

Aaron watched the two men for a moment, waiting for them to laugh. When they didn't, he shook his head in amazement. It was a wonder that the men were still alive with such a captain.

"I know what you're thinkin'," Randolph said, "but you're wrong. The captain gets a little confused, sure, but

I'd guess he's just about the best damned sailor that ever lifted an oar—not that he does a lot of that, mind."

Balen nodded, "Me and the kid here would have been friendly with the fishes years ago if not for the Cap."

Randolph took in Aaron's confused expression and smiled, "Balen means that we'd be dead. You see, lots of folks think there's not much to sailing besides tugging on ropes, and drinking ourselves into a stupor when we're on land leave, but they're wrong. Not that we don't do some of that, you understand, but that's not all there is. You see, Sheza is a temperamental goddess. Why, between pirates, sea monsters, and good old fashioned dumb-assery there's thousands of ways a man can die on the water."

Aaron frowned. "That's comforting."

The first mate barked a laugh, "Ain't nothin' to worry about, friend, not so long as the captain's here. Why, that man ain't met a pirate he couldn't outrun or outsmart, a stupid mistake he couldn't turn to his good, or a sea monster he wouldn't spit in the face of before he showed it our back 'end and made it eat our dust. Metaphorically speaking."

Randolph nodded solemnly, "There's not a lot of dust in the ocean," he said to Aaron by way of explanation.

"Yeah, I got that." Strange. He would have thought that the men would have been driven damned near to murder by the captain's erratic behavior and penchant for useless conversation but instead they seemed to trust him completely. *Maybe they just got used to it,* he mused. If that was the case, he prayed to Sheza, mermaid goddess of sailors and boats, that he wouldn't have to spend enough time with the man to find out; he'd sooner get used to a blade in the gut than the unbalanced Parnen. "Does all of the crew feel this way about the captain?"

Balen shrugged, "Couldn't say. This batch here's new." As if reminded, he leaned away for a second, "Trim the jib you lazy bastards, the wind's changin'!" Several men rushed to the task, but Aaron noticed a few sullen looks when the first mate turned back. "Anyway, these fellas is hardly wet behind the ears."

Randolph laughed, "Shit, they're still shakin' the dust off their boots, I'd say." Balen grunted in agreement.

"Why a new crew?" Aaron asked curiously, "If the man's such a good captain, I would think that his men would want to keep working for him."

The two men's expressions grew grim, and Balen hocked and spat over the side of the ship. "High Prince Belgarin, that's why. A couple of months ago, the Cap decided to make the run to Baresh. It's a dangerous trip to the north—with the wars, a man never knows what he'll run into—and few are the captains that'll dare it. Belgarin's got the place sealed up tighter than a duck's ass. I tried to talk the captain out of it. After all, the high prince ain't exactly known for his mercy, and we both knew he wouldn't take kindly to any sailors dumb enough to test those waters, but he wouldn't hear none of it."

Balen's gaze grew distant as he recounted the memories, "I tried to tell him that it weren't worth the risk—after all, the north never has been known for its riches. Keeper, we coulda made twice as much and traveled half the distance if we'da taken the supplies to Telasia or Akren. The Telasian's ain't much for fightin'—shit, they didn't even put up a fuss after their ruler, Geoffrey's death, but they're all for primpin'—not that Geoffrey was much different from what I hear. Not a big lady's man, our dearly departed Prince." He said with a wink, "Nah, powders, perfumes, and silks'll damned near bring a fortune there, and Ophasia's Akrenese ain't much better."

Aaron frowned, "So why do it?"

The two sailors glanced at each other and shrugged. "That's what I asked the captain," Balen said, "I mean, what reason does a crew of smugglers have to go swimmin' with sharks like Belgarin and the rest? Best not to get mixed up in it, I told him, no matter how good the payoff was. A dead man spends no coins, and that's the truth."

Aaron raised an eyebrow, "Smugglers, eh? And here I took you for a crew of simple sailors."

Balen grinned, "Smuggling you and your friends, ain't we? Anyway, the captain weren't about to be dissuaded, he was clear on that." He noticed Aaron's doubtful expression and shrugged, "Well, as clear as he ever is anyway."

Aaron considered this for a moment, "That still doesn't explain why Leomin would risk his crew and his own life on the trip."

The first mate nodded, "Right enough. Now don't get the wrong notion, mister. A lot of times the captain's ideas sound like about the craziest tavern tale a whore ever told." He shook his head, a small smile on his face,

"So crazy—at times—a man'd have to have a deathwish to follow 'em, but you know what? They always seem to work out. No matter how cracked the idea sounds, we always seem to come out the other side not just breathin', but a damn sight richer than we was 'for we went in. Still, bringin' goods to the northerners sounded too much like pickin' sides to me—one of the best ways for a smuggler to get his fool head lopped off—and I told the Cap so." The man met Aaron's gaze, "Do you know what he told me?"

"No," Aaron said, leaning forward, interested despite himself, "what?"

The man's grin widened, "I ain't got a damned clue. Ain't you ever heard the man talk? No, I ain't got no idea what he said, but I think I got a pretty good idea of what he meant by it. I think what the captain meant, more or less, was that, sooner or later, if a man didn't pick sides, a side was gonna pick him anyway. Least this way, we got to make the decision ourselves."

"Still, he decided to put it to the crew, let 'em decide for themselves. Said he wadn't gonna have no ghosts hauntin' him on account of he didn't give them their fair choice. They said—shit, *we* said, that whatever the captain decided was good enough for us. You see, they was good lads, and we'd all heard the stories. We all knew that them folks in the north were starvin'. Down to eatin' beans and boot leather, what with Belgarin's ships patrolling the waters, keepin' honest traders out. We ain't priests or saints mind—bout as far from it as you can get truth be told—but it's one thing to thumb your nose at pompous nobles and their import taxes; it's another to let folks starve to death when you maybe could do something about it."

The first mate shrugged, self-consciously, "Not that that was all of it. Shit, probably not even most of it. The captain said we was going, and so we was going. That was all that needed to be said. So we set out and after a while we met up with a couple of Belgarin's ships."

"You got caught."

The man grinned again, "Those boys couldn't sail for shit. We split 'em, put ol' *Clandestine's* nose in the wind, and left 'em flappin'. Naw, we made it to Baresh, alright. Eladen weren't there, or if he was, his Royal Highness didn't see fit to grace us with his presence. Some man by the name o' Deckard brought some soldiers up and took care of getting the food out to those as needed it—the common folk in the city and surrounding countryside. The nobles complained, 'o course, but any man with the eyes the gods gave 'em could see that the fat bastards weren't goin' hungry—if there's one thing to know about nobles, it's that they'll always eat. Yes sir, they bitched and moaned up a storm, but that Deckard fella weren't havin' none of it. He sent the bastards runnin' like there was a sale on silk." He nodded approvingly, "A good fella that."

"Anyway, we made it out o' port and were about a week out when we ran into 'em, three or four of the big busters, Belgarin's best ships, waitin' on us like they knew what route we'd take. Weren't no way to get away from 'em, not then, and they escorted us to some back water port I still can't remember the name of. Threw all of us 'sept the Cap in cells; him they took off alone. The man in charge—a real fat bastard by the name of Fritz or Ferg, I can't rightly recall—said that we was all to be questioned and then set free. I reckon we all knew it for a lie even before the guards started leadin' the lads off one by one to ask their "questions."

Balen paused then, and the silence stretched so taut that Aaron imagined he could hear it vibrating. When the first mate finally spoke, his voice was rough and slightly hoarse, "A long week that. Couldn't hear much down in that dungeon, but from time to time, you could make out one of the lads screamin' as those boys asked 'em their *questions*." He spat the last word and made a face as if he'd just swallowed some foul brew. "I figure I was about a quarter hour from lettin' go and pissin' myself like some kid sailor in his first bad blow when the Cap showed up out of nowhere. One minute I was tryin' to keep myself from blubberin', the next he was there at the door of the cell, holdin' his finger over his lips. He had a key—gods know how he got it—and he let us out."

"Me and Randolph here was in the same cell—the fat man was savin' the officers for last—and we followed the Cap as he led us out of the dungeon past a pair of unconscious guards." Balen sighed heavily and wiped a hairy arm across his eyes, "I guess I'd like to say I thought we were comin' back for the boys, but I knew better. The Cap was doin' all he could to get us out, sneakin' us past the fat man's soldiers and out of the buildin'. There just weren't no way to save the rest of 'em, and the truth is I was too damned scared to worry about anybody but myself." He cleared his throat roughly, "Too damned scared."

He paused then, his eyes reflecting the deep emotion that the memory brought. "As for the boys, they had to known the score well as we did—but they didn't make a sound. Not a one. Strange when you consider that one of 'em had to have told Belgarin's fat man what route we'd take. No way he would have found us otherwise—like Randolph says, it's a big ocean. Anyway, the Cap led us to some dump of an inn, fed us, and paid the owner for a week's stay. After that, he disappeared and didn't come back for days. My guess is that he meant to go back for the lads and judgin' by the grim look on his face when he returned, I don't guess he did too well on that score—not that I could promise ya for sure. He never told me, and I never asked. Scared to, I reckon."

"All of it past that's a bit fuzzy. All I know is that somehow the Cap got a crew together—not a familiar face among them—we waited till night, and we stole the *Clandestine* back right out from under the fat man's nose." He frowned then, and his eyes were suddenly blazing with anger, "I hope Belgarin's got some serious questions for that bastard, I surely do. Hope he asks 'em hard, too. Damned hard."

Aaron shook his head in stunned disbelief. He didn't know a lot of smugglers, but the ones he did know would have sold their kin into slavery if they thought they could make a profit off the deal. The thought of the crew of a smuggler ship risking their lives to feed some starving people they wouldn't know if they passed them on the street was almost more than he could fathom. As for Captain Leomin? Well, if everything Balen said was true, the man was certainly more than he pretended to be.

Which begged the question. Why? Why the pretense of idiocy? Why risk his life to save strangers? "So you came back to Avarest?" He asked, "To the Downs?"

"And left the boys," Balen said, wiping at his eyes. "I don't guess I'll ever see 'em again. Not old Carl with his breath that smelled o' shit and worse, or Jamie Wuthers, neither." He glanced back at Randolph and gave a laugh choked with emotion, "That boy'd caught just about every disease a woman could give a man I reckon. Made a regular study of it."

Randolph's eyes, too, were glistening with unshed tears, and he nodded before turning to Aaron. "Yes, we went to Avarest. After all, the city is one of the few places left in Telrear that's neutral—or claims to be, anyway. As for the Downs, why not? What better place for a group of wanted, hunted smugglers to run to than a place where almost everyone's a criminal? What better place for us to hide from the world than in a part of it where no decent man or woman wants to look, let alone go?"

"So you were still hiding—"

"When you came." Randolph nodded once, "Yes. We'd suggested some ideas to the captain, but he hadn't really listened. He's been … different of late."

"It's 'cause of the lads," Balen whispered, "You wouldn't know it by the way he acts, but I think leavin' the lads hurt the captain more than it did any of us."

Randolph nodded, "True. In a way, I'm glad you and your friends showed up. I was beginning to think we never *would* leave the Downs, that maybe the captain had decided to stay here, drinking and whoring the years away in an effort to forget about the crew he'd lost, about the men he hadn't been able to save. But when you showed up with those papers, well, it was like the old captain came back all of a sudden."

Aaron glanced over at Balen and saw that the man's eyes were watery and his jaw was working as if he were chewing on something. He guessed that the man probably hadn't cried since he was young enough to piss the bed and get away with it, but here he was barely holding it together. What did you say to a man like that? What could you say? Better, maybe, to say nothing at all.

You could say you were sorry, Co said in his mind, and he could hear the anger and sadness he felt at the pointlessness of it all mirrored in her voice.

Sorry doesn't change anything, firefly. The dead stay dead, and the bastards like Belgarin keep breathing. It's the way the world works. Sorry isn't enough.

It's something.

Aaron sighed inwardly and gripped the first mate's shoulder awkwardly, "I'm sorry about your friends."

"Preciate that," Balen said, snorting and wiping a hand across his eyes. "I surely do." He looked embarrassedly around the ship at the sailors busy about their business and cleared his throat. "Well, guess I'd better see to this batch, 'less you all don't mind winding up stuck in the side of some damned mountain, that is." He nodded to Aaron and walked off, bawling out commands at the nearest sailors who hurried to follow orders.

When Aaron turned back to the second mate, Randolph was watching him strangely. "Well," The hawk-faced man said finally, "I guess I'd best be about my own business."

Aaron watched him go before turning back to the ocean, to the deep blue water that stretched on into eternity, to the waves that lapped against the boat. The sun was bright and warm against his skin, and he could just make out the sound of some water bird, with which he was unfamiliar, cawing and hooting in the distance. He sighed heavily. He felt sick, but it wasn't from the rolling of the deck underfoot anymore. *An entire crew of men dead all because of some prick noble and what's changed? Nothing. Not one damned thing.* The sun still rose, the waves still crashed, men still died, and the world grew older, not caring one way or the other.

For the first time in years, he thought of the words Headmaster Cyrille had told him on his first day in the orphanage. He'd been sitting in his room, crying over his parents, when the Headmaster came to visit him. That was long before he'd discovered the headmaster's addiction to the musky-scented tamarang, long before he received the first of the scars that covered his back.

On that first night, he'd thought the headmaster kind, even wise. The man looked like the world's best grandfather, gray-haired with a jolly face. Cyrille came and sat beside him on the bed and patted his shoulder comfortingly. When he'd turned to look, the headmaster had been smiling. At the time, he'd thought the man was trying to reassure him. "Why do you weep, child?" The headmaster had asked.

Sniffling, wiping at the tears and snot that were running down his face, Aaron had been unable to answer.

"It is because of your parents, is it not?" The headmaster asked, his voice soft, filled with what the child Aaron—naïve and too young to know the hard truths about people, about the world—took to be compassion.

The old man shrugged casually then and his smile turned sharp, cruel, the first signs of his true self. "Men die and the gods watch. It is the way of things. And do you know what the gods do, when they watch, young Envelar?"

Aaron had shaken his head, unable to speak past the lump in his throat. The man had grinned wider displaying a crooked row of brown-stained teeth as he leaned closer, so close that Aaron could smell the bitter, acrid smell of the tamarang, though he'd known nothing of the herb then. He could feel the cloying, sickening warmth of the man's breath against his face, "They laugh. Men die, and the gods laugh, my son. So has it ever been. So will it ever be."

The headmaster had been a cruel man, one who exalted in the perverse depravities he visited on the young girls of the orphanage as well as the severe beatings he administered to the boys. He was a sick, evil bastard. Now he was a dead one and what difference did that make? Those who had suffered or died under his twisted care got none of that which was taken from them back. The dead remained dead and the girls, those girls with the dead eyes and shuffling, lifeless walks, would never get their innocence back.

Over the years, as the headmaster's tamarang addiction grew worse, so too did his rages and degradations. In the end, when Aaron had come for him, he'd barely had enough of his wits left to understand that he was going to die. Aaron had stood and watched as the man gasped his last breath, as his eyes glossed over with the unmistakable gaze of the dead, and he had enjoyed it. Still the man had been right. "Men die and the gods laugh." He muttered as he gazed out over the endless water as it eddied indifferently in the wind.

Aaron was so lost in his own dark thoughts that he had no idea anyone was behind him until he felt a hand on his arm. He whipped around and was surprised to see Adina standing there, watching him with eyes the color of the roiling water, her brow creased with worry, "Are you okay?"

"Why wouldn't I be?"

She shrugged. In the white, clinging silk shirt that she wore, he found that the motion did interesting things with her breasts, and all thoughts of the headmaster and the orphanage where he'd spent the last years of his childhood faded, and the sounds of those child's screams stilled and grew silent. "I called your name three times."

He coughed and forced his eyes away from the view the dress provided, "I ... err... I was thinking."

"Oh?" She asked. "What about?" She smiled a small, knowing smile, and he got the impression that he may have taken too long to look up, after all.

"Just some things Balen and Randolph were telling me."

She raised an eyebrow curiously, and he began to retell the story the two men had told him. Adina waited silently as he did, asking few questions, but he saw the anger gathering in her eyes like the first signs of darkening clouds before a thunderstorm. By the time he was finished, tears were winding their slow, meandering way down her face. "I didn't know it had gotten so bad," she said, her voice a dry, weak whisper, "With Eladen gone, the people must have had nowhere to turn. Claudius is a sniveling coward, a fat buffoon who cares only about himself, but I wouldn't have expected him to let the people starve. There are plenty of farms in the north—it doesn't make any sense." She shook her head slowly, wiping at her eyes, "I had no idea."

A surge of anger flared through him, and although Aaron knew it wasn't fair, he couldn't stop himself. "Why would you? You were too busy giving orders and living a life of luxury in your castle just like the rest of your brothers and sisters. How could you be bothered to know that the common folk were starving to death? They're nothing but cattle to people like you anyway."

She jumped as if struck and took a hasty step back. "That's not true! How can you say that?"

"How?" He growled, grabbing her roughly by the arms, "Because I *know,* that's how. My parents *died* because of people like you. Because of *nobles*, I spent the last years of my childhood getting beaten until I couldn't walk by an old bastard who loved his pipe more than his god. But that was fine wasn't it?" He sneered, "He paid his taxes to your father, didn't he? He kissed all the right asses, was invited to some of the best parties, and shit, he worked wonders for the orphan population, didn't he? Taking those poor, downtrodden girls and boys off the streets? Why, the man was almost a fucking *saint.*"

"Let go of me; you're hurting me," Adina gasped, but he wasn't listening. His mind was traveling back to those days so long ago, to the pain and the impotent rage that had been his constant companion.

He gripped her tighter as he moved closer so that his face was only inches from her, "And hey, if he made the occasional visit to a young orphan girl's room at night? If, during his nightly beatings, he managed to beat some of the younger, weaker boys too badly, so badly that the next day they were just gone? Disposed of like broken toys? Well, what does that matter? They're just orphans, right? Just *commoners.* Of course, no one would ever know anyway because no one ever fucking *asks.* Oh but you nobles care, don't you? Sure, you and your friends put on your new dresses and go to dinners and talk about how you pity the common man, about how you abhor his suffering. All the while, you sit your pampered asses on fluffed pillows and cover yourselves in silk, but at least you're *sorry*"

She tried to jerk away again, but he pulled her back with a growl. One of her arms moved, and before he knew it she was holding a small, thin blade against his throat. "I said let *go* of me."

He barked a harsh laugh, "Or what? You'll kill me?" He leaned against the blade, a feral grin splitting his face, and her eyes widened as blood welled up against his throat. "Go ahead, princess," he snarled, "Your kind have been killing my kind for years. Why stop now?"

She tried to pull away again, and this time he let her. "I hate you," She observed, her voice cold and calm despite the flush of red in her cheeks and forehead. She turned and started back toward the cabins.

"I'm surprised, princess," he called after her, "I didn't think us commoners mattered enough to warrant anything but your pity."

She stopped and stood with her back toward him for several seconds before looking back. "I came to tell you that Captain Leomin has asked us to dine with him two nights from now." Her voice was as hard as iron, as cold as the icy mountains of the north, yet he noticed that her hands were shaking.

"Speaking of us," he said, "where's your other servant?"

Her jaws clenched tightly, and she took a deep breath before answering. "Gryle says that he wasn't made for the sea. Based on the buckets he's gone through in the past hours, I'd be inclined to agree." She turned and walked away.

What was all that about? Co asked in his mind.

None of your business, firefly. He said, his eyes still locked on the door through which she'd gone.

She didn't deserve that, the Virtue admonished.

His smile had no humor in it. "If not her, then who? Besides, in my experience, lightning bug, people never get what they deserve." Despite his words, he'd taken two steps toward the door the princess had disappeared through, an apology on his lips, before he realized what he was doing. He hesitated, his hand on the door, mulling over the words he would say for several moments before her words from the night before ran through his head. *Don't try to act human now*, she'd said. And that was right, wasn't it? Commoners were nothing more than ill, misbegotten beasts to her and her kind, creatures placed on earth to serve and amuse them, easy targets for their sick, perverse indulgences.

After all, Cyrille hadn't always been alone in his nighttime frolics, had he? He'd often brought "friends," the same men who spoke with such eloquence about the plight of the commoner, men dressed in rich doublets and trousers, with arrogant swaggers, calculating smiles, and eyes colder than winter frost. He turned away from the door in disgust and walked away. He'd had his fill of nobles.

CHAPTER FOURTEEN

THE NEXT FEW DAYS aboard the *Clandestine* passed uneventfully for Aaron. Adina took pains to stay as far away from him as possible, and never once did the chamberlain venture out onto the deck, instead spending his time filling buckets as if he was getting paid to do it. As for the crew, the men were polite enough to Aaron's face, if in an off-handed, distracted sort of way. When he spoke to them, they answered, but they seemed to use as few words as possible, and always there was some urgent task that required their attention elsewhere. When they thought he wasn't looking, he saw them sizing him up as if spoiling for a fight. He wasn't much surprised; he had that effect on people.

As for Captain Leomin, Aaron hadn't seen the man venture onto the deck since he and the others boarded. He'd begun to think that the Parnen didn't plan on coming out of his cabin until they put into port when he finally showed himself. Aaron was standing at the edge of the ship, watching the moonlight reflect off the passing water like a field of shifting diamonds, as a skeleton crew of sailors saw to the ship's needs in what felt like brooding quiet. Somewhere out there, a ship was still following them, and despite the first mate's boasts of the

Clandestine's swiftness, the ship seemed to be gaining on them, though it could have been his imagination.

He was grimly wondering who would kill him first, Aster or Belgarin's men, when someone cleared their throat behind him. He turned, his hands balled into fists, expecting to find one of the sailors had finally decided to try his luck. Instead, he was surprised to see Captain Leomin standing before him. The Parnen was smiling widely, and what appeared to be small gold and silver bells twinkled in his long, dark hair. "Oh," Aaron grunted, "it's you."

Leomin smiled wider, "It is good that you are here to tell me. I had begun to wonder. Now, if only someone would tell me what it means to *be* me, I would be most thankful."

Aaron frowned, "Listen, I appreciate you taking us out of the Downs, but I'm not in the best mood, and if you don't have anything to say ..."

"Let us say, then, that I do have something to say," the man said, tilting his head first one way and then the other and setting the small bells to jingling as if to punctuate his words.

Aaron sighed. "Okay then." The captain grinned, saying nothing. "*Well?*"

"Oh!" The captain said as if surprised, "you mean now? Very well. Well, let me begin with a question for you, Aaron Envelar, formerly of the Downs. A riddle of sorts. What do all men, smugglers or kings, covet?"

"Silence?"

The captain's laugh was rich and mellifluous and despite himself, Aaron found that he had to fightt back a smile. "Money, Mr. Envelar," the captain whispered, as he stepped beside him and stared out at the sea. "Men covet money. Sure, there are other, passing lusts, but they soon lose their ... shall we say, luster. For an old man, late in his years, even beautiful women hold little appeal, but all men, young or old, rich or poor, covet money—even if they don't know what they would do with it if they had it. They yearn for it in the way an alcoholic craves a drink, or a sneak-thief a moonless night. Money, like power, is one of the ways in which all men are made or broken— one of the paths by which we are all tested."

"What are you talking about?" Aaron asked, realizing, with surprise, that he was interested in what the man had to say. Not for the first time, he was amazed by the fact that the man could speak complete nonsense, but do it in such a way that Aaron felt compelled to listen, as if he was some legendary prophet of old instead of the insane captain of a smuggler crew.

"I am *talking*," Leomin said, "about five thousand gold coins." Aaron tensed at that. The captain's smile was still in place, but it appeared wooden now, and it didn't touch the limpid depths of his eyes.

Five thousand gold coins. The *exact* amount that the man, Aster, had put on Aaron's head. He *knew*. Somehow, the man knew about the price Aster had put on Aaron's head. His hands drifted slowly toward the handles of the blades at his sides. How the captain had figured out didn't matter. What mattered was that he had, and that he was obviously planning on collecting. *Reliable my ass, May,* he thought.

"Relax," the captain said, his midnight gaze never leaving Aaron's, "we are two men talking, nothing more." He glanced around as if to make sure that none of the sailors had drifted within ear shot. "Still, such a sum would cause many men to act … crazy." Normally, such words coming from the odd Parnen would have been a cause for laughter, but Aaron had no time for humor. He was busy considering whether or not to draw his blades and slit the captain's throat. Maybe he was going to die, but he'd make damned sure he'd have company when he walked Salen's Fields. The Parnen smiled knowingly as if he could read the sellsword's thoughts.

"Well," Aaron growled, "so you know. What do you plan to do about it?"

The captain leaned back, and the bells in his hair set to tinkling once more. "Me?" He asked with a smile, "Why, I am the captain. I intend to do exactly what is best for those of us upon this vessel; we brave souls who have thrust ourselves into the mysterious depths of Sheza's playing ground, throwing caution to the winds and reservation to the waves." He gave a flourish of a silk-covered wrist, "In short, I intend to have dinner. Tomorrow night. You are, of course, going to attend?"

Aaron opened his mouth to tell the man that he'd rather attend his own execution, but the Parnen had already started away, waving his long hair, whistling along to the jingle of the bells as he headed below decks. "Five thousand gold coins," Aaron muttered to himself, still amazed at the sum. It was a funny thing to realize he was worth more dead than alive.

He glanced around at the sailors tending the rigging and working the lines. It could have just been his imagination, but he thought that they were glancing at him more frequently than what would be expected. And what was all that talk about men who were *untested?* What had that fool of a Parnen been trying to say? He realized, with a groan, that the best way to find out would be to accept the captain's invitation. "Son of a bitch." His mood quickly growing from bad to worse, he headed below decks.

CHAPTER FIFTEEN

THE FOLLOWING NIGHT, Aaron found himself outside the captain's cabin. *What throw of Iladen's dice has landed me here?* He thought miserably and not for the first time. Inside his head, Co giggled, but he did his best to ignore it as he reached out and knocked.

He heard grumbling from within and the door opened upon the Parnen captain. The man was frowning, "Yes, yes, welcome. Come in and be seated."

Aaron followed Leomin into a cabin that was at least eight times the size of his own. The air was redolent with the smell of cooked meat and vegetables. The room, like the captain himself, was adorned with ostentatious, glaring decorations of every possible color and shape. Ornately-made diamond chandeliers hung from the ceilings and drapes of richly colored cloths hung against the wall. Interspersed between these were several mounted animal skulls, many of which he didn't recognize. A massive, kingly table stood in the center of the room, and Adina sat in one of its high-backed chairs.

Ignoring the princess's scowl, Aaron walked across the room and took a seat across from her. The captain reclined leisurely in a chair at the head of the table, draping an arm over its back. "It is a poor, destitute time when a captain must *not only* open his own door to his guests, but must also serve his own food." The Parnen grumbled. "I've a mind to sit here until I wither away to a dry husk. Perhaps *that* would teach Balen the error of neglecting his duties." He glanced at the princess knowingly, "Good help is *so* hard to find these days. After all, what good is a first mate if the man can't even serve dinner on time?"

"I'm sure, Captain Leomin, that Balen has some good excuse for being unable to attend," Adina tried carefully.

Leomin rolled his eyes with a sigh, "Oh please. 'Sir,'" he began in a terribly inaccurate mimicry of Balen's thick accent, "The lads tell me that the ship that's been following us is closing in, and I must see to it." He snorted, "An obvious attempt to shirk his duties." He shook his head in annoyance, and Aaron was thankful that the captain had at least taken the bells out of his hair. He was sure that if he'd had to listen to them jingling through the entire dinner he would have taken his sword to the Parnen and damn the consequences.

"It's as if the man was born without any sense of decorum, whatsoever!" The captain exclaimed.

Aaron cleared his throat. "It seems to me that evading that ship would be more important than having a servant for dinner."

The captain nodded pityingly, "It is precisely *because,* my dear sellsword, you have never had a servant, that you would even contemplate such a statement. Forgive me, but through no fault of your own—a man without servants can't be expected to understand them—you lack experience, and therefore credibility, in this particular area."

He opened his mouth to tell the captain just what he could do with his experience and credibility, but the princess spoke first. "Do not let it bother you, Captain Leomin. I suspect that there are *many* areas in which Mr. Envelar lacks experience. Particularly," she said, shooting an angry glance at Aaron, "areas involving any type of human interaction that doesn't involve stabbing someone or hitting them over the head with a wine bottle."

Aaron smiled his best, most winning smile at her, "Well, it's kind of you to say so, princess. I find people easier to deal with when there's a blade at their throat, and I've made some of my best friends from wine bottles."

"I didn't think you had any friends," she snapped back, all pretenses of decorum gone.

Captain Leomin cleared his throat, "Yes, well. I am sure that we can come to some sort of agreement on the matter. As for her part, the princess is correct that men—in general, mind—are less sensitive to the human arts than the fairer sex." He resolutely ignored the scowl Aaron directed on him and pressed on hastily with the air of a man trying to avoid a war, "As to Mr. Envelar's point, I must agree that I, too, find men most agreeable after they have been thoroughly stabbed. Less useful, perhaps, but certainly more ... *pliant.*"

"Yes," Adina hissed, "and better to knock women over the heads with clubs than to imagine that they have their own *opinions* isn't that right, Aaron?"

He grinned again and shrugged, "You won't get any argument from me."

Her face turning a deep crimson, the princess was starting out of her seat when the captain rose, "Yes, yes," he said as if oblivious to the argument, "let us all have a toast." Aaron rose, smiling, and lifted his wine glass. He wondered, idly, whether the captain himself or the princess had poured it. If it was the latter, he suspected strongly that it would have spit in it, but he refused to let his discomfort show as he held out the glass to the captain's own.

Adina's eyes narrowed at him, but after a moment she reluctantly lifted her own glass from the table and touched it to the others. The captain let out an audible sigh of relief before he spoke, "A toast. To new friends who we pray will not be enemies, to old enemies who we pray are not friends, and to old friends, who are," he glanced meaningfully at Aaron, "most certainly, the worst of enemies."

Aaron and the princess turned away from each other, their anger momentarily forgotten as they tried to work out exactly *what* they were toasting. The captain sat his glass, now drained, down on the table. Finally, Aaron shrugged and drank, and Adina followed suit.

They all had just seated themselves again when there was a knock on the door. The captain let out an angry huff, "Who is it?" He shouted. The door opened, and a grim-looking Balen walked in.

"Sir, sorry to disturb you, but—"

"I sincerely doubt that, Balen," Leomin said, frowning, "but what is it that requires my attention so much that I must risk total and utter destruction at the hands of *starvation* to see to it?"

The first mate bowed his head in apology, "It's the ship, sir. They've caught us."

"Impossible!" Leomin exclaimed, "Why, they'd have to be, well ... *faster* than us to do that."

Balen blinked and nodded slowly, "Yes sir."

Leomin sighed heavily, "Well, I do suppose such a craft *may* exist, though I suspect it all the more likely that you drank milk before bed—you do know how it gives you strange dreams."

The first mate continued as if the captain hadn't spoke, "They say that they want us to hand over our passengers to them." He shot an apologetic look at Aaron and the princess, "The man aboard, a man that goes by the name of Aster, has promised five thousand gold pieces to each of us in return for the three of them."

Go ahead and try it, Aaron thought. He liked the old first mate—as much as he liked anyone, that was—but the man was crazy if he thought Aaron would just be handed over for his execution like a misbehaving child to be punished.

He was just about to get out of his chair and draw his blades when Co spoke in his mind, *Wait. Let's see what the captain says.*

Fine, Aaron thought, *but if we wind up as shark shit you've only yourself to blame.*

The Parnen raised his eyebrow curiously, "And what is to be the consequence should we fail in this ... *request*?"

Balen made a sound in his throat, "He says he'll kill us all."

Leomin rolled his eyes, "How crass. Tell me, Balen, have we, as sailors of Sheza's mighty seas, accepted these, our passengers, in good faith?"

The first mate grinned widely, "Yes sir, we have."

The captain nodded distractedly, "And is it, thereby, in your personal and professional opinion, our duty to see to their safety as best we are able while they yet reside among the *Clandestine?*"

The man nodded again, "Yes sir, it is."

Leomin stared hard at the first mate, and Aaron was sure that he saw anger flash in the Parnen's gaze, but when he spoke, his voice was as calm as ever, "Very well. It seems there is nothing left for us, but to regretfully decline this Aster's offer."

Balen nodded, "Of course, sir. I will tell him that you will speak to him in a moment."

The captain snorted a laugh, "And ruin a perfectly good dinner? Truly, Balen, sometimes your lack of decorum astounds me. No," he said, shaking his head, "it would be nothing short of criminal to let this meal—one which Henry sweated and toiled over I do not doubt—go to waste."

"Very well, sir. I will see to it." The first mate bowed his head first to the captain, then to the others, before turning and walking out the door.

"Curious," Leomin muttered to himself as the door closed behind the departing first mate, "truly curious." He seemed to be in deep thought for a moment before finally turning to Adina, "I wonder, princess, where is your man? Oh, what was his name, Eddard?"

"Gryle. He's not feeling well, captain. He has been battling sea-sickness since we boarded the ship, and I fear that he would be poor company just now."

The Parnen captain nodded slowly, rubbing a hand across his chin, "Right, Gryle. Still, it would do us quite well to have a servant present. Yes, quite well. Would you be so kind as to ask him if he would join us?"

The princess frowned, turning first to Aaron then to Leomin, "Now?"

"Now?" The captain asked as if she'd suggested it, "why, yes," he said, nodding thoughtfully, "I think that would be for the best."

Aaron expected the princess to say no, and he was surprised to see her nodding thoughtfully. "Well," she said, "I suppose it would do Gryle good to get out of that room. Still, I'm not sure—"

"It's settled then," Leomin said rising. He moved to slide Adina's chair out from behind her, and she had no choice but to stand, "I beg of you, do not be gone long, my dear, sweet lady, for we shall both be lessened by your departure."

"Speak for yourself," Aaron muttered, and the princess shot him an angry look before allowing herself to be led out the door.

Leomin looked down both sides of the hall before closing the door and sitting back down at the table. "There. Now, we may talk freely, or, at least, as free as any one man ever may to another, constrained as we are by those around us." He frowned and glanced around the room as if expecting to find someone hiding behind one of the cloth tapestries, "Those who sit idly by, listening, and waiting." After a moment, he turned and met Aaron's gaze. Gone, was the absent-minded look Aaron had begun to associate with the man. For the first time since he'd met the captain, the Parnen appeared completely focused. Focused and troubled. "For there are always those *listening,* waiting to see what we will say, what we will do, do you not agree, Mr. Envelar?"

Aaron growled in frustration, "There is a ship of men who have just threatened to kill you and your crew, and you talk gibberish? By the gods, what is the matter with you?"

"They do not threaten to kill *all* of the crew, Mr. Envelar," the captain replied calmly, "or at least, they would not, I think. As for the crew being mine, you are wrong. They have not been mine for some weeks now—if they ever were—a possibility that I have grown to seriously doubt."

"What are you talking about?" Aaron asked. "Of course they're your crew. You're their captain."

The Parnen revealed his bright white teeth in a humorless smile, "And yet, they are not my crew."

"I don't have time for this," Aaron growled as he rose from the table and started for the door.

"I wonder, Mr. Envelar, have you ever had a best friend?" The captain asked, his voice low and thoughtful, "One that you trusted implicitly?"

Aaron sighed heavily and turned back to the captain, "How is that any of your business?"

"Humor me, please," the captain said, meeting Aaron's eyes with a penetrating stare. Unbidden, memories of his childhood began to crowd into the

Aaron's mind. Before the orphanage, most of his life had been spent in various military camps. While his father ordered drills and commanded Prince Eladen's armies in battle, Aaron spent his time being tutored with other kids who were the sons or daughters of soldiers in Eladen's army. The fact that his father had been the commander of the fathers of the other children hadn't helped Aaron make friends.

At best, the other kids had avoided him in the same way that experienced stable-hands avoided walking up behind horses. It wasn't that they were certain the horses *would* kick, only that they *could.* At worst, the kids—most often the sons or daughters of soldiers his father had reprimanded—took every opportunity they could to make his life a study of torture. Their methods ranged widely, from slipping Rabelia petals into his drinks, so that he spent the rest of the afternoon puking his guts out, to lining his chair with sap from a Satley bush, so that he stuck to it and was only able to stand after ripping large, ragged patches in the seat of his pants.

No one ever came forward to claim responsibility for the tricks, of course. They had laughed and talked about him when they thought he wasn't listening, but they would never take the credit. After all, he *was* the son of General Envelar. In truth, he hadn't had any friends until after his parents were killed and then only one.

For the first time in years, he thought of Owen. After his first beating at the orphanage, as pain traced its way along the wounded flesh of his back like wildfire, he'd been lying on his small cot (on his stomach, of course) filled with anger and trying not to weep. It was then that the door to his room had opened and a small, sickly-looking boy walked inside and introduced himself. In his pain and anger, embarrassed by the tears leaking out of his eyes, Aaron shouted at him, using every threat he could think of to make the boy leave. But he didn't. Instead, Owen had rubbed some sort of sharp-smelling unguent on the wounds, and as he did, explained to Aaron how best to avoid the Headmaster and, therefore, the regular beatings that he administered to his young charges.

Aaron had listened then, though mostly because the unguent did an incredible job of numbing the almost unbearable pain the headmaster's strap had left in its wake, but as time went by he listened and talked to the small boy more and more and eventually they became friends. They would wander the grounds of the orphanage in their rare moments of spare time, talking about their dead parents, dreaming about the days when they would become soldiers or fishermen or even farmers—anything but orphans.

It was their friendship, more than anything, which sustained Aaron through his first year at the orphanage. Knowing Owen made life under Cyrille's twisted reign bearable. That was, at least, until a few months after Aaron's year anniversary at the orphanage. He'd been one of the headmaster's recent picks for a switching, and he lay in his room, his back bloody and raw, his anger building, until the headmaster left to visit one of his noble friends.

When he was gone, Aaron crept to the tool shed and retrieved a hammer and a pickaxe, his fury helping him to ignore the sharp burning agony that traced itself across his back. Owen pleaded with him, warned him of the consequences, but Aaron was too furious to listen, and he left his friend behind as he snuck into the priest's personal chambers and systematically tore them apart. He broke the expensive oak desk into kindling, ripped the costly mattress apart and scattered the soft white stuffing across the room. He smashed several small statuettes and figurines—gifts from some of the headmaster's noble friends—until the piles of porcelain and glass that were scattered across the floor were completely unrecognizable. He kept at it until his hands bled from gripping the pick-axe, until his shirt was soaked in hot sweat and fresh blood. And then he kept going. By the time he returned the tools and crawled into bed, a satisfied, weary smile on his face, the headmaster's quarters looked as if a pack of rabid jackals had been let loose inside.

The next day, he was assigned to work in the garden with several other boys while Owen—who was weakly and often sick—was sent to help the girls with the laundry. The headmaster enjoyed taunting Owen because of his small size, and the task was just another way of going about it. Aaron spent the day constantly shooting glances over his shoulder as he pulled weeds and dug holes, sure that he would turn to see the headmaster with his switch in hand, his old, wrinkled face twisted with rage.

It was with some surprise, then, that the day passed uneventfully. Night came and, giddy with relief, Aaron shuffled into the bedroom he shared with several other boys, too exhausted from worry and relief to meet with Owen and sneak around the grounds as they often did after lights out. It wasn't until the following morning that he learned that his friend wouldn't have been waiting at their spot even if Aaron *had* gone to meet him. The headmaster had, indeed, went wild with rage when he saw what had been done to his personal quarters. He'd stormed into the cafeteria during lunch (Aaron had taken his in the garden), frothing at the mouth like a wild animal, laying about himself with the hateful leather switch, cracking noses and blacking eyes as he demanded to know who was responsible.

From what Aaron was told later, someone had mentioned his name. The headmaster had turned and started toward the gardens when Owen jumped up and took the blame on himself, claiming that he'd destroyed the headmaster's quarters alone. The terrified kids could do nothing but watch as the headmaster dragged the boy out of the room, hitting him as he went. No one ever saw Owen again.

Despite his size, or perhaps in part because of it, Owen had been well liked among the kids at the orphanage. He'd been a kind person, kind and innocent, and the other children often assured each other in quiet whispers that he'd escaped, that he'd found a good family to take care of him. It was a lie, of course, and they all knew it, but they said it just the same. The truth was that

Aaron had awakened the headmaster's fury, and his friend had suffered—had died—because of it.

He felt a knot growing in his throat and forced the sadness away with a growl. Owen hadn't deserved what had happened to him, but so what? It was the way of the world. The powerful took what they wanted and the weak suffered. He turned to the captain and when he spoke his voice was tight with emotion, "Yes. I've had a friend before."

Leomin nodded, as if no time had passed at all between his question and Aaron's answer, "I've had a few in my time as well—two, to be exact. I wonder, Mr. Envelar, what would you do if you were to learn that your friend, a man who you thought you could trust with anything, had betrayed you?"

"He wouldn't." Aaron answered at once, surprised by the anger in his own voice.

"Let us assume, for the sake of argument," Leomin said, "that he did."

Aaron considered the question. His first thought would be to make the man suffer, but he thought of Owen, thought of the boy's shy smile, and that first night, where he'd spent the better part of an hour rubbing the numbing unguent on Aaron's wounds. "I don't know."

The captain nodded, satisfied. "We are not so very different then, you and I."

Aaron barked a laugh, "If you say so."

Leomin's mouth turned up in a humorless grin, "I do indeed." He was starting to say something else when the floor lurched beneath them, spilling them from their chairs. After a few dizzying moments in which Aaron was sure he was going to puke, the ship stabilized. The captain climbed nimbly to his feet, dusting off his fancy clothes with an annoyed sniff.

"What in the name of the gods was that?" Aaron said as he rose on unsteady legs and glanced at the spilled silverware lying in the floor.

The captain rolled his eyes with a sigh, "That, I suspect, is our friend Aster boarding us."

"*Boarding* us?" Aaron growled, drawing his blades, "I thought you said he couldn't catch us."

"Normally, he could not. Alas ..." The captain shrugged casually, not bothering to finish his sentence.

"Alas *what?* Is your ship faster or isn't it?"

Leomin stared at him as if he'd just discovered the man he was talking to wasn't right in the head and gave a long-suffering sigh, "Do you not yet know? We have been betrayed, Aaron Envelar. *I* have been betrayed." Suddenly, the cabin's door flew open. In the same instant, the captain whipped a rapier from somewhere under the table with a speed Aaron wouldn't have credited him and pointed it at the newcomer. "Ah, it is our dear princess and her man," he said in a calm, welcoming voice as he let the rapier's point fall, "I am glad that you could make it. Things are about to get ... shall we say, interesting."

The chamberlain's face was pale and covered in sweat, and he covered his mouth with one hand as Adina led him into the room by the other. "Just what is going on here?" She demanded, "what was that? I nearly broke my neck."

"Aster and his men coming aboard," Aaron said, "apparently the crew have taken it upon themselves to overrule the captain's decision.

The princess's eyes went wide, "They can't do that!" She exclaimed incredulously.

"Well, you're more than welcome to tell *them* that, *Your Highness*, but I don't think they're in the mood to listen."

The princess turned to Leomin, "What are we going to do?"

The captain was just opening his mouth to speak when Balen barged through the door. "You!" Leomin hissed, his normally amiable face twisted in rage. He sprang forward, lightning fast, and was about to plunge the blade into the man's chest when he came to an abrupt stop.

"Balen?" The Parnen asked, confused. It was then that Aaron realized what Leomin was staring at. Balen's hands were clasped against his stomach and blood was leaking out between his fingers.

"S-sir," The first mate groaned, "y-you've got to get out of here. It's—"

"Captain, stay away from him!" Randolph exclaimed as he rushed into the room, a crude, blood-smeared sword in his hand. "Balen is a traitor. He's sold us out."

Balen tried to speak, but he couldn't seem to force the words out as he slipped down to his knees with a pained sigh. Leomin only stared at him, "Why, Balen? Why? I trusted you above all others."

The first mate tried to talk again, but his words turned into a wracking cough as he hacked out blood, swaying weakly.

"Let me finish him, sir," Randolph said, stepping forward.

Leomin stared between the two men, his expression thoughtful. Finally, he nodded grimly. The second mate started forward, and Aaron winced in anticipation, but just as Randolph was raising his sword, Leomin exploded in a burst of movement, lunging forward with the rapier and stabbing it through the hawk-faced man's chest.

Randolph let out a shriek of surprised pain, and his sword dropped to the ground as he took in the length of steel impaling him with wide, disbelieving eyes.

With a sneer of contempt, the captain ripped the blade free, and Randolph fell to his knees beside Balen, his face a mask of confusion and agony as he stared up at the captain. The Parnen leaned in close, his voice little more than a whisper, "Did you think I wouldn't know?" He asked, genuine surprise in his voice. He gave the wounded man a push and Randolph crumpled to the floor. "I have been stupid, yet you must think me a complete fool to believe that I wouldn't notice your deceit when it was right under my nose." The second mate opened his mouth to speak, but before he could the captain's arm whipped forward again and his blade pierced the man's heart.

Randolph convulsed once and then lay still. Leomin sighed and turned back to Aaron and the others, "You must go. They will be here in moments. I will see to Balen."

Aaron didn't bother pointing out that, judging by the amount of blood covering the first mate's shirt and pants, the only person likely to be seeing to him in the near future was Salen himself. "Love to," He said, forcing his eyes away from the now unconscious first mate, "but unless this ship's got a back door then I'd say we're pretty well screwed."

Leomin nodded, walked over to the wall and pulled aside a blue and gold tapestry revealing a small door. He turned back to the others a hint of his usual smile appearing at the look of surprise on their faces, "Any captain worth his salt knows that it's always good to have a backup plan. Follow the corridor; it will eventually come out on the side of the ship where, hopefully, a rowboat awaits your departure."

"Hopefully?" Aaron asked with a frown.

"Just so," the captain said, staring at his unconscious first mate, "Hoping is the best any of us can do, Mr. Envelar." They all turned at the distant sound of approaching footsteps in the hall. "Quickly now unless you wish to be this Aster's guest tonight. I suspect he will not be as pleasant a host as myself—not that many are."

"Alright then," Aaron said as the footsteps drew closer, "time to go." He opened the door onto a dark corridor. When he looked back, the captain was kneeling beside Balen, tearing off a piece of his own shirt to staunch the flow of blood from the man's wound. Gryle was staring wide-eyed at the first mate, his mouth working soundlessly. "Gryle!" The man didn't answer. "*Chamberlain!*"

The fat man jumped as if struck then turned to Aaron with a terrified expression. Aaron beckoned him and Gryle hurried past him and into the corridor. Adina started forward as well but stopped at the door. She turned and looked back at the captain, "Come with us. They'll kill you both if they find you here."

Leomin smiled at her, but there was a hardness in his eyes and voice that surprised Aaron with its strength, "Don't count us out yet, princess. The *Clandestine* is hard to catch, but those few who have caught her have lived to regret it. Besides," he said, his voice regaining its distracted, almost whimsical quality, "a good captain never abandons his ship."

She hesitated on the threshold before finally slipping past Aaron and into the darkness. *They're coming, Aaron,* Co said in his head. He started into the corridor but turned back, "Good luck, Captain."

"And to you," Leomin answered as he cradled the first mate's head in one hand and held the bandage to his stomach with the other. "Perhaps we will meet again."

Not likely, Aaron thought. "He's a good man," he said, glancing at Balen.

Leomin looked up at him, unshed tears glistening in his eyes, "Yes, and a good friend."

"You're sure you don't—"

"I'm sure, Mr. Envelar."

Aaron nodded then, reluctantly, he turned away from the two men, shut the door behind him, and followed the others into the waiting darkness.

CHAPTER SIXTEEN

THE ONLY SOUNDS IN THE PITCH-black corridor were those of Gryle's panicked breaths and the steady susurration of the ocean currents. As they walked, Aaron kept glancing over his shoulder expecting to see the faint light of the door being opened as Aster's men charged after them, but there was only him and the others and the darkness that wrapped around them, hugging them tight. After what felt like hours, they came to a dead end. Squinting, Aaron could just make out the light of the moon as it came through cracks in what must be the opening. *Tricky bastard, that Leomin,* he thought, shaking his head. From the outside, the door, he was sure, would look like any other part of the ship.

He hurried forward, dug his fingers into the thin crack, and heaved. At first, the wood refused to budge, but after a strained, anxious moment, the door gave and began to slide open. Aaron was mildly surprised to find the boat waiting, just as the captain said it would be. The man seemed a good enough sort, and clearly his men loved him, but Aaron was still reasonably sure he was mad. Clever, true, but mad nonetheless.

He followed the others into the boat. The two ropes that held it aloft ran through a winch mounted on the craft. He grabbed hold of the winch's lever and began to lower them down to the distant water, wincing as the unoiled, damp metal squeaked in protest. The wind was heavy, blowing his hair around wildly and rocking the boat as they descended, and in the darkness he could barely see the others around him. He was glad of that darkness, though. Better that than that bastard Aster and his men spot them.

Finally, after what felt like an eternity spent floating in a sea of night, the boat settled into the water. He unfastened the rope from the winch, grabbed the oars, and began to row. "Aaron," the princess began.

"Shh," he said softly, "not yet." There was little chance of them being heard over the gusting wind and the roiling water, but he wasn't about to take a chance, not when they were so close to escaping.

He continued to work the oars, and it wasn't until the ship was little more than a distant smudge on the dark horizon that the princess spoke again. "Aaron?"

"What is it?" He asked between strokes.

"Do you think ... the captain and Balen—"

"They'll be fine." He said, knowing it was a lie even as he said it, "Leomin's a crazy bastard, but he's a clever one too. He wouldn't have left himself no way out."

She considered this in silence for a moment, then, "Where are we going?"

He shrugged before realizing she wouldn't be able to see the gesture in the darkness. "According to what Balen told me, the *Clandestine* was taking a course mostly parallel to the eastern coast. If we continue in this direction, we should end up on land before long. As for where that will be ... only Iladen knows." He left it unsaid that if they'd gone too far north, they ran the risk of running into a ship that owed its allegiance to Belgarin. And wouldn't *that* be interesting?

They pressed on through the night, taking the oars in shifts, so that they each had a chance to rest. Aaron was pretty sure they lost more than they gained on Gryle's turns, but the look of determined effort on the chamberlain's face, combined with his own mounting exhaustion, kept him from saying so.

Time dragged on like a dying animal as they continued, and each of the three constantly glanced behind them in fear that Aster would be giving chase. The sun had been in the sky for over an hour, and Aaron was resting, lying back in the small boat as best he could, his eyes closed against the painfully bright reflection of the sun on the water, when Adina's voice raised in excitement, "Look!" She was taking her turn at the oars. Early in the night, Gryle had offered to take both her shift as well as his own, but the princess had declined. It was possible that she wanted to do her fair share but Aaron thought it more likely that he wasn't the only one who'd noticed the chamberlain's lack of skill.

Gryle, who'd been curled up in the bottom of the boat and snoring heavily, jerked up and managed to whip his head in every direction except the one that Adina was indicating. "What's wrong?" He asked, "did they find us—" He stopped speaking as he finally noticed what Adina and Aaron were already looking at—a rough, rocky shore and, further in, a forest of trees. No people in sight, but what did that matter? It was land. Aaron grinned. Despite the chamberlain's best efforts, they'd made it back to land.

Another hour passed before they made it to the shore and clambered out of the row boat onto wobbly, unsure legs. Once they'd stretched their weary backs and muscles, Aaron looked around and took stock of their surroundings. Large oaks and pines loomed overhead, their leaves stirring under a gentle breeze. Here and there, birds flitted through the treetops, singing happily. "Where are we?" Adina asked from beside him.

He shrugged, still smiling, "Only one way to find out."

"Surely you don't mean *now*," Gryle said, "we haven't slept or ate, and I err ... that is ... the princess needs to rest."

Adina shared a glance with Aaron before turning to the chamberlain, "I *am* tired, Gryle, but I think I can make it, truly. Besides, who knows? There may be a town close. I know it doesn't matter much to you men, but I would much rather sleep on a bed than the hard ground."

Gryle frowned, considering. Finally, he nodded, "If you say so, Mistress."

Aaron nodded, "That settles it then." He started toward the forest and the others followed after.

"Of course, we will need to make sure to take breaks," Gryle huffed behind him, "it wouldn't do for the princess to tire herself unnecessarily."

Aaron ignored the man as he pressed on under the canopy of trees, still amazed that they'd made it away from Aster. He felt like a man sentenced to death that awakens on the fateful day to discover that his executioner has come down with a bad case of the shits and that he'll have to reschedule. Still doomed, sure, still on his way to the gallows, but for now his feet were on steady, unmoving land, the air in his lungs was crisp and clean, and that was fine. And if the first mate Balen and the Parnen captain had suffered for helping him, well that wasn't his fault, and the tightness in his chest was nothing more than sore muscles complaining from overuse. It wasn't the first lie he'd told himself, and it wouldn't be the last.

CHAPTER SEVENTEEN

THEY TRAVELED A STRAIGHT COURSE through the densely-wooded forest, often forced to push their way through bushes and climb over fallen trees. After a few hours, they came upon a well-worn wagon trail. They followed it for another hour, and Aaron was seriously considering the pros and cons of strangling the complaining chamberlain when they came to the entrance of a small town. A sign on the trail named it Kaser. *Town my ass,* Aaron thought, glancing around him at the dirt path and ramshackle buildings. As a sellsword, he'd spent most of his time in cities. After all, the more people in a place, the better the chances that someone would pay good coin to hire a man like himself. The small, spare buildings and nearly deserted streets of the place made him feel far more conspicuous than he liked. "Watch yourself, Gryle," he murmured as an old woman scowled menacingly at them from the door of a nearby house, "this is the type of place where they make sausages out of people."

The chamberlain's cherubic features twisted in alarm, "Y-you're kidding, aren't you, sir?

Aaron shrugged, "I guess we'll see."

Ignoring the chamberlain's squeak of fear, he started through the town. They passed a few women washing clothes in big basins and hanging them to dry. In the distance fields, they could just make out men hard at work, tending their crops. The princess tried to speak to several of the villagers but instead of words of greeting, the travelers received cold, sullen stares and silence.

"These people don't know royalty when they see it," Aaron observed with a laugh after the princess tried to speak to several women working in a garden and was chased off by a barrage of curses and rotten tomatoes.

"I don't understand it," the princess said as she wiped some of the stinking evidence of her latest attempt off of her shirt, apparently too bewildered to take offense, "what's wrong with all of them?"

Aaron shrugged, "Guess they don't like tomatoes." Before the princess could respond, he started through the town again and after a time they came to a squat building that was considerably larger than the simple homes. A sign hung above the door. *"The Cows Utter,"* Aaron read aloud, shaking his head. "You've got to be shitting me."

He stepped inside and was greeted by the smells he'd grown to associate with bars: ale, sweat, cigar smoke and, beneath it all, the faint but distinct miasmas of decades of urine and vomit. Ignoring the angry, suspicious stares of the patrons that sat scattered about the room, he walked to the bar and took a seat, the others following behind him.

The man tending the counter was incredibly thin with sallow, sunken cheeks and hands that would have looked more at home on a skeleton than a living person. He turned at the sound of their approach, his mouth twisting in disgust as if he'd just found maggots crawling in his apple pie, "What do you want?"

Aaron shrugged, trying a smile, "A drink would be nice."

The man grunted, "We're all out," he said then turned away and began busying himself with cleaning the bottle racks behind the counter.

Aaron glanced at a nearby table where four men in tattered clothes watched him darkly over full mugs of ale, before looking back to the bartender. "Let's try this again. My name's Aaron. What's yours?"

The thin man turned with a scowl and leaned close to Aaron, "Listen, mister," he began in a whisper, "You see those men over there?" He indicated the four men with a nod of his head. "That's Glenn and the boys. Now, Glenn ain't got much patience for your kind, and in another minute or two he's gonna come over and let ya know it. I've got half a mind to let it happen myself, but this here inn's all I got. It's the only thing you bastards ain't managed to take yet, and I don't want it broken up on account of you. So, how about you forget the drink and get your ass out of here while you still got an ass to take with ya?"

"What do you mean *our* kind?" Adina asked, more confused than angry.

The bartender turned to her, "Look, lady, we might not be as book learnt as some of you city folk, but we ain't stupid either. This is a small town. We don't get a lot of visitors. By that I mean we don't get *any* visitors, 'sept, of course, when that bastard Claudius decides to send one like yourself to take what little we have. 'Taxes for the good o' the people' he calls it while our children go hungry. Well, we ain't got nothin' left for you bastards to take, you understand? Now do yourselves a favor and walk out that door while you still can."

Aaron was just considering what the bartender said, wondering at the speed of the *Clandestine* to have brought them so far in such a short time that they'd made it into Eladen's—*Claudius's*—territory, when a voice rose from the table at the end of the room. *"Hey. Hey, you."*

The bartender shook his head, as if to say he'd warned them, but Aaron didn't miss the small, cruel smile on the man's face. "Too late."

Aaron rose from his stool and regarded the four men as they approached. The largest of them walked in front. Judging by the man's broad shoulders and stocky frame, Aaron supposed that he'd been formidable once, but lack of good food to eat had taken its toll, and he looked withered, wasted, as did the other three men behind him. "Glenn, I presume?"

"You got it." The man said, popping his knuckles.

Aaron glanced at the man then around the room. He thought about telling him that he had it all wrong, that they hadn't been sent by Claudius but decided against it. Glenn and the three with him had already decided they were going to have a fight, and it would take more than the truth to change their minds. Not that he could much blame them. Fighting wouldn't fill their bellies, wouldn't take away the drawn, shrunken look of them or take away their hunger—something he knew from experience—but it *would* make them forget it for a time and sometimes that was as much as a man could ask. He sighed heavily, "Alright." He beckoned the men forward, "Come on then. Let's get this over with so I can have my drink."

"You prick bastard," Glenn growled, starting forward.

"Wait," Adina said, stepping forward, "we're not here for your money. Aaron, tell them!"

"I don't think they've a mind to listen just now," he said his eyes shifting as the men fanned out around them.

Then make them, Co said in a matter of fact tone as if it were the simplest thing in the world.

Great idea, firefly. They look like reasonable people. I'm sure, if we promise them that we really really mean it, they'll believe us.

Listen, Co said in his mind, and he gasped and stumbled backward, barely managing to catch himself against the bar, as a storm of emotions swept over him with the force of a hurricane. Anger was a part of that storm, as was a grim satisfaction at being able to fight back, to hurt someone else, but they weren't the biggest part. The biggest part was a bitter, wretched grief that nearly buckled his knees. A wave of grief so high, so powerful, that it threatened to drown him and, spread throughout it, riding on the crest of it and churning in its depths, a name. Someone's name. Something, some—

"Marla." Aaron gasped, feeling as if the name had been ripped out of him, "her name's Marla." Glenn and the other men froze, staring at him with wide, frightened eyes.

"What the fuck did you just say?" Glenn asked, his voice little more than a whisper.

Aaron grabbed his temples against the impossible pressure that was building there, searching in that roiling maze of emotions, of feelings, for more. "I-it's your daughter," he said, "Marla. She's sick, isn't she?"

Someone in the inn cursed. Someone else, Aaron thought it was the bartender, called on the name of Nalesh, Father of the Gods, and keeper of the world, in a hoarse whisper. Glenn glanced nervously at his friends before turning back to Aaron. The anger was gone from his expression, replaced by a wary confusion. "How ... how could you know that?"

"No, not just sick," Aaron said, wincing as the man's emotions pushed against him, "dying. She's dying, isn't she, Glenn?" It's the medicine. You were saving for the medicine, but the tax collectors, they took it didn't they? They took it all. But she doesn't have to die, Glenn. You can still save her. It's not too late."

"What do you know of it?" The man said, his voice bitter, "Claudius increased taxes, said that if we didn't pay we'd lose our land, but if I lose my land, how am I gonna pay? How am I ever gonna get her the medicine she needs?"

Aaron breathed a sigh of relief as the roiling sea of emotions receded, and he wiped an arm across his forehead that was suddenly bathed in sweat. "How much does it cost?" He asked, leaning against the bar, suddenly feeling more exhausted than if he'd run for miles. For a moment, the big man just looked at him stupidly. "The medicine, Glenn. How much does it cost?"

"Seventy gold," Glenn finally said and there were grumbles of discontent from around the room.

Seventy gold, Aaron thought, surprised. No wonder the man was pissed. That was more money than most farmers made in a year's worth of work. Only half conscious of what he was doing, he reached into his pocket and withdrew the small bag he'd been carrying, tossing it to the man who caught it with a look of surprise that turned to confusion as he heard the unmistakable jingle of the coins inside. "There's a touch over two hundred gold there, Glenn. Make sure that Marla gets all the help she needs, alright?"

Glenn's eyes narrowed suspiciously. Slowly, as if he expected a snake to jump out at him, he reached into the bag, and he grunted in surprise as he withdrew a handful of gold coins. "W-w-why?" He asked, "Why would you do this?"

"Because I know what it's like to watch someone you love die and not be able to do anything about it," Aaron said, thinking of his mother and father lying in pools of their own blood," and because, like the lady said, we're not tax collectors."

"Thank you," The big man breathed, his face working with emotion, "Thank you." Abruptly, the hard lines of his face disappeared beneath a wide smile, "I'll go right now! You hear that?" He shouted, looking around at the stunned expressions of the others in the inn, "She's going to be okay." After a moment, the stunned silence turned into clapping and cheers, but Aaron doubted Glenn heard; he was already running toward the door and barreling through it with a speed and strength Aaron wouldn't have credited him with. *Just as well I didn't have to fight them,* he thought. Then a hand touched him on the shoulder, and he turned to see the barkeeper looking shamefaced, his eyes studying the ground.

"I uh ... I'm sorry, mister. I had you wrong. I thought you were one of those tax collector assholes."

"Oh, I'm an asshole alright," Aaron said with a small smile, "Just not one of those assholes."

Several of the people in the crowd laughed at that, nodding at him and grinning as if they'd all been friends for years. *Always surprising,* he thought as he nodded back, *how a little money can change things.*

And a little kindness, Co spoke in his mind.

Let's not go too far, firefly. "We all thank you for helping Glenn, stranger," the bartender said, ringing his hands like a man who's trying to explain to his wife that the maid just *happened* to fall into the bed and, no, no he didn't have any idea why her shirt had come off and her skirts were bunched around her waist. "Kaser's a small town," the man continued, "and like a lot of small towns, I guess we look at one another like family. Glenn weren't the only one shed a tear or two over little Marla; I can promise you that." Several of the bar's patrons voiced their agreement to this. "We took up donations," the bartender continued, "but truth to tell, it's all we can do to eat, and we can't do much of that, what with the way Claudius has been taxin' us to the bone." The man's eyebrows drew down thoughtfully, "Still, I'd be mighty interested in how you knew about little Marla, what with you bein' a stranger and all."

Aaron froze for a minute then, finally, he shrugged, "A man gets a certain look when he's got a sick loved one. As for knowing the girl's name, well, I heard some folks talking about it on my way through town."

The bartender let out a self-deprecating laugh, "Course you did," he said shaking his head, "course you did. I mean how else could you've known?"

Aaron smiled, "How else?"

The man reached across the counter and offered his hand. "Name's Herbert Barton. Folks 'round here just call me Herb."

"Nice to meet you, Herb. I'm Aaron," he said, shaking the man's hand and taking his seat at the bar once more, "Now, how about that drink?"

CHAPTER EIGHTEEN

ADINA WATCHED, STUNNED, as Aaron and the bartender, Herb, talked and joked as if they'd been best friends since childhood. A few minutes ago, everyone in the common room had been studying them as if they carried the plague. Now, they were grinning and talking in excited whispers, a few of them even going so far as to come up and shake the sellsword's hand.

For his part, Aaron took the attention in stride, as if it was the most natural thing in the world. Gone was the suspicious, greedy sellsword she'd first met. In his place, was a smiling, laughing man who seemed completely comfortable with everyone and everything around him. In fact, he looked as if he was actually enjoying himself.

"Good at this, isn't he?" Gryle asked in a whisper. "There are few men or women who can put a room at ease so smoothly. Do you think, mistress, that he might be of noble blood?"

Not likely, Adina thought, feeling a stab of jealousy. She'd been trained since she was a child in all of the noble arts including diplomacy, yet she doubted that even she could have done as well as the sellsword, and she knew that it wasn't just the coins. The money had made them like him, true, but judging by the looks in several of the women's eyes, and the jovial pats on the back from several of the men, they were well past liking. "I'm sure you would know more of that than I, Gryle." She answered, struggling to keep her tone neutral.

The chamberlain must have heard something in her voice because he cleared his throat nervously. "He is, of course, not close to my lady's own decorum and grace."

Adina nodded at the chubby man to set him at ease, but her gaze didn't leave Aaron. The man was maddening. Every time she was sure she had him figured out, he did something that went completely against everything she thought she knew about him. It was a disturbing, disconcerting situation for a woman who'd been taught her entire life to see past people's masks to their true intentions. If her childhood in her father's court had taught her anything, it was that most people were nothing if not accomplished liars and charlatans when it suited them, and nobles often the most deceitful of all.

She'd thought herself a master of seeing past such conceits, but Aaron insisted on proving her wrong again and again. It was as if the man had made a full time job of making her feel like a fool.

Why *had* he given the farmer with the sick child all of his gold? It didn't make sense. Not that that was the worst of it, of course. What she couldn't wrap her head around was how he knew about the little girl at all. She supposed it was possible that it had happened as he'd said; that he really *had* heard someone mention the child, but she was with him the entire time, and she didn't remember anything of the kind. But if he *hadn't* heard then ... no. He must have. There was simply no other explanation.

"Isn't that right, Gertrude?" It wasn't until Aaron nudged her in the side, jerking her away from her own thoughts, that she realized he was talking to her.

"I'm ... I'm sorry?"

He rolled his eyes long-sufferingly and winked at the innkeeper. "You'll have to pardon my sister, Herb. She's bad about disappearing into her own little world from time to time. When we were kids, she pretended to be a princess. Now that we're adults, I hesitate to imagine what she fantasizes about." The bartender barked a laugh, and Aaron turned back to Adina, a mischievous glint in his hazel eyes, "Herb was just offering us a free place for the night. I was telling him that we really don't have the time. We've got to be on our way."

Adina felt her face flushing an angry red. *I'd like to take the time to knock that smug grin off your face, you pompous bastard.* The thought helped relax her, and she didn't have to try hard to summon a smile of her own, "Of course, you're right, dear brother," she said in a voice that thoroughly oozed sweetness, "Sadly, we do not have the time. As for my mind wandering, I apologize. Sometimes, I find that if one wishes to find interesting people she must imagine them, lest she go mad with boredom."

Herb laughed again, apparently not noticing the sellsword's frown, and patting his stomach in a way that must have been habit back when there'd been plenty of food, and he'd had a stomach to pat. "You've got a live one there, Aaron. Got a little fire in her, your sister does."

"True," Aaron said after a moment. He smiled then, but this time it appeared forced. "She's made a habit of rudeness. It's no wonder she's still single."

Adina opened her mouth, preparing a scathing retort, but Herb, not noticing the anger flash in her bright blue eyes, continued on as if nothing had happened, "What is it that you're in such a hurry for, anyway?" He glanced at the blades at Aaron's side, and the sword sheathed on his back, as if seeing them for the first time, "Hold on a minute. Let me guess. You're heading for Baresh."

The princess felt Gryle tense beside her. Aaron's smile remained in place, but his hazel eyes got that suspicious, searching look she was beginning to know well. "Why do you say that?"

Herb shrugged as if it was obvious, "We're simple folk here in Krase, Aaron, but even a fool of an innkeeper knows that nobody around these parts could afford the kind of steel you got strapped to you unless he decided to try a year without eatin'—not that we're far from it, mind. That's why we took you and your friends for tax collectors before. Every time they come, Claudius sends one or two men with 'em to protect em. Really sour looking sons of bitches they are too. The way I see it, if you ain't here to take our money—don't worry, I know you're not now—then you're heading to Baresh for the tournament."

Aaron took a pull of his ale, "Tournament?"

Herb laughed as if he'd just told a joke. When the sellsword and the others didn't join in, he raised his eyebrows in surprise, "What, you been livin' under a rock or somethin'? The contest that bastard Claudius is holdin'. Me, well, I reckon it's hard enough for a man to survive in this world without risking getting his fool head beat in over a few of gold coins, but what do I know, eh?"

"How much is a few?" Aaron asked, a hungry look in his eyes that Adina didn't like at all.

The bartender shrugged, "A thousand? Maybe two? When it gets so high, it all seems meaningless to me. Why, a hundred or two would get you everything I own and the shirt off my back in the bargain. Anyway, aside from the money, the winner gets to have an audience with Claudius himself." He snorted, "Personally, I'd tell 'em to keep their money if it kept me from having to talk with that fat bastard."

"A thousand, maybe two," Aaron mused, running his hand across his chin, "and an audience with Claudius himself. You said it's going to be held in Baresh?"

Herb nodded, "That's right. They say it's on account of Claudius has some important announcement for the people after the event. Not that I know how much truth there is to that, you understand."

The three shared a worried look. There was only one thing they could all imagine Claudius would want to tell his people. *Hey guys, so I hope you enjoyed the competition. No? That's great. Hey, listen, remember how Eladen fought against Belgarin? Well, turns out Belgarin's your new ruler. Have a nice day.*

"He must be out of his mind if he thinks Eladen's people will follow him" Adina whispered disbelievingly. "Gerald and Ophasia were one thing; Eladen is quite another. He cared deeply for his people, and they cared deeply for him. They won't sit idly by—" Aaron grasped her arm warningly and she came to a halting stop. She looked at Herb and saw that the bartender was watching her suspiciously. "Or ... that's what I think anyway," she finished lamely.

"You'll have to pardon my sister," Aaron said, shrugging his shoulders and giving the bartender a -- *women-what-can-you-do?* look, "she makes a past time of studying the different princes and princesses. Don't ask me what for. I always figured that there were two things that a man would be a fool to try to figure out—politics and women—and in my experience it's a lot more fun trying to understand the latter. Not to mention," he added, staring at Adina, "that talking about politics doesn't make a lot of friends."

Adina held her breath, not having to pretend at the deep, embarrassed blush that crept up her cheeks. Herb studied her for another moment through narrowed eyes then nodded and turned to Aaron, "You've got that right. As far as I'm concerned, all the royal bastards could take a quick trip through the Keeper's Fields, and the world'd be better for it."

The princess opened up her mouth to tell the man just how much she cared about his opinion, but the sellsword's grip tightened on her arm, and she remained silent. He winked at the innkeeper conspiratorially, "Still, there's that one ... what's her name ... Adina? That one's pretty enough to make a criminal out of an honest man and an honest man out of a criminal the way I hear it."

Herb snorted, "I don't give a damn if the woman shits gold and spits sunflowers; a man would be crazy to get mixed up with any of her kind. Besides, I doubt she'd have ya. Word is," he said, leaning in conspiratorially, another gesture which Adina was beginning to suspect had become a habit, "the brothers and sisters spend more time together than is strictly ... *proper,* if you catch my meanin."

Aaron cleared his throat. "This tournament," He said, deciding it was time to change the subject, "Just when is our esteemed leader, planning to hold it?"

The bartender shook his head wonderingly, "You really must have been living under a rock. Folks have been flappin' their jaws about that damned contest so much lately it's a wonder that there's any air left for breathin'. It's supposed to start in a fortnight. They say that Claudius has went all out for it, that he's spending gold like it's piss. I don't guess we gotta guess where the money's coming from."

Aaron grunted in agreement, "No, I don't guess we do."

Gryle let out a squeaking, exhausted yawn, and Herb shook his head. "You sure you folks don't want to spend the night? I'd be happy to have ya. Like I said, the rooms are free, of course. After what you done for Glenn, it's the least I can do."

Aaron considered for a moment, "You said that the contest is in a fortnight?"

Herb nodded, "That's right."

"And how far is Baresh from here?"

"Less than a week's travel."

Aaron glanced questioningly at the princess, and she nodded. "We will stay the night," she said, "but we'll pay for our rooms." Her voice was tight with barely restrained anger, but if the innkeeper noticed, he gave no sign.

Herb shrugged, "Suit yourself. I won't lie and tell you that I couldn't use the money, but truth is you'd be doin' me a favor. Some of the town folk used to come, drink more than was wise, and rent a room for the night instead of makin' the trip home, but now, what with money so scarce, folks has been takin' their chances on the roads. It ain't right for a room to stay empty so long. It gets … well, it gets a certain feel to it."

"We'll pay just the same," Adina said.

The bartender nodded, "Alright then. I imagine you're hungry. We ain't got much—cabbage stew with more water than cabbage—but it takes the edge off anyway. You're welcome to it."

Adina pursed her nose, "No th—"

"We'd be happy to have some," Aaron interrupted, "it's kind of you to offer, Herb. You're a good man."

The innkeeper snorted, "Bite your tongue 'for somebody hears you." He turned to a small door behind the bar, "Paula. *Paula.*" A young girl, no more than ten summers, stepped into view, and Adina winced out how painfully thin she was. She wore a simple cotton dress, and the arms and legs that the princess could see looked like little more than twigs. "What's the matter, girl," Herb asked, "you got cotton stuffed in your ears again?"

"No, daddy," the girl said, smiling.

Herb smiled back his gruff exterior gone, "Listen, sweetheart. You think you could show these folks to their rooms? There's a piggy back ride in it for you if you do."

The girl's eyebrows drew down, "I'm too old for piggy back rides, daddy," she said, her voice serious, "Momma says I'm almost a young lady."

The bartender grunted a laugh, "Well, maybe *I'm* not too old for 'em, what do you say to that? As for you becoming a young woman, well, gods help the man who picks you to marry."

The girl crinkled her nose in disgust, "I'm not going to marry. Boys are dumb and they smell."

Herb put on a hurt expression and sniffed himself thoughtfully.

Paula rolled her eyes, "Not you. You're not a boy. You're daddy."

"Alright then," Herb said, leaning over and kissing her on the forehead, "You think you can show these good folks to their room for your dumb and smelly dad?"

The girl giggled again, "You're silly, daddy." She turned to the others and raised her nose in the air, a gesture that displayed her too thin face and neck, "This way if you please." She said with the tone of a great queen escorting privileged guests through her castle.

Adina forced back the tears that were threatening to spill out, "After you, madam," she said with a curtsey. The girl nodded, as if this was her just due and headed toward the stairs.

CHAPTER NINETEEN

ALONE IN HER ROOM, Adina washed up in a small basin of warm water Herb had brought up, luxuriating in feeling clean for the first time in what felt like forever. She took her time, enjoying the comfort the warm water brought to her sore muscles. Once she was finished she lay down in the room's small, simple bed and was surprised by how comfortable it felt; more comfortable, in fact, than she ever remembered her own silk-sheeted bed being. Time passed and despite her body's weariness she found herself tossing and turning, unable to sleep. Through the wall, she could hear Gryle snoring so loudly that it sounded as if a small thunderstorm was taking place in the next room. Gryle had been her father's chamberlain before he was her own, and his snores had been nothing short of legendary in King Marcus's court, yet it was her own racing thoughts, not the chamberlain's heavy breathing that kept her awake.

She found herself thinking of the young girl, Paula, of her sunken cheeks and her dangerously thin arms and legs, of Claudius and the approaching contest, and of the Parnen captain and his loyal first mate, but mostly she thought of Aaron. The sellsword liked to pretend that he didn't care about anyone else, yet he'd saved her on the rowboat when the man attacked her, and he'd been quick enough to offer Glenn the money to help his little girl and, come to think of it, how *had* he known about that anyway? The more she considered it, the more she became convinced that no one had been talking about it on their way into town. But how else could he have possibly known?

He couldn't have, that was all, yet he had. It didn't make sense, and if there was one thing Adina hated, it was when things didn't make sense. She wanted to, no she *needed* to know. Frustrated, she rose, got dressed, and crept quietly down the hall to Aaron's room. She froze, her fist balled to knock, realizing that he was probably asleep. A moment's thought was enough for her to decide that she hoped he *was* asleep. It would serve him right for the way he'd talked about her to the innkeeper, not to mention the outrageous way he'd treated her on the *Clandestine,* as if all the world's problems were her fault. When she knocked, she might have done so a bit louder than was strictly necessary.

"Come in," he called from inside, and she was disappointed to note that he sounded completely awake.

She walked through the door and closed it shut behind her. He was sitting on a stool, his face lathered with soap, a small knife in one hand. A bucket of water sat on the counter in front of him. He turned and raised an eyebrow at her, "Oh, it's you. I thought it might have been Herb's girl bringing the soup."

"Paula," she said, her face heating. He'd taken his shirt off to shave, and her eyes were drawn to the sculpted muscle of his arms and chest, and to the taut flatness of his stomach. She shook her head as if to clear it, "Her name was Paula."

He nodded, continuing to shave, thankfully not having noticed her stare, "That's right, Paula. Funny, I wouldn't have taken Herb for a family man, but he's good wi—"

"How did you know?" She blurted, pulling her eyes away from his muscled frame with an effort.

"How did I know what?" He asked as he sat the blade down and splashed his face with water from the bowl.

"About the girl, Marla. How did you know she was sick?"

He grabbed a hand towel off the counter and began to dry off. He hesitated, then shrugged, "I told you. Someone in town was talking about it when we went by."

"I don't remember anyone saying anything about it."

He met her eyes for a second then shrugged again. "I guess you must not have been paying attention."

She sighed. There was no point in asking him further. True or not, she knew what he would say, and the fact was his explanation was the only thing that made sense. That, or that he was some sort of mystic who could pull the thoughts out of a person's mind. "Fine, but why did you give Glenn the money?"

Aaron grunted, "What else was I gonna do? Did you see the look on their faces? Make no mistake, princess, everyone in that inn meant to see us dead."

Adina was shaking her head before he was finished, "That's not why," she said sharply, surprising herself with her anger, "You gave it to him because you wanted to help the girl. Why won't you just admit that?"

He flicked a hand carelessly as if shooing away a fly, "What do I care about a girl I've never met?"

Adina took a step closer to him, "You don't mean it," she said, her voice a quiet, pleading whisper, "I know you don't. Downstairs, you told them it was because—"

"I told them exactly what they wanted to hear," he growled, his eyes hard, "I told them what I needed to to keep breathing, and if they think it was because of some sick little girl, well, all the better."

"*Liar,*" Adina shouted and before she knew it, her hand lashed out, striking the sellsword across the face. "What's *wrong* with you?" She shouted as everything that had happened in the past few weeks, her brother's death, learning of the people in the north starving, and nearly being killed herself, came crashing down in her mind like jagged bolts of lightning, "How can you be so cruel?"

Aaron didn't move. He just stood, watching her with that blank, dead stare. "*Damn you,*" she snarled, "don't you *feel* anything?" She reached out to slap him again, but he caught her hand casually, as if she were no more than a child. "People are dying and you don't even care."

She thought she saw something flash across his eyes then, a thinly-veiled grief so vast that it was like seeing the peak of a massive underwater mountain, but in the next moment it was gone, and the cold, uncaring hardness had returned to his eyes.

"Enough," he said, his voice hoarse as he jerked her close to him, so close that she could feel his breath on her face, could feel the heat of him and the hard muscles of his chest pressed against her, "that's enough."

She felt tears spilling from her eyes and down her cheeks, and she was furious with herself for crying in front of him, furious with him for *making* her cry. She lashed out with her other hand, but he caught it, too, and pulled her closer still, so that their faces were only inches apart, "Let *go* of me," She hissed between sudden tears, "You're not even a man. You're a ... a monster!" She tried to say something more, but the tears were coming heavier now, coming in great, racking sobs and he held her against him as she buried her face in his chest and cried the way she hadn't since she was a child.

"I am what the world's made me," he said in a whisper so low that she could barely hear it, as if he wasn't speaking to her at all but to himself.

He paused, as if he was going to say something more, but he did not, and he held her in silence as she cried tears for Eladen, for Ophasia, and Geoffrey, and all of the people who had suffered because of Belgarin. After a time, she managed to get herself under control, but she did not pull away. He felt so real against her, so alive, the warmth of his chest and the beating of his heart that she could feel as if it were her own, and in that moment there was no Belgarin, was no war or hunger, no suffering or uncertainty. There was only the two of them, wrapped in a bubble of time, a bubble so fragile that she was terrified to move lest she break it. "Please, Aaron," she mumbled against his chest, "I saw you, I heard your voice. I know you meant it." She glanced up into his eyes and again she imagined that she could see a terrible grief there, a great, crippling loss that no person should have to endure, and she cupped his face in one of her hands. His eyes closed for a moment, and she felt him lean into her touch. "You don't have to be alone, Aaron," she whispered, "You don't. It's okay to care." He swallowed hard but didn't answer.

She craned her neck and met his gaze, not the cold, hardened stare of the man he thought he wanted to be, the man who cared for no one, who *needed* no one, but the man he was. A man who didn't want to care, a man who was too terrified to care and then, without thinking, she leaned forward, closing her eyes and letting her lips brush against his softly, so softly, like the faint trace of a feather on bare skin. "You're scared to get close," she whispered, knowing it was true as she said it, "You're scared to let anyone know you." She ran her other hand through his hair, down his neck, and slowly, gently, down the ridged scars on his back. "But I'm close. I know you."

He tensed beneath her hands, opened his mouth to speak, then suddenly snarled as he tore himself out of her grasp, breathing hard, his eyes wild like those of a wounded, cornered animal. "You don't know *anything,*" he shouted, and Adina took a shocked, frightened step back. "What?" He asked in a harsh voice, "You think because you've seen my scars that all of a sudden you've got me figured out, huh? Just another commoner to be pitied, another mongrel dog that you can toss some food to and then go riding in your palanquin to one of your fancy balls and feeling good about your *charity?*"

"T-that's not true," she stammered, "I know you. I know that you care about that little girl. I know that you care about—"

"No, I don't," he shouted, cutting her off. "I care about your money, and I care about being left alone, now how about you just--" He stopped abruptly, closing his eyes. When he opened them again, the wildness that had been there was gone. In its place was the same blank, dead stare that made Adina's skin go cold. "You should leave," he said in a tired, hoarse voice, "I'm tired, and I'm going to get some rest. That's if I can with your chamberlain snoring like a bear in heat."

"You don't want me to leave," she said, shaking her head, "I know you don't. There's a reason why you're here. You could have left by now."

He snorted in disgust, "Just how stupid are you, lady? I'm here because you *pay* me. All I care about is making money and keeping breathin.' You can go slumming with some other fool."

Her mouth dropped open in surprise, and she brought a hand to her chest, "Is that what you think? Is that ... forget it. Fine." She turned, opened the door and stopped, her body trembling. "After you finish the job, I don't ever want to see you again."

He shrugged, "Fine with me."

She took a step then glanced back at him, "If all you care about is money and staying alive, then what's the point? Did you ever think of that? What's the *point?*"

Aaron stared to respond, but the princess was already gone, the door slamming shut behind her.

He stood there, staring at the door in silence, his chest heaving with some great emotion. After a time, the Virtue started to speak, *Aaron, w—*

"Mind your own damn business, firefly," he muttered, his eyes still locked on the door, part of him hoping that Adina would come back, part of him praying that she wouldn't. She did not return and eventually he walked to the small bed and slumped onto it wearily, resting his head in his hands.

You try so hard not to care, but you do anyway. Why? Why do you insist on living your life alone?

He took a deep breath and crossed his hands behind his head as he leaned back in the bed, "What do you know?" He asked, suddenly more tired than he ever remembered being. Unbidden, his mind drifted to the way Adina's lips had felt, soft and moist and *right*. He pushed the thought away angrily. "In this world, everyone is out to take what you have," he said in a whisper, not sure if he was talking to the Virtue or himself and not caring either way, "Better not to have anything worth taking. Better not to have anything at all."

CHAPTER TWENTY

THE NEXT MORNING, he walked downstairs to find the princess and the chamberlain already sitting at the bar. The tables of the common room were empty save two old men who sat and talked in hushed whispers, hunched over their mugs of ale protectively. At the end of the counter, a young, red-haired boy of no more than fifteen was speaking with a pretty, older woman whom Aaron suspected was Herb's wife. Adina pointedly avoided his gaze, and Gryle was too busy yawning heavily and rubbing a meaty fist at his eyes to notice him walk up. "Hey, Aaron," The innkeeper said, pausing in cleaning the bar to smile at him.

Aaron nodded at him, "Mornin' Herb," he said, "Hey, I was wondering, are there any horses for sale in this town?"

The innkeeper's brow drew down in thought for a moment. "Not for sale, no, but I've got a couple of mules I use to go to the city when we need supplies. Why do you ask?"

Aaron winked, "I need to get to Baresh in a hurry. I hear tale of a contest where a man could win his fortune. I'll buy 'em from you for a fair price."

Herb shook his head, "No, you can't buy 'em, but I'll let you use 'em, sure enough. After you and your sister's kindness, it'd be my pleasure."

Aaron glanced at Adina, wondering what "kindness" she had shown, but she didn't meet his gaze. He turned back to the innkeeper and nodded, "Alright then."

"Good," Herb said, "that's settled. Now we'll just have to find someone to guide you there, that and bring my mules back, of course."

"I'll do it." They all turned to see the fiery-headed youth rush forward, nearly tripping in his haste. The boy puffed out his chest, and Aaron noted that he kept glancing at Adina nervously, as if for approval. *Great,* he thought with an inward groan, *just what I need.*

Herb grunted, a hint of a smile on his face, "Peter, doesn't your pa need you on the farm?"

The boy's face twisted in anger, "Not now he don't. We can't afford seed to plant most of the fields on account of the collectors. Besides, I'll be back in less than a fortnight, and I know the way better'n most—pa's sent me on supply runs to Baresh for the last three years runnin'." He flashed a quick, shy look at the princess, "I can get 'em there safe."

Herb grinned and winked at Aaron. "Well, it's up to you three. The boy knows the way, that's certain, and he's got a good head on his shoulders—as much as a boy his age can, anyway." The red headed youth's chest puffed out even more at the innkeeper's words.

"I don't know—" Aaron began.

"That would be perfect," Adina interrupted, "thank you, Peter, was it?" She smiled at the boy, and Aaron fought back the urge to frown. *Careful, kid,* he thought, *I've seen that smile before. Next comes folks trying to cut your fool head off.* "I'm sure," the princess continued, "that we'll make it there safely with your help."

The boy's face turned a deep crimson, "Y-yes, ma'am."

She turned to Aaron with a smirk, "We'll let you *men* finish the details. Peter, would you mind showing me and my friend to the carriage?"

"Excuse me, Miss," the boy said nervously, "but it's not much of a carriage. More of a cart really, and not a very b—"

"That'll do just fine," she interrupted sharply.

Peter nodded quickly and headed out the door, the princess behind. Gryle glanced thoughtfully between Adina's departing back, and Aaron before shrugging helplessly at the sellsword and following her out.

Herb waited until the door closed then barked a laugh, "Gods help you I think the boy's got a crush on your sister."

Aaron sighed, "So it would seem."

"Tell me," the innkeeper said, his voice suddenly serious, "are you really considering entering the contest?"

"Why not?"

Herb shook his head, "You know your business, of course, but I'd be careful, Aaron. That kind of gold will attract swordsmen and knights from all across the country. Men who have spent their entire lives training for competitions just like this, and with that kind of money on the line they won't be pulling any punches."

The sellsword grinned, "I hope not. That wouldn't make things very interesting, would it?"

Herb snorted, "You're a good man, Aaron, but you're a crazy bastard. Just make sure to be careful up there, and come back and visit us if you can. We can always use more folk like you in town."

Aaron nodded and rose from the stool, "Alright then. Thanks for letting us borrow your cart, Herb. I'll be seein' ya." He started toward the door and stopped, "Oh, and Herb."

"Yeah?"

"I don't mean to tell you your business either, but if some men should happen through, some more strangers, and they start askin' questions about me and the others, you tell 'em what they want to know, alright?"

The innkeeper frowned, "What sort of men?"

Aaron considered a moment, "The sort that can ask hard, you understand?"

Herb nodded, the pleasantness gone from his face, "Folks in Krase ain't real good with strangers sticking their noses where they don't belong. These people come by askin' their questions, they'll get some answers—just might not be the ones they're wantin'."

Aaron shook his head, "Not these men, Herb. Trust me on this. You tell them what they want to know, and get them out of your town as quickly as you can. These aren't the kind of people you want to screw with. Especially not when you have something to lose. Promise me."

The innkeeper and his wife shared a worried glance then both of them glanced at the door where, Aaron suspected, their daughter was sleeping. When Herb turned back to the sellsword, his face was grim, "Alright, Aaron. Whatever you say."

Aaron nodded, satisfied, and left.

CHAPTER TWENTY-ONE

A BIRD WHISTLED HAPPILY in one of the trees surrounding the road, and Aaron was barely able to resist the urge to shout at it. They'd been traveling for hours now and his mood was steadily becoming worse. The air was frigid, much colder than he was used to, and his tattered cloak did nothing to keep it at bay. This, however, was not the reason why he could feel his temper rising. It wasn't the bouncing cart that made his back and ass ache, nor, even, was it Gryle's constant snoring—how the man could sleep on the bumpy trip was beyond him. More than anything, he felt himself growing angry as the boy, Peter, continued to ogle Adina like she was a goddess come down from the heavens. With the amount of looks the boy kept flashing at her, it wasn't surprising that the cart managed to hit every damned rock or root sticking out of the road. *Truth to tell,* Aaron thought as the boy smiled shyly at the princess again, *we're lucky the bastard's managing to stay on the path at all.*

Jealous? Co asked in an amused voice.

His frown grew deeper. *For her? Hardly. I'd just rather the boy spent more time worrying about getting us to Baresh in one piece than eyeing her highness's tits, and the way she's treating him, smiling and chatting away like they've known each other for years isn't doing anything but encouraging him.*

Uhuh. So definitely not jealous then.

Aaron pinched the bridge of his nose and took a deep breath. It wasn't enough that he and the chamberlain had been stuck in the back of some turnip cart while the princess and the boy rode up front like royalty, now he had to deal with Co's taunts. In his time bonded with the Virtue, he'd learned that all women—even ones that were floating balls of light—could be a real pain in the ass. *Even if I did care about her—which I don't—I wouldn't be worried about some hick boy with a face full of acne that can't even shave yet.*

I see, the Virtue said in a reasonable tone that made Aaron even angrier, *they do seem to be getting along famously though.*

Aaron glanced at the front of the cart, and saw that the princess was laughing, one of her hands on the boy's shoulder. For his part, Peter's ears had turned as red as his hair, and his gaze—for once—was locked on the dirt trail in front of them. *Like I care,* Aaron thought back. Suddenly, the chamberlain's snoring was more than he could bear, and he gave the man a shove with one of his boots. The fat man shifted in his sleep and the deep, thunderous snores cut off.

"Thank the gods for that, at least," Aaron muttered, scowling, but no sooner were the words out of his mouth than the chamberlain's snoring started again. Aaron sighed resignedly and readjusted in a vain effort to get comfortable. It was going to be a long trip.

CHAPTER TWENTY-TWO

IT WAS NEARLY DARK by the time Peter pulled the mules to a stop on the side of the road. Aaron's muscles complained loudly from the bumpy ride, and his head ached as if it was going to split in two. "There's a small clearing through here," the youth said, "it's not much, but we could have a fire and rest for a while if you'd like. I've used it before."

Aaron was sure the question was directed at the princess, but he'd be damned if he was going to be bounced around anymore today. "Sounds good. Lead the way."

The boy glanced at the princess then clucked to the mules and began leading the cart into the trees. In a few minutes, they came upon the clearing he'd spoken of. Aaron winced as he stood up in the cart and stretched his aching muscles. He'd wanted to borrow Herb's mules because they'd make better time than walking, and with Belgarin's men no doubt hunting him—not to mention that crazy bastard Aster—they needed all the help they could get, but he was regretting the decision just the same.

He gazed down at the sleeping chamberlain with narrowed eyes, and kicked him. This time, Gryle let out a startled yelp, and jerked up to a sitting position in the cart. "W-what's happening?" He squeaked, "What's wrong?"

"That's a long list," Aaron said, "and we don't have the time. Now, come on. You've got first watch."

"Watch?" Gryle whined, rubbing a meaty paw at his eyes, "is that really necessary?"

"Yes, now move your ass."

Aaron had never been this far north, and now that the sun was nearly down he was surprised at how cold it was. The wind cut through his clothing like daggers made of frost, and he and the others hurriedly gathered wood from the nearby forest and started a fire. As they sat around warming their hands on the small blaze, they helped themselves to dried jerky and bread. The food tasted like road dust to Aaron, and he washed it down with a bottle of ale that Herb had sent with him. The ale worked wonders on his sore body, not eliminating the pains, so much as covering them over with a pleasant numbness that was beginning to spread through his limbs.

"So," the princess said as they all ate, "how do you like living in the north, Peter?"

"I-it's good, I guess," the boy stammered, obviously uncomfortable with being the center of attention.

"Well, that's nice," Adina said.

There was a pause before Peter spoke again. "That's ... maybe that's not true. It *used* to be good until a month ago, when Prince Eladen up and disappeared and Claudius took over. My pa says that most nobles ain't worth a spit, but the prince is different. The prince actually cares about us commoners, and my pa says that as soon as he gets back from wherever he's gone, Claudius is going to have a lot to answer for."

Adina felt a pang of sadness at the thought of her brother, at the thought of all of his people waiting for him to return, not knowing that he was dead, and she felt a surge of rage at gods who would allow a man like Eladen to die while her brother, Belgarin, lived and forced an entire land of people to suffer because of his own greed. After a time, the anger passed, leaving her feeling empty and exhausted in its wake. She rose, walked to the cart and removed her bed roll. "I'm going to go to sleep. Goodnight everyone."

Aaron watched Peter stare after her, and despite the dim light of the fire, he could make out the boy's expression of embarrassed hurt. Despite himself, he felt sorry for the youth. "Don't worry about it, kid," he said, surprising himself with the words, "She's had a long day."

The boy nodded silently, retrieved his own bed roll, and lay down.

"Are you going to get some rest, sir?" Gryle asked beside him.

"Later." They lapsed into silence, and Aaron sat, gazing at the fire as it whipped back and forth in the wind. Despite his best efforts to the contrary, his mind kept returning to Adina. The woman was damned bossy at times—no surprise that—and he'd lost count of the times she'd almost gotten him killed, but he had to admit that she had some backbone. What's more, despite the fact that she'd no doubt spent her years being pampered and sleeping in the finest beds, she hadn't complained once about sleeping on the hard, rocky ground. Suddenly, a thought struck him and he turned to the chamberlain, "Why didn't you leave, Gryle?"

The chamberlain started at the sound of the sellsword's voice, "Sir?"

"When Adina's other servants were bought out by Belgarin, why didn't you leave? For that matter, why didn't you take Belgarin's coin yourself?"

There was a pause, and when Gryle spoke, he sounded angry for the first time Aaron had ever heard, "I would never betray Her Highness."

He nodded, "So why not just leave? I doubt Belgarin would have spared any trouble going after you."

"Because the Princess needs me," Gryle answered, as if it was the most obvious thing in the world.

"And starving people need food," Aaron said, thinking of Herb's daughter, Paula, "but they don't always get it. You've got to know that the longer you hang around with her, the more likely it is that you'll be killed."

The chamberlain didn't respond at first and when he did his voice was little more than a whisper. "I'm scared. Of course, I'm scared. I'm no warrior, like you." He took a deep, hitching breath, "I'm a coward. But ... King Marcus, before he died—gods protect and keep him— once told me something that I'll never forget. He said, 'A man has a right to fear death, Gryle, the same way he has a right to breathe, but if he has nothing that he'd be willing to face that fear for, to *die* for, then he's not really a man, but an empty shell and of no use to anyone.' I believe, I *know,* that the princess cares for her people, that she only wants to make the world better, and I pray to the gods each night to watch over her."

Aaron grunted, "I used to hear my father say something similar to my mother sometimes. It was the reason he followed Eladen; why he wanted to help him unite the whole of Telrear."

"Your father sounds like a wise man, sir."

Aaron hocked and spat, "My father's dead. He and my mother were killed because he chose to follow the prince. No, my father wasn't wise. He was a fool. As for the gods, pray if you want, Gryle. You aren't the first, and you won't be the last, but you know something? People keep dying, anyway."

"Sir," the chamberlain said with a frown, "I really don't thi—"

"Forget it," Aaron said, suddenly angry, "I'm going to get some rest. Wake me when it's my time for watch." He started toward his bedroll and turned back, "Oh, and Gryle?"

The chamberlain blinked his eyes owlishly in the firelight, "Yes sir?"

"You're not a coward; a fool, maybe, but not a coward."

CHAPTER TWENTY-THREE

THE NEXT DAY PASSED UNEVENTFULLY. They rose, ate in near silence, and got back on the trail. After a time, the road took them out of the forest and into hilly grasslands that stretched on as far as Aaron could see. It rained that night. The sweeping fields offered no shelter. They got wet. They rose the next morning, all of them ill-tempered and out of sorts except for Gryle who was, at least to Aaron's mind, annoyingly cheerful, constantly commenting on the fine, autumn weather or the surprising comfort of the cart.

It was on their third day in the grasslands, the fourth since leaving Herb's, that they topped a hill and first saw the dust cloud stirring behind them in the direction from which they'd came. "What is it, do you think?" Adina asked, "Someone else heading to the capital?"

"Could be," Aaron said, meeting her gaze meaningfully, "but I don't think so." He turned to Peter, "How far from Baresh are we?"

The youth turned away from the road, his face screwed up in concentration, "We should make it to the capital around tomorrow night—no later than that. That is, if we don't stop at Naya's." He smiled, apparently not noticing the worried expressions on the faces of the others, "Naya's is a waystop for travelers, an inn of sorts. She makes the best sugared lemon tarts you'll ever have. It sure would be good to—"

"I don't think we'll be stopping," Aaron said, frowning back at the growing dust cloud. Whoever it was, they were traveling fast. It was nearly impossible to tell from this distance, but he thought that there were three, maybe four of them. According to the boy, they had a day and a half before they reached Baresh; a long time to ride in a rickety old cart. Too long. Whoever was following them—and despite what he wanted to think, it would be foolish to think the riders weren't following them—would be on them in the morning, mid-day at the latest. A thought struck him, and he turned back to the pimple-faced youth, "How far is this Naya's?"

Peter glanced up at the sky in thought. "If we stop for the night at about the same time as we have been, we should reach it an hour or two after we start out in the morning."

He nodded, "Alright then. Keep going."

Peter finally noticed their nervous expressions. "Do you know who's behind us?"

"Better than I'd like to," Aaron said, "and if they catch us so will you. Best keep going." They traveled on, speaking little. The youth didn't say anything, but based on the stiff whiteness of his hands where they gripped the reins, and the punishing pace he was putting the mules to, he'd apparently decided that, while eyeballin' the princess's goods was an enjoyable pastime, breathing was an even better one.

In the afternoon, they crested another large, grassy hill. Aaron looked back and spat in frustration. Despite the cart's increased pace, the riders had got closer. A lot closer. "Bastards must be killing their horses," he muttered. "Alright, lad, let's slow it down some."

"Slow it down?" Adina asked incredulously, "Are you crazy? They'll catch us."

He shook his head, "Not tonight they won't."

"And after that?" Adina asked, "You heard Peter; we won't get to Baresh until tomorrow night."

Ignoring her, Aaron turned to the youth, "You want to make it home to your family, boy?"

The red head's face was pale, his eyes wide with fear. He swallowed hard and nodded, "Yes sir."

"Alright then. Slow it down. Give the animals a chance to catch a breath. It won't do us any good to run them to death."

Peter stared at him with those wide, terrified eyes, "Are they gonna catch us, sir?"

Aaron glanced behind them again. "Probably." He turned back to the terrified youth. "Relax, boy. Just do as I tell you, and we just might get out of this with our guts in place."

The boy nodded and eased the pace of the mules. Adina shook her head in awe, "You're out of your mind."

He felt for the handle of the sword at his back, ensuring himself it was there, then turned to her, a grim smile on his face, "You have no idea."

CHAPTER TWENTY-FOUR

HE HAD PETER PUSH THE MULES past the time when they normally would have stopped. They went on until the nearly-full moon hung in the sky, bright and pregnant, until he judged the men no more than a couple of hours behind them, then he ordered the youth to stop the cart.   "What is it?" Adina asked, and though she masked it well, he could hear the fear in her voice, "Aren't we going to keep going?"

Aaron climbed out of the cart and took a moment to stretch his aching muscles, wrapping his cloak around him for what little protection it would afford him against the growing cold. He turned to Adina and nodded, "You are."

Realization dawned in her blue eyes and they seemed to sparkle in the moonlight, "You can't be serious. You don't know how many there are."

"I think I may. Besides," he said, shrugging, "does it matter?"

"But *why?* You don't care about us—you've made that clear," she said, her voice a mixture of anger and hurt, "why would you risk yourself?"

"Look, we don't have time for this," Aaron said, feeling precious seconds slipping by, "We both know what those men want—what they'll do. Now, we can sit around here arguing about this until they slit our throats, or you can get moving."

"No," she said, shaking her head, "it's not right."

He barked a harsh laugh, "Nothing is." He took in the princess's angry, worried face and sighed, "Look, relax. It's probably just a scouting party. Two or three men, four at the most. Besides, I don't plan on letting myself get ghosted just yet—not until I get paid, anyway." He turned to Gryle. The chamberlain's face had paled visibly, and he was rubbing his hands together anxiously, "You keep going until you reach Naya's. If I'm not there by first light, you and the others rush to Baresh like the Keeper himself is on your tail—because he is."

Gryle was shaking his head before Aaron was finished, "We can't leave you, sir, it wouldn't b—"

"*Listen,*" Aaron said, "We can either wait for them to run us down tomorrow morning like fucking animals, or you can do what I tell you and maybe we can survive. You do want your mistress to survive, don't you, Gryle?"

The chamberlain nodded slowly, "Of course, sir, but—"

"No buts," Aaron said as he withdrew one of his blades and offered it to the chamberlain, "Here, take this." He met the man's eyes, "Run if you can, but if it comes to it, use it."

Gryle eyed the blade askance, as if its touch was poison. "I ... I don't think—"

The chamberlain let out a squeak of surprise as Aaron grabbed a handful of his shirt and jerked him closer, "*You're not a coward, remember?*"

Gryle's mouth worked silently for a moment, "Y-yes sir."

Aaron watched him for several seconds then nodded, satisfied, "Good. Remember, first light—not a minute more."

"First light," the chamberlain repeated.

"*No,*" Adina said, "We're not going to leave you alone."

Aaron frowned, rubbing his chilled hands together, "No, better that we all die together? Better that we leave all of Eladen's people to their fate, is that it? With no one to stop him, Belgarin will be king, and I guess that'll be the end of it, huh, princess? Hundreds, maybe thousands die in the quelling all because you felt left out?"

"P-princess?" The youth asked, but neither of them paid him any attention.

"You bastard," Adina said furiously. "Fine, get yourself killed. Do what you want. What do I care?"

He shrugged, "You'll have to do better than that, princess. Bastard's what my friends call me." He turned to the youth, "Now go as fast as you can but be safe. Now's not the time to break one of the mules' legs by leading them into a hole."

Without a word, the boy barked a command to the mules, and the cart lurched into motion. Aarno watched them go, Adina staring at him with a strange look on her face, Gryle still gawking at the blade like it was going to bite him.

He kept watching until they disappeared over another hill. Then he sighed, and glanced back in the direction they'd come. In the wake of the receding cart, the night was eerily silent and still. It was as if the whole world waited on him. It was also cold, bone-chilling, goose-bump raising cold. On a night like this, a man would be more worried about staying warm than anyone coming up on him in the dark. Or so he hoped. He wrapped his cloak tightly around him—the tattered cloth provided meager shelter against the stinging wind, but it was better than nothing—and started down the road.

It wasn't long before he could make out the orange glow of a fire in the distance. Grunting in satisfaction, he headed toward it. *This is a very stupid idea,* Co said in his mind.

"You're as bad as the princess," he muttered.

I'll take that as a compliment.

He sniffed and brushed an arm across a nose that felt like a chunk of ice, "Take it how you want to. It doesn't matter to me. But let me ask you a question, firefly. You think a hunter ever wonders what the deer is thinking?"

There was a pause, then, reluctantly, *No.*

"Neither do I," he said, struggling to keep his teeth from chattering, "because he's the hunter. His job's killing, and the deer's job is dying, right?"

That is a rather crude way of putting it, but I suppose. Is there a point to this?

"My point, lightning bug, is that, to these men, we're the deer. Men don't have a lot of expectations of their prey. They expect them to be scared, to run, to hide, and, eventually, to die. What they *don't* expect is for them to sneak up on them while they sleep and slit their fucking throats."

And what if there are more than you expect?

He shrugged as he continued forward into the howling wind, "Then we'll be at it all night. What the Pit else do we have to do?"

CHAPTER TWENTY-FIVE

HE WALKED for what felt like an eternity. The fire was little more than a dull orange glow on the horizon, and his fingers and toes felt frozen, but he bared his teeth and pushed on, the wind and the cold cutting through his clothes like blades made of ice.

After a time, he was close enough to see the shape of the flickering fire. The flame whipped back and forth in the wind, as if performing some ritualistic dance reminiscent of the days when the world was still young, back in a time when fire was man's only ward against the darkness, against the things that waited in the shadows.

He didn't' know how long he stood, watching it, a frozen revenant who'd forgotten what it was to be warm. Then, he caught himself and shook his head as if to clear it. *Damned cold must be getting to me.* Jerking his attention away from the mesmerizing flame, he stalked closer, wincing at the crunch of the frost-laden grass beneath his feet. As he drew nearer, he could just make out the shadowy forms of two men lying in the darkness. Two horses had been staked to the ground nearby. Their ears perked up at his approach, but they appeared exhausted, and they made no noise.

Two, he thought, *two at the least.* Some men would have moved in then, satisfied that there were only the two, but not him. There were plenty of fools living in the world, but there were a lot more dead ones. Instead of giving in to the temptation to get it over, to get it done, he waited. In the cold, in the darkness, he waited.

He might have stood there for minutes or hours, in the darkness and the cold, he'd lost all track of time. He waited, the darkness wrapped around him like a cloak, schooling his breathing and listening to the steady *pop* and *snap* of the fire, scanning the fields to see if some other hunter shared the night with him. When he was finally satisfied that there were only the two and decided to move forward, his knees protested painfully and small shivers ran through his body.

He crept around the shadow of the camp, forcing his numb legs to move, until he stood above one of the men. This close, he could see that the cloak the man had wrapped himself in before he went to sleep was a deep crimson, and despite the accumulated dust on it, the golden slashes on the cloth were still visible. He sighed silently to himself. They were colors that brought out shouts of pride and cheers of joy from some men, while sending others scurrying into their homes like rats trying to outrun a flood. They were Belgarin's colors, Belgarin's men. He glanced back at the other, ensuring himself the man still slept. He wondered idly how the prince had found out that they had traveled north but pushed the thought aside for later. There were things that he needed to be about just now.

Silently, he knelt down, drawing his remaining blade. As he did, the soldier rolled over in his sleep, so that he was facing toward the sky, toward Aaron. The flickering firelight revealed the face of a youth that was certainly no more than a year or two older than the boy, Peter, if that. It was probably the boy's first outing, the first time he was trusted with anything more than cleaning the latrines and mopping up after the real soldiers.

Scouting duty—if that was what this was—and judging by the fact that there were only two of them, Aaron was confident in that assumption, was one of the most hated tasks of enlisted men. Nine out of ten times, it was a complete waste, and more often than not, you returned with nothing to show for the trip except for a saddle-sore ass and a desperate need of a bath. The veterans had probably done everything they could to avoid it. But not this one. No, this one would have volunteered readily, excited to become more than just the errand boy around camp, excited to prove to himself—as well as the others—that he was a soldier in his own right.

Yeah, nine out of ten times the boy would have made it back to camp empty-handed. Empty-handed but safe. No doubt, even now, there were men scouting in all directions from the town of Krase, finding nothing and grumbling themselves to sleep. But not this one. No, not this unlucky bastard, who was still young enough, still stupid enough, to think life was a fairytale, and that he, unlike everyone else, was immune to the Keeper's Call. Aaron raised the blade above the boy's throat and positioned his other hand so that he could keep the sleeping man's mouth shut as he bled out. It was a damned messy job—he knew this from experience—but he couldn't risk waking the other—not yet.

He was just about to open the young soldier's throat, when something about the youth's features struck him as familiar, and he hesitated. For a moment, he couldn't think of what it could have been that had triggered the feeling, but then he knew. The boy's nose was thin, and canted to the side where it had obviously been broken. It looked exactly the same as Owen's had, so many years ago. Owen had got his broken nose from his abusive, drunken father, and ever since then it had held the same crook. That was, before the old man decided to take on a bottle of poison in a game of chicken—the poison won. Death always did. Aaron couldn't help wondering where this boy had gotten his.

What in the name of the gods is wrong with me? He thought angrily. *Sooner started sooner done.* He leaned forward and brought the blade within an inch of the youth's throat. There was a rustle at his side, and he whipped his head around, sure that the other soldier was bearing down on him. Instead, he saw that the man had only rolled over in his sleep. Satisfied, he turned back and saw that the boy was staring at him with wide, terrified green eyes. A green he knew well. "Owen?" He whispered, dumbfounded. "It can't be."

"P-please," the soldier pleaded in a whiny, child's voice, "don't."

Aaron felt his arms break out in gooseflesh. He blinked once, then twice, and stared back at the soldier. "Owen, you know I'd never—" *Wait,* he thought, *just wait a damned minute. Owen would be older than this.* With that thought, suddenly his vision seemed to clear. This man wasn't Owen. His ears were small—Owen's ears had been massive, much too big for his face—and this man's hair was black, where his childhood friend's had been a brown so light it was almost blonde. It had been nothing but his mind playing tricks. He must have been more tired than he'd realized.

Still, the look of terror in the boy's face filled him with a nagging sense of shame. *Why the fuck should I feel guilty? I wasn't the one chasing him.* "You were chasing *me,*" Aaron whispered.

"I-I was ordered to," the boy whimpered, his bottom lip quivering, "I didn't—I wouldn't have hurt you. Please don't kill me."

Irritated at himself, Aaron realized something. Despite the fact that he knew it was foolishness, he couldn't kill the boy, not now, not with those stupid green eyes pleading, begging him to stay his hand. He was a sellsword, after all, not a monster. "I'm not going to kill you, kid," he whispered, cursing himself in his head as he did, "Not this time, but don't you let me see you again. The next time, you'll suffer before I bleed you out, you understand?"

The boy's head jerked in a tight nod, "Y-yes sir, of course."

Aaron grunted quietly as he rose, his breath pluming out into the cold night air and vanishing like a dream. He sheathed his blade and pulled the hood of his cloak back over his head. "Go to sleep, boy. Go to sleep and this'll all be gone when you wake up, nothing but a nightmare on a night made for them."

"Yes sir, thank you, sir," the boy stammered. Aaron only stared at him until the youth swallowed hard and closed his eyes.

You're making me soft, firefly, he thought wearily as he turned, *too damned soft.* He'd taken no more than two steps when he heard the tell-tale rustle behind him. *"Damnit,"* he hissed. He lunged to the side, and it was this desperate burst of action that saved his life. Instead of taking him in the base of the brain stem, the blade plunged deep into his shoulder. He bellowed as pain lanced through his body, fierce and jagged and hot. He whipped around to see the boy stumbling away from him, his eyes wide. The youth's hands were covered in blood. His blood.

"You stupid bastard," Aaron said in disbelief, lurching toward the boy on suddenly unsteady feet.

"I got him, Carl! Carl, wake up, I got him!" The boy shouted, his voice cracking. His eyes were wild as he stumbled back another step, his hands out in front of him as if to keep the sellsword at bay.

"Huh?" A gruff voice, thick with sleep, asked from the other shadowed bundle.

"I *got* him," the boy repeated, and although his voice was full of fear, Aaron could hear the pride in it.

He stumbled toward the boy, swaying drunkenly as the pain ripped through him. If the other man came fully awake and came from behind him, Aaron knew he was finished. He growled in frustration and took another halting, excruciating step.

The youth, his eyes locked on Aaron, wasn't paying attention to what was behind him as he shuffled backward. His foot snagged in his bed roll, and he let out a yelp of surprise as his legs came out from under him. He was still wrestling with the covers, trying to get himself untangled, when Aaron dove on top of him. The boy cried out in panic, wriggling in Aaron's grip like an eel, but Aaron grabbed a handful of the youth's hair in one hand, his chin in the other and let out a growl of fury and pain as he wrenched the youth's head to the side.

There was a *crack* as the boy's neck snapped, and his eyes opened so wide that they looked as if they would pop from the strain. He sputtered and choked, struggling, and failing, to draw a breath. Aaron turned away from the youth's look of horror, hating himself as he tore the boy's weakly pawing hands off of his shirt. With a grunt of effort, he pulled himself to his feet in time to see the other soldier, a man who looked to be in his early forties with a brown beard specked with gray, staring at him in shock.

"You—you killed him," the man said, "You killed the lad."

Aaron felt at his left shoulder gingerly, and discovered that the knife the boy had used was still in him. Blood loss was making him lightheaded, and he knew that if he passed out with this man still alive, he'd never wake up again. "Yeah, I killed him," he gasped, a deep self-loathing settling over him, "now are you just gonna stand there like a ... a fucking idiot, or are you gonna do something about it?"

The man growled, and drew a knife from his belt that was twice the size of the one sticking out of Aaron's shoulder, "Oh, I'll do something about it you son of a bitch." He snarled as he started closer. The soldier was nearly twice Aaron's size, but he consoled himself with the fact that, in his currently weakened state, he'd barely be able to overpower a child in hand to hand combat anyway. It didn't help.

Gritting his teeth, he gripped the handle of the blade in his shoulder and tore it free. There was a sickening, sucking sound as it came loose, and fresh blood blossomed out of the wound. Breathing in rasping grunts, Aaron stumbled awkwardly, barely keeping his feet as a wave of dizziness swept over him. The older soldier grinned cruelly, "You'll suffer for what you done to the boy. I'll see to it."

"Come on then," Aaron said, trying, unsuccessfully, to blink away the darkness at the corners of his vision.

The man let out snarl of rage and rushed forward. Aaron tried to dodge the soldier's first strike, but the man was a skilled fighter, and Aaron's wound made him too slow. The knife cut across his side, and he bellowed in pain, nearly losing his footing on one of the dead boy's legs as he reeled away.

The soldier was on him in an instant, swinging the knife in vicious cuts and stabs. Aaron put all of his dwindling energy into avoiding the strikes, giving no thought to attempting any counter attacks with his own, blood-smeared blade. He managed to kick the man away and grimaced as he pressed his unarmed hand to a fresh cut across his stomach. *This isn't working,* he thought resignedly, *he'll have me soon.*

I am blocking what I can, Co said in his mind. Her voice sounded strained, tired.

He'd figured as much. Without the Virtue's help, he was certain that he'd have lost consciousness minutes ago, but, magical flying orb or no, the loss of blood was making him disoriented and slow, and it would only be moments before the soldier managed to close the distance and get in a strike that Aaron wouldn't walk away from.

The grizzled man circled him, a hungry expression on his face. He feinted with the knife, and Aaron lurched to the side in a desperate attempt to dodge a thrust that never came. The soldier smiled a cruel smile, "Not much good when your opponent's awake, are you, sellsword?"

Aaron set his jaw with grim determination, "Are you going to sit there and talk, or are we going to get this done?"

The man nodded, "Alright then, bastard. Say hello to the Keeper for me." Then he rushed forward, swinging his knife in a vicious arc.

Instead of trying to evade the blow, the sellsword stepped into it, throwing his forearm in the way of the oncoming blade. He bellowed in pain as the sharp steel plunged deep into his arm and struck bone. With a savage snarl, he called on what little strength he had left, lunging forward and slamming his own knife up and into the man's gut.

The soldier let out a grunt of surprise as the steel sheared through his flesh. He gave a jerk on the blade in

Aaron's forearm, trying to pull it free. Aaron cried out as the knife dug at the bone in his arm, but it was stuck fast and did not come out. He took another step closer to the man, growling, his eyes wild and feral, then ripped his knife free and slammed it into the man's stomach again.

The soldier gasped, and took a step back, his eyes wide with shock and a dawning fear. Aaron pursued him forward, plunging the knife home again and again, paying no attention to the blood splattering him. A few more strikes, and the man's legs gave out from under him, and he crumpled to the ground. Aaron followed him to the ground, bringing the blade down again and again. The knife pistoned up and down, up and down, blood fountaining out, nearly black in the firelight. For a time, he was aware of nothing except the feel of it on his hands and face, warm enough to be almost hot, and the rhythmic push and pull of the blade.

By the time he came to a panting stop, his good arm was aching fiercely, though the pain paled in comparison to the wounds in his shoulder and forearm. He let the knife fall free of his numb fingers onto the crimson-stained grass. For several seconds, he sat there, trying to get a handle on the pain that raged through him. Then he took a deep breath and started to his feet.

Before he was halfway up, the darkness which had been creeping into the edges of his vision surged forward as if with a mind of its own, and he crumpled to the ground under the weight of it. *This is how it ends,* he thought, and then there was the darkness and nothing but the darkness.

CHAPTER TWENTY-SIX

HE FLOATED IN A SEA OF DARKNESS, on waves of darkness, and it was alright. Soon, he knew, he would sink beneath those waves, would fall into the still greater darkness waiting beneath, and that was alright too. There was no pain, there, no hunger or thirst. Only the darkness. That and nothing more.

--UP. AARON, YOU HAVE TO GET UP NOW! The words sounded strange, as if they were coming from some great distance, from some small, unremembered place, and he thought he could just make out some light in the distance, a weak, flickering thing that the darkness had not yet touched, had not yet consumed. But it would. He knew that now. It always did.

A man could light his candles, could lock his windows against the night, and huddle beneath the covers like a child, yet still it came, and when it did, there was no denying it. If a man was living, he was dying. *Go away,* he thought to the voice, *leave me alone. I'm dying, can't you see that? Why won't you just leave me alone?*

The voice said something else, but it was farther away now, quieter and weaker, and he couldn't make out the words. That was alright. He couldn't remember what it wanted, but that was alright too.

--OU'LL DIE IF YOU DON'T GET UP NOW.

He winced inwardly at the frantic, screeching sound of the voice, *Don't you get it?* He thought, trying to make the owner of the voice understand the uselessness of it all, *I'm done. I've been done for a while, I think, and what does it matter? Men plan and the worms feast; it's the way it's always been, and what's left for me there anyway? Pain, that's all. More pain than you can imagine.*

I can imagine it, the voice replied, *you are not the only one that feels pain. I think you've forgotten that somewhere. Life is pain, but that is not all it is.*

Oh? He thought, wishing the voice would just go away, *could have fooled me.*

No, the voice answered sadly, and this time it sounded as if it spoke directly into his ear. *Life is joy too. You do remember joy, don't you?*

He started to say no, no he *couldn't* remember joy, but stopped as a vision unfolded before him. No, not a vision, a memory. A small boy sat at the top of the stairs of his home, looking between the wooden railings to the room beneath where his mother and father danced, unaware of their audience. There was no instrument playing, no singer to accompany their movements, but if they noticed the lack, they did not show it. The woman laid her hand on the man's shoulder, and they held each other close. And they danced.

That's it, the voice said reassuringly, *you remember.*

I remember nothing, Aaron thought back, turning away from the terrible, wonderful memory, turning back to the darkness, *I don't know that boy.*

But you do, the voice countered, *it's you, Aaron. The boy's you.*

I'm telling you I don't know *him damnit.*

What of loyalty, Aaron? Do you know nothing of it as well?

Another vision appeared in front of him, faint at first, but growing until he wasn't looking at it anymore, but experiencing it. He was in a massive room, a cafeteria, it appeared. The tables were filled with young boys and girls with bowls of some gruel in front of them. They ate soundlessly, their eyes locked on their own bowls as they shoveled food in their mouths mechanically. Somehow, the place seemed familiar to him, and for a reason he didn't understand, he was glad that they were silent. Here, in this place, it was important to be quiet, to be still, to not be *noticed.*

All of the kids turned, and he felt his own heart lurch in his chest as the main doors of the cafeteria burst open. He cringed inwardly as Headmaster Cyrille, marched in, a wicked, familiar switch in his hand. "Who *dared* to do it?" The man screeched, his face crimson, his eyes wild with anger as they swept the room. "Which of you ungrateful ingrates *dared?*"

The boys and the girls cowered in their seats, and Aaron, like them, wished that he could disappear. He desired only for whatever was about to happen to be over, so that they could keep living. Living wasn't much to any of them, not in that place—one only had to look at the vacant, dead gazes of the girls or the careful, shaking movements of many of the boys to know that—but it was all they had. All that hadn't yet been taken from them.

"Answer me you stupid little bastards!" The man screamed, his hands knotted into tight, pale fists at his side, "Or I will make every last one of you suffer, do you understand me?" Silence reined, thick and pregnant with dreaded expectation.

The old man turned to the nearest child, a nine year old girl with soft, doll-like features and blonde hair so fine it seemed to flow around her face like rain, and brought the switch savagely across her face. The girl let out a cry of pain as her nose snapped beneath the taut wood, and she was flung out of her seat. She landed on the floor with a *thump*, her hands covering her broken nose as she sobbed in desperate, keening whimpers.

The man took a step toward her and brought the switch up again. "I know who it was," A voice squeaked.

The gray-haired man stopped in mid-swing and whipped around to the young boy who had spoken. "What did you say, Thomas?" He asked, his voice suddenly deceptively sweet. "Please, go on my boy. Tell me again. I will not hurt any of you anymore; I just want to know who did it, that's all. A boy or girl like that, well, they could ruin things for all of us, don't you understand?" Somehow, though he knew he wasn't there, Aaron could smell the sharp, acrid tang of the Tamarang herb floating about the man, and he knew that the man's words, like the place itself, were a lie.

"I-it was Aaron," the boy stammered, "P-please, sir. Please don't hit her anymore. It was Aaron Envelar."

"Are you sure, Thomas? You wouldn't lie to me, would you?" He asked, his voice little more than a whisper.

"O-of course not, M-Master Cyrille. It was him. He did it."

"No he didn't," a new voice said. The headmaster turned to the other boy who'd spoken. The boy's hair was so light it was almost brown, and his nose was bent to the side from a past break that had never healed right. "It wasn't Aaron, sir. It was me."

"*You?*" The headmaster asked, surprised, "Owen, it was *you?*"

The boy's eyes were wide with fear, but he nodded, and when he spoke his voice was determined, "Yes sir. I did it. I'm sorry, but I did."

"Tsk tsk," the headmaster said, shaking his head, "and after all I've done for you," he gestured expansively across the room with the switch, "after all I've done for *all* of you, this is the thanks I get? Well, we will just see about that." The boy trembled as the old man started toward him, but he did not cry out or beg as the headmaster grabbed him by the collar and drug him out of the cafeteria, slamming the doors behind him.

Once the doors were closed, the kids did not speak. They all liked Owen, but what could they do? It was better not to speak of it, to forget it, to keep on living. They turned back to their food and ate. You had to eat to live.

In some distant place, Aaron felt a tear slide its way down his cheek. *I didn't mean it,* he thought, *I didn't mean it. Why did he do it? Why? It should have been* me!

What of loyalty, Aaron? The voice asked as if he'd never spoken, *do you remember loyalty?*

No! He cried soundlessly, *Don't you see? They're all dead. My parents, Owen, all of them dead. There is nothing in the world but pain and waiting for the pain to stop.*

You're wrong, Aaron, the voice said sadly.

Stop saying my name. You don't know me!

I know you, Aaron Envelar. I know you better than you know yourself. What of love? Does love mean nothing?

Stop it, he begged, *leave me alone.* But the voice did not. Instead, a series of visions flitted through his mind in rapid succession. Visions of a woman with dark brown hair and eyes so fiercely blue that they seemed to burn with it. A woman that waited on the docks when he would have ran, a woman who hesitated with a blade when he would have struck, the same woman who had come to him at the inn, despite all of his cruelty, to let him know that she cared. *Adina,* he thought, *her name is Adina.*

Yes.

Suddenly, the darkness that surrounded him, gathered and waiting, seemed abhorrent, greasy and cloying. He shook himself free of it the way a drowning man might struggle against the pressing water, with a desperate, frantic determination.

When he'd given everything that he had, when he was convinced that it wouldn't be enough, his eyes flitted open, and he winced at the brightness of the fire. "C-Co?" He croaked.

I am here, Aaron, the Virtue answered, the relief clear in her voice.

He gingerly felt the wound in his shoulder. The flow of blood had lessened but had not stopped. With a momentous effort and despite his body's protests, he managed to struggle to a sitting position. He rested there for a second, his head spinning, his eyes struggling to focus. Then, he took a deep breath and tore a piece from his tattered, bloody shirt—a task made almost impossible with one working arm—looped it around the wound, and grunted in pain as he pulled it tight.

He waited another moment then tried to push himself to his feet. He was sure that he wouldn't make it, that he would fall, that his eyes would close for a final time and that would be the end of it. It was with some surprise, then, that he realized with a shock that he was standing. He was swaying drunkenly, in danger of tipping over at any moment, but he *was* standing. *Alright then,* he thought as he fought off a fresh wave of dizziness, *alright.*

He wondered, as he closed his eyes and took a slow, steadying breath, how much worse the pain would be if Co wasn't there to lessen it. *Too much,* he thought, *far too much.* He glanced at the fire and saw that it was burning low, almost burned out. *But not dead,* he thought fiercely, *not yet.* He stumbled toward one of the soldier's horses and, after the third try, managed to scramble into the saddle. The horse let out a neigh of displeasure as he tugged on its lead. "Come on then, boy," he said, turning the beast toward the road, toward Naya's and the others. "We don't want to keep them waiting."

CHAPTER TWENTY-SEVEN

ADINA ROSE FROM HER SEAT near the fire and peered out the window for what must have been the hundredth time. Outside, the darkness huddled around Naya's small waystop, and Adina felt a deep foreboding settle over her. There was still no sign of Aaron. Gryle stood by another of the building's windows, wringing his hands nervously, his gaze locked on the pale moon. *He dreads the sun,* she thought sadly, *dreads the moment when those first rays of light will pierce the darkness, and we will leave Aaron behind. I know because I do as well.*

She sighed heavily and walked back to her seat by the fire. On their trip here, Peter had been so excited about the visit, going on and on about Naya's lemon tarts, and how kind the old woman was. It had taken all of Adina's training in diplomacy to keep herself from strangling the youth. While he was worried about filling his belly, Aaron was out in that darkness. For all they knew, he could be dying. *Don't be a fool. For all you know, he's already dead.*

No. I won't believe that. She swallowed hard and wiped at her eyes. "It'll be okay, dear," Naya's kind, age-wizened voice said beside her, "you'll see."

Adina nodded and forced a smile as she turned to the woman. Though Peter's incessant yammering had brought her nearer the point of murder than she'd care to admit, he hadn't been wrong about the proprietor of the waystop. Naya was a short, stooped, elderly woman, and though she walked with a cane, she'd moved around surprisingly quick when they'd arrived, fixing them a meal of cooked meat, bread, and, of course, her famous lemon tarts, despite the late hour and without complaint.

"Thank you again for taking us in so late at night," Adina said, struggling to sound grateful past the lump of fear and uncertainty that seemed lodged in her throat.

The old woman waved a wrinkled hand dismissively, "Never mind that, dear. I've always been a light sleeper, and I've found that it's grown worse with age. Why, I'm lucky to get four hours a night, what with my old bones aching like they do. My husband, Ed, he could have slept straight through if a tornado'd come a'knockin, but I've never had the knack. I would've been awake whether you folks had stopped by or not. At least this way, I don't have to sit around by myself." The old woman casted her milky gaze around the small waystop, "The place has been too quiet since my Ed was taken by the fevers. Much too quiet for my likin'. It does my old heart good to have some young people here."

The princess smiled, "Well, I thank you just the same." She glanced over at the red-headed Peter who, even now, was chewing contentedly on a lemon tart, lost in his own world of sugary sweetness, "and I'm sure Peter thanks you too."

The old woman chortled, "That boy eats like it's his last meal."

Adina winced at the woman's words, thinking of Aaron somewhere out there alone. And what had his last meal been? Dried travel rations, nothing more, and he'd walked away with her words, spoken in anger, following him.

"Is something wrong, dearie? I'm sorry," Naya said, patting her hand, "that was a fool thing to say. Sometimes my mouth runs off before my mind has a chance to catch up. Ed used to say that I could talk the stars down from the sky. At the time, I took it as a compliment." She snorted and shook her head, "Now, I think maybe he meant that they'd choose suicide over listening to my rambling."

The princess laughed weakly. "I'm sure your husband meant nothing of the sort."

"Why don't you tell me about him."

Adina turned and glanced at the woman, surprised. "We never told you we were waiting on anyone."

Naya coughed a laugh, "Come now, child. I've been around long enough to know that there's only two things will put that look in a woman's eyes, a man or bad memories, and you're too young for many of those. Besides," she said, gesturing at Gryle, "your man there has been staring out that window like his eyes are glued to it since you all got here. No," she said with a small shake of her head, "I know how waitin' looks. I ought to; I've been doin' it for a long time now."

"What have you been waiting on?" Adina asked curiously.

The old lady smiled, "Death. No, now don't look at me like that, dearie, I'm not lookin' to die, but I'm ready for it, and when the gods decide to take me I'll go willingly. Fred's awaitin', and he never was a patient man. Nicest one a woman could ever ask for, but tell 'em he had to wait on somethin' and his foot'd be tappin' a mile a minute 'til the waiting was done. Why, I reckon he's probably wore a hole clean through his shoes by now."

Despite her fear, Adina didn't have to fake the smile, "You must have really loved him."

Naya nodded, "And still do, dear. Now, why don't you tell me about your man. I ain't the best at talkin', but I can listen, sure enough."

The princess opened her mouth to correct the woman, to tell her that Aaron *wasn't* her man, but decided against it. After all, what difference did it make? She thought of the sellsword, of the look in his face and eyes when he'd spoken of Glenn's sick daughter, of the way he'd given the man his gold without even a second thought. He would have her believe that he'd done it because it was the best way to keep from being killed, that he didn't care about the girl one way or the other, but she knew that was a lie. She'd seen the look of anger and sadness in his hazel eyes, had seen his fists clench at his side as Herb's girl, Paula, had come out from the back with her painfully thin limbs, and hair falling out in patches. "He's ... he's difficult," she said finally, "and stubborn. I didn't think someone could *be* so stubborn."

The old woman cackled good-naturedly, patting her chest with a wrinkled hand.

Adina smiled uncertainly, "Did I say something funny?"

Naya shook her head, running a finger across her eyes as she finally gained control of herself. "Oh, nothing dearie. You've just described every man that was ever born is all. My Ed could have taught a mule a thing or two about stubbornness, and that's the truth. No, I mean what makes your man special to you?"

Adina considered this. "He doesn't treat me like everyone else ... for all my life, people have treated me like I was made of glass, like I'd break if I wasn't watched. He doesn't do that. And he has a good heart. He doesn't know it, but he does."

The proprietor smiled, "Then I guess you'd better show him when he comes back hadn't you?"

The princess smiled, "I guess s—" she cut off as the doors of the inn burst open. Gryle let out a squeak of surprise and stumbled back. He tripped over his own feet and nearly impaled himself on the blade Aaron had given him as he fell to the ground. Cold air wafted through the door making the fire dance frantically. Adina felt her heart leap to her throat, sure that somehow the soldiers had gotten around Aaron, had pressed on through the night and found them.

They all watched, frozen, as a shadowed figure lurched through the door and into the orange glow of the fire. She gasped as Aaron shuffled into view. He was covered in so much blood that it looked as if he'd taken a bath in it, and a knife stuck out of his left forearm which dangled uselessly at his side. He swayed drunkenly as he surveyed the room with an unfocused, distant gaze.

Finally, his hazel eyes, mad and feverish, settled on her. "I killed him," he croaked, "I killed Owen." As if the words were a cue, his legs buckled beneath him, and he crumpled to the ground.

CHAPTER TWENTY-EIGHT

HE DIDN'T SO MUCH WAKE as drift into a state of semi-consciousness, carried on eddies of delirium and pain. *I killed Owen,* was his first thought, but even as he had it he knew that it was wrong. The youth hadn't been Owen, just some kid playing at being a soldier. *He was soldier enough when he damn near killed you.* He tried to sit up and pain tore through his body. He fell back into bed gasping and feeling as if he was about to pass out.

You live, Co said in his mind, her relief clear in her voice.

If you'd call it that. He forced his gummy eyes open, blinking against the harshness of the sun being filtered through a window. He was in a small bedroom he didn't recognize, and a yellow quilt embroidered with white flowers had been laid atop him. Sighing heavily, wincing at the pain in his shoulder and arm, he closed his eyes again. *Firefly, make yourself useful. Tell me where I am.*

You're at Naya's. You have been here for the last three days.

Three days? You've got to be kidding me.

I am not in a kidding mood, the Virtue answered, her voice in his head thick with anger and fear, *you took a stupid risk, and you've spent the last three days unconscious as a reward. The proprietor, Naya, is a skilled healer—lucky that—but you very nearly died just the same.*

For a moment, he was silent, surprised at the emotions he could hear raging in Co's voice. Then he remembered the boy, remembered deciding to let him live and the feel of the knife as it entered his back. He clenched his teeth against a building fury of his own. *I almost died because of you. You had me thinking all those stupid thoughts about that kid. Because of you, I tried to let him live. Because of you, I was weak, and it nearly got me killed. From now on, how about you stay the fuck out of my business?*

You think mercy is weakness? Co asked dangerously.

Look at where it got me! He thought back, *before you showed up, I was living the easy life, taking jobs and making money. Now, every time I try to do what needs to be done, I've got you screwing with my head.*

You're wrong.

The fuck I am. Mercy is for fools. In this world, you take what you want, keep what you can, and to the Fields with everyone else.

You misunderstand me, the Virtue responded, her tone cool, *I didn't make you feel anything.*

Of course you did! Why else would I—he paused, frowning.

Yes, the Virtue said, *you begin to understand. I am not the one that made you 'weak' as you call it. I am not the one, Aaron Envelar, who staid your hand, who chose mercy. You are. You are not quite the monster you pretend to be.*

He was just about to tell her exactly what he thought of *that* when there was a rustle beside the bed. He opened his eyes again and managed to turn his head a fraction in the direction of the sound. It wasn't much, but it was enough for him to see the princess seated beside him. Her legs were curled underneath her, and her head was lying on the back of the chair, her dark hair covering most of her face. Now that he wasn't distracted by Co, he could just make out the faint sounds of her breath as she slept.

He watched her breathe in and out softly, thinking of the visions the Virtue had shown him while he lay near death. *She has spent almost every moment here,* Co said. The anger was gone from her voice, something like affection having replaced it.

Why?

Do you not know?

He stared at Adina, at the soft fall of her hair, the gentle lines of her face and did not answer. Finally, he cleared his throat.

The princess stirred and glanced over at the bed. She let out a gasp of surprise at seeing his eyes open, "Y-you're awake." She reached a hand toward his where it lay over the quilt, then hesitated, no doubt remembering how he'd acted the last time she'd gotten close.

"It's okay," he croaked, wincing at the dryness in his voice and trying to smile.

She placed her hand, soft and warm on his, "Naya said ... I didn't think--"

"That I was going to live?" He asked softly, "Me e—" he started, then cut off as he was overcome by a coughing fit.

"Wait, I'll get you some water." She went to the nightstand and poured him a glass of water. By the time she came back, he'd managed to get his coughing under control.

"Slowly," she said as she brought the glass to his lips. The water was cool and refreshing, and he thought he'd never had any better. Despite her warning, he drank greedily, and she was forced to jerk the glass away as he broke into another fit of coughs.

When he'd finished, he saw that she was smiling at him, "You don't like to listen, do you?"

"Look, Adina, about the way I've treated you—"

"It's fine," she interrupted, "you should really save your strength. We can talk about it another time."

"No," he said, meeting her gaze, "this is important." He waited for her to argue. When she didn't, he took a deep breath and spoke, "You see, the thing is ... well, it seems like for all my life anything good I ever got was taken from me. First my parents, then Owen ... I didn't kill him by the way, he was already dead. Or, that is ... probably. He's probably dead, but I didn't do it." He saw her confused expression and went on, "Well, I *did* kill him, but he wasn't Owen—I only thought he was, and I tried not to, really. But that," he felt himself growing angry at the memory, "that son of a *bitch* stabbed me in the back. He stabbed me in the *back.*"

"Uhuh," she said, starting to rise, "maybe I should get Naya. She'll want—"

"Wait," he said, grabbing her hand, "please." He took a deep breath and sighed, "Damnit. I'm not very good at this. Look, what I mean to say is that you were right, I do—"

Just then she pressed a finger softly against his lips and smiled. "Shh. I know, Aaron. It's okay."

She moved closer, so that their lips were only inches apart. "I know," she said in a whisper. Just then, there was a loud *creak* as the door swung open, and she jumped back into her seat.

An old woman, Naya, he assumed, walked into the room, a glass in one hand, a cane in the other. She was too busy ogling the sellsword in shock to notice the princess's deep blush. "Well, may the gods be praised," she breathed.

Aaron lay there, uncomfortable under the woman's gaze for several seconds before he cleared his throat, "I'm Aaron. You're Naya, I take it?"

The old woman shook her head as if to clear it, "Sorry, it's just that I ain't seen many folks cheat the Keeper his due. The name's Naya and don't worry; I know your name. I reckon I know about everything there is to know about you," she winked conspiratorially at the princess who blushed and looked away.

He smiled, "Well, I thank you for patching me up. Now, if you two will help me up, we need to get going."

He was just starting to try to rise, when Naya took a menacing step forward, "You're a big fella, young man, but you won't move one muscle off of that bed if you know what's good for you. I didn't spend all my time *patching you up* as you call it just to see you ruin all my hard work by getting the notion in your fool head that you were going to jump out of bed and go on a bloody march."

Aaron frowned but didn't move. "Fact is," the old woman went on, either not noticing or not caring about his expression, "that you're lucky to be alive. No, lucky don't even cover it as far as I'm concerned. Boy, I've seen corpses that look a blessed sight better than you do even now. Why, when you arrived, I'm pretty sure you had more blood on ya than in ya, and for the life of me I can't see how you managed to walk in here on your own two feet."

"The walking was fine," he said with a smile, "as I recall, it was the standing that did me in."

The woman frowned at him through furrowed brows, "Yeah, well. You're lucky you've got a good woman that cares about you. As far as I'm concerned, any man fool enough to get himself stabbed not once, but two times, not to mention cut up like a slaughter hog, deserves his fate, so don't you give me no trouble, or I'll make what happened to you seem like a picnic, you understand?"

Aaron swallowed hard and tried to look properly admonished under the woman's stern, milky gaze, "Yes, ma'am. Well, I thank you just the same."

The woman walked over to the stand beside the bed, sat the drink down, and looked at him meaningfully, "You can thank me by drinking every bit of that tea. Tastes like horse leavings, but I won't have you takin' fever and dying – not after all the work I've put into you."

"Thank you, Naya," Adina said.

The old woman's scowl vanished in an instant, replaced by a kind smile as she patted Adina on the hand, "That's alright, dear. It was my pleasure." She glanced back at Aaron, "Now, if he gives you any trouble you let me know, alright?"

The princess smiled, "Yes ma'am."

"That's a good girl." The old woman glared at him once more before she turned and shuffled away. "Patching him up," she muttered and snorted as she walked out the door.

Once she was gone, Aaron glanced at Adina, his eyebrow raised. "I don't think she likes me much."

The princess laughed, "You think? No, Naya is just … protective. She's been looking in on you constantly, you know. You should have seen her that first night, Aaron. For a woman who shuffles like she can barely walk, she moved like lightning when you came in. All the rest of us were terrified but not her. She got Peter and Gryle to lift you onto the table and started to work on your wounds like it was the most ordinary thing in the world." She shook her head, her smile vanishing, "I still can't believe she managed it. When I saw you like that, all covered in blood with a knife still in your arm, I thought … Well, I thought—"

"I know."

Several moments passed before either of them spoke. Finally, Adina took a deep breath and asked the question she'd been dying to ask, "Why did you go, Aaron? We could have run … we could have hid."

He thought of the orphanage then, of the days he'd spent doing his best to avoid the notice of the headmaster, the days he'd spent letting the man's atrocities continue, too scared to try to stop them. "Because I decided a long time ago that I wouldn't run anymore, that I wouldn't hide. Leaving the Downs, that's one thing, fleeing like a rabbit from a couple of soldiers, well, that's more than I'm willing to do."

"So what happened out there?" She asked, and he could hear the reluctance in her voice. It was a question she thought she needed to ask, but one that she didn't really want to know the answer to.

"I made a mistake," he said, thinking of the youth with the green eyes, begging for his life. "It's one I won't make again."

She nodded, relieved. "I'm just glad you're alive."

"Alive isn't good enough. If what Herb told me was right, it won't be long before the contest starts in Baresh, and Claudius means to hand the country over to Belgarin after it's over."

She shook her head, "Surely you can't mean to enter, not after what you've been through. Why, you can barely even move, and Naya says it'll be at least a month before the bone in your left arm's healed."

He smiled, "It's a good thing I'm right-handed then."

"No, Aaron. You can't. There's got to be another way."

"If you know one, name it."

She opened her mouth to speak but closed it again. He nodded, "It's been a long time since I've let myself care about anybody else, Adina, and I'll admit that I'm one of the world's biggest assholes, but those people don't know what's coming. They're already starving, sure, but that'll be the least of their worries if your brother takes control. You know that don't you?"

She nodded but didn't speak.

"If there's another way, we'll find it," he said reassuringly, "trust me, I don't relish the thought of fighting one handed. That kind of money is going to bring in some quality contenders, not just the normal group of strutting peacocks these kinds of events attract, but some real blades. If I'm stuck going up against a master with a bum arm, I won't last five seconds."

She frowned at him, "You're not making me feel any better."

He laughed at that, and was still laughing when there was a knock on the door. "Who is it?" He asked, pretending not to notice the princess's glare.

"It's Gryle, sir," answered the muffled voice of the chamberlain from the other side of the door, "M-may I come in?"

"Well, come on then."

The chubby man walked in, his gaze never wavering from the ground in front of his feet, "I-I heard that you were up."

"Well, I wouldn't say I'm up," Aaron said, "but I'm breathin', and there's something to be said for that."

The chamberlain didn't answer. Instead, he fidgeted from one foot to the next, his gaze staying on the ground. To Aaron, he looked ashamed, like a man needing to get something off his chest and, judging by the furtive glances he kept casting in the princess's direction, he didn't want her present when he did.

Adina must have also noticed Gryle's unease because she rose and winked at him, "Don't forget to drink all of the tea Naya brought. I'll be back in a few minutes. I'm going to see if Naya needs any help in the kitchen."

When she was gone, Gryle breathed an audible sigh of relief, and risked his first glance at Aaron himself. "Sir, I'm glad that you're okay. We were all worried about you."

"Thanks." Aaron caught a whiff of something foul and frowned, glancing in the direction of the tea sitting on the nightstand. He could smell the pungent, herbal odor from the bed, but the old woman had been very specific. He sighed, motioning to the glass with his chin, "You mind handing me that?"

Gryle handed him the glass distractedly, too absorbed in his own thoughts to notice Aaron's wince as he barely managed the monumental effort of forcing his unresponsive fingers to grasp the cup. As soon as the cup was taken from his grasp, the chamberlain began wringing his hands nervously. He opened his mouth several times, as if about to speak, only to shut it again.

While he waited on the chamberlain to spit out whatever was bothering him, Aaron took a deep, preparatory breath, and took a long drink of the tea. He sputtered, spilling some of it on the quilt as he gagged on the foul-tasting liquid. It felt like oil in his throat, thick and cloying, and though he tried to force himself to drink it, he was only able to get down a small amount of the sharp, tangy mixture before he became certain that anymore would have him heaving all over the flowered quilt. When he was sure he wasn't going to puke, he looked back at Gryle. The man had paid no attention to his suffering, too busy mulling over whatever it was he was thinking of. "Alright, damnit, I'm the one having to drink sewer water, but you look like a man on the hangman's block. What's eating you?"

"I was going to leave you," the chubby man blurted, his face turning a deep red, "I was going to take the princess and leave you. I wanted to go back, but ... but I had to make sure that she got to safety."

He looked at the man, confused, "Didn't I tell you to leave at first light?"

The chamberlain nodded pathetically, refusing to meet his eyes, "Yes."

"Look at me, chamberlain. Damnit *look* at me." Slowly, cowering as if he was about to be struck, Gryle met his gaze. Aaron noticed with chagrin and more than a touch of impatience that the chamberlain's bottom lip was quivering. "You did what I told you to do, nothing less. You did what you were *supposed* to do. There's no reason to beat yourself up about that."

"I-it isn't right, to leave you like that. It isn't right." Gryle said miserably, his chubby face screwed up in an effort to keep from crying.

Aaron barked a laugh, "Maybe not, but what does that matter?" The chamberlain glanced at him curiously. "If there's anything I've learned, Gryle, it's that what most people consider the right choice can get a man killed. Leave it to the priests and the politicians to die for their beliefs. For us normal men, the right choice is the one that keeps us breathing a little while longer."

Gryle frowned at him, "Y-you don't believe that, sir— you can't."

Aaron smiled, but there was no humor in it. "Don't I? Let me tell you something, chamberlain. When the darkness comes, when a man lies awake for fear that it will be *his* night, *his* turn to visit the Keeper's Fields...." He thought of Owen and paused. When he spoke again he did so through gritted teeth, "At a time like that, a man doesn't give a fuck about morality or being a good person. All he cares about is seein' the sunrise."

Gryle considered this for several moments. When he finally answered his voice was little more than a whisper, and he eyed Aaron with a look of expectant dread, as if he was sure that he was going to skewer him for his words, despite the fact that with the way his body felt Aaron would be lucky if he managed to take a piss by himself, "I-I don't believe that, sir," The chamberlain answered. "I won't believe it. Breathing's not enough; it can't be. The gods watch us, and they know our hearts. They protect those who serve them."

Aaron grunted, suddenly exhausted. His eyes closed of their own accord, as if lead weights had been tied to the lids, and he wondered when they'd gotten so heavy. "Well."

"My, I'm sorry, sir," Gryle stuttered, "here I am talking to you when you're supposed to be getting your rest. I'm so sorry; I'll leave right now."

Aaron was sure that if he opened his eyes he would see the chamberlain wringing his hands anxiously, but the effort wasn't worth it. "You did the right thing, Gryle."

The chamberlain didn't answer, but Aaron could hear the man's shuffling steps as he made his way to the door, "Oh, and Gryle?"

"Yes sir?" The chubby man asked, his squeaky voice sounding distant as the darkness of exhaustion and weariness began to settle over Aaron like a thick, heavy mantle.

"It's good that you have your beliefs," He said. His tongue felt too big, wooly, and he could detect a slur in his speech, but he was too tired to care. "My father told me once that a man without any beliefs wasn't a man at all."

"T-thank you, sir," the chamberlain said, and Aaron heard the distant sound of the door closing as he left.

Left alone with his own thoughts, he remembered the boy who wasn't Owen, remembered the way his green eyes had pleaded, so desperate to live. He thought of the way the young soldier's neck had looked, the bone pushed out to the side in a swollen clump, his eyes wide and blank in death, his arms and legs splayed out wildly as if he wasn't a man at all, but some grotesque marionette whose strings had been cut. *And aren't we?* He thought bitterly, *aren't we all just the puppets of the gods, waiting for them to tire of us and cut our strings?* He sighed heavily, "That's alright," he said, his voice little more than a whisper, "it's good that he believes in something. Even if it is a lie."

CHAPTER TWENTY-NINE

HE AWOKE FIGHTING FOR HIS LIFE, choking and gasping as some terrible poison was forced down his throat. He struggled, but his muscles were weak from his wounds and it did little good as the liquid coursed down his throat like liquid fire. It was the soldiers, it had to be. They must have crept up on them at Naya's while everyone was asleep. He tried to spit up the vile brew, but a hand, strong and merciless despite its thinness, clamped down on his mouth, and he was forced to swallow or drown.

"Please, that's enough," A woman's voice, fraught with worry.

Slowly, reluctantly, the hand pulled away. Aaron gagged at the slimy, cloying foulness coating the inside of his throat and waited for death to claim him. When it didn't, he slowly opened his eyes and stared in surprise. Instead of the soldiers or assassins he'd expected, the stooped, gray-haired proprietor of the waystop, Naya, stood above him. The old woman's hair was pulled back into a bun so tight that it stretched her leathery, wrinkled face. She was frowning, "I never would have took a big man like you for such a baby. Why, Ed used to love my

Shalta tea, used to wake up every mornin' and ask for it. Besides, I told you, you have to drink it all."

Aaron was just opening his mouth to tell the old hag that asking for the tea had been her husband's idea of suicide when Adina spoke, "I'm sure he just forgot, Naya. It was my fault—I kept him up talking too long yesterday."

The old woman shook her head as she turned to the princess, "You're too soft on him, dear. It does a man good to suffer every once and a while," she glowered at him with her milky, gray eyes, "keeps him from doin' a fool thing like runnin' off and getting himself carved up like a fairday turkey."

"*Ouch!*" Came a shout from the other room, and the old woman sighed, "That Gryle seems a good enough sort, but he's got less sense in the kitchen than the gods gave a rock." She tsked, "A woman's work is never done. Dear, do you need anything while I'm keeping that kind-hearted fool from killing himself?"

"No, thank you," Adina said.

The woman nodded once before glancing back at Aaron. "As for you, I'll be bringing by another cup of Shalta in a few hours—you've lost a lot of blood, and you need to get your strength back. I'd remind you to drink it all up, but I don't think you'll forget again, will you?' She grinned, displaying her few remaining teeth, "Not unless you liked your wakin' this morning, that is." Not bothering to wait for a response, she turned and shuffled out of the room. Aaron could hear her shouts as she headed toward the kitchen. *Poor Gryle,* he thought, but he was just glad that someone else would be bearing the brunt of her attentions for a while, at least.

"That old hag works for Belgarin," he said, "I'm certain of it. Probably his chief torturer."

Adina let out a soft, throaty giggle, brushing a strand of dark hair behind her ear, and he found himself smiling despite the foul taste in his mouth. "Naya's not so bad. She's just worried about you."

He grunted, "Trying to drown me's a funny way of showing it."

She smiled, "Listen, Aaron. Naya says that it will be another two or three days before you're able to move around much. We tried, no one can say different, but we're going to have to find another way to get to Claudius."

He glanced at his bandaged shoulder and arm and flexed them, wincing at how stiff they were. "There's not another way, Adina. We both know that." He took a deep breath and swung his legs over the side of the bed, straining with the effort. He paused a moment to gather himself, ignoring the cold sweat that had broken out on his forehead as he levered his way to his feet.

He swayed dizzily for a moment and was forced to catch himself on the nightstand. Adina moved forward to catch him, but he waved her away, taking a deep breath and trying to accustom himself to the bright, hot pain that seemed to fill every muscle, every joint. "I'm okay," he said through clenched teeth, "and if I can walk, I can ride. We leave now."

CHAPTER THIRTY

THE OLD WOMAN SHOOK HER HEAD as she studied the three of them scornfully, "It's a foolish thing to travel when you're on the mend. I don't know why you're in such a hurry, but you'll undo all of my hard work for nothing."

Aaron sighed, "I understand that you don't like it, ma'am, but we have to go just the same." Of course he understood. It would be impossible not to considering that she'd spent the last hour telling him exactly how much of a horse's ass he was for leaving while they were preparing for the journey. "And trust me," he said, glancing at Adina's worried expression, "It's not for nothing."

Naya's wrinkled face screwed up in a frown and she hocked and spat, "Well, the only thing more foolish than a fool is the man that tries to reason with one as my Ed always said. At least that boy, Peter, was smart enough to get away from ya while he could. "

From what the princess and Gryle had told him, Peter had left shortly after Aaron's bloody arrival. Not that he blamed the youth. There were plenty of ways for death to find you without going and courting it. He was thankful, however, that the youth had been kind enough to leave them the cart and mules—extracting a promise from the chamberlain that he'd send them back to Kraser as soon as possible—before borrowing a horse from Naya and hauling ass back home. In truth, Aaron was glad the boy was gone. Better that than having to watch him gawk at the princess for another day or two. He forced a smile and nodded to the old hag, "Your husband must have been a wise man."

The proprietor of the way stop snorted, "Ed was a fool, like every man I've ever met, but I loved him anyway." She glanced at the princess meaningfully, "You be careful, dear, and if you ever need help, you just call on old Naya."

Adina smiled her radiant smile, ""Thank you, Naya, for everything that you've done. He would have died without you."

The woman dismissed the thanks with a wave of her hand, nodded, and without another word disappeared inside, closing the door behind her.

"She scares me," Gryle said, his voice little more than a squeak.

Aaron started to laugh, but he remembered the woman's grin as she'd poured that horrid drink down his throat, and his humor vanished. *Me too,* he thought. "Come on. We don't have any time to lose."

Gryle and the princess had to help him climb in the cart, but after a lot of grunting and cursing, they managed it. They traveled for the rest of the day, pushing on as the sun sank into the horizon, and the darkness spread out around them like a sable quilt. Aaron had just about decided that it was time to stop despite the feeling of urgency that had been building in him since they left Naya's when they crested a hill, and saw Baresh in the distance.

He let out a low whistle. Though Eladen's capital was still some distance ahead, there was no missing it. The massive, sprawling city was full of thousands of lanterns, torches, and fires, their glow mingling together so that it didn't look like a city at all, but like some massive star that had fallen out of the sky and that, even now, was burning with its own silent heat. "A hard place to miss."

"It appears as if Claudius has gone all out for the tournament," Adina said, her voice stiff with anger.

Aaron nodded, staring at the city in the distance, at the lights flickering there. Since meeting the princess and taking the job, he'd lost track of the amount of times he'd nearly been killed. If he was being honest with himself, he'd never expected them to make it to the city at all, had expected them to die along the way, but his sense of relief was blunted by a growing anxiety. Among those dancing lights sparkling in the distance like fool's gold, in a castle guarded by hundreds of soldiers, the object of their journey waited. He took a slow breath, forcing the fear down. It was not the thought of his death that frightened him, not really. It was the thought that he would fail. That, when the moment came, he wouldn't be fast enough, clever enough, and they would all die for nothing.

Somewhere in the night that surrounded them, Belgarin and his army marched toward the city, preparing to take it and its people over. Somewhere,

Aster and his men combed the countryside in search of Aaron and his companions. Too many enemies. Too many men that would be happy to see him and those with him hang or worse. "Ah, to the Keeper with it," he said, "we've made it this far."

"What was that, sir?" Gryle said.

"Nothing," Aaron said, flexing his bandaged left arm at the stiffness brought on by the wound. He fought back a grimace at the pain, turned to the others, and gave a single nod. "It's nothing. Let's go."

CHAPTER THIRTY-ONE

Two BORED LOOKING GUARDS stood in front of the massive wrought-iron gates of the city. They wore Eladen's colors, blue and white, and as Aaron and the others approached, they stepped in front of the mules, forcing them to stop. One of the guards held a torch that blazed fitfully in his hand. He moved to the side of the cart, and Aaron squinted eyes accustomed to the darkness as the guard held the torch high, studying them. "What is your business in Baresh, strangers?" He asked, and by the bored, almost annoyed way he said it, Aaron could tell it was a question he'd had to ask often lately.

"Good evening, sir," Aaron said, holding a hand up to block the worst of the light, "We've come for the contest."

The guard ran a hand thoughtfully through his thick, coarse black beard and eyed the three of them, his gaze lingering on Adina. "All of ye?"

"Just me. This is my wife," he indicated Adina. "And this," he said, gesturing to Gryle, "is our servant."

The guard nodded slowly as he scrutinized Aaron. "Lookit, Garl," he said, turning to the other guard, "we've got us another would-be champion." The man named Garl chuckled at this, and the talkative guard nodded, "Well, best of luck to ya. How about you leave your woman with us for a while?" He winked lasciviously at the princess, "We'll be sure to show her a good time while you play at soldiering."

Adina's hand on his stopped Aaron from drawing his sword. "I've always heard," the princess said, her voice calm, "that Baresh was one of the safest cities in Telrear, and it's leader, Eladen, one of the most noble men in the land. I wonder how he would feel if he learned that his gate guards were harassing visitors to his fine city?"

The guard's smile soured, "Got a tongue on ya, haven't ya, lass? Seein' as you haven't heard, the prince hasn't been around the city for some time. The way folks tell it, he turned coward and ran. I don't guess he'd have much to say about it one way or the other."

"And what of General Deckard, the Captain of the Guard?" Adina asked innocently, "has he also disappeared?"

The man's frown deepened, but he motioned to a man in the guard house and, in a moment, the heavy, wrought-iron gate began to rise. The guard stepped out of the way of the cart and motioned brusquely, "Get you and your woman inside before I change my mind— though I'd probably be doing you a favor. Some of the finest blades in all of Telrear have come for the tourney, even a few of the masters like Nico Swiftblade and Boris Braveheart themselves—Garl here seen 'em with his own two eyes." The man smiled then, but there was no humor in it, "What chance does a country bumpkin like yourself have against the likes of them, do you reckon?"

Aaron smiled back, "I guess we'll see won't we? You boys stay warm out here."

Though it was approaching midnight, the streets of the city were packed with visitors from all over Telrear. Children ran between the carts crowding the lane and the gathered people, laughing and chasing each other, oblivious of the cold or the thick press of bodies, unconcerned with the world that existed outside of their game. Aaron watched them, wondering if he'd ever been so young.

They led the cart past a group of southerners, their skins the color of burnished bronze from hours spent under the blazing sun of their homeland. They wore the thin, one-piece garments known as Calavars that left little but their eyes revealed. The fine material allowed them to maintain their modesty in the scorching temperature of their homeland without passing out from heat exhaustion, but, judging by their appearance, it did little to warm them in the frigid, northern night. They stood in the street shivering, wrapping their arms tightly around themselves as they gawked at the dozens of stands lining the road.

Merchants selling goods ranging from roasted sticks of beef and meat pies to charms that promised to ward off ailments for something as simple as the common cold to something as permanent as death itself, shouted at passersby. As they continued down the avenue, Aaron saw men and women from the land of Parnen wearing simple, unadorned clothes and walking in the quiet, unobtrusive manner characteristic of their race, their eyes on the ground in front of them, their shoulders hunched as if in expectation of a blow. He wondered, idly, what they would make of the captain, Leomin. If, that was, the man was still alive.

He pushed the thought behind him, and they continued on. It was slow going with the crowd, but eventually they passed the last of the merchant's stalls. Here, away from the outer edges of the city, less people walked the streets, and those who did didn't share the wide-eyed excitement of those closer to the gates. Instead, they walked with tired strides, no doubt locals or visitors who'd had a rough night making their way to their lodgings. Here and there he could make out the graceful, purposeful strides of fighting men and women, no doubt come to prove themselves in the tournament. He stretched his wounded arm, wincing at the tight stiffness of it, and sighed. In his current state, he'd be lucky to make it past the first round, let alone come in first place.

Perhaps there will be another way, Co said.

Yeah, like maybe Claudius will choke on a turkey leg and save us the trouble. Still, I think I'll sharpen my blades just in case.

Sometimes you can be truly vexing, the Virtue said, annoyed.

Aaron smiled, *I'll consider that a compliment, firefly.*

Co didn't respond. *Pouting doesn't suit you,* he thought, satisfied, but there was no answer. He headed further into the city, not sparing a second glance for the expensively ornamented inns they passed. "Why aren't we stopping?" Adina asked after they passed *The Gilded Rose,* the largest and finest yet.

"I'm looking for The Downs," Aaron answered, never taking his weary gaze from the street.

"Uh, sir ..." Gryle's voice was nervous as if he was sure that the sellsword had finally lost his mind, "we're in the wrong city for that. The Downs were in Avarest, remember?"

"You're wrong, chamberlain," Aaron said, scanning the street in front of them, "every city has its Downs. They go by different names, but the place is the same; a place where people go to disappear, where a man can be anyone he wants to be, do anything he wants to do, as long as he has the coin for it."

After a while, they came to a place where, the lanterns that had hung on the outside of almost every building became less frequent, and the shadows clung to the corners and entrances of the side alleys like living things, swaying in their melancholy, and he nodded, satisfied. He'd found the Downs. He wasn't surprised by the lack of lanterns, after all, what little light there was only served to illuminate ramshackle, decrepit buildings that appeared as if they were about to fall over. Not that it mattered much; none of the people Claudius wanted to impress—namely Belgarin himself—would demean themselves by venturing into the slums. At least, not in the daylight.

Aaron nodded to a ramshackle building, "This'll do." The sign, which hung crooked from the building's front, named it *The Lost Coin.* Aaron found himself smiling, feeling in his element for the first time since leaving Avarest. "The stolen coin more like," he muttered. He eased himself off the cart and hitched it to a post outside of the building then he and the others walked inside.

As they entered the inn, the steady rumble of conversation came to a halt and hard-faced men and women studied the three companions as they made their way through the crowded room. It wasn't until they were at the bar that the tense silence was broken as the inn's patrons apparently decided that the three of them, dressed as they were in their travel-worn, tattered clothes, weren't worth their attention. "What'll it be?" The heavy-set man behind the bar asked, his bored, unconcerned manner belied by the way his shifty gaze played over the three travelers. *No doubt deciding if we look like heavy sleepers,* Aaron thought, *the kind of sleepers who keep their coin purses out of reach. Damn, it's good to be home.*

"We'll need rooms for the night," He told the bartender, "and there's a cart out front that needs to see its way back to Krase, if you've a man for the job."

The man scowled, "Krase, eh? I don't think you'll have a lot of luck finding a man that's willing to travel to that little backwater, and we're all full up on rooms."

Aaron shrugged, idly grabbed several gold coins out of his pouch, and shifted them in his grip so that their shining surfaces reflected in the lantern light. "Oh? Too bad." He was beginning to tuck the coins back into the pouch when the bartender held up a hand, his eyes locked on the gold.

"Just hold on there, stranger. If you could find it in you to part with a few of those coins, I just might be able to find someone willin' to take your cart back for ya."

"And the rooms?"

The bartender hesitated for a moment, his gaze flicking from Aaron's face to the coins, "I can manage you one, but no more than that. I wasn't lying to ya, the inn's full up, what with every money hungry bastard in all of Telrear coming to compete in the contest. I'll have to kick someone out as it is."

Aaron shrugged, tossing a few coins onto the bar, "One will have to do then, but make sure that cart makes it back."

The man nodded distractedly as he eagerly scooped up the coins in his dirty, hairy hands. Only once the coins had disappeared into the pocket of his apron did he look past the travelers into the main room, "Oy, Ella!"

A middle-aged, chubby barmaid turned at the innkeeper's voice. Her lusterless blonde hair was in disarray, and she had deep, dark circles under her eyes as if she hadn't slept for days, "Yeah?" She said, shuffling to the bar.

"Grab Oscar; I've got a job for him."

"He's asleep," she said, "and I don't mind that a bit. I've been groped enough by that drunken bastard for one night. I'll be just fine if he never wakes up again."

"I didn't ask you for your damned opinion," the innkeeper said, "now get your ass up there and wake him up. If he gives you any argument, you just tell him to come see me. Tell him I've got a job for him and there's good money in it."

The woman's eyes narrowed for a moment, but finally she nodded. "Alright, but if he touches me again I'll cut his fucking fingers off."

Jacob Peppers

The innkeeper shrugged, his smile revealing a set of crooked, yellow teeth, "Just as long as you leave him enough to lead a cart with, I don't give a damn what you do." He waited until the woman turned and left before turning back to Aaron. "There you are. Now, you wait here just a minute, and I'll get that room ready for ya," he said, then he turned and walked away.

He sure isn't any Herb, Aaron thought.

No, Co said, her voice sounding disgusted, *he most certainly is not.*

The barkeep returned a few minutes later pulling a short, spectacled man in one greasy hand. "But I paid good coin for my room," the man said as the barkeep led him to the door, "this is ... this is an outrage and I'll—"

"Aw, shut your yappin' or *I'll* put my foot in your ass to help you along," the innkeeper said, and before the man could respond, he tossed him out and into the street, slamming the door shut behind him. He walked back over to Aaron and the others, rubbing his hands together in a gesture that did nothing to remove the grease and dirt from them. "There we are. Your room'll be ready now."

Aaron glanced at Gryle and the princess who was frowning at the innkeeper. He thought she might protest the stranger's treatment, but she only nodded.

"Alright," Aaron said, "show us." They followed the burly man up a creaking set of stairs to a room that smelled faintly of urine. A single bed dominated the space barely leaving enough room to move around.

The innkeeper noticed their frowns and cleared his throat, "It's not much, but it's all I've got."

Aaron glanced at the door, "No lock?"

"No sir.," the innkeeper said, breathing out a long suffering sigh, "Would you believe some bastard stole the lock right off the door?" He shook his head sadly, "Folks will do anything for a little coin these days."

"I've noticed," Aaron said, meeting the innkeeper's gaze until the man grew uncomfortable and looked away. "We'll want breakfast brought up."

"Of course, sir."

"Alright then." The man turned to leave, and Aaron stopped him with a hand on his shoulder.

"Sir?" The man asked, his smile doing little to mask the base cunning that flashed through his brown, mud-colored eyes.

"Be sure that whoever brings our food in the morning announces themselves. You see, I've got a bad habit of slitting the throat of people who come into my room uninvited and unannounced. Why, my sleep befuddled mind might accidentally take them for a robber or sneak thief. Although I'm sure that no such crime would ever happen in such a *respectable* establishment as yours, I'd hate there to be a misunderstanding. "

"O-of course, sir," the innkeeper said, staring between Aaron and the others uncertainly, "As you say, I don't want any ... misunderstandings."

Aaron nodded, "Alright then. Sleep well."

"Until the morning," the man grumbled, not meeting Aaron's eyes as he walked out and closed the door behind him.

"There now," Aaron said, turning to the others, "maybe we'll be able to get a good night's sleep, after all." He looked back to the room, taking in the single bed and sighed. "Or maybe not."

CHAPTER THIRTY-TWO

IN THE MORNING, the serving maid—a fat, steely-haired woman with crow's feet etched into the skin around her eyes—came with breakfast, but she refused to enter until Adina opened the door for her. The maid hurried across the room, shooting nervous glances at Aaron as if he was some wild animal that might pounce at any moment. She sat the tray holding three bowls of beef stew down on the nightstand and was out the door and gone in another moment. Adina raised an eyebrow at Aaron, but he only shrugged. The innkeeper had obviously told the woman what he'd said the night before about any unwanted visitors in their room and that was alright. They'd be staying at the inn for the duration of the tournament, and it was better for the woman to be scared than Aaron and the others have to lie awake at night for fear of someone sticking a knife in them and running off with what little money they had left.

They ate in silence as each of them considered the day—and the dangers—that lay ahead of them. Aaron found himself in a dark mood. Between his wounds, watching Adina lying in the bed from his own spot on the hard wooden floor, and Gryle's snoring, he felt as if he hadn't slept at all.

When they were finished eating, they went downstairs, and Aaron ignored the wary stare of the innkeeper as they made their way through bustling common room. Outside, wincing at the brightness of the north's cold sun, Aaron found his mood getting worse. The streets were alive with the sound of people shouting and laughing as well as the complaints of horses and mules as they pulled carts through the crowded press. Aaron stared out at the hundreds of people in the street with a mixture of annoyance and wonder. People from all over the breadth of Telrear had made their way to the city for the tournament and were, even now, pressing and pushing against each other in an effort to get to the contest grounds.

He looked up the street and saw that the press continued toward the tournament grounds as far as he could see. He sighed, rubbing his hands together to warm them and wrapped his ragged brown cloak around himself, pulling the hood down in a vain attempt to keep out the biting wind. According to Adina, Eladen had commissioned the tournament grounds to be built outside the city years ago claiming that physical contests satisfied man's baser inclination to violence without the requisite bloodshed that so often followed. Personally, Aaron thought it more likely that the northerners used the contests as a means of distracting themselves from the constant, bone-chilling cold.

Even in the early morning with the sun shining brightly, his face quickly went numb, and he could see his breath in the air in front of him, a foggy reminder—if one had been needed—of just how far away from the Downs they were, of just how far they'd come to die. "How much farther?" Gryle asked, his own face bright red from the cold.

Aaron frowned, "Like I told you the first five times you asked, the innkeeper said it was outside the eastern gate of the city. It shouldn't be long before we reach it, that is, of course, if these bastards will *move!*" He pushed past a young couple who had apparently decided that they couldn't spend the time it would take to get off the street before they started groping and kissing like they were in a brothel.

It took them nearly two hours to make it to the tournament grounds. As he and the others waited in the crowded enlistment line, Aaron—in an effort to avoid stabbing one of the people that kept bumping into him from behind—studied the arena. Despite his steadily darkening mood, and the aching stiffness in his wounded arm, he couldn't help but be impressed. Ascending rows of benches stood in a circle around the tournament grounds and pavilions of various colors and sizes stood erected along the outer edges of the arena. Long cloth banners seemed to hang from everywhere, their colors and emblazoned figures representative of the various knights and swordsmen who'd entered the competition. It was clear, judging by the pavilions and the clothes of those inside the arena that one side of the grounds had been reserved for nobles, another for the commoners.

On the noble side, young men strutted around in their brightly colored garments like peacocks putting on a show while the women in their fancy, frilly dresses smiled and hid their giggles behind delicate silk handkerchiefs. One section of the seats was cordoned off by scowling guards, and inside of it, surrounded by fawning noblemen and women, a grotesquely fat man sat plucking food from a servant's tray and stuffing it into his face.

The man's head was bald, and even from this distance Aaron could see that the man's fingers, which looked like nothing so much as thick sausages, were covered in so many rings that the flesh beneath barely showed. He wore a white and blue doublet with matching stockings. One particularly ambitious young noblewoman whispered something in his ear, and the Duke grinned, taking the opportunity to paw at the woman's breasts with grease-covered hands. Aaron felt an unexpected surge of anger as he realized who the man must be.

"Claudius," Adina breathed beside him as if following his thoughts.

Aaron frowned. While his people starved, Claudius was busy getting so fat that he took up nearly three chairs on his own. "Bastard likes his food, doesn't he?"

The princess nodded, "You could say that."

"In fact, you could say a lot more than that, princess," Gryle said. "Even since he was young, Claudius has always had a ... *weakness* for food. I once had reason to speak with his chamberlain, and the man assures me that the good Duke never eats less than three men at table."

"What in the Keeper's name possessed your brother to make such a man his second?" Aaron asked incredulously.

Adina sighed heavily, "The people love Eladen now, but it was not always so. In the first years after my father's death, the nobles and merchants were ... resistant to Eladen's rule. Not openly, perhaps, but enough to cause him increasing difficulties as he tried to lead his portion of Telrear to prosperity. The appointment of Duke Claudius Ergyle to his right hand was a concession to the nobles and the merchants both. It satisfied the nobles because Duke Ergyle's noble blood reaches back more generations to count in the north, and it satisfied the merchants because Claudius has ever been a proponent of the Merchant's Guild. Not surprising, really, when you consider the man's luxurious and extravagant lifestyle. It is said that the only thing that can match the Duke's insatiable hunter is his lust."

Aaron raised an eyebrow, "The food I can understand—the man obviously appreciates a meal like few others, but the women? Why, they'd be taking their life in their own hands getting in bed with that fat bastard."

Adina's mouth twisted in disgust, "You'd be surprised what many will do for a chance at increasing the prestige and standing of their own house. No, I doubt a day has gone by without the Duke, who is one of the richest men in Telrear, not to mention the current ruler of my brother's lands, not being offered the chance to bed any number of *eager* women."

Aaron snorted and shook his head, "I'll never understand nobles."

The princess nodded slowly, "Neither will I."

Disgusted, he turned away from the fat man and examined the rest of the grounds. On the other side of the field, hundreds of simply dressed peasants laughed and talked in loud, excited voices. Many of them looked weary, no doubt from a hard day's work, and several of the children and women that Aaron saw looked malnourished, but despite this they all seemed much happier and carefree than the nobles who were too busy trying to look unimpressed to enjoy themselves.

He'd been to tournaments before and, in his experience, the peasants were usually made to stand or sit on the ground. It was a point in the dead prince's favor that he'd spent time, effort, and money crafting serviceable seats even for the lowly born. "*Event?*" An annoyed voice asked.

Aaron turned and realized with surprise that they'd made it to the entry gate. A man and woman sat behind a small table with large stacks of paper in front of them. They held quills poised, waiting for his response with bored, impatient expressions.

"Single combat." Aaron said.

The man frowned as he made a new line on his paper. Already, the woman was waving someone else forward. "Name?" The man asked.

"Flynn," Aaron said, surprising himself, "Flynn Daltan."

The man looked him over once, "Never heard of you."

"Maybe we can change that."

The clerk rolled his eyes and shook his head as he jotted the name down. "Weapons?"

"Sword."

"Noble or commoner?"

"Commoner."

The man craned his neck to look at him, nodded perfunctorily, and made another note on the paper before holding out his hand, "Entrance fee?"

"What fee?" Aaron asked.

The clerk gave a disgusted look, "You didn't think that the tournament was *free* did you? Why, the noble Duke Claudius wouldn't want his tourney overran by a bunch of farmers with pitchforks and more dreams than sense, would he?"

"Of course not," Aaron answered, schooling his anger. "What better way to determine a man's worth than how much gold he has."

The clerk nodded, satisfied, apparently not detecting the sarcasm in Aaron's voice. "The fee is two hundred and fifty gold to be paid before entry."

Aaron bit back a curse. Adina nodded to Gryle who stepped forward, handing the coins over with obvious reluctance. The clerk took the money, stamped a sheet of paper, signed it, and handed it to the Aaron. "Go through the gate and bare left. The melee circle is on the far end of the stadium. There are several waiting rooms set up for the contestants. Go to one—it doesn't matter which. Once there, you'll be outfitted with a blunted blade, and will wait with the other contestants until your name is called."

The clerk paused and eyed the Aaron's frayed, dusty clothes doubtfully, "If you cannot afford armor of your own, they may be able to find some that will fit you. The contest is single elimination. You'll fight twice a day, once in the morning, again in the afternoon. Should you manage to win all of your matches, you will continue through the third day. On the fourth, the finalists will duel. The winner will be given the immense honor of being presented to Duke Ergyle himself as well as a purse of gold for his victory." The clerk spoke the last in a quick, distracted manner. Clearly, he didn't expect Aaron to make it past the first round, let alone receive the reward.

Pompous prick, he thought, but kept himself from saying. The last thing he needed was to attract attention. "Alright then," he said and started off in the direction the man had indicated, Gryle and Adina following in his wake.

They had to push their way through crowds of people that were trying to find their seats as they walked past the rows of benches. It took them nearly half an hour to navigate their way through the mess, but they finally arrived at the group of buildings that had been set aside for the contestants. Two well-armored men dressed in the white and blue of Eladen's house stood guard outside the doors of each, their hands never straying far from the thick broadswords sheathed at their belts.

Aaron stopped a short distance away from the two guards and turned to the others. "Well, I better get going."

"Sir, there must be another way, surely—" Gryle began to protest.

"There's not, and we all know it," Aaron interrupted, "besides, it's nothing to get worked up about. You heard the man at the gate; we'll be fighting with blunted weapons. People compete in tourneys and contests all the time; it's nothing to worry yourself to death over."

It was Adina who answered, "True, but they don't compete when they barely have the use of one of their arms, or when they almost died a few days ago. Aaron, there *has* to be something else we can do. We should go back to the inn. I'm sure we'll think of some other way to stop Claudius before Belgarin comes."

"Five days, Adina," he said. "You heard the clerk. Five days before the contest is over. Five days before Belgarin accepts the rule of Baresh and all of Eladen's holdings. With the might of the north behind him, how will anyone be able to stand against him? So far, he's been mostly subtle, choosing scheming and assassination over outright war, but how long will that continue once he's consolidated your late brother's power? How long, once he's in control of over half of the fighting men and women of Telrear before he decides to throw away the subtleties and hunt you and your remaining brothers and sisters down like dogs in the street?" His words came out in an angry growl at the end, "No. I can't let that happen. I won't lose y—" he shook his head, "No. I've spent enough time worrying only about myself. I can't do that anymore. Not now."

The princess opened her mouth to speak, but no words came.

"Be careful, sir," The chamberlain said into the silence, "I will pray to the gods for your victory."

Aaron smiled, "I doubt they're listening, but you go ahead and pray, Gryle. It couldn't hurt." He turned back to Adina's worried expression, "It'll be okay. It's only a tournament. Besides, I'm feeling better, almost back to normal," he lied. "That sewer sludge the old hag gave me must be magic. Still, I call it an even trade."

"You can't even move your left arm," Adina said, folding her arms across her chest.

He laughed, "Of course I can." He slid his cloak aside and flexed the hand of his wounded arm into a fist, turning his arm first one way and then the other."

Adina's eyes widened in surprise, "Wow, you really can move it."

Aaron smiled, "I told you, it'll be fine. Besides, I doubt there'll be a good fighter here. I'll probably spend the next five days fighting pampered nobles who entered for a chance to strut around and model their newest clothes for the crowds. I'd be surprised if any of them even knows how to hold a sword, let alone use one."

"Alright," she said, "but promise me that if you start to hurt or to feel weak that you'll stop. It won't serve anyone for you to pass out or die because you pushed yourself too far too soon."

Smiling, he bowed his head, "Of course, Princess. You have my word."

"Okay," she said reluctantly, "Then ... I guess we'll see you after your first match."

He offered his hand to the chamberlain who took it. He pulled the man close, so that he could whisper in his ear, "Watch out for her, Gryle. We haven't seen any of Aster or Belgarin's men recently, but that doesn't mean they're not here. When his scouts didn't return, I'm sure Belgarin sent men out in search of us. You stay quiet, and stay low, and if you see anybody that looks out of place, you take the princess and run like your feet are on fire and your ass is catchin', you got it?"

Gryle swallowed hard and nodded. "Yes sir."

Aaron released him and winked at the princess, "Alright then. You two kids stay out of trouble. I'll see you in a bit." With that, he turned and started toward the armory, waiting until he was out of their hearing before he finally released a gasp of pain and gritted his teeth at the pain lancing up his arm. He uncovered his wounded arm enough to see that it was shaking badly, before throwing his cloak over it again. He was surprised by the deep sense of guilt that spread through him as he replayed his words to the princess. After all, a well-told lie was as much the tool of a sellsword as his blade and often more dangerous. *Especially when you've only got one good arm.*

Despite what he'd told the others, he knew that it was a great risk he was taking, but what choice did they have? Even if he *did* somehow manage to make it past the dozen or so guards surrounding the fat bastard—an impossible task—he damn sure wouldn't make it out. The soldiers would come in swinging and *their* blades wouldn't be blunted. So it was time to take a chance; it wasn't like he hadn't done it before. Still, the thought gave him little comfort. It was almost as if he could hear Iladen's dice rattling in his godly cup, and he thought he knew what the roll would be.

CHAPTER THIRTY-THREE

INSIDE, TORCHES HAD BEEN PLACED in brackets against the wall, and the reddish, orange glow spilled over the floor and everyone inside, making them look as if they were covered in blood. He stumbled and plopped down on a nearby bench, using the tail of his cloak to wipe cold sweat, what his old master had called pain sweat, from his forehead. *Stop if I feel weak or tired,* he thought, shaking his head, *that's a joke.*

Flexing his hurt arm against the pain building here, he glanced around the room. Men of all shapes and sizes crowded the benches or stood by themselves putting their blunt weapons through practice strokes. Several groups of two or three nobles, smiling and richly-dressed as if for a ball, bragged to one another as they shot disgusted or pitying looks at the commoners in the room. *"I feel sorry for them,"* One young dandy said, laughing and nudging one of his friends, *"Perhaps, if the weapon was a hoe or a shovel they'd stand a better chance. It seems unfair."*

Aaron shook his head as he glanced around the room at the lean, hard-faced commoners of which the youth spoke. *Hard faces and hard men,* he thought, and the boy would have to be blind not to see it.

They are blind, Co said. *Blind to the suffering of others and their own shortcomings.*

Yeah, Aaron thought back, *in my experience, firefly, gold has a way of doing that.*

He turned away from the nobles and raised an eyebrow as he noticed a man in the corner of the room. The man had to be at least seven and a half feet tall with shoulders as wide as three of the nobles standing side by side. The man noticed Aaron watching him and his eyes drew down in a scowl before he popped his knuckles and spat. Aaron ignored the challenge and looked to the man sitting on a bench near the giant, a thin man whose long, filthy hair hung in his eyes. The man was reclined against a support beam, his eyes closed as if in sleep.

On the other side of the room, a short, stocky man with a thick jagged scar across his throat knelt in prayer. The man had been hung—that was certain—but apparently it didn't take. Except for the nobles—to whom all of this was only a game—all of the men in the room shared a look in their eyes and the sets of their jaw that he knew well. It was the look of a killer, or of a man who was prepared to become one. Aaron had been given occasion to see such looks before.

To the nobles, five thousand gold pieces was nothing, but to the commoners that were gathered in the room, it was a fortune, enough so that they'd never half to spend any more days digging and rooting in the muck like an animal, enough so that their sons and daughters, their wives and parents would never go hungry again. *If that's not enough to make a man a killer,* he thought to himself, *what is?*

You told the princess that there would be no men to fear in the contest, Co reminded him.

A lie, he answered simply, *and not the worst I've told. Surely you must have known that. You couldn't have existed for hundreds, thousands of years and not gained a better understanding of men than that. Shit, there are plenty of men who would murder their own family for that kind of money. How much easier to beat to death some man you've never met?*

I had thought that, perhaps, you knew something I didn't, Co answered, the annoyance clear in her girlish voice, *I didn't think you'd be foolish enough to take on would be murderers wounded.*

Aaron laughed inwardly, *the man who taught me the sword once told me that we are all murderers in the making, firefly. We're just waiting for the thing that is more precious to us than another man's life. For some, it is gold, for others women, for most pride, but make no mistake it is always something. Besides, being capable of killing someone is quite different from being able to. You worry too much.*

The last time you told me I worried too much you ended up with a knife in your back and another in your arm. Maybe you don't worry enough.

He scowled at that but chose not to respond. Instead, he rose, took a moment to steady himself against the pain the movement brought on, then began to inspect the beaten weapons and ragged suits of makeshift armor hanging by hooks in the center of the room. He tested the weight and quality of several of the blades until he finally settled on a long, thin sword. The grip had been wrapped tight with leather, and the steel of the sword was beaten and nicked from use. Still, the weapon was surprisingly well-balanced.

Satisfied, he walked back to his spot and sat down, leaning his newly-acquired blade on the bench beside him. *What of armor?* Co asked.

What, he thought back, *those tin cans? No thank you. It would only serve to slow me down, and I doubt I could heft the damned things right now anyway.*

You're determined to get yourself killed.

Aaron smiled a tight, humorless smile and lay back on the bench. Co made a frustrated sound in his mind, but he paid it little attention. Instead, he closed his eyes, and waited for his name to be called, wondering idly if he'd be able to raise himself off the bench when the time came.

CHAPTER THIRTY-FOUR

"HE'LL BE OKAY, MISTRESS."

Adina turned to the chamberlain and tried to force a smile, "Thank you, Gryle. I pray to the gods that you're right." All around them, the benches were packed with people chattering eagerly, laughing and bragging about their favorites in anticipation of the bouts to come.

"You heard him," Gryle continued, "he said that—" the rest of what he said was lost in a sudden roaring cheer from the crowd that was so powerful that it shook the bench beneath her as an announcer, dressed in the white and blue of Eladen's house, made his way into the melee circle. He stopped in the center and turned to face the nobles. He held his hands up for silence and the cheering subsided.

"Gentlemen and gentle ladies," the man shouted in a nasally voice that carried to everyone present as he spread his hands wide to encompass all of the nobles seated in front of him, "I welcome you to one of the largest tournaments Baresh has ever seen, where some of the world's best warriors are gathered to pit themselves against one another in three contests, single combat, general melee and, of course, the joust, for your entertainment!"

The commoner side of the arena erupted in shouts and cheers. A few of the nobles, those not too preoccupied with appearing bored or unimpressed, clapped half-heartedly. "Our noble Duke Claudius," the announcer said, bowing in the Duke's direction before continuing, "is offering an unheard of purse of five thousand gold to the contest winners as well as --" He paused as the commoner side of the arena broke out in wild applause again at the mention of gold. Once the cheers died down, the man continued, "As well as an audience with the Duke himself!"

This time, it was the commoners turn to remain silent while the nobles clapped loudly. *All seeking favor with their new ruler,* Adina thought angrily, *fawning and posturing while their true ruler lies dead.* Not that they knew that of course—no doubt Claudius himself was aware of it, but Belgarin would have commanded him in no uncertain terms to keep it a secret until he took power—but she was still disgusted at how quickly the loyalty of the nobles had shifted. Perhaps Aaron wasn't wrong about them, after all.

Still, it was no great surprise. Eladen had been one of the few rulers who treated the common folk like people instead of livestock, treating them as equals to the nobles themselves, a fact that rankled those pompous lords and ladies of old blood who thought themselves as different from commoners as men were from dogs. Eladen had allowed the commoners to bring their issues and grievances to court, had often even punished nobles who mistreated their workers, a thing unheard of in other parts of the world.

Up to a week ago, when she'd first arrived in Avarest and met Aaron, Adina had thought that her brother was foolish for so often taking the side of commoners over nobles. To her, it served to alienate the nobles—men of power and wealth in a time when he needed both to overcome Belgarin's armies—for no purpose. It wasn't six months ago, in fact, when she'd argued with him about it. She'd been angry and rash with her words, but Eladen had only smiled the same warm smile she remembered from her childhood and said, *"The 'commoners' grow our food, working long, hard days so that their families, as well as ours, might not starve. While the nobles boast of our certain victory in the war it is the commoners who give up their sons, their fathers and husbands, to fight it. Which seems more noble to you, dear sister?"*

At the time, she'd been furious with him, amazed that he couldn't understand the importance of the old blooded families and their wealth. After all, it took money to make weapons, money to feed and clothe armies, but she'd finally given up, storming out of Eladen's palace and leaving for Edrafel without so much as a goodbye. It was the last time she'd ever seen her brother alive. She shook her head and wiped angrily at the tears that had begun to gather in her eyes.

If only you'd listened, El, you might still be alive. She hated herself for the thought; she was beginning to understand that her brother had been right, after all, but that didn't change the fact that one, possibly several, of those nobles on the other side of the arena could have known something about Eladen's assassination before it happened. Those men and women dressed in rich silks and velvets that laughed and preened, the women fussing over their hair and their clothes while the men no doubt spoke vehemently about the glory and honor of battle—though most of them had never fought in one themselves—might have saved her brother's life. She knew, as she had the thought, that she was right, and she hated herself for it.

She frowned, staring angrily across the tournament grounds at Claudius. The duke was laughing at some joke told by one of ambitious lackeys as he stuffed his face with some sweet meats. *You'll pay for what you did,* she thought bitterly, *even if I have to die to see it done. I swear by Nalesh, Father of the Gods. You'll pay.*

She was so caught up in her own thoughts, her own fury, that it wasn't until two warriors emerged from different armories and began to make their way to the center of the circle that she realized the announcer had called for the first contestants.

The crowd whispered in hushed disbelief as the two contestants stopped in the center of the circle, facing each other. One of the fighters was a big, brutish bull of a man with a thick neck and massive hands that looked like they could crush stones. His head was shaved bald revealing a thick, ugly scar that ran down his forehead to his jaw. The man's massive, slab-like muscles pressed tightly against the dirty linen shirt he wore, as he popped his neck, his grin displaying rows of rotten teeth.

The other contestant, an old gray-haired man that couldn't be any taller than Adina herself, looked unconcerned at the hulking savage towering over him.

He must be insane, she thought sadly. *"Give up now, and I'll let you live, old man,"* the monster growled, and despite her fear for the small, gray-haired contestant, Adina was impressed—and more than a little unnerved—by how well the arena amplified the sound, so that it seemed as if the man had spoken from right beside her.

The old man pulled his long pony tail of gray hair over one shoulder, smiled and nodded his head, saying something that she couldn't hear. *"Hah!"* The giant barked, "There won't be enough of you left for your family to bury when I'm done with you, you stupid bastard! That money's mine!"

The old man's casual smile remained in place as the announcer made his way to the center of the circle and stood in front of the two contestants. Once again, he turned to address the nobles, "The rules are simple: The contestants will fight until one man yields or is unable to carry on. The winner will be allowed to leave until later this evening when he will participate in his second match. The loser will be eliminated." He turned to the two fighters, and spoke in a normal voice that was still loud enough for everyone in the arena to hear, "Are you both ready?"

The big man reached behind his back and withdrew the massive two-handed sword strapped there, and Adina let out a quiet gasp of surprise. Blunted blade or not, the old man would surely be killed with one hit of that blade. She clenched her jaws, why wasn't the fool wearing armor? Why did he enter the contest in the first place? He looked like someone's favorite grandfather, not a warrior.

The small man took a step back and withdrew his own long, slender sword. "Begin!"

Adina winced expectantly, as the big man growled and charged forward, bringing his blade down in a vicious blow that would decapitate the small man despite the blunted edge. A sharp intake of breath from the crowd made it clear that Adina wasn't the only one watching in dreaded expectation, but when the huge sword cleaved through the air where he'd been standing, the old man was no longer there.

She had just time enough to register the look of surprise on the bald man's face before the gray-haired contestant, who'd stepped neatly to the side, whipped his sword around and under the man's throat. "Do you yield?" The old man asked, his voice surprisingly calm.

"Fuck you!" The big man growled, shoving the blunted blade away with one hand and swinging his own weapon in a wide arc meant to cave in the old man's face. Instead of retreating, the old man ducked smoothly under the blow with less than an inch to spare, and countered with his own blade, slamming it into the side of the man's leg.

The giant let out a grunt as his leg gave out underneath him, and he fell to one knee, his sword slipping out of his fingers and clattering to the ground. He started to rise and again the old man's blade was at his throat. "Do you yield?"

The giant shouted wordlessly, grabbed the dull blade, tore it from the man's grip, and threw it away. The old man backed up as the other contestant waded toward him, his fists swinging wildly. Finally, the small man stepped to the side of one of the other contestant's haymakers, and his own fist lashed out like lightning and connected with the man's temple.

The giant staggered drunkenly for a few steps, a dazed look on his face, before crumpling to the ground, unconscious. For several seconds, the arena was impossibly silent as everyone took in what had happened. Then the crowd erupted in cheers and laughter so loud that Adina thought her head would burst. "Did you see that?" Someone close to her shouted, "He knocked that big bastard down like he was a stripling!"

For their part, Claudius and the nobles gathered around him appeared bored and, Adina thought, cheated, as if they'd been hoping to see the old man's brains dashed out with the giant's claymore.

The announcer beckoned to two men standing on the sidelines. They rushed forward, grabbing the giant by his legs and under his arms, visibly straining under his weight as they carried him off the field. When they were gone, the announcer moved forward with a strut of importance, and motioned the winner forward. He draped an arm across the old man's shoulders as if they were lifetime friends, turning him to face Claudius and the other nobles, "Ladies and gentlemen, the winner of the first bout," there was a pause as he leaned toward the contestant and asked him something in a whisper. He nodded as the wiry old man answered, finally turning back to face the crowd of nobles once more. "The winner of the first bout, Rashan Caltier!"

The old man turned to face the commoners and bowed low, and the cheering and hollering grew louder still. After a moment, the wiry old man rose, tossed his long gray pony tail over his shoulder, and walked away from the circle without sparing the nobles a glance.

There'll be trouble for that, Adina thought as she noted the frowns of Claudius and the other around him. It was, after all, one thing for the nobles to act uninterested in everyone else, it was quite another for everyone else to act uninterested in them. If there was one thing she'd learned from the years spent in her father's court, as well as her own, it was that nobles were worse than children when it came to jealousy.

Finally, the commoners grew silent, and the announcer called for the next two contestants. Several more bouts took place, and Adina had begun to grow restless—not to mention cold, how *did* these northern women stand it?—when the announcer stepped into the circle again, avoiding several new splatters of blood on the ground and waiting for the two men to drag another unconscious form away. At least, Adina hoped he was unconscious, but the blow he'd taken to the head could have easily been fatal.

She jerked forward in her seat as the announcer called for Flynn Daltan, the name Aaron had used. After a moment, the sellsword appeared, walking out of the armory and toward the circle, and though he didn't limp she noticed that his jaws were clenched tightly. *He's hurt more than he said,* she thought worriedly.

"He'll be okay," Gryle said beside her, "he'll be okay," and she nodded despite the fact that she got the distinct impression the chamberlain was talking more to himself than her.

She quailed as she saw Aaron's opponent walk out of an adjacent building. The man wore an intimidating suit of dark green plate armor with a fig tree emblazoned in gold on its front. The visor of his helmet was raised revealing sharp, hawk like features that weren't unhandsome, and an expression of disdain that said more clearly than any words could what he thought of his unarmored, commoner opponent as he swaggered to a stop in front of the sellsword before finally dropping his visor.

As soon as the announcer gave them leave, the noble waded in, swinging his sword in vicious arcs meant to end the farce early. With each strike, Adina's heart leap in her throat for fear that Aaron's wounds would slow him down too much and that one of the wild blows would connect. Instead, each time the knight swung, Aaron's sword was somehow there in the last second, deflecting the blow and sending it harmlessly to the side or knocking it up high as the sellsword circled around the man, keeping him at a distance. Each time he sent the man's sword wide, she waited tensely for him to counter as she had so often seen her father's soldiers do when she was younger.

Instead, Aaron continued to evade the man's blows by a hair's breadth, ducking and rolling out of the way at the last second. *Attack!* She thought wildly, *Why isn't he attacking?* Aaron's movements appeared to be growing more sluggish with each passing moment. All it would take was for one of those blows to land, and he would be finished. The knight swung again, but reversed direction on the blade and sent it back at the sellsword. She gasped in fear, but instead of taking the blunted blade in the face, Aaron ducked with a grace she wouldn't have thought his weary frame could muster and stepped smoothly under the swiping steel, coming up behind his opponent. She leaned forward, sure that this was it, that he was going to finish it now, but instead of rushing forward, the sellsword backed away as the knight turned ponderously around and started toward him.

"He waits," a voice that wasn't Gryle's said beside her. The chamberlain let out a squeak of shock. Adina turned and was surprised to see the old man from the first bout sitting next to Gryle. The man's face was leathery from years spent in the sun, and crow's feet surrounded his eyes and mouth.

"Excuse me, sir?" She asked suspiciously, suddenly painfully aware of the tournament guards that patrolled back and forth in front of the benches in search of trouble. Was it only her imagination, or had that last one been eyeing her too closely? "Were you talking to me?"

He smiled, "To both of you, actually," he said, nodding to Gryle. He gripped hands with the chamberlain, then took the princess's and kissed it softly. "You may call me Rashan Caltier. And yourselves?"

"I'm A-Naya," she stumbled, cursing herself silently, "and this is my servant, Edward."

Apparently not noticing her slip, the man smiled. "It is nice to meet you, Naya. Edward."

"N-nice to meet you too, sir," Gryle stumbled.

"That is your man, is it not?" He asked, gesturing at Aaron who, even now, came within inches of getting struck with an overhead slash that would have knocked him senseless as he stepped to the side.

"Why do you ask?" She asked distractedly, her hands clenched into fists at her sides as she watched the bout.

"No particular reason," the man answered, his own eyes locked on the combat, "please, forgive an old man the pleasantries."

She turned to study the man for a moment. He sounded sincere, and he didn't *look* like a soldier who would work for her brother, but there was no way to be sure. Still, there was no point lying to him. Clearly, he'd already seen her with Aaron. She shot a quick glance at the chamberlain before turning back to the old man, ready to bolt if he made a move for her, "I'm sorry," she said, "I'm just nervous. He's almost gotten hit several times now."

"You're wrong in that," the man said, flashing her a smile that seemed to know too much, "your *husband* has got his opponent's measure now. It won't be long."

Adina felt her stomach lurch uncomfortably. Had she imagined his emphasis on the word husband? She couldn't tell for certain. "What do you mean he has his measure?"

"Watch," the man said, gesturing at the two contestants as the sellsword knocked aside another blow of the knight's sword, "Do you see how he lets the other contestant tire himself? A man in heavy armor can't keep up a pace like that for long—trust me. Soon, he'll begin to slow. His strikes will become sloppier, and he'll begin to neglect to cover himself against a counter. No, your husband has done this before, madam."

Adina drew in a sharp breath as the knight's sword passed within an inch of the sellsword's face, "If he knows what he's doing then why does he let him get so *close?*" She demanded angrily.

"It's better that way. Let the hound smell the blood, let him get so close he can nearly taste it. Let him go mad with the scent of it." Adina noticed that, indeed, the armored man's vicious attacks had slowed. His armored feet dragged noticeably, and the acoustics of the arena were such that she could hear his panting, labored breaths even from her spot on the bench. "And once he's weak," the man continued, his dull gray eyes locked on the battle, "once he's overcome with exhaustion and has no fight left, when he least expects it, that is when you strike."

As if on cue, Aaron dodged to the side of one of the knight's overhand strikes, but instead of circling out of range as before, he raised his blunted sword with both hands and brought it down in a brutal chop to the man's extended arm. The knight let out a howl of agony, and his sword fell out of nerveless fingers. He bent over, apparently trying to retrieve his blade despite the fact that his arm must have been smarting terribly, but Aaron surged forward, bringing his sword into the back of the knight's knees in a vicious sweep.

The man cried out again as his legs gave out beneath him, and he crumpled to the ground in a crash of steel.

Aaron took a few steps forward and laid his sword across the back of the fallen man's head. The knight cringed beneath the blade, and though his helmet was twisted crookedly from the fall and muffled his voice, his pained words were clear enough for everyone to hear, "I yield."

Aaron nodded and started back toward the armory, ignoring the calls of the announcer who stepped into the center of the circle as his two helpers began the task of getting the armor-laden knight to his feet, "Flynn Daltan, my good people!" The commoners roared louder than they had yet, laughing boldly, and she heard whispered jokes about how a peasant had defeated an armored knight. "And now," the announcer continued, shouting to be heard over the applause, "we will take a four hour intermission."

"You were right," she said, chagrined that the stranger could know so much more about what the sellsword was doing despite the fact that she'd spent nearly the entire last week with him. She turned, and let out a gasp of surprise as she noticed that the old man was no longer there. "Gryle?"

The chubby man made an effort and finally managed to jerk his gaze away from the knight who was only now getting up from the ground with the help of the two struggling men. "Princess?"

"Where did he go?"

Gryle looked around in surprise, "I-I thought that he was just there, Mistress. I never heard him leave."

"Me neither," Adina said, goosebumps breaking out on her arms. Why had the man sat next to them? Why had he insisted on speaking so much? Suddenly, she was sure that when he'd been talking about Aaron's strategy, he hadn't *just* been talking about that. In fact, the more she thought over their conversation, the faster her heart began to beat. Was it possible that the man worked for Belgarin, or even Aster, and had been toying with them? But to what purpose? It didn't make any sense, but the thought did little to thaw the foreboding that had settled into her stomach like a chunk of frozen ice.

CHAPTER THIRTY-FIVE

AARON SIGHED, EXHAUSTED, as he finished strapping his real sword back in place and threw his cloak over it. He fingered the worn leather handles of the blades hanging at his side, reassuring himself of their presence. He'd hated having to leave them, even for the bout, but there'd been no choice. Belgarin's men couldn't be far behind, and the last thing he wanted was to get caught with nothing but a blunted blade of poor quality to protect himself and the others with.

He flexed the fingers of his left arm and winced. Co was doing everything she could to keep the pain back, but the arm still felt stiff and weak, and no matter how hard he tried, he couldn't stop it from trembling. The two handed blow he'd struck the knight hadn't helped matters, and his arm was protesting strongly even now, reminding him that he was pushing himself too far, too soon. Naya had been right about that. Still, what choice did he have? *None,* he thought sourly, *and that's the truth of it.*

He made his way past other contestants gathering their gear toward the armory's exit. As he opened the door, he was confronted with a crowd of people who'd apparently taken the intermission as an invitation to crowd the tournament grounds, congratulating and shaking hands with their favorites. He kept his head down, avoiding their gazes as he worked his way through the jostling people. Several commoners slapped him on the back and congratulated him on his victory, and he nodded, thanking them, as he continued past. He didn't care for their attention—it was just another way for him to stick out, another way for his head to end up on the business end of a noose or an executioner's axe—but not responding to the commoners would have made him stick out even more. After all, a man who'd joined the tournament for the money—as all of the commoners had—would be content after his first victory, not sullen, not eyeing everyone around him as if he expected a knife in the back—never mind the fact that he did.

"Not graceful, perhaps," a voice said beside him, "but effective."

Aaron turned, and his eyes widened as he took in the man who'd spoken. It had been over ten years since he'd last seen Master Darrell, the man who'd taken him in and taught him the blade when he'd been nothing but a starving runaway in the streets of an unfamiliar city, but he recognized him instantly. True, his old master's midnight black hair had gone to gray, and there were leathery wrinkles around his eyes and mouth that Aaron didn't remember, but the man had the same reserved manner, the same cool gray eyes. "Ma—"

"My name," the short, wiry man interrupted, meeting his eyes with a hard gaze, "is Rashan Caltier. A pleasure to meet you."

Aaron frowned for a moment, then finally nodded, "The pleasure's mine," he said, offering his hand, "You may call me Flynn."

The man took his hand and smiled. "So," he said as he clapped Aaron on the back, "does Baresh's arena suit your tastes, stranger?"

"What are y—"

"An interesting fact," the man went on as if Aaron had never spoken, "you may have noticed that the announcer needed to only speak in normal volume to be heard all throughout the arena. It is said that Prince Eladen designed the theater that way so that there would be no chance that a man would ever try to yield and not be heard." He shrugged, "True or not, it cannot be denied that the arena amplifies sound incredibly. Why, I don't doubt that any man or woman sitting in the stands could hear individual conversations as if the men involved were standing right beside him. Interesting, don't you agree?"

Aaron nodded slowly, "Very."

Darrel grinned, "I managed to catch a bit of your fight. It was ... interesting."

Aaron snorted, "I won. It's enough."

The swordmaster shrugged, "I suppose you are right. Still, a wise man once said that grace is the mother of combat, and the beauty of battle a thing more spectacular than the smile of a new born babe."

Aaron grunted, unable to hide his smile, "I never held much with poets or philosophers; fools and boy lovers the lot of them, I think."

The old man laughed, "History, as well as the future, is written by such fools, my friend. I shudder to think what the man who trained you must have suffered through with such a … shall we say, stubborn, attitude to work with."

The sellsword nodded as they maneuvered around a group of laughing nobles, "Perhaps it was a trial for him," he agreed, "but I doubt he minded much. He was a good enough sort, but I got the distinct impression that he was touched in the head."

"Oh?" Darrell said, a look of surprise on his face, "and here I thought the man must have been granted the wisdom and patience of the gods themselves, not to mention their kindness, to have dealt with such a single-minded pupil as yourself. Truly, he must be a remarkable and talented man. One to be revered, I suspect."

"I doubt he still lives. The man was ancient when I knew him and that was years ago. By now I imagine he's feeding the worms or tottering around on a cane, rambling about the invisible gnomes that keep peeing his bed to any unlucky soul that happens by."

The old man laughed, but then his eyes grew serious. "Either way, he must be commended for his efforts. After all, he did teach you a considerable amount of skill with the sword. It is no easy task to take down a fully armored knight with a blunted weapon. Especially," he said, leaning in and clapping Aaron on his wounded arm hard enough to make him wince, "when wounded. Why, a man would have to be very desperate or very stupid to enter into such a grand tourney with an arm that was barely of use."

Aaron frowned back, "Desperate times make desperate men."

"This is true," Darrell agreed, "and I'm sure I'm not the only one to have noticed. Why, anyone with eyes to see would be aroused to curiosity. A great way of drawing attention to one's self if that is the goal. Perhaps, it would help to talk about it."

He detected the disapproval in his old master's voice, and it took all he had to restrain himself from telling this man who had been like a father to him for many years, everything that had happened. It wasn't only the fear of being overheard that stayed him, however, but also the knowledge that to inform Darrell of everything that had happened would only put him in danger, and he deserved better than that for all that he'd done for a starving young boy who'd lost his way.

"I'm sure that all will be clear in time," he said cryptically raising a hand to Adina and Gryle as they finally extricated themselves from the pressing bodies and started toward the benches.

"Speaking of time," the gray-haired man said casually, "did you know that Belgarin himself is supposedly visiting Baresh?" Aaron felt himself tense at the prince's name, but the old man went on as if he didn't notice, "It's the talk of all the inns and bars. In fact, they say that the prince was initially supposed to arrive in five days, but that he's due to arrive early, some say as early as the day after tomorrow."

Aaron felt his stomach lurch, but he struggled to appear calm as they continued through the crowd, "Oh?

Why would Prince Belgarin visit Baresh? I thought that he and Eladen were at war."

His old master shrugged, "So did I, but the rumors are plentiful enough that they are hard to doubt. Strange, indeed. Especially considering the fact that no one has seen or heard from Eladen in over a week's time. Perhaps, Belgarin comes to seek peace with the noble Duke Claudius."

Aaron's mind was too awhirl with ideas and the impending threat of Belgarin's early arrival to respond, and before he knew it they had arrived where Gryle and the princess waited. "Are you okay?" Adina asked, and he could see the worry in her and the chamberlain's gazes.

He nodded, "I'm fine. The man barely knew what end of his sword to hold. He was just here to show off his fancy armor more than anything, I imagine."

Adina frowned, the man had *seemed* competent enough, and whether it had been Aaron's strategy to wear the knight down or not, she was pretty certain that at least a few of those blows had almost connected. "If you say so."

"I do," Aaron answered, "trust me, the man was hopeless. If the rest are no better, it'll be a boring tournament."

"Truly, my lady," Darrell said as he walked out from behind Aaron and gave a bow, "the man had no chance."

Adina stared at the man warily, but Aaron didn't appear to be bothered by the stranger's presence. In fact, there was something about the way the two of them seemed completely comfortable with each other that struck her as odd. From her experience, Aaron wasn't the type of person that made quick friends, and this man, whom she'd taken for a stranger, was already taking up for him. What was *that* about? "Do you two know each other?" .

The two men glanced at each other in surprise. It was the old man who spoke first, "Well, that would be quite a coincidence, my lady. No, this is my first time meeting," he paused, looking embarrassed, "I'm sorry, sir. What did you say your name was?"

"Flynn," the sellsword answered, and Adina was sure she'd seen Aaron smile for a second, "Flynn Daltan."

The gray-haired man nodded as he gripped Aaron's hand, "A pleasure to meet you, Flynn."

"You as well."

The princess eyed them silently, and their innocent smiles cracked and then disappeared as they avoided meeting her gaze. Something wasn't right here, she was sure of it. "Wha—"

"Well," Aaron interrupted, turning to the gray-haired man, "we really must be going. Good luck in the tournament, Rashan. Perhaps we will meet again."

The stranger nodded, a smile playing at the corner of his mouth, "If the gods will it."

With a grunt, Aaron turned back to the others, "Come on, let's go." The princess bit back her questions as she and Gryle hurried after the already departing sellsword.

CHAPTER THIRTY-SIX

BACK AT THE INN, Aaron sighed as he unstrapped his blades and propped them in the corner of the room. The princess had sent him up to rest while she and Gryle got some food from the kitchen below and brought it up. Normally, the innkeeper assured them, their food would be brought to their rooms, but it was all he and his two serving women could do to manage the bar downstairs, what with the massive crowds the contest had attracted.

He'd tried to put on a grim expression when he'd spoken of it, as if he regretted the busy crowds, but Aaron had seen the smile in the man's eyes, and why not? The crowds meant more people to buy the hard bread that had appeared to be dangerously close to molding and what Aaron suspected were week-old sausages. Not to mention more people to rob. Of course, even fresh, meat would have been suspect in an inn such as this. After all, good beef could be hard to come by, but there was never a shortage of stray cats and dogs in a city like Baresh, and in Aaron's experience, such animals always seemed to find their way to the shadier, less scrupulous parts of the city.

He stretched his aching muscles, being sure to do so carefully so as not to tweak his wounded arm. He looked at it sourly. The damned thing's trembling didn't seem to be getting any better. In fact, he was beginning to think it was getting worse.

It is, Co said, *you are pushing yourself too far. Much more of this, and you'll end up killing yourself.*

"Come on now, firefly," he muttered, "it's not so bad as all that. You sound even worse than the princess."

Mmm, Princess Adina is an intelligent woman, but I have the added advantage of knowing when you're lying. You forget that I feel your pain as if it was my own. You were barely able to stand after your fight, no matter what you say. You can't go on like this.

As if I have a choice, he shot back. He walked across the room, slid the door open quietly and looked both ways. Assuring himself that the hall was empty, he reached into the pocket of his trousers and withdrew the note that his old master had given him when they shook hands.

That had been dangerous, sneaking a note past the princess even as she was watching them, but Darrell had always enjoyed his subtleties. To Aaron's mind, it was one of the man's biggest flaws. He unfolded the small piece of parchment and nodded along as he read.

I find that when I am troubled, it often helps to talk to the gods. Nalesh, in particular, seems to listen. Surprisingly, the poor district of Baresh has a small, but not totally inadequate church. Should you need comfort, it is as good a place to start as any.

There was no signature. Aaron sighed heavily. The man enjoyed his games too much. It wasn't as if someone was going to get hold of the note. He snatched a look out the window. Based on the sun, he still had three hours or so before he needed to be back at the tourney grounds, and he was certain he'd seen the church Darrell spoke of on his way into the city. If he was right, the place was no more than a fifteen minute walk away. Based on how crowded the downstairs of the inn had been, and how harried the serving girls and single cook had looked, he suspected that Adina and the chamberlain would still be waiting some time yet. He should have plenty of time to run over to the church, meet Darrell, and be back before the others ever knew he was gone.

You could just tell her, the Virtue said disapprovingly.

It's better if I don't, he thought back. *Darrell was a good man, but a lot can change in ten years. For all I know, he could be working for Belgarin right now. It seems like too much of a coincidence that he just so happens to be here, and I don't like coincidences. No, it's better to wait. I don't want to involve Gryle or the princess until I know one way or the other.*

And if he is working for Belgarin? What then? You just walk right into an ambush, wounded, and hope to escape with your life?

"In the words of a once great general," he said, "When all choices are shitty, a man must pick the one most likely to leave him alive to wash."

There was a pause, then, *You made that up.*

He grinned as he started toward the door, "Possibly."

CHAPTER THIRTY-SEVEN

HE APPROACHED THE SMALL CHURCH warily, eyeing the back alleys for concealed soldiers. If anything, Baresh's poor district was even more haphazardly constructed than The Downs. Hundreds of short, bisecting alleys and pathways honeycombed the district, as if made by some mad engineer who'd made it his sole purpose to confuse anyone who dared travel its streets. The alleyways were probably useful to most people, but for him, just now, they only served as possible hiding places for men bent on ambush.

The street the church was on was in even worse disrepair than most, and with the contest drawing so many people to the tourney grounds, it was completely deserted. Not surprising, perhaps, since it dead ended into the church of Nalesh. There had been a time, hundreds, possibly thousands of years ago, before the birth of many of the other gods, when humans had worshipped Nalesh, the Father God, and no other, but that time had long since passed.

Now, most people worshipped one of the descendants of the Father God, the major gods—sons and daughters—or even their sons or grandsons, the minor gods, those who represented specific things. Instead of praying to Nalesh, a god not known for his mercy or his compassion, for fertile soil or a better yield, farmers prayed to Nalek, the God of Growing Things, or even his daughter, Kalia, goddess of agriculture and farming. In this way, men and women felt that they prayed to gods who cared specifically about *their* concerns, and *their* problems. Not that Aaron had ever seen any evidence, of course, but he understood the human need to categorize.

He walked up to the run down church and opened the door, noticing the print his fingers left on the dusty door knob as he closed it behind him. Inside, the church was dark and smelled of must and decay. The only light came from a single candle that burned on a rough wooden altar. Above the altar hung a simple wood carving of Nalesh. Despite the rough material from which the carving was fashioned, the Father of the Gods managed to appear noble as he held the Book of Life in his left hand, and the quill that he supposedly used to create it in his right.

At the foot of the altar, the candlelight illuminated Aaron's old master on both knees, his head bowed, as he whispered a hushed prayer. He turned as Aaron took another step into the room, his expression serious, "Ah, you came."

"Yes."

The small, gray-haired man rose nimbly and started toward Aaron with a grace that few would have credited a man of his age. Aaron noted the man's narrowed eyes and clenched jaws and wondered yet again if he'd stumbled into an ambush. His former master stopped a pace in front of him and eyed him warily. He felt his heart begin to speed up under the man's steely-eyed scrutiny until, abruptly, Darrell's face broke out into a wide grin and he clapped Aaron on the back and clasped his hand warmly. "By the gods, but it's good to see you, boy!"

Despite his earlier wariness, Aaron felt himself smiling back, "And you, master."

The old man rolled his eyes, "Oh, don't start with that nonsense. It's been many years since I was your master, and you didn't listen worth a damn even when I was."

"Sure I did," Aaron protested, his own grin widening, "at least when you told me something that had some sense to it."

"What is, is." Darrell said meaningfully, "A man must find meaning on his own."

Aaron quirked an eyebrow, "More philosophy?"

His old master shrugged, "I find myself growing more thoughtful in my old age. For instance, I wonder why you did not bring the woman or that man with you?"

Aaron opened his mouth to speak and stopped. Noticing his hesitance, Darrell nodded in understanding, "I see. You thought it safest to leave them alone until you discovered if I was a threat."

Guilt washed over him at the note of understanding in his old master's voice, "I didn't mean t—"

"Of course you did, lad," Darrell said, "and I can't blame you. Why, I'd have been forced to question my own teaching if you'd have trusted in me whole-heartedly. After all, it has been over ten years."

"Forgive me, sir," Aaron said, "it's just that ... well, seeing you here ... it seemed like too much of a coincidence."

Darrell nodded, "Of course. Still, I can't help wondering what kind of situation you've managed to get yourself into this time." He sighed teasingly, "I always did tell you that that mouth of yours would get you in trouble."

Aaron barked a laugh, "And you were right, but that's not the problem—not this time."

"Oh?" His old master asked as he led Aaron to a nearby bench, "and what is?"

"I can't tell you."

"Can't or won't?"

"It's better if I don't."

"Is it still that you don't trust me, lad?"

"No sir," Aaron said, shaking his head, "it's not that. It's just ... well, it's safer for you if you don't become involved."

It was his old master's turn to frown. "I have only ever taken one apprentice in my life, lad, you know that as well as I do. Many have come to me for training, and I denied them all. I chose you because you had something the others didn't."

"Strong jaw line?"

The gray-haired man snorted, "Not hardly. I chose you because you have a strong spirit, boy, a strong heart. When I first met you, it was buried beneath a river of hate and anger, true, clouded by wasted thoughts of revenge, but still there for anyone to see if they looked closely enough. Though you picked up the blade faster than anyone I've ever seen, my biggest regret is that I was never able to pierce that hate of yours, so tightly did you wrap it about yourself. Yet now you seem ... no you *are* different. I wonder ... what has changed? What is it that has taken the place of all of that hate?"

Aaron shrugged, suddenly uncomfortable, "Something more important, I guess."

His old master's eyes narrowed for a moment then he burst into a fit of laughter. "What's so funny?" Aaron said, frowning.

Darrel wiped tears from the corners of his eyes and managed to get himself under control. "Why, boy, for a moment, you sounded like you were talking about a cause. Funny considering that you always used to tell me that there was nothing worth giving your life for, that a man who dedicated his life to something besides himself and his own happiness was the worst kind of fool."

"I don't see how it's funny." Aaron muttered.

Darrell watched him for several seconds then his eyes widened in realization, "You're serious." Aaron didn't respond. "Well," the man said smiling, "what about that. Praise the gods."

"You can if you want. Personally, I wouldn't waste my time—they never listen."

The old man sighed, "Some things never change. Still, just because you don't see the gods doesn't mean they aren't there, boy. After all, we humans have a way of missing things, don't we?"

"What are you talking about?"

The swordmaster shrugged, "I'm just saying we miss things. For example, does your lady know how much your wounds are really bothering you?" Does she know how close you came to being beaten in your first match?"

"I was fine."

"Don't you lie to me, boy," the man answered, his gray eyes narrowing, "you *weren't* fine. You were nearly beaten by some noble fool who couldn't tell his ass from a hole in the ground. The only thing that snobby bastard knows about sword fighting is what he heard in the stories his wet nurse told him when he was on her tit, and he almost bested you. *You,* a pupil I spent years training, almost beaten by a pup whose blade's never tasted blood."

Aaron started to protest and thought better of it. He'd spent a lot of time with the swordmaster, and he knew from experience that the man rarely grew angry, but, when he did, it was best to stay quiet and wait for the storm to pass. "Now let me help you, Aaron. Whatever it is, it's clearly important enough for you to enter a tournament when you can barely move your left hand. Yes, that's right, I know of that too. Why, a man would have to be blind to miss how it shakes."

"I can't, sir." Aaron said, "I can't. You went through enough trouble for me in the past. I won't mix you up in this too."

Darrell sighed and sat back, "Alright then, lad. Have it your way. But keep something in mind, not everyone in the tournament is a pampered dandy. Sooner or later, you'll run into someone with some real skill, and what do you plan on doing then?"

"I'll figure it out."

Darrell shook his head sadly, running a hand wearily across his lined face, "Well, you'd best be going before you're missed." He rose from the bench and Aaron followed suit. "I'm staying in Midtown, an inn called the *Absent Bard*. You come find me if you need me, okay?"

"Yes sir."

The swordsmaster met his eyes for several moments. Finally, he nodded. "Whatever you're up to, be careful, boy. I'll see you in a couple of hours."

"Alright."

Without another word, Darrell walked out of the church. Aaron frowned as he watched his old master go, suppressing the urge to stop him and tell him everything, knowing that it would only put the man at terrible risk for no reason. He waited, giving Darrell time to get a lead so that no one would see them leaving together.

He turned back to the altar, gazed at the carving of Nalesh and frowned. The Priests said that the Father of the Gods wrote the story of each and every person's life in his book, creating and destroying thousands, hundreds of thousands, in a story that stretched onward into eternity. He was known as the world's first, and greatest, author, but Aaron didn't see why. To his mind, if life was a book, it was nothing short of horror. And poorly done horror at that.

CHAPTER THIRTY-EIGHT

HIS FEET FELT HEAVY as he started back to the inn. He was happy to have seen his old master again, but their conversation had brought back the reality of everything he'd let himself get mixed up in. In trying to rescue the prince, he'd managed to make enemies of the most powerful man in Telrear, a man who could send legions after Aaron and the others if he decided to and who had enough money to hire any amount of assassins to do his dirty work for him. He frowned down at his left arm. Not that the man would need an army of assassins to get the job done just now. In Aaron's current state, an old lady with a broom would probably suffice.

What the fuck am I doing here? He thought, not for the first time. *A man would have to be insane to hang around in the very place he* knows *Belgarin will be.* He waited, out of habit, for Co's reply, but the Virtue apparently didn't deem his thoughts worthy of an answer. He could feel, even as he walked down the deserted streets, the men closing in, hunting him like a wild animal, and instead of hiding, like he had some sense, he was competing in a damned tournament that he had no chance to win for a shot at murdering a man he'd have no chance of murdering.

A fool's errand, one that would certainly end up with a walk through the Keeper's Fields. Still, he found that what bothered him more wasn't the thought of his impending death, but the thought that he was going to fail Gryle and Adina. They were counting on him, and he was going to fail.

He turned a corner and started down the main road. Here, the foot traffic was much heavier with people heading into or out of the better part of the city or haggling at one of the many merchants' stalls crowding the lane. Among the milling press of bodies, Aaron picked out guards patrolling the street in ones and twos, placed there, no doubt, to keep order among the increased population of the city's poor district. He snorted at the thought. From his experience, the bastards were probably the worst criminals in the city.

Then again, for all he knew, one of those slack-faced, shabbily clothed men, one of those women with the dead eyes, or the children with their hungry stares, could be killers hired by Belgarin. He felt the hairs on the back of his neck rise, and the space between his shoulder blades began to itch. *There!* That man at the nearest stall pretending to argue with the merchant over some trinket, he'd been staring hadn't he? There was a sound to his left, and he whipped his head around to see two children running past, playing at a game of chase.

He realized that his hand was gripping the handle of one of his blades so tight that it ached, and he forced himself to take a deep, calming breath as he remembered words his master had told him, so many years ago. *"Fear has killed more men than all the swords and arrows ever* made." It had seemed like foolishness at the time, and he was pretty sure he remembered making some flippant, smartass remark about it, but now he understood all too well as he struggled to calm his rapidly beating heart.

Don't stop. You're being followed, came Co's urgent voice.

Aaron started down the street again, resisting the urge to turn and look. *Who?*

I don't know, the Virtue said, her voice sounded tense, scared, *there's too much ... too much noise I can't ...*

That's fine, he thought grimly as he turned down an empty side alley. Let them follow. He may be wounded and hunted, but damnit he wasn't dead yet. Despite the light of the day, shadows clung to the walls of the buildings on either side of the alley. He put his back against one of them and slid his sword free.

Several tense seconds passed before he was able to make out the sound of approaching footsteps. *Aaron, wait!* Co said.

Not now, firefly, be quiet. There was another step, then another. Judging by the sounds, there were two of them. *That's alright,* he thought, a cruel grin spreading across his face. Wounded or not, he was sick of being chased around the whole damned country, and these two bastards were about to find out just how sick.

Wait, Aaron, Co thought, *you can't—*

Enough! He shot back, blocking out her words, *they're the ones chasing me, now let me do my work.* There was a flash of cloth as the first one stepped around the corner, and Aaron let out a roar of anger as he shot forward, swinging the sword overhead.

Short fucker, he thought as his sword continued its lethal sweep. Someone let out a whimper, and his eyes shot down. He stared in shocked realization at the person in front of him. Not a soldier or assassin at all, but a young boy that couldn't have been more than ten summers of age. He grunted as he tried to arrest the forward motion of his blade. He managed it, but only barely, and the blade quivered inches above the blonde haired boy's head. There was a frozen second when the kid stared, wide-eyed at the blade mere inches from his face. Aaron's nostrils filled with the sharp, pungent smell of piss and a puddle began to grow at the youth's feet. The moment passed and the kid collapsed to the ground on his butt, screaming in terrified, screeching whimpers as he inched his way backward along the pavement.

Suddenly, the owner of the second pair of footsteps, a heavy-set, middle-aged woman with limp, dull brown hair tied up in a bun, came around the corner. The woman gasped in shock and fell beside the boy, hugging him tightly against her heaving bosom. "What did you do?" She demanded of the sellsword, piercing him with an angry gaze.

Aaron stared, confused, "I ... I don't—"

"You don't *what?*" The woman shrieked, as the boy cried against her, and he realized with growing dread that the red-faced, thick-jowled woman was the boy's mother. "What's *wrong* with you, you bastard? Does it make you feel like a man to wave your sword at children?"

"What? No, of course not. Listen, I thought—"

"Oh, I very seriously doubt you *thought* much of anything," the woman shot back, and he noticed people staring curiously down the alley as they walked by.

Perfect, he thought, *just what I need.* "Well what were *you* thinking?" He demanded, suddenly angry, "why were you following me?"

"He saw you fight!" The woman screamed, "You were his favorite. He just wanted to *see* you, you ... you *monster!*"

I tried to tell you, Co said.

Aaron sighed heavily as he knelt down in front of the kid. He looked into the boy's watery gaze, saw that his bottom lip was trembling. "Listen, kid. I'm sorry, I didn't mean to—"

"Don't you get near *him.*" The woman was back to her feet faster than Aaron would have thought possible given her weight, and slapped him in the face, hard. She jerked the boy behind her and began to back away from him, waving a sausage-sized finger at him in warning, "Don't you come near us. *Guards.* I want the guards!" She shouted, turning toward the street, "Someone get the guards, this man tried to kill my son!"

"*What?*" He asked, shocked, "Lady, what in the name of the gods are you *talking* about?" But the woman was too far gone now, screaming and wailing at the top of her lungs for the guards. He noticed with dismay that a crowd was beginning to gather, drawn by the mother's screams like flies to shit. It was only a matter of time, he knew, before the whale got her wish and the guards began to show up as well.

He opened his mouth to try to explain what had happened, but shut it again when he looked into the faces of the crowd and saw the anger building in their scowls and the hard set of their jaws. They, like the woman, were past reasoning. The woman was screaming as if he *had* killed her boy, and in answer to her shouts, the kid had begun to wail loudly. He considered waiting for the guards so that he could explain what happened and immediately dismissed the idea. In his experience, guards cared little for the truth at the best of times, and with the excess of people and no doubt crimes the contest had drawn, they'd be even less willing to listen than usual. If he was lucky, he'd end up spending the night in a cell for his trouble; a cell that, with all of the people chasing him, he'd never make it out of alive. More likely, though, they'd hang him and have done. So, instead of waiting for his fate to come to him, he employed a skill that any successful sellsword cultivated. He ran.

He darted down the alley, slammed into a wall as he made a sharp turn and kept going, leaping over beggars and ignoring their cries of shock as he wound his way through the maze-like side streets, putting as much space between him and the crazy lady as he could and heading, in what he thought was the direction of the inn.

Finally, he emerged out of the alley and onto the main road of the city, panting and gasping for air. He glanced behind him and was relieved to see no mob of angry, kid-loving fat women barreling after him. He propped his hands on his knees and tried to get control of his breathing. A few passersby took in his sweat-covered face and heaving chest with strange looks, but not *murderous* looks, so that was alright. He looked around and saw, with relief, that the ramshackle inn was only a short distance up the lane.

He forced himself to take calm, measured strides as he headed for it. The last thing he needed was to attract attention. Well, any *more* attention at any rate. "What in the name of the gods was I thinking?" He muttered angrily to himself.

I think—Co began.

"Best you stay quiet just now, firefly," he interrupted gruffly.

Adina and Gryle were sitting at the bar waiting on him. As he entered, they both jumped up from their stools and hurried toward him. "Where have you *been?* We thought—" Adina paused as she glanced around the room. Deciding that the inn's patrons were too busy drinking or swatting playfully at the harried serving girls to pay her any attention, she turned back, "We've been worried sick."

"I'm alright," he lied. *Pulling a sword on kids? Charging down alleyways like a damned maniac? Buddy, you're about as far from alright as it gets.*

The princess looked at him dubiously, as if she could read his thoughts. "But where were you? Why are you so sweaty? Did something happen?"

He hesitated, "You could call it that, I guess."

"Sir," Gryle said, his face apologetic as he looked between the two of them, "what my m—" he winced and his mouth worked soundlessly for a moment before he cleared his throat and tried again, "What your *wife* means to say, is that she is glad you're alright—we both are—but if you still intend to fight in the tournament, we'd best be heading to the arena. It won't be long before the matches start again."

Aaron nodded, struggling not to let his relief show on his face. He'd done a lot of pretty shitty things in his career as a sellsword, but he was just fine not sharing the fact that he'd pulled his sword on a child. Even if the kid was a whining brat. "You're right. Come on, let's go."

He could feel Adina frowning at his back as he led them out into the road and started toward the tourney grounds. "What happened, really?" She asked, and the determined look in her eyes assured him that she wasn't going to let it go.

As they walked, he told them about the note and about his meeting with his old master. They didn't interrupt him as he relayed the tale, but as he spoke he noticed the princess getting angrier and angrier. By the time he was finished, she looked ready to chew iron and spit horse shoes. "I *knew* you two knew each other."

He nodded, "I would have told you, but I couldn't, not in the arena where anyone could hear."

"Oh?" She asked, her eyes flashing, "So why didn't you tell me about the note? We could have come with you. What if it had been an ambush?" He didn't answer, and she grabbed him forcing him to a stop, "Tell me why you didn't tell us," she demanded, and he suddenly thought he knew how her servants must have felt, but though her voice was angry, her eyes were pleading, "Why didn't you *trust* us?"

"Trust you?" He asked, incredulous. "*Trust* you?" He shook his head angrily, "Him!" He hissed, "Don't you get it? I didn't trust *him*."

Her eyes widened in shock, "You mea—"

"Yes!" He interrupted, "I didn't tell you about the note, and I didn't take you two with me because for all I knew it *was* an ambush, and if it was, there was no point in all three of us being killed, was there?" She didn't answer. Instead, she stood staring at him, a strange look in her deep blue eyes. "What?" He asked, "Look, I might be an asshole, but I'm not a monster. I couldn't just let—"

Suddenly, she reached her hands behind his neck and pulled him into a kiss so deep, so all-encompassing, that he completely forgot what he was going to say. Instead, he reached his arm behind her back, and pulled her closer, all his thoughts and worries vanishing as he felt her body, soft yet firm, yield to his embrace. He had no idea how long they'd been at it when he felt a tug on his shoulder. "Sir, we really should be going." *I'll kill him,* Aaron thought.

The princess pulled away, her cheeks and face flushed, "O-of course, Gryle, you're right. I'm sorry I ... I don't know what came over me."

Aaron frowned at the chamberlain then back at Adina, "You sure he's right?"

She smiled, and he could see the laughter in her blue eyes, "Come on. We wouldn't want you to be late." He stared after her as she turned and started down the street. He turned to Gryle, and the chamberlain must have seen something in his eyes because he cleared his throat uncomfortably and hurried after.

Aaron watched him go and sighed heavily as he started after them. "Yeah, you're right," he muttered, "Wouldn't want to be late."

CHAPTER THIRTY-NINE

As SOON AS HE STEPPED OUT of the armory and got a look at the other contestant, Aaron knew he was in trouble. The man that approached the center of the circle from the other armory had dull brown hair, a face and build that was completely unremarkable. He was both shorter and smaller than Aaron himself. He wasn't handsome or ugly only very ... plain. He was the type of person that people forgot the name of minutes after meeting him, uninteresting in every way. None of these things were what bothered Aaron. What bothered him was the man's walk.

His father, years ago, had told him that you could tell a lot about a man from how he walked. Did he shuffle along, his head down, each step taken as if it was a chore, avoiding people's eyes, or did he swagger, staring at those around him in silent challenge? At the time, his father had been trying to educate his young son on the importance of understanding people's motivations and, therefore, how to best lead them, imparting a small bit of knowledge that, he claimed, was invaluable for any general or leader.

Back then, Aaron hadn't thought anything of it. It hadn't been the first time his father had given him a strange lesson, and he'd just been happy to be able to spend time with him, but later in life he'd discovered that his father had been right. In fact, many people of similar backgrounds shared the same walk. Farmers, merchants, nobility, they could all be identified by the walk they used, and so, too, could soldiers.

The walk of a fighting man wasn't the weary, purposeful walk of a farmer, nor was it the sauntering, vain strut of a noble. Instead, it was the confident stride of a man who knew how to handle himself, a man who had shed blood before, who knew he would shed it again and wasn't much bothered by that. The man's hands never strayed far from the sword at his side, and his dull brown eyes took in the crowd in the stands, the announcer, and Aaron, in an assessing, calculating manner, as he stalked into the circle. *Not the walk of a soldier,* Aaron thought, revising his opinion as he entered the center of the circle and stared into the man's eyes, *the walk of a killer.*

The brown-haired man smiled at Aaron revealing straight, white teeth. *He knows he has me,* Aaron thought as he frowned back, *knows it like he knows the sun is shining. Knows it like I know it.*

"Ladies and gentlemen, I give you Flynn Daltan and his opponent, Rodrick Elarn." The announcer shouted, and then jogged toward the edge of the circle to the wild applause of the crowd.

"Just me and you," the man said as he slid his sword free of its scabbard.

Aaron pulled his own sword free in reply. *"Begin!"* The announcer shouted, and before the word was finished the brown-haired man shot forward with alarming speed, his sword blurring as he attacked with a flurry of jabs and slashes. Backpedaling furiously, Aaron only just managed to avoid getting his stomach cut open. By the time he brought his own blade around for a strike, his opponent had already backpedaled away.

They began to circle each other and the brown-haired man smiled. "Are you scared yet?' He asked in a low voice that only Aaron could hear. "You know that you can't beat me, don't you? You know that you're not good enough, especially not wounded like you are."

How does he know that? Aaron thought, *is it really as easy to see as Darrell said?* The man dashed forward once more, and all thought was pushed from Aaron's mind as he was forced back under the heavy rain of blows.

CHAPTER FORTY

ADINA GASPED AS SHE WATCHED Aaron retreat from the other contestant's fearsome barrage of strikes and lunges. *"Come on, Aaron,"* she whispered fiercely, her hand tightening on Gryle's, "Come *on.*" She took a relieved breath as the sellsword managed to circle away from the other contestant, batting his sword aside in a desperate parry and putting some distance between the two of them.

"He won't win," a voice said beside her, and she turned to see the old man, Aaron's one time master, beside her on the bench. The man watched the combat with a resigned expression, and to Adina's eyes, he looked as if he'd aged twenty years in the last few hours.

"You don't know that," she shot back angrily, "You don't know."

"But I do," he said, his voice sad. "Look at him. His wounds have stolen his strength." Adina turned back to the fight and saw, with dismay, that Darrell was right. Aaron's chest was heaving, and his feet were moving sluggishly. Gone was the smooth grace she'd seen him use when fighting Lucius's two bodyguards. "No," the old man said beside her, his voice angry, "this fight should have never happened. Please, dear," he said, meeting her gaze with his steely, gray eyes, "tell him to yield. Yell it to him, before he gets hurt worse. The blades are blunted in tournaments, but mistakes have happened before. Please. He may listen to you."

Adina hesitated, unsure, and the other contestant waded in behind a flurry of flashing steel again. Aaron worked his sword through desperate parries with more skill than she'd ever seen from any of her or her father's soldiers, but he was weak from his injury, slower, and in a burst of movement the other contestant knocked Aaron's blade wide, and brought his sword in a slash across the sellsword's chest. Aaron shouted in pain as the sword cut across him, and he reeled away drunkenly. The princess felt her breath catch as the sword came away dripping red.

Even from this distance, she could see that Aaron's shirt had been sliced cleanly through and was staining crimson from his blood. "It can't be," she whispered, "the blade is supposed to be blunted." Her own thoughts were echoed in the confused mutters and whispers of the crowd. She turned to the old swordmaster, "It shouldn't have cut so easily, should it?"

"No," he answered, his lined face grim, "no, it shouldn't have. Something's wrong."

"We have to do something," Gryle whispered fiercely beside her, "Sir Aaron is in trouble and needs our help." The heavy set chamberlain rose from his place on the bench and was immediately pushed back down by a thick-necked, bull of a man, who seemed to have appeared out of nowhere. The man wore no colors, but plain, simple leather trousers and jerkin. A sword was belted at his waist.

"If I was you, fat man," he said, gesturing to six, similarly clad men who'd moved up to stand behind him, "I'd worry about myself. I'd say you've got plenty enough trouble on your own," he turned to Adina with a cruel grin, "wouldn't you, Princess?"

CHAPTER FORTY-ONE

AARON TOOK TWO STUMBLING STEPS BACK and glanced down in shock and pain at the bloody cut across his chest. Luckily, it wasn't deep. The steel had only just made contact. Another couple of inches, and he'd be a dead man. He turned back to the brown-haired contestant, and saw that the man was still smiling. "Who are you?" He asked, keeping his blade between them as he circled warily.

The man feinted with his blade once, twice, grinning as Aaron brought his blade up to parry blows that never came. "Doesn't matter who I am, does it?" He asked, as he circled, his blade low, confident that Aaron had nothing left. "What matters, is what I'm here for, and I think you know that, don't you?"

"You came here to kill me."

"Oh?" The man asked, his eyebrows raised in an expression of mock surprise, "and why would I do that?"

"Because you're one of Belgarin's soldiers."

The man's eyes narrowed, "I'm not anyone's soldier, fool," he hissed, and then abruptly he was smiling again. "Then again, I guess you could say that I'm everyone's soldier. As long as the price is right."

Aaron nodded as the man confirmed what he'd already known. "An assassin."

The man shrugged, "So many bad connotations to that word. I prefer to think of myself as a problem solver, and *you* are a problem that a certain someone is willing to pay handsomely to get solved." He grinned wider, "Funny thing. When I took the job, I thought that the hardest part would be finding you. After all, the north is a big place, and I didn't relish the idea of freezing my balls off in this frozen wasteland just to dust some asshole that managed to piss off the wrong person. Imagine my surprise, then, when I track you here, to Baresh?" He laughed and shook his head, "You must be one dumb bastard," he taunted, "It's like you wanted to die."

Co, he thought, *if you can do anything for the pain, now's the time.*

I'll try, but I won't be able to hold it back for long, the Virtue answered, her young voice sounding impossibly tired and strained. Immediately, the pain lessened, didn't disappear, but lessened enough so that he could move his left arm, and he could no longer feel the cut on his chest at all despite the blood that still leaked from it.

"I'm not dead yet," he answered the assassin.

The man grinned, "Not yet." Even before he was finished speaking, he was dashing forward, his blade whistling as it darted through the air toward Aaron's throat.

Instead of retreating as he had before, Aaron lunged forward, ducking under the blade and whipping his blunted blade around at the man's midsection. The brown haired man grunted in surprise and just managed to get his own blade back in time to stop the strike. The air rang with the sound of metal striking metal, and they stood there, their swords locked, each of them struggling to force the other's blade aside. "Just die, you bastard," the man growled, his smile gone.

Aaron didn't waste energy talking. Although Co was alleviating his pain, he was still weak, and it took all he had to keep the smaller man's sword at bay. Still, he knew that it wouldn't last long. Already, he could feel his strength leaving him, and he knew it wouldn't be more than a matter of seconds before the assassin managed to knock his blade aside and finish it.

"You've already lost," the man snarled, "you just don't know it yet. Your woman, and the fat man, both of them are as good as dead. See for yourself."

Aaron shot a glance over his shoulder, and saw that Gryle and Adina were no longer sitting on the bench, but being forced back toward the entrance of the arena by a group of rough looking armed men, and though several of the people in the crowd were staring curiously, even angrily, no one made a move to stop it. *Gods no.*

He pushed harder, forcing more strength against the other man's sword, so that the assassin had to exert more pressure of his own. Then, without warning, he pulled his left arm away from his sword. The second that he did, the man grinned and knocked his sword aside. He was still grinning when Aaron let out a growl of rage and smashed his fist into the man's face. There was a loud *crack* as the assassin's nose snapped, and he bellowed in agony as he tumbled backward, his sword tumbling to the ground.

Aaron dove on top of him, "Kill me will you?" He drove his fist into the man's face again. The assassin's head rebounded off the tightly packed earth, and Aaron clamped his hands around the man's throat and began to squeeze. A small part of his mind noted that the arena had grown eerily silent. The only sounds to be heard were his own growls and curses of rage and the assassin's choking gargles. *"Stop!"* An unfamiliar voice shouted. *I'll be damned if I do,* Aaron thought, and he didn't flinch as the assassin struck him in the sides, didn't feel the pain at all. Instead, he squeezed harder, digging his fingers into the man's throat.

He felt a twinge in his side and looked down to see a knife sticking out of it. *Must have been hiding it in his tunic, the bas*—the rest of his thoughts were blasted from his mind as Co suddenly let out wretched, agonized scream so intense that he was sure his head would shatter from it. The Virtue's tortured wail stretched out, impossibly long, and soon he was shouting himself, not at his own pain—the Virtue was still blocking that—but at the impossible, gut-wrenching dimensions of Co's agony, an agony that he somehow felt without *feeling,* an agony that he knew was supposed to be his own.

He snarled, feeling as if he'd go insane from the terrible sound of Co's scream, but his grip on the assassin's throat did not relent. The man's lips were turning blue, and his eyes bulged from his sockets, but he still managed to get his hand around the blade and twist it. The pain was a faint, distant thing, but Co's tormented scream rose in pitch, threatening to drive all rational thought from his head. He held on to one thought with the desperation of a drowning man struggling for the surface. Adina. They were going to kill Adina.

He didn't know how long he crouched there, growling and cursing and squeezing, his eyes closed against the Virtue's agony, but when he finally looked down the man's dead eyes stared back at him in a look of surprise, and his own hands trembled and shook violently.

Aaron, the Virtue whimpered, *I can't ... hold it back anymore.*

Not yet, Co, he thought back, *not yet. They have Gryle. They have Adina.* He struggled to his feet and took several, shuffling steps in the direction of Adina in the others. Then, without warning, an agony like nothing he'd ever felt tore through his body, a roaring inferno that drowned out everything else. The strength went out of his legs, and he crumpled to the ground, howling in rage and pain.

Get up damn you, he thought fiercely, but his legs wouldn't respond to his demands. Snarling, he started forward at a crawl, his expression set in a grimace of twisted rage. His chest heaved and his straining effort caused fresh blood to pump out of the wound in his side. Darkness started to creep its way steadily into his vision, and he fought against it as he drug himself across the dusty ground, heedless of the bloody trail he left in his wake.

The darkness grew deeper, so that his vision consisted of a thin, rapidly shrinking tunnel. Then, like some beast that had been lurking, waiting for the right opportunity, the darkness reared up, relentless and implacable and pounced. As he slipped into unconsciousness, he could just make out the sound of footsteps beside him. "Get him," a man's voice said, and then it was gone, and there was only the pain, and the darkness, and then nothing at all.

CHAPTER FORTY-TWO

THE MEN LED ADINA AND GRYLE toward the arena's entrance. Adina tried to think of some way to escape, but her thoughts kept going back to Aaron, to the bloody cut across his chest, the last thing she'd seen before the men had taken her. And that scream. Had that really been Aaron? Was he dead already? *Please,* she thought desperately, *please let him be okay.*

It's your fault, a part of her said as hot tears glided down her face. *If not for you, he'd be safe in the Downs. If he's dead, you killed him as much as the man with the blade.* She'd wanted to make the world a better place, a place where people didn't have to live in fear of Belgarin and his men, but she had failed. Eladen had died, Aaron was most likely dead, and it was all her fault.

She was so overcome by her brooding thoughts that she wasn't aware the men around her had stopped until she bumped into one of them. The soldier turned and slapped her contemptuously across the face, and she cried out in shock and surprise, a hand going to her bloody lip. "Watch where you're going, bitch," he hissed before turning back to gaze at something she couldn't see past the soldiers in front of her.

"Get out of our way, old man," the leader growled.

"Let them go, and I'll be happy to," a familiar voice said.

"I don't have time for this shit," the leader said, drawing his sword, "Kill the stupid bastard." As the men fanned out, Adina saw that the old man, Darrell, stood facing them, his sword held low at an angle to the ground.

The soldiers started forward in confident swaggers, and the old man watched them come, his face expressionless. The closest of them brought his blade up to strike, and Darrell exploded into motion. He lunged forward, impossibly quick, and his sword lashed out and took the soldier in the throat. His unlucky victim took a fumbling step back and his sword clattered to the earth. Before the others had a chance to react, the old man took two quick steps back, out of the range of their swords. The man he'd struck wavered drunkenly then fell to the ground in a thrashing heap, the hands he'd brought to his throat staining crimson in moments.

The soldiers glanced at each other, stunned, ignoring their dying comrade. "Watch her," the leader said to the man closest to Adina. Then, as one, he and the remaining three roared and charged and the old man disappeared in a flurry of swinging and stabbing steel that flashed with deadly promise in the sunlight. Adina watched, terrified, expecting the old man to be cut down. Instead, he weaved in and out of the storm of blows like the wind, ducking slashes, sidestepping thrusts, and knocking the blades of the soldiers harmlessly aside. To the princess, who'd often watched her father's and her own soldiers practice, he didn't appear to be fighting at all, but performing some intricate, elaborate dance.

"Kill him!" A frightened, whining voice shrieked. *"He's ruining it! He's ruining everything!"* Adina turned and saw Claudius standing out of his seat, a turkey leg still in his hand. The fat man's face was deep crimson with anger, and even from across the arena, Adina could see his jowls shake as he waved the piece of greasy meat like a sword and pointed it at Darrell, *"kill him and bring the princess to me!"*

At the Duke's command, guards began to rush out of the benches and across the grounds like ants swarming out of their hive. More than twenty men all told, sprinting across the grounds toward the old swordmaster who was too busy fending off the attacks of the remaining soldiers to notice. "Look out!" She shouted, as a young, blonde haired man—faster than the rest—charged up behind Darrell, and the old man moved just in time to avoid a blow that would have split him in two.

"Run girl!" He shouted, his voice hoarse, as he parried another blow and kicked the nearest man in the stomach sending him to the ground, "You and your man get out of here now!"

Adina knew that the old swordmaster was right. She should run, survive, bide her time. Belgarin might soon gain control of the north, true, but he hadn't won yet, and as one of the royal line, she was better equipped to undermine her brother's schemes than anyone else. She also knew that, though she'd had some training with a blade at the hands of Jon Harvend, her father's Captain of the Guard (her father had insisted that all of the royal line knew enough to protect themselves) she would die if she stayed. Perhaps, given a dueling rapier and matched against one of them, she might have had some small hope, but they'd never give her a chance. Once they finished with Darrell, they'd cut her down with no more thought than a butcher slicing hog's flesh. And that if she was lucky. These men were not nobles or duelists, and she doubted very seriously if they'd ever even heard of *Eralian's Treatise on the Proper Etiquette of Formal Dueling.* In truth, she would have been surprised if any of them could read at all.

Better to run, to hide, to survive. She knew all of this, yet she hesitated, her eyes locked on the doomed swordmaster as he fought an unwinnable fight. When her feet finally did move, she was surprised to find that it wasn't in the direction of safety, but toward the carnage. She'd taken only three steps when a hairy arm wrapped around her neck and jerked her back. In an instant, a knife blade was poised scant inches from her eye. "Move and die, bitch," the remaining guard growled into her ear, and she almost gagged at the overpowering, rotten whiskey-stench of his breath.

The chamberlain took a step toward her, and the soldier tightened his grip, bringing the knife to her throat, "Not another step, fat man or the bitch dies, princess or not." Gryle froze, and Adina just had time to notice that the chamberlain wasn't looking at her or the man, but over their shoulder, behind them, when the soldier let out a grunt of surprise. He fell, taking her with him and landing on top of her.

The air was knocked out of her, and she struggled wildly for several seconds, anticipating the feel of sharp steel tearing into her before she realized that the man wasn't fighting back. Finally, she managed to push herself out from under the soldier. Breathing hard more from fear than exertion, she scooted backwards across the dusty earth, trying to put some distance between her and her guard. She looked to see how close he was and froze in shock. Sticking out of the back of the man's neck was a dagger that looked as if it should be hanging in some collector's show room. The handle was adorned with gold and at its base held a large, sparkling ruby. Blood, sickeningly similar to the color of the gem, pulsed from the wound in spurts. "Wha—" she began, then hands were grasping her by the arms, pulling her to her feet.

"Come on, we have to go," A voice urged, and she let out a gasp of surprise as she saw that her savior was no other than Celes, the blonde-haired, blue-eyed bartender from May's club back in Avarest.

"You!" Adina exclaimed, "but how—"

"No time for that," the blonde answered grimly, the playful, flirtatious manner she'd shown in the Downs nowhere in evidence, "If you want to live, we've got to get you and your man out of here. Now."

Adina let herself be pulled along several paces before jerking her arm away and turning back to where Darrell fought desperately for his life. "Wait. What about him?" More guards had arrived, attacking in unison, and the old man's sword was a blur as he struggled to keep the web of steel at bay. Three soldiers lay dead on the ground, another two writhing and screaming as they gripped the bloody stumps where their sword hands had been moments before. Still, the swordmaster wasn't having it all his way. He bled from a cut across his chest and one of his arms was cradled against his side, stained crimson from a long cut on his forearm. A short way off more armed men were rushing toward him. "We can't leave him. He saved me."

The blonde woman pulled at her, "Dar knows what he's doing, now come on. Don't make it for nothing!" She hissed angrily.

Reluctantly, Adina forced her eyes away from the older man and followed the bartender, looking back once to make sure that Gryle was close behind. "We have to get Aaron," she said, as they pushed their way through a gathering crowd of stupefied, slack-jawed onlookers.

"For a girl who can't even save herself, you sure do have a lot of foolish ideas," Celes snapped, "now stop acting like a spoiled princess who expects everything to go her way and *come on!*"

The woman burst into a sprint, tugging on Adina's arm, and the princess was forced to follow or have her arm ripped from its socket. Soon, they were out of the arena grounds and running through the empty streets. They wound their way through so many back alleys and side passages that by the time Celes slowed to a walk in one of the wealthier parts of Baresh, Gryle and Adina were both panting heavily, pouring with sweat, and Adina, at least, was hopelessly lost.

"This way," the woman said as she led them up to the wrought iron gate of an expensive looking house.

"We can't break in here," Adina thought, "I've seen these kind of gates before. You won't be able to force them."

The blonde arched a delicate, perfectly-shaped eyebrow at her, "Break in? Of course not." She turned back to the gate, and in moments an elderly bald man appeared and opened the gates. "Mrs. Celes, welcome back. They're waiting for you inside."

"Thank you, Olo," she said, as she led the confused princess and chamberlain up the cobbled walk, past richly colored and meticulously maintained gardens to the front door of the sprawling home. She knocked once, and the door swung open.

"I-it can't be," Adina breathed, as a familiar face smiled back at her.

CHAPTER FORTY-THREE

Aaron DIDN'T WAKE SO MUCH as get torn out of unconsciousness by the many pains and hurts that he'd acquired over the last couple of weeks. By themselves, each was enough to explain the film of cold sweat that covered his body and convince him that his time of finally come. Soon he would begin the Last Walk through the Keeper's Fields and would become nothing but another slave toiling under the God of Death's yolk. He thought of Adina and felt a deep pang of sadness. Sadness, but not surprise.

Salen's Priests claimed that their god was the most powerful, the most worthy of worship, because everyone who was living was steadily marching toward death. Aaron supposed if that was true then, given his lifestyle and profession, he'd been flat out sprinting. The truth was, he'd known his death was coming—had known it for a long time. He'd never deluded himself into thinking he'd die old, surrounded by loving children and squalling grandchildren to mourn his passing. If he was surprised at all, it was only that it had taken this long.

"There now," a rough, male voice said beside him, "relax. It's alright."

He tried to open his eyes, but he found that he didn't have the strength. It was as if weights had been tied to his eyelids. "Drink this," the voice told him, and he felt something pressed against his lips.

His supposed that it was poison. For a moment, he considered drinking it. At least it would make the pain stop. It was a mixture of thoughts of the princess and his own stubbornness that kept his lips tightly sealed. The bastards could kill him if they wanted—he was in no shape to stop them—but by the gods they were going to have to get their hands bloody doing it. *Co,* he thought, struggling to keep his thoughts coherent past the waves of pain on which they floated, *where are we? What's happening?*

The Virtue didn't respond.

Co?

Still there was no answer, and Aaron began to worry. What if she'd absorbed too much of his pain, taken too much of it into herself and, so doing, had died. There'd been a time that he would have laughed at such a thought. After all, how could a glowing ball of light die, and what did it matter to him if it did? Well, the fact was, it *did* matter now, and that was enough.

The glass pressed against his mouth more urgently, "Drink," the owner of the voice said, "it will help. It will help the pain go away."

I don't doubt it, he thought, but he was too weak to reply even if he wanted to. The question was, was there something in the drink that would kill him, or only some remedy that would bring relief to the hot agony that coursed through his body. He decided that it didn't make sense for it to be poison. After all, if Belgarin's men wanted him dead, all they had to do was stick a knife in him and be done.

More likely, they wanted him to get better so that they could question him about everything that had happened. Not much point in torturing a man that was already dying, after all. He considered not drinking it anyway. Why give the sons of bitches the satisfaction? The problem was that the pain was growing worse, more insistent. Reluctantly, he opened his mouth and let the liquid pour down his throat. "That's good," the disembodied voice said approvingly, "Drink all of it." Whatever the mixture was, it tasted bitter and left a sharp after taste in his mouth, but he complied readily nonetheless. He hadn't realized how parched he'd been until he tasted the cool liquid.

The voice said something else, but he couldn't make it out. The dark river of unconsciousness on which he'd floated suddenly surged up, pulling him under, and he gave in gratefully.

CHAPTER FORTY-FOUR

HE AWOKE LATER TO THE VOICE asking him to drink again. He did without hesitation, and realized that the all-encompassing pain he'd felt before was nowhere near as bad as it had been. He still felt impossibly weak, and his side throbbed where the assassin had plunged his knife into him, but he could think past it now. *Co? Are you there?*

Still no answer. Once he finished drinking, the glass was pulled away, and the owner of the voice made a satisfied sound. "How are you feeling?"

Like death warmed over, he thought, but didn't answer.

"Well?"

He tried to speak but all that came out was a dry croak. He swallowed and tried again. "I-I'm okay." He was shocked by how frail his voice sounded.

"You're many things, I reckon, but okay's not one of em," the voice responded, "not yet anyway."

"Who," he paused to clear his throat, "who are you?"

"Why don't you open up yer eyes and see for yerself."

Slowly, reluctantly, Aaron did, and let out his breath in surprise. "It can't be. You're dead."

"Well, now," Balen said, grinning widely, "there's dead, and then there's dead. I'd think you more than anybody would know somethin' about that."

"I'm not dead," he muttered, wincing at the rawness of his throat, "I'd be a lot more comfortable if I was."

The first mate grinned, "As you say."

"But how?" Aaron asked disbelievingly, "When we left Aster and his men were boarding the ship. How did you get away?"

"As to that," the first mate said, rubbing a hand across his chin, "I'm not so sure as I understand it myself. One minute, the bastards were comin' aboard, fixin' to cut us down, then Leomin took that Aster fella aside and talked to him for a minute. Next thing I knew, I was laid up on a table getting' sewed up by one of his men. Mind you, the man weren't no doctor," he grimaced at the memory, "if anything, I'd guess he's a blind butcher, but he managed anyway."

"But how did Leomin talk his way out? That Aster is crazy. I know. I've met him."

Balen nodded, "You're right there, the man's a few fish short of a full string, but he let us go just the same. Even gave us some money to help us on our way." He shook his head in disbelief, "As to what the captain said, I ain't got a clue. I was in pretty bad shape there for a while and not much up for listenin' to too much of anything. Besides," he said, grinning, "ain't you ever heard the Cap talk? The man could talk mermaids out of the water."

Aaron frowned. It was true that Leomin had a way with conversation that made him hard to understand,

and that he also had a way of getting people to do things they didn't intend to do. He'd seen that readily enough when the captain had somehow managed to talk the princess into going and getting Gryle when all she really wanted to do was throttle Aaron, but he still couldn't believe that the man had somehow talked his way out of Aster's hands. There was something strange about that, but he couldn't worry about it just now. His thoughts were on the last thing he'd seen before he'd lost consciousness, Adina being led away by soldiers.

Balen must have seen something in his face because he patted him on the shoulder reassuringly, "You're worried about your woman. Don't be. She's safe as can be. Why, she spent so much time by your bed here I figured she was about to sprout roots, that man of hers too. Finally, the boss made her go on and get some rest, said it weren't doin' no one a bit o' good for her to kill herself waitin'. She didn't want to, but she finally did it anyway. Got a real stubborn streak in her that one does."

Aaron opened his mouth to speak, but stopped as the shouts and cheers of what must have been hundreds of people sounded outside. "They've found us," he hissed, clenching his teeth, as he stared across the room at the window. It was too far for him to see out of, but he had no problem imagining the mob gathering below them in the street, only too excited to welcome their new leader with a celebratory execution.

The first mate glanced at the small window in confusion. "What are you ta—Oh! No, no, you got it wrong, Aaron. That ain't nobody come to get us. Why, it's just the parade."

Aaron frowned, rubbing at his temples, "Parade?"

Balen nodded with a frown of his own, "That's right, for Belgarin. Since Claudius announced him ruler of Baresh and all of it's outlyin' lands there's been one every day. Near as I can tell, the prince means to hold a week's worth of the damned things, just in case there's some poor blind, deaf bastard out there who missed it the first five times."

"Five?" Aaron asked incredulous.

"That's right. One a day since he was crowned."

"But that means ..." he hesitated in disbelief.

"You been out the better part of a week," the first mate confirmed. "The tournament's over and done, and Belgarin sits at the Seat of Baresh. Leastways, until he heads back to his own country."

"So we failed," Aaron said in an emotionless, dead voice. "I failed. Belgarin's been crowned."

"You're livin'. There's somethin' to be said for that."

Suddenly, Aaron wished desperately that Co would speak. Though he'd been loath to admit it (still was, in fact) talking to the Virtue had, in many ways, been a comfort. *But she's dead,* a voice in his mind said, *dead and gone like so many hopes and dreams.*

He felt a black mood descending upon him and, suddenly, he felt more exhausted than he ever had in his life. "Talks Aster into letting you two live *and* manages to get Adina to do what he wants ... your Parnen certainly has a way with words, Balen."

"Huh? Oh, no, sir. It weren't the Cap who convinced her to leave yer side. Why, he wields words like a blademaster wields swords, but I doubt even he could have managed that. No, it was the *boss,* you see."

Aaron looked at the man blankly, blinking heavily, "What are you talking about? Who's the boss?"

Balen grinned, "Well, might be I'll leave that for you to find out on yer own. After you've had some rest, that is."

Aaron nodded, letting his eyes fall shut. "I am tired."

The first mate snorted, "Why, of course ye are. You been lyin' around all day."

CHAPTER FORTY-FIVE

THE NEXT TIME HE CAME TO, Aaron opened his eyes and was greeted with the sight of Adina staring down at him. Her dark hair was a tangled mess, and her blue eyes were bloodshot and wet with unshed tears. He thought that he'd never seen anyone or anything so beautiful. She leaned in and kissed him warmly and for a moment he forgot all about the pain, all about the failure that hung over his head. "You're awake," she breathed, finally pulling back "Balen told me that you were, but I couldn't believe it."

"The gods must have a sense of humor," he said, smiling.

Adina was starting to say something else when the door swung open and Captain Leomin strutted in. The Parnen captain was wearing a massive purple hat with feathers in it, a bright green silk shirt, and black leather trousers, "Our hero awakens," he said, grinning widely and displaying his bright white teeth. "Balen tells me that soon you'll be fit enough to trim a sail or swab a deck. It is good for a man to rest, but sometimes he must rest from his rest, must he not?"

Aaron grinned back at the Parnen despite himself, "I have no idea what you're talking about, but it's good to see you breathing just the same."

"Yes, well," the captain said, adjusting his hat and appearing embarrassed, "it is a state which I find most agreeable."

"Balen was a little foggy on the details," Aaron sadi, "but I can't understand it. How *did* you manage to get away from Aster?"

The captain hesitated, then smiled knowingly at Aaron. "Oh, we all have our little secrets, don't we? A man can't go around telling everything there is to know about himself. Why, he would appear vain, and I make it a point to *never* appear vain."

Aaron started to laugh, but paused as the door opened again. He watched in shock as confusion as a familiar figure walked inside the room. "May?"

The club owner wasn't dressed up in the expensive clothes and jewelry that she was known for. Instead, she wore a simple woolen shift, and her long hair was tied into a pony tail. She smiled widely at Aaron, walked to the bed, and wrapped him in a tight embrace, "Silent. I'm so glad you're okay."

Aaron was suddenly struck by the certainty that he must be dreaming, either that or he was dying and even now his mind was wrapped up in an elaborate death vision. What else could explain the presence of these people here, in Baresh, weeks of travel away from where he'd left them? "I don't ... I don't understand."

May smiled kindly, "Oh, Silent. It is so good to have you back. I—*we*," she said, glancing at Adina, "were worried sick."

"We all were," Leomin said, nodding his head to Aaron.

As if reminded of the captain's presence, May turned to frown at him, "I thought we had agreed, Captain, that you wouldn't bother him until he was well. Why, your idle chatter will convince him to take his own life before you're through."

The captain put a hand to his heart, "My dear lady, I assure y—"

"Why don't you go check on Herb and Balen and the others?" May interrupted with a frown, "Poor Olo's probably got his hands full trying to keep them from burning the whole place down."

The captain scooped his hat off of his head and bowed deeply to May, winking at Aaron as he did. "I am happy to see you awake, Mr. Envelar, but I find that my presence is required elsewhere." He began to saunter leisurely out the door. May growled, low in her throat, and the captain cringed visibly before rushing out of the door. Aaron laughed despite himself. It was good to see his friends again.

Once the Parnen was gone, May shook her head, smiling. "Leomin is a good man, and a damned bit smarter than he lets on, but his talk is enough to drive one of Nalek's priests to murder. Not to mention, he's more stubborn than any pack mule I've ever seen." Adina laughed, and May glanced at her, arching an eyebrow, "I don't know what you're laughing at; you're not any better."

Adina stared at the ground as if properly chastised, but her lips spread in a smile and despite their failure, despite the fact that he'd very nearly died, Aaron felt himself smiling back. Sure, they may not have been able to keep Belgarin from taking the north, but he no longer felt as badly about that as he had. They'd lost a battle—that was all. There would be others to fight before it was done, and he decided then, basking in the innocent beauty of her smile, the laughter in her bright blue eyes, that he would be there for that. As his father had often said, there was more than one way to plow a field, but nothing ever got done without work. Here the work to be done called for a sword not a plow and that was fine. He didn't know the first thing about farming.

A thought struck him and he turned to the club owner, "Wait a minute. Balen said that the "boss" convinced Adina to rest."

May raised a perfectly shaped eyebrow, "And?"

"I don't understand."

The club owner smiled widely, "Not yet, Silent, but you will. Let's just say that you, Gryle, and the princess here aren't the only ones who don't want to see Belgarin seize power. In fact, you're all kind of late about getting into this whole rebellion thing. Why, we've been at it for years."

"We?" He asked. He glanced at the princess suspiciously, but saw that she looked just as confused as he felt.

The club owner let out a throaty chuckle, "Well, you didn't really think that I could afford such beautiful dresses just from the money I make off the club, did you?"

He hesitated, "I ... I guess I never thought about it."

She sighed heavily and glanced at Adina, "Men. They never do." She turned back to Aaron, "Why, Silent, I love the club, certainly, and I wouldn't trade it for the world, but the truth is it started as little more than a front. For years now, I—*we,* have been working against Belgarin, undermining him as best we can with what little resources we have. It isn't much but--"

"That's not possible," Adina cut in, "my men keep—" she paused then, and a look of anger and loss passed across her face, "*kept* track of all of the rebel groups in the major cities. I remember specifically sending a group to search in Avarest. It was thought that one of the realm's only remaining neutral cities must surely contain a rebel faction. In the end, nothing was found."

The bartender laughed until she saw the hurt look in the princess's face. "I'm sorry, hon. It isn't that you or your men were incompetent, but the people of the Downs spend most of their lives hiding or fleeing. It would take a lot more than a couple of soldiers dressed in rags to get the better of people who have stayed alive only by making an art of not being noticed."

"But," Adina frowned, "if that's true, you could have helped." Her stare grew hard, her eyes like twin chunks of glacial ice, cold and forbidding. When she spoke, her voice shook with barely restrained anger, "If you would have come to us, helped us, my brother might still be alive."

May's expression grew sad. "Prince Eladen, your brother, was a good man—a man of compassion. Rest assured, princess, that we did everything we could to save him. Everything, that is, except for giving ourselves away."

"You didn't do anything," Adina said, her voice angry, "You were so scared of showing yourselves that you let those bastards kill my brother when you could have helped him!"

It was the club owner's time to be angry, "Yes, we could have shown ourselves, but that would have done nothing but get a lot of good people—people who have supported Eladen and worked against Belgarin for *years*—killed for no good reason. People with families, with lives of their own. If we'd shown ourselves, how long before Belgarin's squads showed up in the Downs? Avarest may be neutral and so removed from the majority of the chaos the war brings, but even we know what your brother does to people who get in his way. If we had, how long before those people and their families were jerked from their homes and put to the sword? The Downs doesn't make warriors, princess—it makes survivors. We have our strengths, to be sure, but the greatest of these is our anonymity. Without that, we are no more to your brother than an itch on his royal ass and as easily remedied. We are not soldiers." She regarded Aaron, "Well, most of us anyway."

"But surely you could have done *something*," Adina said, and it was not anger that choked her voice now, but grief.

May walked to her and embraced her and the princess dissolved into quiet but wrenching sobs. Aaron started to speak but decided against it. The club owner was comforting the princess, patting her back quietly and whispering soothing words of assurance better than any he could offer. Adina's grief made his own heart lurch in sympathy, but he didn't know what to say. He'd spent his entire life learning to kill, to steal, and to make it away clean. He knew dozens of ways to murder a man ranging from poisons to brute force. He'd devoted years to mastering the tools of pain and death. He'd never given much thought to cures.

After a few minutes, Adina pulled away from the club owner and nodded slowly, wiping at her eyes. "I'm sorry. I didn't mean to lash out at you ... I just miss him."

May shook her head sadly, "You have nothing to apologize for, dear. The truth is, it was safer for everyone for us to keep our secret hidden so we did. That doesn't mean any of us liked it. Still, we did try to help you."

"How? I don't remember anything."

The club owner smiled, "Tell me, princess, why did you choose to hire Aaron and not some other sellsword? As I've said, the Downs doesn't have many, but the richer parts of Avarest contain dozens of warriors that would have eagerly accepted your coin."

Adina paused, and shrugged with a puzzled expression, "Everybody said he was the best."

May nodded sharply, "They better have. They were paid well enough."

"Wait a minute," Aaron said, "just wait a damned minute. You're saying that you ... what? *Paid* people to recommend me?"

May rolled her eyes at Adina, "Men and their egos." She turned back to the sellsword, her expression serious, "Silent, you're good. Gods, you're possibly the best fighter I've ever seen—and I've seen some real masters in my day—but you're not exactly a people person, and witnesses to your skill have a sometimes inconvenient way of ending up dead. I wanted to make sure that the princess hired you not only because I think you're the best, but also because I knew that—despite all of your bluster and bitching—you'd dedicate yourself to the cause completely."

Aaron was too amazed and curious to offer any sharp remark. "But why now?" He asked, "If you've been a rebel leader all the years I've known you, why haven't you tried to involve me before?"

The club owner's face turned red, and for the first time since he'd known her, he was amazed to see that she actually looked embarrassed. He watched her for a moment, wondering what was wrong, then the truth hit him like a club in the face. "It isn't the first time you've had me work for the rebellion," he said, and as the words left his mouth he found that he was certain they were true, "those jobs you hired me for, they were all to further your rebellion."

May had the good grace to look ashamed, and she would not meet Aaron's angry gaze, "Not *all* of them, but most, yes," she said, her voice nervous and clipped, "Still, don't forget Aaron, it isn't *my* rebellion anymore, but *ours*. You've chosen it yourself of your own free will."

"Leomin, Balen. They both work for you."

The club owner swallowed hard and nodded, "As do Celes and Herb, the innkeeper you met in Krase. Though he didn't know who you were when you arrived. Thanks to the gods that you didn't kill him."

Aaron stared at her, stunned. He knew that he should be angry, furious, in fact. May had manipulated him and used him to further her own agenda with no care to what she was getting him into. But that hadn't been enough. She'd gone a step farther, maneuvering him into working for the princess and effectively putting him in opposition to the most powerful man in the kingdom, a man who had armies at his command and who wiped his ass with rich silks and the hopes and dreams of commoners like Aaron. He knew he should be angry. But he wasn't.

Later, he would have some very pointed words for the meddlesome club owner but not here, not with Adina so close, with the memory of her kiss still fresh on his lips, and not with Leomin and the others down below. They'd manipulated him, there was no arguing that, but they'd also risked their lives to save him and the others, and in the end there was no harm done. True, he'd been a puppet and very nearly a dead one but somehow, as unlikely as it was, he'd survived. Even more amazing, he'd found something he'd thought he'd never have or want again—friends. "We're going to have a long talk about this later," he said, and the club owner winced, nodding. Then Aaron took a deep breath and smiled at the two women, "So what now?"

"Well," May said, relieved, "we're going to have to talk about that, but not yet. In another day or two, perhaps, but for now you need your rest. You've got a bad habit of almost getting yourself killed."

He managed a stiff shrug, "There are worse things than almost."

The club owner made a sound of agreement, "Well, we'll let you rest." She turned a meaningful stare on the princess, and Adina rose reluctantly, kissed him lightly on the lips, and followed her out the door.

Aaron watched them go, and when the door shut behind them, he found that he was grinning. Despite the pain, despite their failure, or the fact that he had no idea what they were going to do next, he felt good. His only regret was that Co wouldn't be able to share it; Co who had been patient with him even when he'd been a pain in the ass, Co who'd saved his and the others' lives more than once. If not for her, he never would have made it out of The Downs alive. He thought of the scout camp where he'd almost died and how the Virtue had used his memories to pull him back to life. The truth was, she'd saved more than just his life, and he felt a pang of desperate sadness at the fact that he would never be able to tell her that.

It's good to be appreciated.

"Co!" Aaron said, "Thank the gods; I thought you were dead. Is it really you?"

It's me, the Virtue assured him in a voice that was at once weary and cheerful, *Now. You were saying?*

THE END

BOOK ONE
OF
THE SEVEN VIRTUES

BY JACOB PEPPERS

Drop me a line!

I hope you've enjoyed *A Sellsword's Compassion.* You can read more of Aaron and his comopanions in **The Silent Blade: A Seven Virtue's Novella.** If you would like to be the first to know when the next Seven Virtues adventure is out, you can visit my website and sign up to mailing list at www.jacobpeppersauthor.com. If you enjoyed the book, please take a moment and leave me an honest review—I'd love to hear your thoughts!

Stop by and say hi!

If you want to reach out, you can contact me on Twitter at @PeppersJacob or on Facebook.

About the Author

Jacob Peppers lives in Georgia with his wife and three dogs. He is an avid reader and writer and when he's not exploring the worlds of others, he's creating his own. His short fiction has been published in various markets, and his short story, "The Lies of Autumn," was a finalist for the 2013 Eric Hoffer Award for Short Prose.

Note from the Author

Although a lot of the actual production of a book is done alone, the final product is one in which many people have had their hands.

I would like to take the time to thank those people now, including the many who took the time to beta read *A Sellsword's Compassion.* This book would have been a much different (and much worse) one without their critiques and their help along the way. So thank you, to all of you—you know who you are.

I would like to thank my mom, dad, and brothers who were there for support and advice whenever I needed it (which was often; we writers are a needy breed). Also, thanks to BJ and Tim, two close friends of mine who spent many hours listening to me go on and on about the book and never complained (aloud, at least).

Huge shout to D.W Hawkins, a friend of mine who is a great author in his own right. If you haven't started reading his series, *The Seven Signs,* you really should. They're great books, and he's a stand up guy, another who helped me immensely, sharing his knowledge and showing me how to navigate the intricacies of formatting and publishing this book, again without complaint.

I would also like to thank my incredibly patient and supportive wife who has endured a distracted husband during the writing of this book and made sure that I didn't succumb to starvation by reminding me that feeding the dream is good but feeding yourself is necessary.

And the last thanks? Well, that goes to you, dear reader. After all, without you, the rest is just a magic show without an audience, isn't it? I may bring the props and the stage, I might even hire a good-looking assistant (not *too* good looking, mind you, I'm married, and I'd like to stay that way) but you? Well, you bring the magic—and without that none of the rest is possible. Thanks, and hey, I'll see you soon.

Printed in Poland
by Amazon Fulfillment
Poland Sp. z o.o., Wrocław

25382442R00233